03/11

THE ROAD WARRIORS:
DANGER, DEATH, AND THE RUSH OF WRESTLING

BY: JOE "ANIMAL" LAURINAITIS
WITH: ANDREW WILLIAM WRIGHT

FOREWORD BY: "PRECIOUS" PAUL ELLERING

". . . the Road Warriors are the most recognized name in the history of tag team wrestling, and more importantly, Animal and Hawk were great guys—just fantastic people."

—"NATURE BOY™" RIC FLAIR®

"The Road Warriors revolutionized the way we all looked at characters in our industry."

—"THE AMERICAN DREAM" DUSTY RHODES

"All I can do is shake my head and smile at the memory of a spiked up Joe saying, 'Tell 'em, Hawk!' and Mike with that crazy mad look on his face, his tongue hanging out, barking out, 'Oh . . . what a rush!' Both Joe and Mike were first-rate pros who were loved and respected by all who knew them."

—BRET "THE HITMAN" HART

"Joe and Mike weren't polluted by politics, maintained the ethics of the business when it needed it most, and their convincing style made people proud to be wrestling fans. No one could've done a better job."

—"ROWDY" RODDY PIPER

"The first time we saw them on TV, my brother (Stevie Ray) and I were like, 'Whoa!' Hawk and Animal were way bigger than anyone else we'd seen, and they were just killing everybody. And that's what people wanted to see. . . ."

—BOOKER T

"The first time I witnessed Animal and Hawk entering the arena to take care of business, I was in awe. From their hardcore music to the welcoming roar of the crowd, I felt the immense energy build as they approached the ring, and I had no doubt that these guys earned massive expectations from their fans. And the Warriors didn't disappoint.

. . . Animal and Hawk earned legendary status with their extensive careers and have influenced wrestlers for many generations to come."

-ROB VAN DAM

". . . they'll be remembered by historians of professional wrestling as one of the all-time great tag teams."

-JIM ROSS "J.R."

"Animal and Hawk are unmatched by any other team in wrestling. . . . The Road Warriors were . . . the most dominating force to ever come out."

-"THE RUSSIAN NIGHTMARE" NIKITA KOLOFF

". . . the Road Warriors were two tough, take-no-shit guys with the right look and just exploded onto the scene. . . ."

-"THE LIVING LEGEND" LARRY ZBYSZKO

"The Warriors will go down forever as the greatest, most imitated, most influential tag team of all time, and you can't just say that about anybody. . . . At the end of the day, it's the people who decide who the best is, and they chose Hawk and Animal."

-SEAN "X-PAC" WALTMAN

"They came out with those spikes, that look, and that size and completely changed professional wrestling. . . . I think tag team wrestling died when Mike passed. It was the end of not just a great life but a big chapter in the wrestling history book itself as well. . . . They took on a bigger-than-life status and carried it like pros, always making sure the crowd was just as much of the match as they were, and that was the difference."

-TERRY "WARLORD" SZOPINSKI

THE ROAD WARRIORS:
DANGER, DEATH, AND THE RUSH OF WRESTLING

BY: JOE "ANIMAL" LAURINAITIS

WITH: ANDREW WILLIAM WRIGHT

FOREWORD BY: "PRECIOUS" PAUL ELLERING

MEDALLION
P R E S S

Medallion Press, Inc.
Printed in USA

Published 2011 by Medallion Press, Inc.

The MEDALLION PRESS LOGO
is a registered trademark of Medallion Press, Inc.

Copyright © 2011 by Joe Laurinaitis with Andrew William Wright
Cover design by Adam Mock
Edited by Emily Steele

Cover, back cover, and interior photography by Bob Mulrenin
Photos on pages 6, 142, 366 courtesy of Pro Wrestling Illustrated / Kappa Publishing Group, Inc.
Photos on pages 2, 16, 158, 198, 346 courtesy of the Laurinaitis family.

Typeset in Adobe Garamond Pro
Title font set in Misproject

Cataloging-in-Publication Data is on file with the Library of Congress.

Printed in the United States of America

10 9 8 7 6 5 4 3 2 1
First Edition

DEDICATION

For my wife, Julia, my kids, Joe, James, and Jessica,

and my partner, Hawk. May he rest in peacc.

CONTENTS

THE MONSTERS OF THE MIDWAY WERE READY TO SMASH EVERYWHERE WE WENT, EVEN THE PARK! SPRING '84.

FOREWORD
MONSTERS OF THE MIDWAY

With great pleasure, I take this opportunity to tell you about an unbelievable human being and a good friend. Animal, aka Joe, became a world-class athlete by being dedicated and tough. He was the Legion of Doom's rock and continues to inspire and encourage all who have known him.

In the course of human events, when the fusion of time—past and present—occurs, those talented and lucky enough carry the banner of the new generation and become the face of the new paradigm.

In 1983, Animal, Hawk, and "Precious" Paul had an appointment with destiny. Cable TV was spreading across the landscape of America. Macroeconomic realities became the catalyst for the change to come in wrestling. The Road Warriors were positioned to become a pop culture phenomenon.

Wrestling requires a willing suspension of disbelief, right? Then along came the mavericks, stunning in their boldness, who altered the face of the game. Fans could not believe their own eyes. The Road Warriors personified the pursuit of pleasure from misery.

Promoters, being human, naturally balked. They tried to mold us, not understanding that conventional wrestling theory was flawed.

Chemistry bonded Animal, Hawk, and me like the three musketeers. "All for one, one for all." We went independent and became the greatest attraction in the business. The boys were the train; I was the whistle. I became their last shooting manager as Animal and Hawk went forward with courage and confidence.

Behind the scenes, a complex web of interrelationships characterized life for the three of us in our wrestling family. We lost our brother Mike in 2003, and hardly a day goes by that I don't think of him. Life for Mike was a circus and the Fourth of July all rolled into one. It's why everyone liked him. Joe and I learned forgiveness being around Mike.

Thanks for the ride. I enjoyed my years being the punctuation mark at the end of the sentence.

Here's to the greatest tag team of our time.

The greatest of *all* time.

—"Precious" Paul Ellering,
mastermind of the Legion of Doom

ACKNOWLEDGMENTS

First and foremost, I would like to thank the wrestlers who paved the way for Hawk and me to have the opportunity to become wrestlers. Some are still with us, and some have passed but should never be forgotten. Without them there would be no wrestling business. Because of them, there is a Road Warriors story.

I would like to thank my wife, Julia, and my three children, Joey, James, and Jessica, for their patience and understanding with this project. They were my motivation.

I would also give thanks to Bernie J. Gernay of PSI Marketing Group, along with Margaret O'Connor-Chumley of Renaissance Literary & Talent Agency, for believing and realizing the potential for success from the start. Andrew Wright should be a brother in paint, as he researched and delivered an amazing Road Warriors book; his knowledge and impeccable job writing add to its without-a-doubt success. Adam Mock, a true believer whose friendship and understanding of the wrestling business were so instrumental in this process. The Medallion Press staff, great people and a pleasure to work with; I can only hope this is the first of many creative projects to come.

Thank you. God bless!

—Joe Laurinaitis, Road Warrior Animal

I'd like to thank my parents, John and Martha Wright, for their unending love and support; Bernie J. Gernay and Margaret O'Connor-Chumley for helping take the vision of this book to Adam Mock at Medallion Press; and, lastly, Joe Laurinaitis for the opportunity to capture and present the career of the Road Warriors for all time.

—Andrew William Wright

HAWK AND I WERE POISED AND IN CHARGE AS THE **NWA** NATIONAL TAG TEAM CHAMPIONS. SPRING '84.

PROLOGUE

August 26, 1991. SummerSlam. New York City. There we were, Hawk and Animal, the mighty Road Warriors, the Legion of Doom, putting our gear on in the dressing room at Madison Square Garden. Then it hit me: we were taking on the Nasty Boys, Brian Knobbs and Jerry Sags, for the World Wrestling Federation (WWF) Tag Team Championships. I looked at Hawk, who was strapping his boots up tight. "Hey, man, can you believe this?"

"Animal"—Hawk looked up with a smile—"I'm shaking, brother."

I looked at his hands as he buckled the last strap. They were trembling. I looked at mine. They were shaking, too. It was crazy.

There was a knock at the door, and Captain Lou Albano came barging in. He reeked of booze. "Hey, Animal. Hey, Hawk." He was huffing and puffing, out of breath. "Holy shit, fellas, did you see the crowd out there?"

We hadn't.

"Twenty thousand. Sold out," he said. "They're hanging from the rafters." His eyes were wide, and he was nodding. "Kick some ass tonight, boys." And he bolted out the door.

Hawk and I started laughing.

Then there was another knock. The door barely cracked open when a voice announced, "Five minutes, guys."

This was it. Hawk and I stood up from the bench and grabbed our trademark spiked shoulder pads. We slipped them on over our heads, snapped the clasps, and walked into the hallway.

As we marched down the corridor to the staging area, everyone saw us coming and pressed their backs against the walls to give us room. We could hear the sound of the fans. The people in MSG sounded like they were having a full-scale riot above us. You could feel the stomping of their feet shaking and swaying the foundations of the building, like 20,000 soldiers marching across a small suspension bridge. It was pandemonium out there.

When we finally came to the Gorilla Position,[1] our boss came up to wish us well. "Good luck tonight, boys," Vince McMahon said in his deep baritone voice. A big smile stretched across his face. "This is your night. Remember this moment."

The Nasty Boys had already gone down to the ring for their entrance and were getting booed relentlessly, giving us the perfect setup. In a flash, I heard our theme music start with Hawk's unmistakable growl, "Ooooooohhhhhh, WHAT A RUSH!" When the guitars and drums kicked in, the MSG crowd erupted into a deafening crush of noise. My arms and back exploded into chills.

Hawk yelled, "Are you ready for this?"

I hollered back, "Hell, yeah," and we burst through the curtain.

Hawk led as we stormed the short distance to the ring, making

---

1. Staging area named after WWF great Gorilla Monsoon's usual backstage spot.

our way through a sea of reaching arms and open hands. When we climbed through the ropes and looked around at the crowd, it was overwhelming. I remember thinking, *It doesn't get any bigger than this.*

And it doesn't. MSG was the holy Mecca of professional sports, and so many great moments happened there. Ali feuded Frazier for the first time there. WWF legend Bruno Sammartino wrestled "Nature Boy" Buddy Rogers there. WrestleMania started there. And now the Road Warriors were there.

After we climbed through the ropes, Hawk and I each went to a corner and climbed the second turnbuckle to pose for the crowd. When we hopped down, I looked over at Knobbs and Sags, who were defiantly staring at us and yelling trash from the other side. I said to Hawk, "Let's throw 'em out!"

We ran over, grabbed each one of them, and sent them sailing over the ropes to the floor. *Boom!* The match was on.

I went after Knobbs while Hawk went for Sags with vicious chops and punches. I quickly took Knobbs by the neck and rolled him back into the ring and followed. He was waiting for me and we locked up, with Knobs whipping me into the ropes. I came running back full steam, ducked his clothesline, hit the ropes on the other side, and came back with a big kick to the stomach. *Bam!* While he was bent over, I shoved his head between my legs and picked him up for a huge powerbomb, then smashed him down. I went for the cover but only got a two count before Sags kicked me in the head.

From that point, the action was all over the place and completely nonstop. This particular match was a Chicago Street Fight, a no-rules contest we specialized in, named after our hometown billing of Chicago. Within seconds, the crowd was chanting "LOD,

LOD!" and it was the only thing we could hear. I remember Sags had Hawk in the corner at one point. Knobbs and Sags' manager, "Mouth of the South" Jimmy Hart, threw a can of hair spray up to Sags, who sprayed Hawk all over his face. Blinded, Hawk dropped and rolled out of the ring as if he were on fire.

In one of the most memorable spots of the match, Sags followed Hawk down to the floor, reached for a big cooler of freezing cold ice water and soda, and dumped it all over him. Hawk was writhing in agony, still blinded, and tried to get away by rolling back into the ring. For the next five full minutes, I watched helplessly as the Nasty Boys double-teamed my partner over and over while Hart distracted the ref. Every time I came charging in to help, I'd get sent back to my corner. The crowd was going insane, and so was I.

Finally Hawk was able to make it over to me and fell down as he gave me the hot tag. The people went nuts as I jumped through the ropes and took both Nasty Boys on at the same time. Punches, kicks, and clotheslines were flying everywhere as I cleaned house. I threw Knobbs into the ropes, caught him with a great powerslam, and went for the pin. Only two. I took Sags' boot to the head and was now getting double-teamed.

As Hawk was still recovering down on the floor, Jimmy Hart threw a motorcycle helmet up for Sags to hit me with while Knobbs kept me down. Knobbs covered me, and I kicked out at the two count. I pushed Knobbs up so hard he went flying out of the ring. While I was trying to get my bearings back, Hawk was back on his feet and went running after Hart. He threw him to the ground and grabbed the helmet Sags had been using. Hawk launched it into the ring. As soon as I caught it, Hawk smashed Sags in the back of the head. This was it!

As Sags hit the mat, I looked at the capacity crowd and gave them a double thumbs-up high in the air. They knew what was coming: the Doomsday Device. The Doomsday Device was our finishing move: I'd duck down behind an opponent and pick him up on my shoulders. As soon as he was balanced in an upright position, Hawk would come off the top rope with a big clothesline and knock the guy for a backflip. Our victim crashed to the canvas in a spectacle that more than lived up to its name.

With adrenaline pumping through me, I grabbed Sags and lifted him up so quickly he felt like a little kid, and Sags was a 280-pound guy! As I saw Hawk jump up from the floor to the side of the ring, I turned Sags to face the nearest corner. In a flash, Hawk was on the top turnbuckle and leapt into the air, catching Sags with a perfect clothesline. Sags went head over heels in a spectacular flip, landing in a crumpled heap. I pinned him. One, two, three!

Announcer Howard Finkel came over the PA system with an announcement I'll never forget: "Here are your winners and new WWF tag team champions, the Legion of Doom."

Pandemonium erupted.

Hawk and I hugged as the people in MSG gave us the most uproarious standing ovation we'd ever received up till that point.

"Never forget this moment, Animal," Hawk yelled to me.

And I never would.

As we stood in the ring on that fateful summer night making history, I thought of how far we'd come. Hawk and I had been in every major wrestling organization across the world and won every championship dangled in front of us. Winning the WWF titles was the last of the great accomplishments we had yet to achieve. This was the pinnacle, the top of the world.

But things weren't always this great. There was a humble beginning. In the '60s, the seeds of a future Road Warrior Animal were planted in a punk kid on the streets of Philadelphia. That's when and where I cut my teeth.

I can remember it like it was yesterday.

1
ANIMAL'S ABRIDGED PREHISTORY

I'm no dummy. There's no question that everyone who picks up this book wants to jump right into the story of Animal and Hawk and read the tales of the Road Warriors through the good, the bad, and the unbelievably ugly. So I've smashed my early years down to size for you here.

I was born Joseph Michael Laurinaitis to proud Lithuanian parents Joseph Anthony and Lorna Ann in Philadelphia on September 12, 1960. Following not too far behind me were my two brothers, John (1962) and Marc (1965).

As I grew up, I had memorable times learning how to play street hockey and football, squashing everyone who got in my way, including my poor brothers, and girls, too. I also developed a monstrous taste for fighting anyone who messed with us, whether they were coming from rival streets to take our toys or making fun of my last name (you can imagine). I also went to Catholic school, where the nuns' rulers brutalized my knuckles. My offense? Being my good ol' charming self.

When I was thirteen, we moved from Pennsylvania to Tampa, Florida, where I perfected my baseball skills, was voted best-looking guy in school, and discovered the world of weight lifting. The last discovery changed my life forever.

But as I was settling in, not even two years later, I had to trade my flip-flops for snow boots as my dad was transferred again, this time from Florida to Minnesota. It was like moving to Mars. I hated it . . . at first.

Everything started making sense when I quickly proved myself at Irondale High School in Minnesota. At sixteen years old, I bench-pressed 300 pounds, beat out the baseball team's captain for his catcher's position during tryouts, and on the football team went from tight end to starting fullback my senior year. I was also still beating the hell out of anyone who messed with me and my brothers. Ask the poor sap who thought it would be funny to egg John's prized '66 Mustang.

In 1978, after being offered a partial scholarship to the football program, I entered Golden Valley Lutheran College in Golden Valley, Minnesota. By now I was six feet one and 225 pounds. As offensive guard, I was slamming the defense, helping our team go 6–0 my first year. By the end of my second and final year, I was twice named First-Team Junior College All American guard and a Second Team linebacker.

While at Golden Valley, I also met a guy named Scott Simpson, my cocaptain, my best friend, and the future National Wrestling Alliance (NWA) professional wrestling star "The Russian Nightmare," Nikita Koloff.

But everything changed before I was to begin my junior year

at Brigham Young University. My serious girlfriend from Golden Valley, Nancy, was pregnant. I dropped out, got a dead-end job, married Nancy, and on February 22, 1981, welcomed my first son, Joey, into the world.

After six months, both Nancy and I realized we were in way over our heads and agreed we could do the best job raising Joey separately. We shared equal custody.

At twenty-two years old, I was making a name for myself as a potential powerlifter. I weighed around 250 pounds and was benching 500 pounds. A couple of guys at The Gym, the most popular facility in the area, introduced me to the anabolic steroid Dianabol. Soon my strength and size skyrocketed even further.

At this point, my life really picked up steam, so hold on tight and prepare yourself for a hell of a ride . . .

I WAS ONE CLUELESS ROOKIE IN GEORGIA CHAMPIONSHIP WRESTLING AS THE ROAD WARRIOR. 1982.

2
BOUNCING AROUND AND TAKING A CHANCE

One night I had finished repping out a set on the incline bench press with 365 pounds and was sitting up to stretch, when I felt an open-handed whack in the chest. *Crack!* That got my attention really fast. I looked up and saw this guy with the curliest mop of orange hair and a funny-looking goatee. He was staring at me and smiling, and it took me a second to figure out who he was.

Then I heard his booming, grizzly voice. "Hey, Laurinaitis, how you doin'?"

I started laughing. I knew this guy. It was Mike Hegstrand, the future Road Warrior Hawk. Although we didn't really know each other that well, we were both bouncers on the local scene with reputations of not taking any crap. Back then, guys like us were always aware of each other.

Mike told me he'd heard how big and strong I'd been getting, but when he actually saw me, he couldn't believe it. "You're not right," he said. "You ain't supposed to be doin' 100 pounds more than me."

I might have been stronger than him, but Mike had been growing, too, and he looked great. He had these traps practically growing out of his ears, these big, ripped arms, and that orange hair. At six feet two and about 240 pounds, Mike was a sight to be seen.

After talking for a while, we exchanged numbers and agreed to get together soon for a workout. The next time we met in the gym, we talked about getting even bigger and stronger and decided to see what a regular steroid regimen could do for us. Mike suggested we talk with a doctor friend of his first to make sure we knew exactly what we were getting ourselves into. We took a very cautious approach to steroids, working our asses off in the gym between cycles to maintain our gains.

Mike and I had very different goals in the gym and, therefore, very different approaches to training. I liked to go extra heavy and spend a few hours in the gym. Mike would be in and out within an hour. He called it "fast and furious" training and was interested in getting ripped. I wanted to get as massive and strong as possible. My workouts were intense. If I didn't throw up on any given night, I didn't accomplish my goal and would be disappointed with myself.

In a short amount of time, I developed a real respect for Mike and we became good friends. Mike's reputation had preceded him. I'd heard he was an absolute wild man with a mean streak. The rumor went that it didn't take much to make Mike lose his temper and start swinging for the fences. He'd freak out, hit like a mule, and get in anyone's face that got too close. He was the perfect guy to bounce with.

When I first met him, Mike was working at this real dive strip joint called Roaring '20s. It was a tough, dingy old dump. It was the kind of place where when people would come in and sit down, you'd go over with a bat, tap the table, and say, "Okay, you've got three choices. Buy your booze here now, over at the bar now, or get the hell out *now*." Seriously, that's the kind of place it was and why they had people like Mike working there. He was in his glory in that kind of environment.

While Mike was laying down the law there, I was at a place called Thumper's. This is where I had my most memorable run-in with a bar patron. It was happy hour, maybe about five in the evening, and a group of girls came in. Before you knew it, this sloppy, drunk creep made his way over to their table and made himself known.

By the looks on the girls' faces, it was more than obvious that they weren't interested. Eventually he started becoming loud and belligerent, so I walked over and asked him if there was a problem. He said no and walked away. Fine. I returned to the front door and resumed a conversation with a cop who'd stopped by. Less than a minute later, I saw the guy walk back over to the table.

I charged right over there. "Hey, buddy," I calmly said, "I asked you before to leave these girls alone. I'm not going to ask you again."

No sooner had the words left my mouth than this guy was reaching up and putting his cigarette out on my forehead.

I saw red! I grabbed him by the throat, lifted him off the ground, and ran him across the floor like a rag doll. Thumper's had these long rows of picnic tables, and I swear that guy's head slammed against most of them on his way to the door.

As I was about to toss my new friend out on the sidewalk, the officer I had been talking with earlier decided to cuff him and take him away instead. To top it all off, after the guy was thrown into the back of the cop car, he thought it would be a great idea to kick out the back windshield. As a reward, he got a nice beating with a police baton before being taken away.

Eventually things took an interesting turn when Mike and I both wound up working regularly at a place called Gramma B's. What a cool place Gramma B's was! It was a pretty good-sized space, with two levels, and although it was only licensed to hold 3,000 people, there'd easily be close to 4,000 jammed in there on a good night.

During the day, they would put plywood on the pool tables so they could run a strip club, but then at night it was an all-out bar atmosphere. Usually upstairs they'd have a rock band, and downstairs they'd have country. But at all times you could count on it being rowdy. Gramma B's was smoke-filled and booze-packed, and anything went, which is why Mike and I were there: we kept a lid on things.

And we had help. There was a literal wrecking crew of us at Gramma B's that you wouldn't believe. It was like all the local badasses decided to get together and work under the same roof. At one point in time, there was me, Mike, and guys like Rick Rood, Barry Darsow, John Nord, and Scott Norton all keeping an eye on things. Each one of us was a notorious powerhouse and future professional wrestling superstar.

Rick Rood was from Robbinsdale and actually went to high school there with Barry Darsow as well as my Golden Valley football buddy Scott Simpson (Nikita Koloff). Without a doubt, Rood was a chick magnet. Girls flocked to him like he was the first man they'd ever seen. He would later flaunt his machismo as Ravishing Rick "Rude," a one-of-a-kind heel[2] who became not only the WWF Intercontinental champion but the World Championship Wrestling

---

2. Wrestling bad guy.

(WCW) International World Heavyweight champion as well.

Barry Darsow was someone I'd seen around at The Gym from time to time, and we got along great. We were both powerhouses near 300 pounds and respected each other without having to say a word. It was like that among big guys in the gym sometimes. Barry is best known today for having been Smash, half of the very successful WWF tag team Demolition. Demolition went on to win the WWF World Tag Team Championships. They were also one of the teams considered to be clones of the Road Warriors.

But that's a story for a much later chapter.

Then there was Scott Norton, who attended Patrick Henry High School with Mike and was a 330-pound super-heavyweight arm wrestling world champion, whose victory in a match with Cleve Dean earned him a slot in the Sylvester Stallone movie *Over the Top*. In the wrestling business, Norton caught on big in Japan, becoming one of only five Americans to hold the biggest honor in New Japan Pro Wrestling: the International Wrestling Grand Prix (IWGP) Heavyweight Championship.

Last but not least was big John Nord, a 300-pound giant, another product of Robbinsdale, Minnesota, who towered above everyone at six feet five. Nord broke into the business first as Nord the Barbarian in the AWA before finding most of his notoriety as the Berzerker in the WWF.

Although we each had a different approach to bouncing, as a group we complemented the hell out of each other. As soon as we'd walk in for a night of work with our Gramma B's T-shirts on, it was time to punch in to see if there was anyone whose lights needed to be punched out.

When it came to bouncing, the six of us ran the place. We

didn't care who you were. Whether you were a Hells Angel who didn't want to take off your colors before coming in or a drunken patron with a big mouth, we took care of business.

Once, a guy didn't want to take his colors off, so we took his ass upstairs and proceeded to grab him by the ankles, turn him upside down, and shake him up and down until he agreed. You had to see it. Some of us wore biker colors, too, and in some cases even knew the guys we had to corner. But at Gramma B's, we were the enforcers and tended to be very hands-on. Hey, we had a job to do, and that was that.

Of all the guys, though, my chemistry with Mike was particularly strong. I remember hearing stories about him long before we actually met. One was about Mike getting rowdy at high school football games. "Hey, did you hear last night? Patrick Henry High was getting killed 42–0, but Hegstrand was 5–0 under the stands knocking heads!"

Working with Mike made me realize I wasn't the only tough guy in town, or the most charismatic. He had personality off the charts and was always on the microphone yelling something crazy. When Mike used to host the wet T-shirt contests, he'd be on the mic rambling all night long, making the whole place roar with laughter. He was never at a loss for words. Ever.

Behind all of this great madness at Gramma B's was a bartender named Eddie Sharkey. Eddie had trained wrestlers back in the '60s and even wrestled for a brief time himself. He had two big claims to fame he'd talk about all the time. The first was that he'd wrestled Harley Race for the National Wrestling Alliance (NWA) World Heavyweight Championship. The other was that he once shot up Verne Gagne's office. That one was my favorite.

Verne Gagne was the owner and promoter of the AWA, and I guess one time after a few drinks, Verne hit on Eddie's wife. Later that night, Eddie responded by driving past Verne's office and unloading both barrels of his 12-gauge shotgun into it. We laughed our asses off when he'd tell that one.

Eddie was quite the character: a real wheeler and dealer. He was this little guy with a big mouth always talking about the new stuff he had that "fell off the truck." Whatever it was you were looking for, he'd have it the next day for you in the trunk of his car. Need a TV? It was in the trunk of his car. A ratchet set? Look no further. Steak knives? A Walkman? Some designer jeans? You guessed it. Eddie's trunk was better than a retail chain.

With his glory days behind him, Eddie had long since gravitated out of the wrestling business and made himself at home behind the bar at Gramma B's. Night after night, Eddie watched as we sent bodies flying over the bar, out the back door, or through the front. I guess he found us pretty entertaining because he was always saying something to us like, "Jeez, Laurinaitis, you're a monster," or "Norton, I'm glad you're on my side."

After work one night Eddie introduced his latest big idea. "Hey, guys, I'm thinking about getting another wrestling camp together. You guys interested?"

We weren't sure about it. In fact, I think the first time he brought it up, I turned and walked away. Another time, I said, "Gee, Eddie, I don't know."

But Eddie was persistent. He kept calling Rood, insisting we let him train us. We all discussed it and figured we'd give it a try. There was nothing to lose. We knew that at one time Eddie had a training school, where Jesse Ventura, among others, had trained.

Ultimately, the decision was easy. If guys like Ole Anderson, Ric Flair, and Jesse Ventura could each make it out of Minnesota as professional wrestlers, we could too.

We didn't think much of wrestlers anyway. From time to time, we'd watch the AWA on TV and see guys like Greg Gagne, Jerry Blackwell, and Jim Brunzell. We took one look at those guys and knew we were a lot bigger and stronger than they were. We figured, if we could've smoked any of them in a real fight, why not try to make some money wrestling them? We wanted to find out.

The first day of wrestling school was hilarious. You have to imagine it. I chauffeured Barry, Mike, and Rood in my microscopic, two-door 1982 Honda Civic hatchback. The comedy began when I pulled up to Barry's. He came walking up, all 280 pounds of him, and when he sat down, I swear the car almost bottomed out. I thought, *Hmmm, this ought to be really interesting.* Then we puttered over to get Mike, who squeezed in. I was kind of laughing to myself as we pulled up to Rood's place. About the same size as Mike, he crammed himself into the back. You practically needed a shoehorn to pack him in there.

What a scene! It was like a bunch of sumo wrestlers contorting themselves into a clown car. I knew it couldn't be good for the Honda. As far as I was concerned, I was driving a ticking time bomb. Before we pulled away, I opened the car door and read the specs posted on the jamb. Again, I had to laugh as I read, "Maximum Capacity Weight: 780 pounds." At a combined weight of over a thousand pounds, we were punishing that little Honda.

Well, after three months of that, the abuse proved too much. One day after I dropped off my son, Joey, at Nancy's, my car blew up. No shit. The poor little Honda threw a piston rod right through the hood, and that was that. Needless to say, I was back in the market for a newer, sturdier automobile. But it didn't stop me from calling the local junkyard first. I got $500 for that pile.

I still remember my overall excitement about the possibility Eddie's school offered. Fame and fortune were going to come my way quickly, I knew, because I was approaching the whole thing like a sport. With my strength, size, and determination, nothing would deter me. Or so I thought.

When we got to the school, though, I had more than a few doubts. Maybe I had envisioned a state-of-the-art facility with all the bells and whistles.

Maybe I was dead wrong.

Eddie's school wasn't really a school at all. It was the dank, cold basement of a church in south Minneapolis. Once inside, we saw the omen of things to come: an old, broken-down boxing ring with stuffing coming out of the pads. It was nothing more than four posts with railroad ties lying across a metal framework with a sheet of plywood and canvas covering the top of it. The ring also pretty much sat right on the floor with maybe only a foot of space between the mat and the ground, giving it almost zero flexion.

I remember first stepping through the ropes and walking on the mat, which was shockingly hard. I'd thought it would feel like a trampoline. No dice. The ring was also positioned with one of the posts sitting in the corner of two walls, and the ropes were so close to the walls that when you were thrown into them, your elbows would smash into the concrete behind you. I still have elbow chips from those walls. To put it mildly, the ring totally sucked and was an absolute death trap with no give to it whatsoever.

This is where we learned to wrestle. It was brutal.

Eddie could see by our reactions that we were less than enthused about working in his ring. "Hey, don't worry about it, guys. We're only going to be training in learning how to take bumps."

Yeah, right. Taking a bump onto your back in Eddie's ring had all of the charm of falling off a building. The Empire State Building.

Our first lessons consisted of simply falling straight back on the mat, making sure to keep our heads up so as not to give ourselves concussions. I quickly found out how it felt to bang your head when taking a bump. Not pleasant. Then we moved onto falling straight back while kicking our legs up to give us air while we took the bump. That added a little dramatic visual and was the way I always took a bump from that point on.

Next, we learned how to do basic moves out of the corner, like a hip toss. I'd be punching Barry, whose back would be in the corner, and I'd hook my right arm under his. Then I'd take a half step, then a big step and flip him over onto his back. It sounded easy at first, but I realized how much of my success in performing the move depended on Barry synchronizing with me. He would have to carefully do the opposite of my footwork by taking a big step first, then a small step and jump in the air doing a flip. In the finished move, it appeared as if I was throwing Barry out of the corner onto his back in the middle of the ring.

There's no question that learning the right timing of a sequence of moves was the key to everything. It had to look effortless. When you're watching a couple of guys in the ring perform a series of spots[3] and it looks flawless, that means you're watching two guys who really know what they're doing.

Eddie was so happy with our progress because we were all getting it the first time around. He'd take a broomstick and hold it out in

---

3. Moves.

front of one of the corners and we'd take turns flipping over the stick onto our backs. *Bam!* We did that every day for a couple of weeks, about fifty bumps per day, to get used to it.

Something else we had to get used to was learning how to throw proper working punches. This was such a gradual process and a lot harder than you'd imagine. We were used to hitting people for real and couldn't grasp how to properly time it. You had to throw the punch while stomping your foot, making every effort to stop short of actually touching the other guy's face. Mike was really adept at it. He used to stomp his feet really hard to get that loud ring sound, making his punches come off perfectly. After a few days, our punching may have improved, but we still had no clue.

We'd be in the ring all pumped up, pretty much swinging for the fences, not realizing the damage we were doing. Everybody was bleeding all the time. Whether I punched Rood in the nose or Mike in the mouth, it was only a matter of minutes before it came my way. Although taking bumps and throwing punches took up most of our time, you never knew what the next lesson would be.

I even learned something on the sidewalk outside of the church one afternoon. I happened to be outside taking a break when Curt Hennig, the future two-time WWF Intercontinental champion as Mr. Perfect, came strolling up the sidewalk. Curt had gone to Robbinsdale High School with Barry and Rood and wanted to stop by.

Just before Curt showed up, I had finished learning how to throw a good working punch, so when I saw him, I couldn't wait. Like a little kid, I ran up and started throwing some punches at him.

A couple of lefts and a right later, Curt quickly started saying, "Kayfabe, brother. Kayfabe. There are people watching us, man."

I didn't know what he was talking about. Kayfabe? What the hell was kayfabe? So he gave me a crash course.

In those days, professional wrestling was protected by the philosophy of kayfabe, which was the illusion that wrestling was real. Guys in the business had to "keep kayfabe" at all times, which meant they had to *live* their gimmicks. It was the bread and butter of being a professional wrestler. One of the greatest examples of kayfabe happened on December 28, 1984.

A reporter named John Stossel was on assignment for the news show *20/20* to investigate the legitimacy of professional wrestling. While walking around backstage at a WWF event at Madison Square Garden, Stossel approached a wrestler named David Schultz with a poor choice of questions. Schultz was a huge guy, like six feet five and 260 pounds, and one of the big heels for the company. When Stossel came up and asked Schultz on camera if wrestling was fake, he had no way of knowing Schultz was in full character.

Stossel had no sooner asked the question than Schultz legit slapped him right down to the ground. *Boom!* Then Schultz asked him if he thought the slap was fake and slapped him again. It was all over the news in a hurry.

Needless to say, there were lawsuits filed and the WWF eventually fired Schultz, but Stossel had unwittingly convinced a lot of people watching at home that wrestling definitely wasn't fake. It was a big victory for the credibility of the business.

And that's exactly what kayfabe was all about.

The days and weeks started to fly by at our little wrestling school, and eventually Eddie decided to put us to the test. It was time for a show. My first match ever was against Rick Rood. Eddie opened up the doors of the church basement for all these little inner-city kids, like thirty of them, so we could show off our stuff. Those kids were great. They knew their wrestling and weren't shy about letting us know it. They'd boo or cheer depending on how realistic our moves were. They were ruthless. I remember busting Rood's nose open and blood gushing everywhere. Those kids were yelling, "That's fake. It ain't real."

Ha. Little did they know Rood was in my ear, saying, "What the hell? Fake? This isn't fake. Look at my nose."

I think we only went about five minutes and didn't even have a winner. They just rang the bell and we were done. Man, we were so blown up and out of breath that we couldn't even talk or move.

My second match was with Barry, who almost destroyed my leg. He had me in a headlock, and I pushed him off into the ropes. He gave me a running tackle so hard that my tibia in my right leg popped out of place. You could actually see the bone protruding against the skin. I thought it was my knee and rolled out of the ring, yelling, "Oh man, my knee. I did something to my knee."

I'll tell you what, the kids in the audience were cheering and having a ball while I thought I'd never walk again. Fortunately for me, my legs were strong and big—probably about 30 inches around—from all of my weight training, so I was able to slightly walk.

On my way out to go home, I took a seat on the church steps for a second to rest. When I got up, grimacing from the pain, I wasn't paying attention and stepped on an uneven section of the sidewalk. As my right ankle turned sideways, the bone popped back into place. I started bending my leg back and forth, relieved beyond belief that I hadn't blown my knee out.

I looked at Barry, who was with me, shrugged, and said, "Hey, that feels pretty good. See you at the gym in two hours for squats?" And I did.

Aside from being impressed by our in-ring training and first couple of matches, Eddie was always taken aback by our size and was convinced we could make it in the business. He would talk about how he knew people in the business like Ole Anderson, who ran Georgia Championship Wrestling (GCW). "Ole would love you guys. I've got to take some pictures of you and see what he could do. I'm telling you, Ole will be interested."

Ole Anderson was a major wrestling star all of us knew from TV. He'd been in the legendary Minnesota Wrecking Crew tag team with his kayfabe brother Gene Anderson. The Andersons had been a main event attraction since the late '60s. They'd won every major tag team championship the NWA territories had to offer, many times over.

By 1981, Ole was focusing more on the business side of things and was a small percentage owner of GCW in Atlanta. He was the booker and the man in charge of everything, including hiring new talent. Eddie was convinced that if Ole liked the pictures of us, he'd stop to see us during one of his trips to visit his parents in his hometown of Ramsey, Minnesota.

We humored Eddie. "Okay, Eddie, whatever you say."

We posed outside of the ring in the church basement for some really rudimentary photos, each of us wearing shorts, our hands on our hips. At the very least, the photos showed how big we were. Add Eddie's slick descriptions of how we were in the ring, and the plan worked.

I'll never forget when Eddie ran up to me one day and said Ole was up from Georgia and was going to stop by Gramma B's for a beer. Now *that* was big news.

Ole showed up on a particularly busy night, which meant he'd get a good show. You see, at Gramma B's there was this big electrical box on the ground outside the front door past the sidewalk. Attached to the box was a midthigh-high wire that we all called the trip wire. Whenever someone got rowdy or outlandish, we'd take him by the back of the neck with one hand and the back of his pants with the other and run him out the front door.

These poor guys would go hurtling through the doorway and, without seeing it, hit the trip wire and either flip and land on their faces or bounce back onto their asses. It was the greatest thing ever, and we all used it as often as possible. Eventually we got to the point where we'd rate each other on the landing of our victims on a scale of one to ten. Rest assured, I always scored a ten.

I had just finished sending some jerk into the trip wire, causing a dazzling flip and smash. I was proud.

"Hmm, that was different," someone off to the side commented. I looked over, and there was Ole Anderson standing with Eddie, admiring my technique. I knew it was him, but I casually walked back inside and resumed my position next to the front door. I was playing it cool, but in my mind I was freaking out. *Holy shit, that was Ole Anderson.*

About twenty minutes later, I heard Eddie shouting down to me from the upstairs office. "Hey, Joe, get Rood and come up here for a minute."

Eddie introduced us, and we shook hands. I was much bigger than Ole, but he was a mountain of a man who reminded me of a rugged old lumberjack. He gave me a strong grip, which I gave right back.

Our meeting was casual and pretty brief. Ole told Rood and

me he liked our pictures and Eddie had spoken very highly of our athletic ability. "We'll have to see how things go," he said, "but I'd like to bring you two down for a tryout in Georgia sometime." He said he'd give us a call, and that was it.

On a Thursday afternoon a few weeks later, I was hanging out at Rood and Mike's apartment. We were all starving and decided to victimize the local smorgasbord restaurant, but as usual, we had to wait on Rood to get ready.

One thing you have to understand about Rood is that he had no shortage of lady friends and loved to look good for them all. His hair and Tom Selleck mustache were always a priority when going anywhere.

Mike and I were getting tired of waiting and went out on the front steps. Finally Rood emerged. As we all started to leave, the phone rang. Mike and I moaned for Rood to let it ring and come on, but he couldn't resist the urge to answer it. After all, he had girls calling day and night.

Rood was in the apartment for a few minutes before coming back out. "Hey, man, that was Ole. He wants me and you to drive down to Georgia and wrestle on the TV tapings Saturday."

The news couldn't have been any bigger. Mike congratulated us, and we all left for lunch.

I could only think about how crazy all of this was—and how long that drive to Atlanta would be. It was already Thursday afternoon, and we had to be there by Saturday morning. We didn't have enough time.

As soon as we got back to Rood's, I called Ole and told him driving might be a problem. He said not to worry and that two tickets would be waiting for us at the airport the next afternoon. In a rush, we packed and got ready to go.

3
EDUCATION OF A
ROAD WARRIOR

Before Rood and I headed toward fame and fortune down in Atlanta, I had to call my folks. It's funny because the day Ole called us, my dad had taped the local classified ads on the refrigerator and told me I shouldn't bother coming home without a job. By that same afternoon, I had the privilege of calling my dad to tell him his son had indeed gotten a job. "Dad, I'm going to be flying down to Georgia tomorrow to be a pro wrestler."

He was incredulous. "You've gotta be kidding me."

"Nope, I'm not kidding. This is what I'm going to do for now and see how it goes."

And that was that. If wrestling had the potential to offer me and my little Joey a good living, I had to check it out.

So Rood and I caught our flight and made it down to Atlanta in plenty of time for the Saturday morning TV tapings. Here we were, completely inexperienced and starting off on GCW's *World Championship Wrestling* TV show. This was the show to watch on cable. It came on every Saturday at 6:05 p.m. on Superstation WTBS 17 and was as big as it got.

We were both a little nervous but excited, too. I was ready, or at least I thought I was. When Ole and I discussed what my gimmick[4] would be, he already had an idea. The Mel Gibson movie *Mad Max 2: The Road Warrior* inspired Ole. The characters had a savage and brutal attitude combined with a neobiker image. I would be Ole's Road Warrior.

The first thing I needed to do was get my image and outfit together—quickly. For whatever reason, I decided my Road Warrior wardrobe would be a little jean jacket vest, black leather gloves, sunglasses, jean shorts, and to top it all off, a Village People-style black police cap.

It seemed right at the time, but looking back, man, was I off.

When I arrived at the studio, Ole quickly hid me in the back. I guess I was kind of like his big secret because he kept me away from everyone throughout most of the taping.

When it was my time to enter the show, Ole made it very clear he wanted me to be vicious as hell: "I want you to go out there and kick the shit out of this guy tonight."

That sounded good to me.

My first match was with a guy named Randy Barber. Randy was a jobber[5] who was short, pale, middle-aged and looked as if he had no business in a ring of any kind. He wasn't intimidating in the least but was a nice enough guy. I felt bad about what Ole wanted me to do to him. I don't remember much about that first experience against Randy other than the audience's reaction to me and how much of a beating I dished out.

Ole and I hadn't discussed anything about how the match

4. Character.
5. A wrestler whose job it is to lose.

would go. "What's the point?" he'd said. "You're going to forget it all the second you get in front of the audience." He was right.

That night is like a series of quick snapshots in my mind, but I can recall walking up to the interview podium across from the ring. In those days, I wasn't allowed to say a word. When I went up to the host, Gordon Solie, for my prematch interview, Gordon said, "Any words from the Road Warrior before the match starts?"

I didn't answer. I stared at him through the sunglasses.

Without missing a beat, the bewildered Solie looked right at the camera and said, "Let's go to the action in the ring."

That kind of noninteraction got a hot response from the little studio crowd, which was comprised mostly of young inner-city kids. They booed me incessantly from beginning to finish. I loved it. My big, mean attitude shined right through, which was the plan from the get-go.

When the bell rang, I quickly charged at Randy, grabbed him by the throat, and pushed him into the corner. As I was choking him, I pushed back his head and then forearm smashed him so hard his chest practically caved in. Poor Randy literally didn't know what hit him. I let him go, and he came groggily walking back. I grabbed him and gave him a giant knee smash to the head for the finish. The match was over almost as soon as it had started, but there it was, my big debut.

As the match ended, all the kids were letting me have it with boos and jeers, so I flipped them all the middle finger. I had so much adrenaline running I didn't know what I was doing. Oops. Thankfully, Ole said they would edit it out of the tape for the evening broadcast.

I didn't even get a chance to see Rood's match. Then, for

whatever reason, Ole sent Rood up to Mid-Atlantic Championship Wrestling (MCW) based out of Charlotte, North Carolina. It was like that in the wrestling business, though. One minute someone would be right next to you, and the next he was gone without a trace. I would see Rood again very soon, though.

Little did I realize that while my big opportunity was unfolding, a power struggle was also developing between Ole and a guy named Jim Barnett over GCW. All I knew was that Barnett was a big player in the business and was another stockholder of the company. It was all a big mess I absolutely had no understanding of. Above that, I didn't care as long as I had a job and kept working. Lawsuits were exchanged, and I remember the constant threat of Barnett trying to shut GCW events down.

As a result of Ole's troubles with Barnett, Ole told me I was going to be shipped off. "Hey, kid. There's a lot of crap going on down here. I need to get rid of you for a couple of months. You'll go up and work at Mid-Atlantic in Charlotte. When this storm blows over, I'll send for you."

I didn't know what to think.

Ole was pretty adamant that he had to shut down operations for a short period and fight to stay in business. "I can either lie down or die trying," he said, raising his hands, "and I ain't lying down."

When Ole told me I was going up to MCW in the Carolinas, I wasn't sure. It sounded to me like going from the big time in Atlanta to some little hillbilly setup in the middle of the sticks in North Carolina. Ole said promoter Jim Crockett would take care of me, but I didn't know.

I called Rood, who'd been up there for a couple of weeks and knew the lay of the land. When I told him my concerns, he said,

"No, man, you've got it wrong. This territory's a hotbed, man. Mid-Atlantic is the headquarters for the whole NWA. Crockett has a good thing here."

Rood sold me.

Jim Crockett Promotions out of Charlotte, North Carolina, owned and operated the MCW territory of the NWA. Jim Crockett Sr. had been promoting wrestling, concerts, and minor league baseball since the '30s and over time built up a local empire. In 1973, when Jim Crockett Sr. passed away, his son Jim Crocket Jr. took the lead.

As soon as I arrived in Charlotte, I met up with Rood and got a small room at this dive motel near the airport. Catching up with him was fun and made me feel at home.

A lot of the other guys stayed there, too. Rood introduced me to Joe LeDuc, a true veteran of the business and a great guy. Joe gave us rides all the time to the studio forty-five minutes away where MCW taped their TV programs. If it weren't for Joe, I don't know what we would've done.

When the time came for my first match, I was surprised and a little relieved to be booked with Rood. At least I knew his style from our days at Eddie's school. His in-ring ability was the same as mine at that point: horrible.

We were the second match on the card in front of a packed house at the Fayetteville Civic Center. We were told to go for a twenty-minute Broadway. That meant we'd have to wrestle to a time limit draw of twenty minutes. I got nervous. Twenty minutes is a long time for a match, let alone a match between two rookies.

Rood and I had no idea what to do. We thought we could randomly throw on moves we'd seen the other guys do in their matches. Man, were we wrong.

Five minutes into the match, Rood threw on a figure-four leg-lock, and referee Tommy Young went nuts on us. "You can't do that. That's Ric Flair's finishing move."

When we got up, I grabbed Rood and put him in a massive bear hug.

"No, no, no. That's Joe LeDuc's finish."

Great. Now what? Rood's and my repertoire consisted of nothing more than running tackles, hip tosses, and body slams, for the most part. We went out there with nothing to work with.

I know the guys were watching us in the back getting blown up, out of breath, and scrambling aimlessly in the ring and laughing their asses off. During the match, you could see all of their heads poking through the curtain in the back so they could catch a glimpse of us. Lord knows none of them ever tried to show us anything. Back in those days, there was very little guidance for new guys. Most of the established guys were too busy worrying about their t in the company to worry about us.

When it was over, Rood and I went to the back and laughed it off as a learning experience.

Soon after, Rood got injured and went back to Minnesota to rest up.

Another important lesson I came to learn during this time was that it didn't matter how big and strong I was. Here I was feeling and looking like a monster, and yet I was wrestling nine times a week for about $150. What did matter was how over with the crowd you were. The more over you were, the more money you made. It was that simple.

I might've been getting a little impatient at my underpaid jobber status, but I knew it was my time to pay dues. Eventually I started getting more comfortable in the ring and occasionally one of the top guys—like Ric Flair, Jerry Brisco, or Ricky Steamboat—would let me get a little offense in, which helped give me some credibility.

I remember when Ric Flair, the NWA World Heavyweight champion, let me body slam him on TV. We locked up early in the match, and Ric whispered, "Kick me in the stomach and slam me." So I did. *Pow!* Then I scooped him up and slammed him down hard. It was a big thrill, even if short lived.

There's no question that each time I had a match with those guys I learned a little more, but my biggest lesson came at the hands of an old-time favorite of the Mid-Atlantic region, Johnny Weaver. Weaver had been around since the '60s and had won single and tag team titles in Georgia, Florida, and North Carolina.

By the time I met up with him in the ring that night, he was pushing fifty years old. I was beating the crap out of him the whole time, and all of a sudden he started shaking his left arm like he was having a seizure. You see, Johnny used to do this thing when he made a comeback during a match. He'd signal to the audience by raising one of his arms straight up, pointing his first two fingers in the air, shaking wildly.

The fans went berserk as Johnny started making his comeback with a flurry of punches to my head. Then he whipped me into the ropes and sank into a sleeper hold. As I was going out, the ref called for the bell, which surprised me.

I mean, I knew from the beginning Johnny was going to win, but I didn't know it was going to be with a sleeper hold. I felt humiliated. I wondered how the crowd could ever believe that a skinny old man like Johnny Weaver could beat my ass, let alone with a sleeper.

I walked to the back, and there was Sgt. Slaughter and Don Kernodle laughing their heads off at me. Slaughter, or "Sarge" as I called him, was always someone I could approach.

"Man, there ain't nobody in the world who'd believe Johnny Weaver could put me to sleep," I said.

Sarge and Kernodle looked at each other and burst into laughter again. "Brother," Sarge said, "you got your next lesson. This business is a total work. Check your concept of reality at the door. Anything can happen and usually does."

Something else I had to grow accustomed to was the traveling, the grueling hours spent driving from town to town in cramped rental cars and staying in roadside motels. This was actually the way most of my time was spent, and there were some memorable experiences to say the least.

Once we were staying at some dump motel in Richmond, Virginia, and a bunch of us were having a few beers and unwinding. Roddy Piper thought he'd break me in a little bit and give me some words of advice.

"C'mere, kid," Roddy said. Then he told the waitress, "Gimme two glasses and a bottle of Jack Daniel's for my friend and me."

I didn't know Roddy from a hole in the wall, but he was a top guy in the company. If he wanted to be generous with drinks, I'd let him. He was sucking that Jack down with beer chasers like it was the last beverage on earth, and he pushed a shot of whiskey my way.

Personally, I always thought whiskey tasted like piss, but out of respect for Roddy, I pounded it down and decided to pick his brain a little. "How do you do it out there?"

Piper was always great in the ring and seemed so relaxed. He looked at me and said, "It's just experience, kid. Experience."

Then I asked him a funny one. "Do you think I could ever make it to your level?"

He leaned back and smiled. "I hope you do well, kid, but it's doubtful you'll ever make it in this business."

Talk about a deflation! I was so pissed that I went back to my room, lay down on the bed, and cursed Roddy Piper's name. *Old bastard*, I thought. *We'll see who makes it.*

When I woke up in the morning, a bunch of wrestlers were running around saying something had happened to Mike Rotunda (WWF superstar Irwin R. Scheister, I.R.S.). I had no idea what the hell they were talking about until Sarge bumped into me and told me the story.

Apparently, Mike had been completely hammered the night before and decided to go skinny-dipping. In order to make it to the pool, you had to scale a chain-link fence. Mike made the initial climb over just fine and had his drunken swim. However, when he was making his return climb over, he caught his dick on a piece of the fence and peeled back all of the skin from top to bottom. Mike was so drunk he didn't even realize it, staggered to his room, and passed out.

It wasn't until the next morning, when Rotunda woke up and saw blood everywhere, that he discovered what had happened. As the story goes, Mike performed a little self-surgery and pulled the skin back into place and held it until he made it to the hospital. What a nightmare!

Eventually, the months of traveling up, down, and around Virginia, West Virginia, and North Carolina were wearing me down. With the pittance I was making, I could only afford a half bag of pretzel sticks and a gallon of milk during any given week.

Fortunately there were those like Sarge who would treat me to Burger King once in a while so I could have a hamburger and fries. He also occasionally took me to shows in his big camouflaged limo, which was cool, but I was having real doubts about MCW. Contrary to Ole's words, Crockett was not taking care of me at all.

My morale wasn't the only thing shrinking. During those three months on the road, my weight dropped from about 275 pounds to 225 pounds. At night I stared at the ceiling and questioned every second of what I was doing. I also wondered how little Joey was doing at home.

While I was gone, Joey stayed mostly with Nancy, but my mom and dad brought him to their house for visits, too. I knew everyone in my family felt my attempt at wrestling was crazy, but I had to try it. I knew I could be a big earner for Joey if things worked out.

Right now, it wasn't working for us. My frustration finally culminated into a meeting with Crockett. I went right into his office and explained my situation.

Crockett didn't even blink when he told me there was nothing he could do. "This is the way the business works." He said he was just doing Ole a favor until things cleared up in Georgia.

Well, I wasn't waiting any longer. I'd had it. I decided to quit wrestling and go home for Christmas. I arrived back in Minnesota burnt out and with a bitter taste in my mouth. Reluctantly, I moved back in with my parents until I could get back on my feet. I imagined my father putting up job postings on the fridge again, and I shuddered. Feeling the pressure, I started doing any temporary work I could find to bring in some cash.

For a while I was loading boxes onto UPS tractor trailers from 11 p.m. to 6 a.m. Believe it or not, I even went back to my dead-end job and worked in what I called "the cave," a dismal room where I had to assemble various high-tech machine parts. I wasn't happy, but it was great to be back home and around Joey. Every time I looked into his eyes, though, I knew I had to get things seriously back into motion.

Back home, everyone wanted to hear about my exploits in the world of professional wrestling. I let my feelings loose and made it clear that going down to Georgia was a horrible mistake and that Ole Anderson had fed me false hopes on the way to a dead end. Word got around quickly, and there was at least one person who took offense and decided to let me know: Rick Martel.

Rick was a well-established French Canadian wrestler who eventually became the AWA World Heavyweight champion before embarking on a run in the WWF as Rick "The Model" Martel. One day while I was working out at The Gym, Rick happened to be there and approached me with his two cents. In his thick French accent, he said, "Joe, I want to give you some advice. I know you went down to Georgia and didn't have a great experience. But you might want to watch what you say about the business. You might get hurt."

Oh, brother. Was he kidding? I cut him off. "Rick, let me tell you something. Those guys down there have my number and address. They can find me anytime. There ain't no one down there I can't handle, and that goes for you, too."

Rick jumped back, surprised.

I didn't mince words as I told him about being shuffled around from Atlanta to the Carolinas, starving. The expression on his face made it clear he didn't care, so I saved my breath and went about my workout.

A couple days later, I was at my parents' house with Joey when the phone rang. I couldn't believe it. It was Ole. I guess his ears had been ringing down in Atlanta.

"Hey, kid. How's it going?"

I wanted to reach through the phone and wring his neck. "You've got a lot of balls calling this house. You brought me down there, pushed me off to Crockett, and forgot about me. *I want to break your neck, man.*" I had so much pent-up frustration toward Ole that I blew up on him. I cussed him out left and right, calling him every name in the book.

To his credit, Ole listened, apologized, and explained things from his point of view. He said how his hands had been tied while fighting with Jim Barnett over GCW, but he assured me that things had been worked out and Barnett was gone. Then Ole asked me the big question: "Hey, Joe, you want to give it another try?"

Wow. I hadn't seen that one coming. Truth was, I didn't know. And that's what I told him. We agreed to talk again down the road.

In the meantime, I went to work. Dropping weight had been depressing as hell. Now that I was eating and lifting normally, my body's muscle memory kicked in and the pounds packed on. Before I knew it, I was close to 300 pounds again and feeling good.

I also got back in touch with both Rood and Mike Hegstrand. While I had been gone on my little adventures with GCW and MCW, Hegstrand and a healed up Rood had unsuccessfully gone to try their luck in Vancouver, wrestling for Al Tomko's NWA All-Star Championship Wrestling. We exchanged stories of our less-than-stellar debuts and had a good laugh.

Mike told me that when those guys in Vancouver got a look at him, they had a revelation: "Let's give this guy an evil

German gimmick." Mike hated it. They made him shave his head, gave him the claw as his finisher,[6] and named him Crusher Von Haig. "Aw c'mon. Not the claw." Mike groaned. "Anything but the claw." It was funny as hell. Crusher Von Haig was a typical, cliché gimmick that paralleled Baron von Raschke, a well-known wrestler in the AWA and NWA territories.

After only wrestling three matches, and vomiting after each of them, Mike had had enough. With Rood in tow, Mike fled Canada and came back to Minnesota. He couldn't get there fast enough. They drove the entire 1800 miles all day and all night until they made it, almost killing themselves several times by falling asleep at the wheel.

Now that the three of us had been reunited, we all picked up bouncing shifts again back at Gramma B's. There we were, working on a typical night, and who was there talking to Eddie again? Ole. Eddie had invited him back to take a better look at the pictures of all of us.

I said a quick hello but kept it short.

As Ole and Eddie were chatting and flipping through the pictures, one of them caught Ole's eye. "Hey, where did you get this shot of Joe?" he said. "I haven't seen this one before."

Only it wasn't me. It was Mike.

"Where was this guy the first time I was here?" He kept holding the pictures of Mike and me side by side. You could tell his wheels were turning. He saw something in us.

"Would the two of you be interested in coming down together? We could make you into a team," Ole said. "I'll make you my Road Warriors."

I was hesitant to have a big conversation about the idea until

6. Trademark final move of a match.

I talked to Mike.

When I did, we both decided that if Ole agreed to treat us right, we'd do it.

Ole and I spoke on the phone, and I made it clear that this was not going to be a repeat of my first trip down to Georgia. "Are you going to take care of me this time?" I asked.

"You two come down here, and I'm gonna make you my champions."

Champions? That was all I needed to hear to give wrestling another chance. After all, the main priority was to be successful and make good money. Becoming champions would ensure both.

So Mike and I packed, said our brief good-byes, and hauled off to the airport. You can imagine the crazy déjà vu I was experiencing.

As soon as we got to Atlanta, Ole made his intentions clear. "You guys are my tag champions. Get ready. Your first match is coming up on TV, and you'll already have the belts."

It was a sudden and shocking revelation. When Ole had told us on the phone that he was going to make us champions, I'd thought he'd meant a little further down the road after we had more experience. Mike and I had to scramble to get ready. I went out and bought us matching outfits that were an upgraded extension of my Road Warrior outfit before. Now we had black leather chaps with long black wrestling tights underneath, matching leather gloves, vests, and hats, black motorcycle boots, and sunglasses (black for me, red for Mike). The image, like us, was raw and in an early stage but much closer to what we wanted to portray: two bad, mean monsters from the streets.

After I got all of our stuff, we went back to see Ole.

"What do you want us to be?" I said. "How do you want us to

act and look? Who are we?"

Ole thought about it for a minute, then smiled. "After what I saw you do to Randy Barber last year, you're going to be Animal."

I liked it, but then we both looked at Mike and wondered what we'd call him.

As I continued to think, Mike shouted it out. "Well, I fly around like a hawk."

I answered right back, "There it is, bro. You'll be Hawk."

And that's how it happened. Right then and there, we would forever be known to each other and the public as Animal and Hawk, the Road Warriors. In and out of the ring, as per kayfabe, we pretty much became our alter egos full-time, and the people never doubted it for a second. It was pretty crazy to be given license to walk around looking and acting like the Road Warriors.

Because we were so green in the business, Ole paired us up with someone who would become an integral part of our lives and career for years to come: "Precious" Paul Ellering. Paul had been wrestling for a few years but had recently blown one of his knees out on two separate occasions. He was looking to step out of the ring but stay in the business. Paul was also a genius with an IQ of 162 and was a former junior powerlifting champion with a re-corded dead lift in the 750-pound range. For the first few months, Paul was our voice while we stood on either side of him as silent, menacing enforcers. We were a complete presentation now.

The time finally arrived for our big TV debut as the Road Warriors on GCW's *World Championship Wrestling*. While we were gearing up in the back, Ole walked up. "We're gonna shock a lot of people today, boys." Then he congratulated us and handed over the NWA National Tag Team Championship belts.

It was just like that. Without even wrestling in a single match, we were champions for the first time. It was an unprecedented move, but Ole had needed to make a quick decision.

As it turned out, Ole had been in a real jam with his most recent champs, Arn Anderson and Matt Borne (future WWF character Doink the Clown). Borne had been accused of statutory rape. The impending publicity wasn't something Ole wanted brought to the company, so he made a change: Arn and Borne were out, and Hawk and I were in.

Officially, it was explained that a few days before our TV debut, we'd won the titles during a tag team tournament in Chicago. It never happened. What did happen was that the Road Warriors became NWA champions without having to wrestle a single match. On June 11, 1983, we made our first ever TV appearance for GCW and came out with the belts around our waists as if we'd always had them.

Having the NWA National Tag Team Championship title was a *huge* deal. It immediately established us with the fans as legitimate forces to be reckoned with, and the boys in the back realized we were going to be around awhile, too.

Ole later told me that from time to time a few of the guys would complain about our stiff style and instant push. "They wanted you gone," he said. "I told them if they wanted you fired to go do it themselves because I sure as hell wasn't going to."

It was still hard to grasp, though. Only a few weeks before, Hawk and I were in Minnesota debating if we should go to Atlanta or not, and now we were champions. We were in the company of other known National Tag Team champion teams like the Freebirds, Brad and Bob Armstrong, and the Wild Samoans,

Afa and Sika.

It really showed how much Ole believed in us, too. He knew we were raw but that with Paul at our side, we'd learn from one of the most brilliant minds in the business. As our manager, Paul developed a vaudevillian carnival ringleader type of gimmick complete with a top hat, blue coat with tails, a pink tie, and his trademark folded up issue of the *Wall Street Journal*.

Paul hyped us during interviews with quick, creative articulation and a deep, gravelly tone. "Here come the Monsters of the Midway," he'd yell. "I'm bringing the world something that's never been seen before. The most dominating tag team of all time! You better run for your lives." Paul was a phenomenal talent and businessman and exactly what we needed. He made the claims, and we backed them up. It was a perfect circle.

One thing many people don't know is that Paul was our real manager. All of the managers in wrestling at the time—guys like Bobby Heenan, Jim Cornette, and Jimmy Hart—were playing a character role. Paul, on the other hand, did everything from booking our appearances, flights, and hotel rooms to sitting us down and strategizing our matches.

Almost every night, Hawk and I watched as Paul would sketch out a ring and stick figures on a piece of paper. "Okay, guys, this is the ring. Now, we don't want to do too much at one time, so pick two moves to add to the match every week. Once you've perfected the timing and execution, we'll move on." Then he pointed with his pencil and gestured with his hands. "Now, Joe, if you're here, bring the guy back to the corner and tag Mike. Then throw the guy into the ropes. As you get down and let the guy jump over you, Mike's going to clothesline the hell out of him."

Paul was so fluid and easy to follow that we learned something new every night. As a result, our confidence started to increase and we were able to elongate our matches.

Paul was more than a manager to us. He was the third Road Warrior.

4
ASSAULT ON GEORGIA CHAMPIONSHIP WRESTLING

When Hawk and I came into GCW as the Road Warriors, Ole said we were going to be killers. He sure wasn't kidding. I remember him saying specifically, "Listen, you guys. You can't wrestle a lick, and you can't talk. Shut your mouths and learn your craft. So for now, let Paul be your mouthpiece and murder whoever's put in front of you."

That was just fine with us. We trusted that Ole knew what he was doing, and I think he really enjoyed shaping our image as indestructible monsters. He liked to throw us into the mix whenever he could to show the GCW audience what we were all about.

One night during a sold-out show at the Omni in Atlanta, Ole decided to have us run in on Dusty Rhodes and make a statement. Dusty was a former NWA World Heavyweight champion and was about the most charismatic star that professional wrestling had to offer at the time. Fans absolutely loved him. So it was only natural that as Dusty was celebrating in the ring after a victory, Hawk and I ran down and started beating his brains out. The people were deafeningly loud, and it was the most exhilarating feeling I'd ever had in the business.

It was also the first time I worked with color.[7] Dusty was notorious for epic displays of blood, and this was no exception. His forehead practically exploded while Hawk and I pummeled him with fists.

"Harder. Hit me harder," Dusty kept shouting. "Open me up."

We were only too happy to oblige.

Dusty was a master to watch as he drew the most sympathetic emotions from the crowd. Many were on the verge of tears. There's no way to accurately explain how emotionally invested wrestling fans were back then. To them, this was as real as it got. Ole wasn't finished with them yet, either. It was time to even up the score for Dusty.

As Dusty was being mercilessly manhandled, Ole had Stan "The Lariat" Hansen run down to even up the score. Hansen was a six feet three, 300-pound wild cowboy known for being stiff as a board, tough as nails, and blind as a bat without his glasses, which he never wore. He came down the aisle wildly swinging his trademark cowbell and hollering up a storm. As he tried to climb into the ring, Hawk and I ran full speed and knocked him onto the floor. The Lariat didn't seem to like that one bit. After grabbing a steel chair, he climbed into the ring and started swinging for the fences.

Earlier in the evening before our rundown on Dusty, Ole had told us about the upcoming spot with Hansen and the chair shots. "Take as many as you guys can. Show everyone what the Road Warriors are made of."

Sounded simple enough, right? Well, when Hansen smashed me across the back for the first time, I knew exactly what I was

---

7. Blood.

made of: flesh and blood. It hurt like a son of a bitch. Hansen wasn't holding back at all.

After a second chair shot, I bailed to the floor and looked up to see Hansen smash Hawk right across the face with a wild clothesline. I thought he was knocked out cold. He rolled out to the floor next to me, and both of us had to dodge cups of piss and dip juice and other trash coming at us from every angle in the stands. I remember some bikers, thinking we were part of the family, handed us Ku Klux Klan cards.

Although Hawk and I were cleared out of the ring, our point was made. It didn't matter who you were or what you were doing. At any random time, you might look up and see the Road Warriors coming up on you. There was nowhere to run, nowhere to hide. Sooner or later, we would find you.

You know, at that point, in 1983, everything about us—even our attitudes with each other—was crude and almost infantile. In fact, one time we actually got into an offstage altercation with each other. Sort of.

I think we were in Atlanta at the airport picking up our luggage and for whatever reason, Mike and I started mouthing off to each other.

"What the fuck did you say?" Mike yelled out.

"You heard me, motherfucker. What are you going to do about it?"

But instead of World War III erupting right then and there at the baggage claim, we let it go and went to the Omni for the show.

While I was in our section of the locker room tightening up my boots and getting ready, Hawk came up and cracked me with a slap to the face. *Wham!* Paul was right there and immediately jumped in front of me as I was about to swing with everything I had. Hawk and I stood yelling threats at each other while some of the wrestlers came to see what the commotion was all about.

I turned and walked away, burning up and thinking, *I'll get that son of a bitch. He'll see.*

Well, a few minutes later, I came back to the scene of the crime to find Hawk about finished strapping his boots on. I didn't think twice. *Whack!* I delivered a nice open hand of my own to my partner's face.

Hawk jumped right up, the veins in his neck ready to burst. "Let's fucking do this now."

As we stood there nose-to-nose, ready to swing for the fences, we looked at each other and laughed. What the hell were we doing? Neither one of us had an answer. We shrugged it off and chalked it all up to being young, dumb, and full of . . . well, you know.

Oddly enough, as ready as we were to kill each other right there in the dressing room of the Omni, I can also remember a time shortly after that when Hawk actually saved another wrestler. After a show in Columbus, Ohio, we were rooming with a guy named Jesse Barr.

Jesse was another guy coming up in the business, and since he was also a heel, we traveled and shared rooms occasionally. Well, that particular evening at about midnight, Jesse wanted to borrow our rental car and find some action at a local bar, so we let him. Sometime around 3:00 in the morning, he came barging into the room and staggered like the big drunken mess that he was and crashed into bed.

Maybe thirty minutes or so later, Hawk and I were startled back awake by a horrifying gurgling sound in the dark coming from

Jesse's area. Hawk sprung up and ran over to Jesse and turned the light on to reveal a sight I'll never forget. Jesse was so comatose that he had vomited several times while lying flat on his back and was in the process of choking on his own puke.

"Holy shit, Joe," Hawk said as he pushed Jesse onto his side. "This motherfucker would've died if we weren't here." Jesse was so hammered that other than a couple of throat-clearing coughs, he didn't even wake up.

In the morning, when we went out to grab something to eat, Hawk and I jumped into the rental car and discovered a gigantic mess. In the middle of Jesse's drunken romp through Columbus with our car, he had managed to stomp muddy footprints all over the floor, ceiling, and seats.

Hawk was fuming. "Joe," he calmly said, "I don't know why I saved Jesse's life last night because now I wanna fucking kill him."

We let Jesse slide for his little escapade, but a couple years later in 1987, Jesse really paid the price for his antics. During a bar fight, Haku, a WWF wrestler, famously popped Jesse's eyeball right out of its socket.

When Hawk and I weren't trying to kill each other or save other wrestlers' lives, we were focused on improving our presentation in the ring. We still needed our hands held when it came to team dynamics and match construction, but Paul and Ole had shown us enough by that point for us to get by. Looking back at a typical match against a couple of jobbers illustrates how elementary our skills were. A good example is our match with Randy Barber and Joe Young.

The bell rang and Hawk started off, grabbing Randy and giving him a strong knee to the stomach before hooking him under each arm and driving him back into the corner. As soon as Hawk had him pinned against the turnbuckles, he unloaded three more knees to the stomach. *Bam, bam, bam!* Randy could barely even stand as Hawk dragged him over to our corner and tagged me in.

I jumped through the ropes, threw an elbow at Randy's head, and whipped him across to his corner, where he crashed hard. As he landed in the turnbuckles, I came charging full force with a knee to Randy's midsection three times before uppercutting him in the face. When Randy fell on his back, I jumped and landed with a gigantic leg drop across his neck and chest. *Crack!*

Fortunately for Randy, his part in our little dance was pretty much over. I picked him up, pressed him over my head, and launched him like a missile over to the other corner. When he landed, Randy almost skidded out of the ring, but he managed to reach up and tag in Joe Young. Joe had a grave look on his face, and for good reason.

I wasted no time grabbing Joe by his neck and walking him over to Hawk. When I tagged him in, we threw Joe into the ropes and ran in for a double clothesline. He might as well have run into a brick wall. As soon as he fell back, Hawk went running to the corner, climbed up to the second turnbuckle, and dove down for a body splash and the pin. The impact we made on our opponents left the audience feeling like they'd witnessed a disfiguring car accident.

Our matches back then were like a smash-and-grab robbery. I don't know what's funnier: the fact that those guys didn't know what hit them, or the fact that we didn't really know what we were doing. The bottom line was that Ole liked what he saw in us and even decided to get in on the fun.

See, even though Ole was booking GCW behind the scenes, he was still an active wrestler on TV. He came to a point when he wanted to turn babyface[8] and figured he could use us to do it. So Ole inserted himself into an angle that had been unfolding since our debut when Matt Borne had been forced to leave the company due to his legal situation.

When Borne had gone out, so had Arn, who'd gone from a prime spot in the company to a state of limbo as he struggled to reestablish himself. When Hawk and I came in, Paul developed a stable of heels around us known as the Legion of Doom, or LOD for short.

A funny side note is that Hawk came up with the Legion of Doom name while we were all sitting around watching TV one afternoon. This cartoon, *Challenge of the Super Friends,* came on and as the intro played and showed all of the bad guys led by Lex Luthor, a voice announced them as the Legion of Doom.

"We've gotta use that," Hawk said.

"Great idea, Hawk," Paul said. "We'll be the Legion of Doom and destroy everything."

The LOD also consisted of Jake "The Snake" Roberts and the Spoiler. Jake Roberts was a second-generation wrestler under his father, Grizzly Smith, and had great runs throughout GCW, MCW, and Bill Watts' Mid-South Wrestling (MSW), winning many championships along the way. Jake understood ring psychology better than any other worker I knew back then. Ring psychology basically refers to a wrestler's ability to read the crowd and call the match spots[9] on the fly according to their reactions.

Jake was a seasoned, classic heel because of his slick, calculated demeanor and was one of those ring veterans who knew how to work the people. A great worker in the wrestling business like Jake or Ric Flair has all of the performance intuition of a successful stand-up comedian. He can quickly determine what material starts to pick

8. Good guy.
9. Moves.

up the audience and manipulate his act on the fly. That's exactly what ring psychology is all about.

Not too long after Hawk and I came into GCW, Jake and I even moved into a small apartment in Atlanta together. It didn't last long. I quickly grew sick of Jake's bad habits, such as his constant drinking and drugging, but it was his cigarette smoking that got the best of me.

Jake had these big ashtrays filled with cigarette butts all the time, and the place stunk on ice. I'd be sitting there trying to eat a good, healthy meal, and there'd be Jake on the couch passing out, looking like a crusty grim reaper. In retrospect, I should've persuaded Hawk to avoid Jake because of his self-destructive tendencies. Little did I know that Hawk would be more influenced by the same type of behavior as time progressed.

Also in the Legion of Doom, aside from Hawk, Jake, and me, was a masked wrestler in the twilight of his career called the Spoiler, portrayed by Don Jardine. During his peak in the '70s in the MCW territory, Jardine was better known as the Super Destroyer, a similar masked character, when he wrestled both Jack Brisco and Harley Race for the NWA World Heavyweight Championship.

Around the time Hawk and I landed on the scene, Paul had been trying to convince the "orphaned" Arn Anderson to join us, letting him know the LOD was the winning team. Paul even suggested Arn call himself Arn Ellering instead of Arn Anderson to further distance himself from Ole, who was also his kayfabe uncle.

Being the ever concerned "uncle," Ole kept coming out and warning Arn he'd be making a big mistake if he joined up with the LOD. It quickly became our job to show everyone that it was Ole who was making the big mistake by getting into our business.

During a Saturday morning taping of *World Championship Wrestling*, Hawk and I paid Ole a visit. Ole was in the middle of giving an interview with Gordon Solie when Paul came out to interrupt him. As Ole got in Paul's face, Hawk and I ran up on him and started hammering him with forearms and punches before throwing him into the ring. We were kicking the crap out of him until Ronnie Garvin and "Pistol" Pez Whatley ran down and made the save.

Just as they arrived, King Kong Bundy, who for the last few weeks had been trying to join the Legion of Doom, came stomping through the ropes on our side, setting up a six-man tag match. It worked like a charm.

The fans sided with Ole, and our heat[10] was off the charts. It was awesome. You should've seen Ole when he came back to the dressing room. He looked as if a bus had hit him. Arn never did join the LOD, and although he pleaded with Paul, King Kong Bundy never made the cut.

It all culminated on TV when Bundy crossed the line and we had to take care of business, Road Warrior style. During an interview with Gordon Solie on *World Championship Wrestling*, Paul was doing one of his typical monologues about how elite of a group the Legion of Doom was. As he brought up Bundy and his vain attempts at joining us, Gordon said it was time for a commercial break.

When the show came back on the air, they cut back in with Paul midsentence as he told Gordon how disgustingly fat and lazy Bundy was. "There's no place for a slob like King Kong Bundy in the Legion of Doom." It was made to look as if Paul didn't realize he was back on the air.

---

10. Negative crowd reaction.

All of a sudden, an enraged Bundy came out of nowhere and grabbed Paul. He had heard everything. Bundy tossed Paul like a rag doll into the ring and started delivering big kicks to his stomach. In a flash, Hawk and I ran out to help Paul.

I remember hitting the ring first and pounding Bundy with a double axe handle so hard that he immediately dropped to his knees. *Whoops.* I didn't mean to do that, seriously. When Bundy started going down, I didn't realize I'd hit him so hard. I felt bad and whispered to Bundy, "Sorry, man. Quick, hit me back even harder."

Without any delay, *bam!* He cracked me with a clothesline harder than I'd ever felt before, and I immediately went down. As I hit the canvas, Hawk and Jake Roberts ran Bundy down and started giving him the boot. I jumped right up and joined in.

As we triple-teamed the hell out of Bundy, in came Wahoo McDaniel and Ronnie Garvin to set up yet another six-man tag match. The crowd went out of their minds cheering for Bundy, who wasn't used to hearing that kind of reaction. It was fascinating to witness. For months, Bundy had been one of the hottest heels in the promotion, and after Hawk and I victimized him, the people embraced him. It was one of my first lessons in ring psychology and story line development.

One night after working a show in Hapeville, Georgia, we were with Ole in his room at the Ramada Inn shooting the shit. He said he'd been thinking about our biker image and said it could use some tweaking. Truthfully, at the time, we looked like hulking versions of the leather guy from the Village People, and we knew we needed a change. Hawk and I were up for anything, so we started shooting ideas out left and right. What we came up with proved to be the first of two major breakthroughs in the evolution of the Road Warriors gimmick.

"Hey," Mike said, "I got an idea for our hair. Why doesn't Joe shave his head into a Mohawk with one big strip of hair on the top of his head from front to back and I'll do the opposite? I'll have one small strip on the top left side and one on the top right. That way it'll look like we could plug our heads into each other and it'd be a perfect fit." I stared at Hawk as I tried to picture it. As crazy as it sounded to me, it really didn't sound that crazy at all. So we did it.

Hawk and I laughed out loud as we cut each other's hair into the designs, questioning what the hell we were doing with our lives. When we were done, we looked at each other in the mirror and analyzed our work. We liked what we saw. It was different; it was perfect. All of a sudden, our appearance took on a ton of raw attitude. Guys our size never had haircuts like these. It became really easy for us to look really dangerous. But our little evolution wasn't over yet.

A few days after we invented our trademark hairstyles, we had a quick meeting with Ole and Cowboy Bill Watts. Watts was a gruff, no-nonsense retired wrestler who had won almost every major NWA title there was in his day, and now he was the promoter of MSW out of Louisiana. Ole and Bill were longtime friends and always worked out deals to trade talent between their territories.

Ole decided Hawk and I were going to work a couple of dates for Watts and wanted to introduce us. When we all met, Watts was impressed with our size and liked what we were trying to do with the gimmick. He even had an interesting suggestion: "Why don't you guys experiment with face painting?"

Hawk and I looked at each other and kind of shrugged, as if to say, "Why didn't we think of that?"

So we bought tubes of red, yellow, silver, black, and blue makeup and started experimenting with designs. I even went back and watched *The Road Warrior* to get some inspiration, which worked like a charm. In the movie, there are guys running around with very primal, almost Native American-style stripes painted on their faces. With those images in my head, I sat down in front of the bathroom mirror and came up with my first paint job.

From the middle of my left eyebrow, I started a red line that curved up and to the top left of my forehead, then repeated the shape with a blue curved line on the other side. The image reminded me of devil horns. From there, I drew an assortment of additional single lines on the sides of my face, under my eyes, and even on my chin.

It wasn't exactly a visionary work of art or anything, but I never really had anything to go on from the start. Hawk's paint job was equally crude: a few red lines here, a blue and yellow one there, and he put a silver circle over one of his eyes.

Hawk and I looked each other over and then started posing and grimacing in the mirror, sticking our tongues out. We didn't know what to think of ourselves, but I definitely enjoyed the extra creativity of it all. One thing was for sure: with the paint on, I didn't feel like Joe anymore; I was Animal. One look at Mike, and I knew he'd also checked out long ago in favor of Hawk.

With only a couple of brush strokes to the face, we could step out of our normal lives and into the boots of Road Warrior Animal and Road Warrior Hawk. As a kid, I'd always wondered what it would be like to have a secret identity and superpowers like the Hulk and Superman. Now I knew.

I'll never forget the looks on the other guys' faces the first time we revealed our new look backstage before TV tapings. We were in Atlanta in the offices of the little studio where we taped *World Championship Wrestling*. The studio had no real locker room to speak of, so the guys just changed in various partitions in the office. When Hawk and I emerged from our cubicle with the new haircuts and the paint, the banter of all the wrestlers instantly died into complete silence. No shit.

As we strode by, guys like Arn Anderson, Iron Sheik, Jimmy Valiant, and Tommy Rich tried to determine what the hell they saw. At that time in professional wrestling, very few of the boys wore face paint, and those who did didn't have a gimmick like ours behind it. Wrestlers like "Exotic" Adrian Street, the Missing Link, who had also recently debuted, and the Great Kabuki were all unique, made-up workers who had found success with an approach completely different from ours.

"Exotic" Adrian Street was a flamboyantly gay character and had been wrestling since the late 1950s. He wore glitter makeup, had colored pigtails, and enjoyed a long and successful run, winning multiple NWA championships in Florida Championship Wrestling (FCW). Interestingly enough, there was a brief time in early 1984 when Paul attempted to recruit Street for the LOD.

The Missing Link was a brand-new gimmick for Dewey Robertson, who had wrestled as a straightforward babyface under his real name for years. He totally reinvented himself as the out-of-control madman by painting his entire face green and only speaking with grunts and screams. Link was an interesting character for sure.

And then there was the Great Kabuki, a Japanese wrestler who achieved great fame not only throughout Japan but in the United States as well, especially in FCW in Tampa and World

Class Championship Wrestling (WCCW) in Texas. Kabuki painted his entire face with white, black, and red in a traditional Japanese theater style and is also credited with inventing the spectacle of spraying mist out of his mouth into an opponent's eyes, which was adopted by later wrestlers like the Great Muta.

When we started entering the ring with face paint, people didn't know what to think. Neither did we. All I knew was that a new attitude was taking over Hawk and me. Our expressions seemed to say, "Get out of our way, 'cause we're coming, and it's gonna be out of control."

With our new image, we not only crossed the line; we went way past the point of no return. Having Ole and Paul constantly telling us to be as unhinged as possible only encouraged us. We didn't miss a beat as we pulverized whoever was in the ring and threw them out to the floor. Those guys always knew it was coming.

Hawk and I also decided we needed a unique hometown billing that complemented our style. Although we were really from Minnesota, so were a ton of other guys, and we weren't interested in having anything in common with anybody. Besides, Minnesota was far too nice of a place to hail from. Besides, "Minnesota nice" is a common phrase that's great to describe regular people, but not the Road Warriors. We looked at a map to see what nearby cities would be cool, and we saw Chicago.

Hawk and I had always heard about how tough the south side of Chicago was, filled with gritty biker bars, gangs, and all sorts of bad news. That suited us fine. Chicago had a notorious history, too, from being almost totally wiped out by fire in the late 1800s to being the old stomping grounds of Al Capone. This town had guts. From that point forward, we were announced "from Chicago," and Paul started referring to us as the Monsters of the Midway during our interviews.

After making our debut with the NWA National titles in June, Hawk and I picked up some serious steam by reinventing our gimmick. It wasn't long at all before promoters from different territories took notice and wanted to bring us in for appearances.

As with Ole and Bill Watts, promoters in those days happily did business with each other and weren't in direct competition. This interaction was the bread and butter of the industry. Each territory had its own regional outreach and usually their own local television show to promote upcoming live events and perpetuate story lines to keep the people interested.

When promoters started seeing and hearing about us, it opened up a whole new world and we never looked back. There was an unending parade of opportunities to make good money and increase our exposure. Calls started coming in from all over the United States to come in and do shots.

Joe Blanchard (Southwest Championship Wrestling in San Antonio), Eddie Graham (FCW in Tampa), Jerry Jarrett (Continental Wrestling Association in Memphis), Don Owen (Pacific Northwest Wrestling in Portland), and Bob Geigel (Central States Wrestling in Missouri) were a handful of the many established wrestling promoters we started frequently appearing for. Not only did we benefit financially, but we also became highly sought after and earned a strong reputation of being a highly dependable commodity.

We also got to work with a lot of great teams outside of Georgia who helped make us seasoned workers. I remember encountering the team of Magnum T.A. and "Hacksaw" Jim Duggan during our very first appearance for Bill Watts' Mid-South Wrestling in

Shreveport, Louisiana. It was a hot August night in 1983 when we came to town to show everyone who the new badasses were.

Magnum and Duggan were the Mid-South Tag Team champions and established studs in their own right. Magnum was a handsome rebel type from Virginia Beach who didn't back down from anyone, and Duggan was a longhaired, bearded wild man who had played for the Atlanta Falcons. The fans were sure to be treated to a brawl they'd never forget.

As we were being announced in the ring, Duggan grabbed the top rope and started stomping his left foot repeatedly to get the fans to clap. It was one of his trademark mannerisms. I smirked and started to mock him by stomping my foot.

I guess Duggan didn't care for my imitation very much as he came running over and started hammering me with stiff forearms and punches. Magnum followed suit on Hawk, and we didn't even have a chance to take our championship belts off before falling out to the floor. The crowd was on their feet the whole time, going absolutely nuts.

We quickly recovered and jumped back into the ring to start the match. Hawk started off with Magnum, and you could tell neither was going to give an inch. I remember watching the playback and listening to the play-by-play with Bill Watts and a young, new announcer named Jim Ross. Watts in particular was really putting Hawk and me over, saying, "They're like the reincarnation of the worst of the Hells Angels and the worst of Charles Manson's Helter Skelter." It was high praise—and accurate to boot.

Though both tag teams put up a big fight, ultimately the referee declared Magnum and Duggan the winners by disqualification. See, there was a certain way business was done. When we were the visitors in another wrestling promotion, we knew we couldn't very well go into someone else's backyard and cleanly defeat their top talent. It would kill their credibility.

At the same time, Hawk and I couldn't be expected to be brought into another company and cleanly lose. It would destroy our mystique. That's why you'd see a lot of disqualifications and double disqualifications. If done right, both teams would come out looking strong and possibly set up another confrontation down the way.

It was also important to stand our ground with the promoters and bookers when visiting another territory. Otherwise, they could take advantage. For the most part, it was their main objective to keep the home talent over and not let some strangers come marching in, get all the heat, and then leave. It would flatten their business.

In fact, right before our match with Magnum and Duggan had been set to start, Ernie Ladd, the booker for Mid-South, had walked in to discuss some ideas. At six feet nine, Ladd, "The Big Cat," was a former American Football League star with the San Diego Chargers and recently retired pro wrestler. He said we needed to put Magnum and Duggan over and really make them look strong during the finish of the match. "At the end, when Duggan's making his comeback against you guys, let him give you like six or seven clotheslines each before you duck out of the ring."

Six or seven clotheslines each? Did The Big Cat have brain damage? "Excuse me, Ernie," I said. "Taking that many clotheslines makes us look weak. We'll take two at the most."

Ladd stared at me, shook his head, and walked over to Hawk. "Yo partnah is a bad link in the chain." Ladd walked out the door.

Hawk and I started laughing.

"Screw him," I said.

Ladd didn't know us from a hole in the wall. In those situations, we had to be smart, speak up, and protect ourselves, or people would walk all over us.

By the fall of 1983, Hawk and I were firing on all cylinders. We were in high demand, still held the NWA National Championship titles, and were constantly working on our tag team dynamics with Paul. Eventually we found a basic rhythm and began to get comfortable.

Things were looking up, and I could be proud of my job when I spoke with my family. In November, I got the news from home that my parents wanted to come down to Atlanta for Thanksgiving dinner. After being away from him for about five months, I was finally going to see my son, Joey, again.

My family arrived at the apartment I shared with Hawk and Jake Roberts. I scooped up Joey, and he started laughing. My parents had even brought Li'l Nan, who couldn't believe her grandson was running around the country as a professional wrestler.

Being with my friends and family was the perfect break from the hustle and grind of the business. It was especially great that I was able to bring Joey to the TV tapings on Saturday morning so he could get an up-close look at what Daddy was doing for work. I know somewhere there's footage of Li'l Nan and Joey at ringside during our match.

Around the same time that my family visited, Hawk and I entered our first notable feud with another team, the Sawyers. Brett and Buzz Sawyer were legitimate brothers who were far more rugged and experienced than most of the teams we'd faced at that point. They were bigger and had a brawling style. To top it off, Buzz was one of the most unpredictable and troubled guys in the business.

Buzz "Mad Dog" Sawyer, as he was known, was notorious for wild mood swings, problems with drugs, and fights with the cops. Not long before this, for whatever reason, Ole had relinquished his own position as booker and given it to Buzz. Now that he was in charge, Buzz naturally wanted to put himself over and take the titles from us. "You guys don't need the belts anymore," he said. "You've got enough heat without them."

Hawk and I agreed. If it made sense, we never objected to doing a job.

On Sunday, November 27, 1983, we dropped the belts to the Sawyers in Cincinnati and immediately rematched them a few days later in Macon, Georgia. Buzz, always the opportunist, decided to exploit his position by messing with us some more. Knowing full well that Hawk and I never went far beyond eight minutes on any given night, he announced that our match would be a sixty-minute Broadway. "I'm gonna make you guys puke," Buzz proclaimed backstage.

I'll give it to him. As coked out and wild as he was, Buzz could go the distance. We saw him go all out many times against other guys, and now he was calling us out. Never wanting to be discounted as a couple of muscle-bound hacks, Hawk and I were totally up for it. We wanted to show we could hang with anyone.

As we made our way down the aisle to the ring, I almost had to rub my eyes. Referee Nick Patrick had been pulled into the crowd right in front of us and was fending off punches from a bunch of guys. It was a classic case of some good ol' boys getting way too drunk and carried away. This kind of stuff was standard fare in those days, though. It went with the territory. Hawk and I dropped character for a second and charged over as fast as hell. We started knocking every head that got in the way between Nick and us and helped him out.

Bruised and pretty shaken up, Nick went back to the locker room, and we continued down to the ring. I grabbed a microphone and challenged anyone to come on down and try to jump us as they had Nick. The people grew silent. No one came. The most important rule of the unwritten wrestler's code is to be safe and to protect yourself and each other at all times. If fans crossed the line, which they did from time to time, they'd better pray the cops got to them first.

The match itself went off pretty much without a hitch. Hawk and I took it to Brett and Buzz back and forth as the fans stood to catch our action. Maybe thirty minutes into the match I was watching Hawk and Brett trade punches when I started thinking with amusement, *Buzz thought he was going to make us puke?*

Right then, Brett threw Hawk out to the floor. I quickly jumped in and started a standoff with both Sawyers, giving Hawk time to recover. As I looked down to the floor, I caught a glimpse of Hawk crawling underneath the ring and then quickly scrambling back. He had a funny look on his face. Brett was walking around in circles, yelling at the fans and waiting for Hawk to return. All of a sudden, Hawk popped up and climbed back into the ring and we finished the match.

Because Hawk and I weren't used to going much more than seven to fifteen minutes in our matches, those sixty minutes seemed to pass like sixty years. We still had such a limited collection of moves between us that Hawk and I must've press slammed and clotheslined those guys a hundred times. What else could we do? At least Brett and Buzz had enough experience that when the action slowed down they'd place one of us in a submission hold on the mat. Being on the mat like that allowed everybody to catch their breath, while at the same time the crowd would start cheering, looking for some momentum to build up again. Really, the Sawyers carried us that entire match, but it was Buzz's idea to begin with, so they knew how much work they had on their hands from the start.

When we got to the back, I asked Hawk about his disappearance under the ring.

"I threw up, bro," he said. "There were buckets of soda and ice there, too, so I rinsed my mouth out before coming back up."

I couldn't believe it. That bastard Buzz was right. He *was* going to make the Road Warriors puke. Well, at least one of them. Puking during a match back then wasn't an uncommon occurrence with Hawk either, which he proved again a couple nights later in Texas.

We were wrestling for Joe Blanchard's Southwest Championship Wrestling (SCW) in San Antonio against the SCW Tag Team champions, Butch and Luke, the Sheepherders (later known as the Bushwackers in the WWF). The Sheepherders were a couple of crazy New Zealanders who had been in the business for twenty years and were well known for their violent and usually bloody escapades.

Tonight, however, the escapades were courtesy of Hawk. Even after a few months in the business, our endurance wasn't quite worked up that well and we still hadn't conquered the nerves of live performing.

About halfway through the fifteen-minute match, Hawk came stumbling over to our corner holding his stomach and breathing hard. He panted for a couple of seconds before announcing,

"Animal, I'm gonna blow." Without any further warning, Hawk leaned over and launched a bucket's worth of bright green vomit out of the ring and down onto the floor.

Fans in the first two rows didn't have any time to react and were splattered by the projectile puke. Some of them started dry heaving as they got up to run away. Hawk looked right back at me with a big smile. "I'm good. Let's go."

Butch looked at Hawk and said, "Atta boy, mate. Atta boy."

Right after that, Butch backed me up into a corner and stuck his tongue completely into my ear. Whoa! It freaked me out big-time. You never knew what was going to happen when you wrestled the Sheepherders.

Back in Atlanta, Buzz's little power trip as booker had reached the end of the line. When Ole came to check things out for himself, he didn't like what he saw. He wanted Hawk and me to have the belts again immediately, so he set up a match in Canton, Ohio. When Buzz found out, he went ape shit.

As I was finishing up my paint job in the bathroom, referee Nick Patrick came up to us and said Buzz was almost foaming at the mouth. "He looked totally insane," he said. "Buzz told me that even though Ole told him to drop the belts to you tonight, you guys were going to have to take them back."

I told Nick, "Give that sawed-off little prick this message: 'Animal said he's going to flip a coin to see if he or Hawk knocks you out first.'"

When Nick reported back, he said that Buzz had stared and then muttered, "Yeah, we'll see what happens," and walked away.

Ten minutes later, Nick came back with a really disturbed look on his face. "I thought you guys should know Buzz is back there taping blades to every one of his fingers. He's a mess, so be careful." Buzz was so out of it that he'd sliced his own hands up pretty good and was bleeding all over the place.

Taping blades was (and still is) a traditional method wrestlers use to prepare for a match when someone is going to bleed from the forehead. They take a single razor and cut the corner off, which yields a short, thin shard of a blade. Then they tape the piece to one finger or wrist with white medical tape. When the time comes during a match to draw color on themselves, they unwrap the tape, grab the blade and while doubled over on the mat or outside floor selling an injury, they slice their head open and, *presto*, they've successfully bladed in professional wrestling.

Up until then, we didn't care about Buzz's personal problems as long as they didn't get in our way, and they usually didn't. But now things were going too far, and Hawk and I were ready to take baseball bats and do some real damage if that's how he wanted to play.

When Brett Sawyer caught wind of what was going on, he went outside and sat in their car. He wanted no part of it.

Fortunately, Ole found out what happened and went to talk some sense into Buzz. When Ole came back, his shirt was a bloody mess from helping take all the blades off of Buzz's cut fingers. We were told Buzz had sobered up enough to go out and work with us. It turned out not to be the case.

The bell rang and the match started, but Buzz wasn't cooperating. He refused to sell any moves, and it really pissed off Hawk. Buzz and Hawk even got into a real wrestling match outside on the floor trying to take each other down, but they eventually broke it up. I can still see Hawk firmly planted outside of the ring near our corner, holding on to the bottom rope with both arms as Buzz kept trying to give him a belly-to-back suplex onto the concrete.

Hawk was looking up at me as if to say, "Is this guy kidding?" The funny thing was that later, back inside the ring during the finish, Hawk nailed Buzz with a successful belly-to-back suplex of his own and got the pin.

Sure, it was a chaotic and uncertain match at times, but at the end of the night we got the win and the belts. I felt bad for Buzz because with us, the Mad Dog's bark was far worse than his bite. Although he'd freaked out backstage and the whole situation was precarious as hell, he really didn't give us any problems during the match. He sobered up enough to finish his job and drop the titles.

Unfortunately, Ole was sick of his Buzz Sawyer problem and fired him from GCW shortly afterward. This was how the Legion of Doom started off 1984. It was one hell of a welcome into the world of professional wrestling.

5
DESTROY EVERYTHING THAT MOVES

As we rang in the New Year of 1984, Hawk, Paul, and I toasted each other to our undeniable success. We were even given *Pro Wrestling Illustrated* magazine's Tag Team of the Year Award for 1983, which was a huge honor because the award winners were chosen by fan ballots and not some group of editors or online journalists. We also went on to win it in 1984, 1985, and 1988, becoming the only team in wrestling history to claim the award more than twice. Paul was even named manager of the year in 1984.

In the span of six months, we had charged into GCW and helped breathe new life into the company. Ole knew how to aim and fire us at the public to keep them trying to catch their breath while wondering who and when we'd strike next. It didn't matter whether you were a babyface or a heel; no one was safe. In those early days, I don't think there was a single TV taping of *World Championship Wrestling* or a live event in Georgia where we didn't interfere with someone's match or interview. It's what we became known for.

Arn Anderson once said that when the boys reported to the studio in the morning to see the call sheet, if they were paired up with the Road Warriors, their hearts sank. Some guys would grab their bags and leave on the spot. All we knew was that we were doing what we were told by the guy who paid us and having a ton of fun in the process. We definitely lived our gimmick full-time, but there was never a direct intention to intimidate the other guys in the locker room. We saved that for the fans.

Depending on what mood we were caught in, Hawk and I delivered mixed results for autograph and picture seekers. Usually right after an event, the fans gathered around the back exits of the arena and waited for wrestlers to come out. Most of the time, we took a minute to pose and shake hands; other times, some unsuspecting fan got more than he bargained for.

One night after a show in Wheeling, West Virginia, Hawk and I were dead tired and hungry as hell. We didn't want anything to do with anybody at that point. Scowling, we kicked the doors open. Even though we had do-rags tied around our heads, people still recognized us. As you can imagine, we stuck out wherever we went, all the time. One fan had the balls to get in Hawk's way and shove a program in his face for a signature.

Hawk grabbed it, autographed it, and coughed up the most disgusting phlegm wad I've ever seen and spat it right onto the cover before throwing it back. "There you go, kid. Enjoy."

When Ole heard about us doing things like that, we'd always get a phone call at the hotel. "C'mon, guys. Cut that shit out."

What did we know? We were just two big dummies figuring it out as we went.

With the NWA National belts firmly around our waists, we

fended off challenges from every team in the company. The Briscos (Jack and Jerry), the Lightning Express (Brad Armstrong and Tim Horner), and Wahoo McDaniel and Mark Youngblood were just a few of the teams thrown in our direction to no avail. The Road Warriors were the new breed, and this was *our* time.

Eventually Ole started looking around some of the other territories to find some main event, money-drawing talent for us to work with. With some help from Paul, he found exactly what he was looking for in Memphis. Paul used to wrestle in Memphis and knew Jerry "The King" Lawler and Austin Idol were about as big as it got in promoter Jerry Jarrett's Continental Wrestling Association (CWA). Lawler was the booker for Jarrett and was coming off of a major feud with comedian Andy Kaufman, who had been making appearances wrestling women. Lawler played it as if he was offended by Kaufman's mockery of the business and set up a match between the two of them, which resulted in Kaufman receiving two big piledrivers and going to the hospital.

The whole thing came to a famous climax on national TV when Lawler and Kaufman confronted each other on *Late Show with David Letterman*. As the two were seated, Lawler shocked the audience when he slapped Kaufman hard across the face for insulting him. The comedian responded by throwing his coffee in Lawler's face. Of course, the whole thing was a work, but it was a good one and raised huge mainstream attention for Kaufman, Lawler, and the CWA.

Austin Idol, the Universal Heartthrob, was a tanned, muscular, and extremely popular babyface who'd won the AWA International Heavyweight Championship title multiple times. He also challenged Harley Race and Ric Flair for the NWA World

Heavyweight title on several occasions. What was interesting about the team of Lawler and Idol was that those guys kayfabe hated each other and had been feuding in grudge matches for years.

Fortunately, Lawler knew it would be a brilliant strategy and even better business opportunity to unite himself with Idol. By putting their differences aside, Lawler and Idol, the babyface heroes of the CWA, could challenge the evil Road Warriors for the NWA National belts in their own backyard in Memphis. It was top marquee billing all the way. To help promote our impending arrival to the CWA, Jimmy Hart approached us with an interesting idea from the "Mouth of the South."

Jimmy was a high-octane manager and creative force in the CWA who had also been right in the middle of the whole Lawler/Kaufman feud. Outside of wrestling, though, Jimmy had also been the lead singer of the '60s band The Gentrys. If you've ever heard that classic bubblegum era tune "Keep On Dancin'," and chances are you have, you heard a twenty-one-year-old Jimmy Hart struttin' his stuff. Jimmy was also one of the key driving forces behind the fusion of rock 'n' roll and music videos into professional wrestling. In 1984, MTV was starting to catch on and Jimmy, having had his career in the music industry with The Gentrys, knew it was the next big thing.

About a week out from our big match against Lawler and Idol, we got a phone call from an excited Jimmy. "Hey, baby, this is Jimmy Hart. I've got this song you need to come here and let me record. We're going to put it on the radio and do a video, too."

Hawk and I thought it'd be fun, so we packed and drove all night to get to Tennessee for our big shoot. When we arrived in Memphis, Jimmy met us and took us to this recording studio downtown. We put our paint jobs on and were wearing cowboy boots, jeans, our leather chaps, custom Road Warriors muscle shirts, and dog collars. Jimmy said he had this rock tune he'd originally written for the former NWA World Heavyweight champion Terry Funk and wanted to give it to us.

Jimmy fed us our lyrics line by line until the whole thing was done. It was like our first wrestling match: we had no idea what we were doing and had to be walked through the whole thing, and the end result wasn't too pretty.

Hawk and I stood together in front of a big boom mic in the studio and took turns singing lines that went something like this: "There's talk in the street. There's trouble coming down. Hawk and the Animal are coming to town. Everybody's talking; they don't say a thing. But everybody knows what the Warriors will bring."

It wasn't exactly a toe-tapping classic, but it worked perfectly. When Jimmy took the song to the local radio stations, not only did they start to play it, but it quickly went to the number one most requested song of the week. The video of us in the studio made the TV rounds on both *Memphis Wrestling* and *World Championship Wrestling* along with promos from both teams about the big match.

When the day finally came for our big showdown in February, Memphis was electric. The public had been eating up the whole buildup of the match for weeks and couldn't wait to see the drama unfold. To be honest, neither could I.

Inside the Mid-South Coliseum, a sellout crowd of 10,000 stood as Hawk and I made our way down to the ring. Lawler and Idol were already waiting for us as we stepped through the ropes and got right up in their faces. Paul was right there, too, waving his rolled-up newspaper in the ref's face, telling him not to get in the way.

The match started off with Lawler and me squaring off, so I launched at him with a kick to the stomach followed by a quick press slam. *Bam!* Lawler bounced off the mat and out of the ring. The crowd was stunned, and quite a few were applauding me as I posed and yelled. Lawler stayed out on the floor for at least a minute before deciding to come back in. I backed him up into a corner, and Lawler started saying, "Punch me. Come on! Punch me."

The last time I'd been in this situation was in Eddie Sharkey's church basement fighting Rood. I'd tried to throw a nice working punch to his face and wound up breaking his nose. Since then, I'd avoided it at all costs. But, at Lawler's request, I tossed a weak little punch toward his face and completely missed—like a strike in baseball. The funniest part was watching Lawler sell it as if I'd hit him with a sledgehammer. Even though I hadn't laid a finger on him, he fell on the ground holding his face as if he'd been shot. He was great.

When I walked over and tagged in Hawk, he and Lawler sized each other up. Hawk kicked him in the stomach, elbowed the back of his head, and then pressed Lawler high in the air before slamming him down. Again the crowd was almost silenced in awe, and again Lawler stalled for another minute on the floor. Right next to him, Paul was yelling in his face, calling him a coward.

When Lawler did decide to get back in, Hawk was waiting for him and they locked up again. This time Lawler was able to back Hawk up into an empty corner and delivered a right fist to the face followed by a hip toss in the center of the ring. As Hawk was getting up, Lawler ran over to him and kicked him in the stomach, setting Hawk up for a piledriver. Lawler reached down, put Hawk's head between his legs, lifted him up vertically, and crashed him down on his head. *Boom!*

The piledriver was Lawler's finisher, and usually no one got up from it. In fact, it kayfabe sent a lot of guys, like Andy Kaufman, to the hospital. Lawler got up and started celebrating as the crowd almost blew the roof off of the coliseum. The "King" had slain the beast. Right? Well, not exactly.

You have to imagine the reaction from the audience as Hawk totally no-sold the piledriver and jumped to his feet as Lawler's back was turned. It was something Lawler had suggested to Hawk before the show. Hawk loved that piledriver spot so much that he added it to his permanent repertoire and probably worked it a thousand more times during his career.

When Lawler turned around and saw Hawk standing and huffing, his eyeballs almost popped out of his head, as if Hawk had risen from the dead. With clenched fists and every muscle in his body tensed, Hawk slowly stalked Lawler around the ring like Frankenstein or something right out of the movies. When they reached an open corner, Hawk leveled him with one punch. Lawler hung there on the ropes for dear life. It was amazing to watch.

Here Lawler was, a longtime respected star in the business, and he was selling and bumping all over the place for a couple of rookies he didn't know from a hole in the wall. It was because of professionals like him and Idol that Hawk and I were able to come off looking every bit the monsters we were billed as.

Lawler knew that by taking all of the punishment we could dish out, he'd also be absorbing huge sympathy from the fans. He crawled around playing the martyr while Idol was always out of arm's reach, pleading to be tagged in. That was the key. A worker like Lawler was brilliant in this type of situation because he knew exactly how to play off of the people desperately wanting him to get that tag.

Lawler would reach toward the outstretched hand of Idol, and then at the last minute Hawk or I would drag him away and pummel him some more. Finally after several attempts to get to his corner and with the tension of the fans at fever pitch, we finally let Lawler break away and give the hot tag to Idol.

Boom! The whole Mid-South Coliseum exploded like a powder keg as Idol jumped through the ropes and began scoop slamming Hawk and me left and right. We probably took about three slams each. As we were walking around dazed, Idol grabbed us both by the backs of our heads and noggin-knocked us face-first into each other.

When Lawler got back into the action, I split off with him in one corner, and Idol and Hawk were in the middle of the ring. I picked Lawler up on my shoulder and started to walk slowly backward. Not knowing Hawk was laid out right behind me, I tripped and fell with Lawler on top of me. Idol, seizing the opportunity, jumped onto Lawler so that I was being pinned by two people. The ref made a two count before I completely launched both of them off me with a big kick-out that impressed even me.

The finish came with all four of us in the ring brawling. At the same time, Paul was trying to hold Idol against the ropes so I could hit him with a running knee. When I jumped toward Idol, he moved out of the way and I nailed Paul instead. Paul got up and tried to climb back into the ring, but the ref was wrestling him to keep him out. Then Paul shoved him down, causing an immediate disqualification. Lawler and Idol got the win, but we kept our belts and showed a whole new audience what the Road Warriors were all about.

When we returned to Georgia, we continued to feud with

everyone who got in our way. King Kong Bundy in particular had such a vendetta against us that anytime Hawk and I were double-teaming someone, you could rest assured Bundy would come running down for the save. Because of his massive size and surprising speed, Bundy was the closest thing GCW had to Road Warrior control, becoming an equalizer of sorts for anyone suffering from our attacks.

In singles matches, Bundy would take on two guys at a time in handicap matches and still win in brutal fashion. He also made the claim that no one could body slam him, offering a $15,000 bounty to anyone who could. Week after week, known strong men like Nikolai Volkoff and Joe LeDuc tried to collect on Bundy's offer but couldn't pick up the 450-pounder for the slam.

On April 1 at the Omni, Bundy got on the mic and asked if anyone in the back had the guts to come out and go for the money. The crowd went ballistic when I started walking down to the ring. Whether they loved me or hated me, those people knew I stood the greatest chance of winning the challenge and making a fool out of Bundy on April Fool's Day.

Bundy and I stood our ground and yelled shit at each other, acting like we were about to go to blows. Then I scuffed my feet, rubbed my hands together, and went for the slam. I picked him up about halfway before I felt him deadweight me, and I had to let go of him. I grabbed my back in kayfabed pain.

When Bundy raised his hands to the crowd as if he'd won, I clocked him in the face and picked him up easily for a perfect slam. *Bam!* The whole ring shook when the big man landed, and I walked around the ring beating my chest like King Kong, which was ironic considering *he* was the one named King Kong Bundy. (By the way, Bundy, if you're reading this, I'm still waiting for my $15,000.)

Bundy was far from finished when it came to his grudge, though. He found a new partner, the Masked Superstar (Bill Eadie). As the Superstar, Eadie was already a true legend if there ever was one, and I don't use that term loosely. At six feet three and 300 pounds, Superstar was a brute force and had held virtually every GCW title many times over. He was also a hell of a great guy. Hawk and I got to know him better when he wrestled as Ax in the WWF tag team Demolition, along with Smash (my pal Barry Darsow).

On May 6, 1984, at the Omni in Atlanta, Hawk and I dropped the National titles to Bundy and the Superstar. It was a phenomenal match against two powerhouse teams who didn't fail to deliver. I quickly realized how strong Eadie was when we locked up and I could barely move him. He was also just as stiff as Hawk and I were, throwing potatoes[11] that could've easily knocked out a lesser man if he wasn't careful.

Near the end, Eadie got his famous cobra clutch[12] around Hawk's neck and started to wrench his whole body back and forth pretty violently. Hawk played opossum for a minute, looking like he was totally out, then jolted back to life and broke out of the hold. It was a big move! (Much like Bundy's $15,000 body slam challenge, Eadie previously had a $10,000 cobra clutch contest and claimed no one could escape it.)

As great of a match as it was, Hawk and I walked out of the Omni without the belts we'd held for almost four months. Bundy had finally gotten his revenge, but it was bittersweet. Eadie dropped out of the team with Bundy and headed to Japan, leaving the titles vacant and up for grabs in a tournament, which Hawk and I claimed.

---

11. Hard punches.
12. A variation of the sleeper hold.

We were happy to have the belts again and not surprised about Eadie's departure. Back in the days of the territory system, there weren't any guaranteed contracts, so guys routinely drifted in and out of various promotions if they saw better opportunities. We knew we'd run into Eadie again.

As for us, in the final match of that tournament on May 20, Hawk and I defeated Junkyard Dog (JYD) and Sweet Brown Sugar to become champions one more time. All I remember of that match was the crazy following JYD had. Whenever we'd take him down, large sections of the crowd chanted, "Who dat? Who dat? Who dat gonna beat that dog?"

As great as things were going for us at the time, the landscape started to change. Both Jake Roberts and the Spoiler had broken away from Paul and us to pursue independent careers again. This left me and Hawk as the only members of the Legion of Doom, which is how we also wound up using the name alongside our Road Warriors moniker.

Far worse, though, especially for Ole, it turned out that things were deteriorating behind closed doors in Georgia Championship Wrestling. For the LOD, they were crumbling beneath our very boots. As Hawk and I had been enjoying the time of our lives being monster heels wrestling all over the place that spring, something else had been going on that we weren't even aware of. The other guys backstage started rumbling about serious problems in the company again.

Hawk and I had absolutely no idea what the hell was going on, but we weren't too worried about it. With our rising fame and success in so many different territories, we knew we could find a place to work.

What did bother me was that Ole was losing control of his baby despite his efforts. Even Ole didn't realize the enormity of what was really happening. The series of events from April to July of 1984 would change the course of history for the professional wrestling industry around the world. And there was one man at the center of it all: Vincent Kennedy McMahon.

McMahon, who had taken over the WWF from his ailing father, Vincent J. McMahon, in 1982, had big ambitions for the territory. When Vince assumed control, he decided to expand the WWF nationally and compete with all of the territories his father had done business with for decades. Once known for being a primarily Northeastern territory with a home base of Madison Square Garden in New York City, the WWF had exclusively run shows and reigned supreme from Maryland to Massachusetts and in Pennsylvania as well. Vince discovered new ways, like home video distribution, to promote his product without even setting foot outside of his region.

The WWF was also the only other company besides GCW that had a national TV deal. *All American Wrestling* was a WWF showcase program airing on USA Network on Sunday mornings. It had great ratings, but that wasn't enough for Vince.

After looking around, Vince found that the only other available time slot that could serve his purposes was none other than a two-hour block starting at 6:05 p.m. on Saturday nights on Superstation TBS. See something familiar there? It was the slot of our very own *World Championship Wrestling*. Crazy, right? Well, when Vince has his eyes on something, he's a machine.

Vince actually went down to Atlanta to see Ted Turner himself about the purchase of the airtime. Without even thinking about it, Turner told McMahon he wasn't interested. It was well known that Turner enjoyed having wrestling on TBS and was proud of its high ratings. Undaunted, Vince started looking for a way around Turner into the time slot—and he found it.

A group of shareholders, including Jim Barnett, Jack and Jerry Brisco, and Ole, owned Georgia Championship Wrestling. Knowing Barnett and Ole would have wanted nothing to do with him, Vince started negotiating with the Briscos to try to buy out their shares for a large sum and company jobs. As part of the deal, the Briscos would have to convince the majority of remaining shareholders to do the same.

They did. Apparently, Jack and Jerry had seen the writing on the wall over the course of the past year or so and wanted out of GCW. With his growing power and money, Vince had begun luring some of the top guys away from the other territories with unrivaled promises of fame and fortune. Andre the Giant, Hulk Hogan, Big John Studd, "Mr. Wonderful" Paul Orndorff, Greg "The Hammer" Valentine, and Rowdy Roddy Piper, among other big names, decided to make the WWE their exclusive home. The Briscos probably thought it was only a matter of time before they were put out of business if they didn't join them.

When the deal came through on April 9, 1984, it effectively meant the end of the forty-year-old Georgia Championship Wrestling promotion as everyone had known it. No one could believe it. Not only was the company sold to the rival WWF, but it was because of the Briscos.

The Briscos were total fan favorites who had wrestled their entire careers in the Southern NWA territories, especially Florida and Georgia. Jack had even been the NWA World Heavyweight champion twice. Instead of cheers from the fans, the Briscos were now receiving threatening phone calls and letters both at home and at their body shop in Tampa. Hawk and I were even asked to hurt them on their way out.

The Briscos had to finish out some remaining dates before they left, and as it turned out, their last scheduled match was against us in Cleveland. Some of the guys in the back offered us $5,000 to exact their revenge and to do some real damage to Jack and Jerry. They actually wanted us to break their legs.

We refused. We didn't need to get paid to legitimately hurt someone; we already got paid to kayfabe it. But there was more to it than that: the Briscos were my friends. I'll never forget how Jack had let me get some offense in when I was a jobber in '82. He was always good to me, and that's all that mattered.

Out of respect, before our match I even told Jerry what had happened. "Be careful, bro. A lot of guys around here are saying some crazy shit, but don't worry about us. We don't have any problems with you."

Then we wrestled them in what proved to be Jack and Jerry's very last match together. Jack retired to Florida; Jerry went to the WWF as an agent.

When June rolled around, panic was in the air from some of the boys. Fearing the worst, some Georgia Championship Wrestling guys scrambled to other territories. Paul had anticipated this, so he got in touch with AWA owner Verne Gagne to gauge his interest in having the Road Warriors jump aboard.

After having lost Hulk Hogan, his biggest star, and a bunch of other wrestlers to the WWF, Verne needed to make some big moves quickly or he could've ended up in a situation like Ole's.

Verne told us he was ready whenever we were and that we'd immediately be thrown into a championship program for the AWA World Tag Team titles. He also said there was a big TV deal with ESPN on the horizon and we'd be a major factor in the network's decision.

We liked what we heard. Verne had a reputation for being a smart businessman and paying his main event guys good money. The AWA was also based right in our backyard in Minneapolis, which made it an even easier decision. We gave Verne a verbal agreement over the phone and then went to speak with Ole about our departure.

By this time, Ole was having a hard time keeping himself together. Thinking guys from the WWF might break in and take his records, he was paranoid to leave his office at the TV studio. I hated seeing him like that.

When we told him we were going to the AWA, Ole more than understood. He said how proud he was of us and talked about how far we'd come. We agreed to drop the National belts on our way out of the company, shook his hand, and even gave him a farewell present. Since Ole was so concerned about the security of his office, Hawk called our old bouncing buddy Scott Norton to come down. Norton was bigger than ever and more than happy to stand guard at the office. Although it never came down to it, Norton was prepared to murder anyone dumb enough to get in Ole's way.

For the rest of June and into July, it was pretty much business as usual without any real sign that the WWF was coming. The rumor was that Vince was going to produce his own show from our *World Championship Wrestling* studio, but the place remained unchanged right up until the day we left. Hawk and I just focused on the few matches ahead of us that we had to finish up before abandoning ship.

We defended the titles almost every night and still made the Saturday morning TV tapings. All along, we wondered what kind of changes, if any, were going to take place. On Black Saturday, July 14, at 6:05 p.m., we found out like everybody else.

The intro to *World Championship Wrestling* started with its usual opening graphics and music, while announcer Freddie Miller, who had replaced Gordon Solie, stood at the podium. After saying hello, Freddie welcomed the World Wrestling Federation to TBS before introducing none other than Vince McMahon.

Having Vince in Atlanta was definitely a surreal moment but not as shocking as his announcement that people would no longer be seeing the stars of Georgia Championship Wrestling on TBS. "We'll be bringing you the very best in professional wrestling entertainment in the world today."

But the fans of *World Championship Wrestling* thought that's what they already had. The backlash from the public was overwhelming. Angry viewers started sending complaints and bombarding TBS with phone calls, demanding to know where their beloved show was. In those days, the WWF didn't go over too well in the Southern states. Its product came off to the people like an over-the-top circus compared to the grittier, more realistic presentation of the NWA.

Fundamentally, though, the biggest issue to Southerners with the big change was the simplest: the WWF was from the North.

You've got to understand something. Southern people are extremely proud of their heritage and still recognize many of the traditional boundaries from the Civil War era, especially those concerning land. Anything north of Virginia is considered Union country and not tolerated very well, if at all. Having *World*

Championship Wrestling taken over by Vince and his Yankees meant war. The emotionally charged fans retaliated by simply not watching the WWE program, sending ratings and advertising revenue into the toilet.

After a few months, the gravity of the situation got through to Ted Turner, who wasn't too happy with how Vince had circumvented his authority. In an effort to calm the situation, Ted approached Ole about coming back on the air at TBS immediately with new and original NWA wrestling programming. Ole was back in business and went right to work developing a new company and show, *Championship Wrestling from Georgia*, which aired Saturday mornings.

Turner wanted Bill Watts in on the action as well and gave him a Sunday morning time slot for his *Mid-South Wrestling* program. Ole and Watts quickly gained huge followings for their respective shows, and when Vince found out he was no longer the exclusive professional wrestling company on TBS, he decided to call it a day. In early 1985, Vince sold the 6:05 p.m. time slot to Jim Crockett Promotions for one million dollars and got out of Dodge. *World Championship Wrestling* returned to TV under the control of Jim Crockett and MCW territory based in North Carolina. Seizing the opportunity to finally go national with TBS, Crockett picked up and moved the operation down to Atlanta.

For a while, everything returned to normal, but the message had been loud and clear: Vince McMahon was going to do whatever it took to become the only game in town. Promoters everywhere started taking precautions, even banding together. Jim Crockett, Ole, and a few other NWA promoters joined AWA owner Verne Gagne and Jerry Jarrett, whose Memphis-based

CWA was an AWA-affiliated territory, forming a new company to compete nationally with Vince. The result was Pro Wrestling USA, a new banner under which the NWA and AWA could copromote super cards featuring each company's top wrestlers all across the country. The key element behind the merger was the national ESPN deal that Verne and Crockett had been negotiating, with Hawk and me, among others, as bargaining chips on the table.

While all of this buyout and merger craziness was going on, Paul, Hawk, and I couldn't have cared less. We were on our way out with golden parachutes in the AWA. About a week before Black Saturday on the Fourth of July, we had dropped the National titles in Columbus, Georgia, to Ronnie Garvin and Jerry Oates. We'd always liked Garvin and Oates and were happy for them, especially Ronnie. He was always cracking me up backstage, and when it was showtime he'd become this wolverine and go toe-to-toe with me with the stiffest of punches and chops you could imagine.

With a fresh opportunity before us, Hawk and I were really focused on the impact we wanted to make for our new company. Verne was excited for our arrival, too, and decided to up the ante. He called to say he wanted us to "hit the ground running" by jumping right into some shows he'd already booked in Green Bay, Chicago, Indianapolis, and St. Paul.

That's right. St. Paul, *Minnesota*. We were floored with the news. Hawk and I would finally have our long-anticipated homecoming. Ever since we'd started out together, we'd talked about what it would be like wrestling in front of a home crowd in Minnesota. Now we'd find out.

To prepare for the big occasion, we took a look in the mirror and decided to make some adjustments. Since day one, Hawk and I were always modifying our paint jobs. The look I was using with the devil horn lines was cool, but it needed something more. I started connecting the devil horn lines on each side of my forehead to the lines on the far sides of my face and under my eyes. With everything drawn together, it created an outline I started filling in with black, red, green, and yellow. The result was a solid, evil-looking mask, a perfect translation of how I felt in character: badass.

Hawk started experimenting with two different looks. The first was what he called the joker, which was a giant upside-down red triangle under his left eye and then a giant spiral of black completely covering his right eye. Sometimes he played around with the colors and the spiral part would be blue or something, but the joker look became the design Hawk would be most recognized for over the years.

His second go-to paint job was a full-faced concept that looked kind of like a flying hawk right on his face. Between his eyes on the bridge of his nose, Hawk drew a point and then flared two big lines diagonally up toward each side of his forehead. Then he took those lines and went almost straight down each cheek, stopping short of the jawline. When Hawk connected those lines back up to the center of his nose and dropped down for a final point down to the tip of his nose, it looked like a cool wingspan. Then he filled it in with solid colors, sometimes all black.

We also went out and bought spiked dog collars, wristbands, and gloves. Hawk quickly realized his neck and traps were so thick he could easily snap off his dog collar with a quick shrug and turn of the head. With only a few days left before our debut, we kept thinking of any and all possible additions we could bring to our ever-evolving Road Warriors gimmick. We needed something else, but I couldn't put my finger on it.

To clear our minds, Paul, Hawk, and I went for a drive to grab a burger. We were listening to the radio when I had a thought. "Hey, we need music, you know? Something that sets the tone when we come down to the ring."

Hawk agreed. "Yeah, we need a badass song."

Since we were billed from Chicago, the first thing that popped into my head was a '70s song by Paper Lace called "The Night Chicago Died." But if you've ever heard that song, you know it wasn't quite what we were looking for. We needed something as heavy and intense as we were.

All of a sudden, we heard a familiar song that immediately grabbed our attention. It started with an unmistakable kicking bass drum: *Doomp, doomp, doomp, doomp!* Then that hanging power guitar chord came crunching in. Hawk and I looked right at each other and knew it was "Iron Man" by Black Sabbath. It was perfect, almost as if it had been written specifically for us.

"I am *Iron Man*," Ozzy Osbourne growled as the music played. Shit, if Ozzy was Iron Man, Hawk and I were definitely the tag team equivalent. Loaded with a ton of new attitude, we started counting down the minutes until July 15 and our debut at the Saint Paul Civic Center.

6

UNLEASHED ON THE AWA

Going to the American Wrestling Association was our best decision for so many reasons. Hawk and I missed our families and were a little burned out from the toll it was taking. Being able to establish a home base in Minnesota was very important, especially to me. Now I could get my own place and take care of Joey and show my parents everything was working out with my career choice, even if it was a little left of center.

Verne Gagne had an impeccable reputation for doing business the old-fashioned way: with a verbal agreement and a handshake. When we first met with Verne about coming in, we weren't sure what he would offer us. Paul made it clear to Verne that we were main event players coming in for main event money. Verne couldn't have agreed more. When we received our envelopes every couple of weeks, the paychecks lived up to Verne's word. Believe me, that's the best trait a promoter can have.

On the media side of things, Verne had been running on KMSP-TV in Minneapolis with his *AWA All-Star Wrestling* program for years. He also had a successful Canadian production called *AWA Major League Wrestling* produced at a station called CKND in Winnipeg, Manitoba.

The AWA was syndicated throughout all of greater Canada and had a huge following. But it wasn't enough for Verne. Like a lot of the other promoters at the time, Verne saw what Vince was accomplishing and wanted in. After Black Saturday slapped everybody in the face and the offer from Crockett came to align the AWA and NWA for *Pro Wrestling USA* on ESPN, Verne jumped in with both feet.

In 1984, ESPN was still a brand-new network trying to establish itself as a credible outlet. They were looking for dynamic programming to fill their air space and knew from the success of the WWE on USA that professional wrestling was worth a look.

ESPN eventually signed a deal that summer for a weekly time slot on Saturday afternoons. With Pro Wrestling USA, fans got a chance to see wrestlers from two of the Big Three professional wrestling companies all on the same show. We came in while all of this was going down, and there was big excitement in the air. It was the new wave of the AWA.

When we were thrown into the mix, we quickly had to get used to the new travel schedule and all of the new cities we'd be visiting. Hawk and I were still fresh off of the Mid-Atlantic and GCW touring loop of Southern states like Virginia, West Virginia, North Carolina, South Carolina, Georgia, and Kentucky. The AWA was a whole new ball game.

Now we were wrestling all over the Great Lakes region, in places like New York, Ohio, Indiana, Illinois, Wisconsin, and Minnesota. The AWA also stretched out to Colorado, Utah, Nevada, and even California, not to mention Manitoba. So when we hit the road, we'd hit a couple of cities in each state, such as Hammond and Indianapolis, then shoot right up to Green Bay and Milwaukee, and up to Brandon and Winnipeg, Manitoba.

When we'd finally hit all of the cities and covered everything in the AWA regions, it was considered finishing a loop. Then we basically turned around and did it all over again. We were wrestling five to six times a week. No matter where we were in the middle of a loop, we'd have to be back in Minneapolis every Sunday morning for the TV taping of *AWA All-Star Wrestling*.

The big wait was finally over, and it was time for our hometown debut at the Saint Paul Civic Center. Because we were from Minnesota, we got huge coverage from the newspapers and TV stations. Even though we were billed as Chicagoans, the native Minnesotans knew better.

Our friends and fans pulled together and escorted us with a huge entourage of fifty loud Harley-Davidsons while Hawk, Paul, and I rode in the back of a vintage Excalibur like the grand marshals of our own Road Warrior parade. It was incredible.

When we arrived at the back entrance, hundreds of fans were outside waiting for us and we didn't know what to make of it. Here we were, the most savage heel tag team professional wrestling has ever known, and we had throngs of supporters chanting our names as we made our way into the Saint Paul Civic Center.

I'll never forget when "Iron Man" started playing at match time. Paul put his arms around us and told us this was the moment we'd been fighting for since the day we'd started on June 11, 1983. He looked at us and said, "I want you guys to leave this locker room and sprint to the ring. Let everyone know this is your night and you're taking it by storm."

If Paul wanted a blitzkrieg, then that's what he was going to get. The crowd went berserk as we launched out from behind the dressing room door and ran to the ring ahead. People were putting their hands out for high fives, but they were getting too close and we had to shove them out of the way.

I couldn't help but remember being here as a fan when Hulk Hogan had feuded with AWA World Heavyweight champion Nick Bockwinkel back in 1982. Those guys had seemed bigger than life as I'd watched from the stands in my Hawaiian shirt and bib overalls. I never would have imagined in a thousand years I'd soon follow in their very footsteps.

When we slid under the ropes and got to our feet, Hawk and I looked around and saw 18,000 people giving us a standing ovation. Even my parents and Joey were in the crowd. Hawk and I prowled around the ring, screaming at the top of our lungs and flexing.

Across the ring, our opponents, none other than my old friend Curt Hennig and his partner Steve Olsonoski, or Steve-O as he was known, jumped out of the ring and let us have the moment. The match itself went by in a flash, but something happened with the fans that none of us expected.

In a case of role reversal, the people were cheering Hawk and me every step of the way, making us makeshift babyfaces. Those fans went crazy every time we started beating the shit out of Curt and Steve-O. It reminded me of Bizarro World from the Super-man comics, where everything was backward. For the most part, we weren't used to anything but hostility from the audience, so it actually made the match hard to work at some points.

In a lot of ways, that first big pop[13] was the defining moment of our popularity. It was an example of the counterculture standing up and rooting for the bad guys. We were the guys you loved to hate. The whole thing was spontaneous and something we'd see more and more as time went on. It was an unstoppable movement like a runaway train.

By August of 1984, a new mentality was developing. The punk scene of the late '70s was pretty much dead, but the angst and rebellion wasn't. It kind of turned into this new wave thing. Mohawks, tattoos, and an I-don't-give-a-fuck attitude were taking over with the disenfranchised youth across the country. With our dog collars, haircuts, and paint jobs, we fit right in with the misfits and antiheroes of the day.

This generation was idolizing popular movie characters like Freddy Krueger from *A Nightmare on Elm Street,* Jason Voorhees from *Friday the 13th,* and Arnold Schwarzenegger's cyborg in *The Terminator.* People took one look at what we were doing and instantly put us in the same category as their favorite science fiction and horror icons.

In the ring that night in St. Paul, the tide began to shift in favor of the Road Warriors for good. Hennig and Steve-O were such great guys, too. They bumped and sold for us all night long and continued to do so for the next few weeks. Wrestling those guys primed us for our upcoming match for the AWA World titles against Baron von Raschke and the Crusher.

But that night in St. Paul, Hawk and I walked out of the arena exhilarated. We hit the town with a few hundred of our newest friends and got hammered until morning.

Now that I was living in Minnesota again, I started working out at all of my old haunts. Hawk and I even became partners with

13. Positive crowd reaction.

Jim Yungner, owner of The Gym, to help finance a new facility. We loved The Gym, and it was a great way for us to get involved in a business outside of wrestling. It was also at The Gym that I started making the acquaintance of a beautiful blonde named Julie.

Julie was a local champion powerlifter from Robbinsdale, and I had seen her around for the last year or so. Gradually she and I started developing a little rapport from bumping into each other. I asked around at The Gym and found out that like me, Julie was fresh out of a relationship.

One day she walked right up to me, a big smile on her face. "Today's my twenty-first birthday."

"Really? Here—take this and go have some champagne on me," I said as I handed her a couple hundred bucks. I told her I had to leave town for a few weeks but that the next time I was in town we'd get together.

A couple weeks later, I gave her a call. "Mind if I stop by?"

"Sure," she said, and it was a good thing, too, because I was right around the corner at a pay phone.

When I got there, Julie got all shy and ran up to her room to put something else on. She was so cute. I didn't know what it was about her, but I knew she was for me. When she came back down, we visited for a little bit. Then I asked for a kiss. She gave me one, and I fell in love right then and there. I even told her I'd marry her.

Julie may have taken guys' hearts before, but now she'd captured the heart of an Animal. If ever there was a time when everything really started falling into place for me, it was then. Julie was amazing, I was providing for Joey, and the AWA was really starting to heat up.

After a couple weeks of running with Hennig and Steve-O, Verne lived up to his word and told us we were winning the World

Tag Team titles from Baron and the Crusher at the upcoming event at the Showboat Sports Pavilion in Las Vegas on August 25.

Before we left Minneapolis, we cut a memorable promo for the big championship match in Vegas. It started with Paul coming out in a blue suit and tie to talk with interviewer Ken Resnick, yet another Minnesota native, while we stood off camera.

In a slow, calculated delivery, Paul went into one of his classic monologues about Hawk and me as we walked on screen. "It could not be denied—275 pounds of muscle and 295 pounds of muscle. Crusher and Baron, you have signed the dotted line, and you have signed away the AWA belts, for destiny lies with the Legion of Doom, the Road Warriors. And your destiny, Crusher and Baron, lies in defeat."

Then Hawk grabbed the mic. "Hey, Crusher and Raschke, listen up. I want you to watch this. I want you to look at this." As he was yelling, Hawk grabbed my arm and I threw a double biceps pose in my custom "I don't care" tank top. "This here thing"—he pointed to my right arm—"I call it the level, and you know why I call it the level? Because that's what you are when it hits you: *level*."

Then I lunged at the camera, mimicking a huge clothesline. It was an early classic, no doubt about it.

When Hawk and I flew out to Las Vegas, we were blown away. On the marquee outside the entrance to the Pavilion was a giant "Welcome, Road Warriors and the AWA." Hawk and I couldn't believe it! All over the casino, posters with our faces on them were advertising the event. It was like what you'd see for a Pointer Sisters concert or something. We felt like big stars.

As soon as we finished painting and gearing up in the bathroom, Paul walked up, smiling broadly. He was slapping his *Wall Street*

Journal against his hand and staring at each of us. "Boys, this is the next step. The AWA titles are the granddaddy of them all. Let's go take what's ours and never look back."

Just as Paul finished, we heard the stomp of "Iron Man" playing in the air and knew it was time. We threw open the door and steamed toward the ring, with Paul right behind us. People were struggling along the aisle to get a glimpse of us as we paved our way through.

When I got inside, Baron and Crusher stood, unimpressed. Those guys had been around the block. Baron was forty-three years old, and Crusher was fifty-eight. Now they'd found themselves as champions one more time. When we arrived, it was like a public changing of the guard. Everyone in the ring and in the audience knew this night was all about the Road Warriors.

As expected, both Baron and Crusher were extremely stiff workers and didn't hesitate to throw heavy punches and elbows. I found Baron von Raschke in particular to be very funny in the ring. Whenever he'd throw punches or kicks, he'd emphasize them with a loud sound effect like you would hear in the cartoons or the noise we'd all make when play fighting. The first time Baron started throwing punches with the sound effects, it startled the hell out of me.

By the end of the almost fifteen-minute match, I was catching the brunt of things. Crusher threw me into the ropes and caught me with a knee to the stomach. Then he started winding up his right arm and hit me in the face with a bolo punch, his classic finisher.

I kicked out, and in came Baron, who wasted no time in also throwing me into the ropes before clutching my forehead with his own finisher, the claw. As I was fighting off his grasp, Hawk came running in and jumped to the second turnbuckle and steadied himself.

On the other side of the ring, Paul was distracting both Crusher and the referee, giving us the perfect double team as Hawk leapt through the air over me and delivered a big clothesline to Baron. Within three seconds, Hawk and I raised our hands with the AWA World Tag Team Championships held tight.

It was the beginning of a new era for us and the AWA. For the next thirteen months, those titles were synonymous with our names. We even had Verne update the style of the belts, which were decades old, worn-out relics. When the new, red leather, chrome-plated belts arrived, Hawk and I kept the originals. I still have mine.

Over the next four months, we feuded on and off with Curt Hennig and Steve-O and Baron and Crusher almost exclusively until we were put into a late fall program with the Fabulous Ones, Steve Keirn and Stan Lane.

The Fabs were from Jerry Jarrett's CWA down in Memphis and about the hottest babyface ticket in tag team wrestling. They both were about six feet tall and 230 pounds with long, blond hair and matching beards. When they came to the ring, they wore bow ties and glittery tuxedo jackets like Chippendales dancers. Those guys were a perfect contrast to our unbeatable monster gimmick, and we proceeded to go around the AWA loop with them time and again.

We'd first encountered the Fabs when we were working for Ole during some shots in Memphis. Man, did those guys know how to work! Up until then, Hawk and I had never seen such intensity from another tag team. They bumped and sold for us like there was no tomorrow, and the fans loved the rivalry. We were perfect "good versus evil." Although they were smaller and we press slammed them from one end of the ring to the other, the

Fabs had heart and never gave up.

After we won the AWA titles, we went right into a program with the Fabs that climaxed about four months later on a dramatic Christmas night in our backyard at the Saint Paul Civic Center. It was a huge, sold-out show for the holiday, and once again almost everyone we knew was there. Even my brothers, Marc and John, home from college on Christmas break, were in the audience. As you can imagine, Hawk and I wanted to put on a really special performance.

While we were going over the plan with Paul, Verne came into our dressing room and said, "We want you guys to drop the titles tonight. The finish of the match will be the switcheroo."

The switcheroo was a move the Fabs loved to use to dupe their opponents. This is how it worked. Let's say at the end of a match Lane was hurt and in danger of being pinned. The referee and the opponent in the ring would conveniently be distracted so that Keirn would slip into the ring and Lane would roll out, leaving a fresh Fabulous One to miraculously jump to his feet and come back for the win. The Fabs got the win, and the losing team came off as idiots to boot. Talk about insult to injury.

The main problem with the switcheroo was that although Keirn and Lane may have had similar features, they weren't exactly twins, and it was a stretch to assume nobody realized there was a different guy in the ring. An even bigger problem, however, especially that Christmas night, was that Hawk and I definitely weren't interested in coming off as the most ignorant jackasses on the planet by falling for the switcheroo in front of our hometown and losing the titles. If we were going down, we'd go down swinging.

When Verne explained what he wanted for the match's conclusion, we nodded as if everything was fine. But it wasn't.

Photo courtesy of Pro Wrestling Illustrated

Photo courtesy of the Laurinaitis family.

Photo courtesy of Pro Wrestling Illustrated

Top: Hawk looks on as I shrug 865 pounds!
Right: I couldn't believe I was an NWA National Tag Team champion.
Bottom: Hawk and I didn't say too much when we first started in GCW.

Photo courtesy of the Laurinaitis family.

"Here's looking at you, kid!" An Animal taking form! Fall '83.

Photo courtesy of the Laurinaitis family.

Hawk in an early shot just after our transformation
with the haircuts and paint.

Photo courtesy of Pro Wrestling Illustrated

Above: On the TBS set of *World Championship Wrestling* trying to get my point across. Fall '83.

Photo courtesy of Pro Wrestling Illustrated

Right: When we stormed into the AWA, Hawk and I had the belts around our waists in no time. Summer '84.

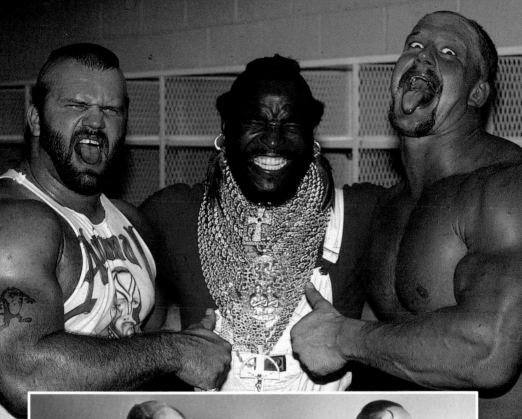

Photo courtesy of Pro Wrestling Illustrated

Photo courtesy of the Laurinaitis family.

Above: Giving a double thumps-up for Mr. T backstage in '85.
Below: Headline News! Hawk and Animal can read! Paul just looked at the pictures. 1988.

Top: Shaking hands with Bill Watts while Hawk shakes hands with Jimmy Crockett after our Crockett Cup win. April 1986.
Bottom: Hawk and I got really used to collecting awards like the PWI Tag Team of the Year, and we owed it all to our fans.

THE ROAD WARRIORS

Top: Minutes after winning the inaugural Jim Crockett Sr. Memorial Cup and the kayfabe $1 million check.

THE ROAD WARRIORS

Photo by Bob Mulrenin

Photo courtesy of the Laurinaitis family.

Photo courtesy of the Laurinaitis family.

Top left: Showing off our brand-spanking-new spiked leather vests and armguards.

Top right: With my good friend Nikita Koloff and our IWGP tag titles. Spring '87.

Bottom: Resting before a match in Japan with "Tiger" Hatori. Spring '85.

Hawk and I were rising to prominence with the Road Warrior gimmick, and we wouldn't let anybody undermine all of our hard work. We tried to appeal to Verne's son, Greg Gagne, booker for the AWA, but he wouldn't compromise. That left us to our own devices and imagination (which could be a bad thing for everybody).

While we were wondering how to handle the situation, Paul in his infinite wisdom stood and told us exactly what we could do. "Listen, boys, you're the ones holding all the cards here. You don't have to do anything you don't want to. If you don't want to go down tonight, change the finish when you're out there. Slam those guys right through the mat."

Hawk and I had never thought of doing anything like that before. To be honest, it was probably one of the most rebellious acts a wrestler could commit. But at that time and place, it sure sounded like a good way out to us.

We decided to incite a DQ finish involving steel chairs. Paul told us he knew Keirn very well from his days in Memphis and whenever Keirn was abused and pushed to the limits during a match, you could always count on him to go get a chair and start swinging like there was no tomorrow.

After both teams came out, the crowd was firmly in our favor. The Fabs weren't used to being heels, but going with what the audience dictates is what ring psychology's all about. We decided Hawk would start things off. I found it funny that Keirn himself was the one who came to the center as the bell rang.

Right before they locked up, Hawk leaned over to Keirn and said, "We're not going for the finish tonight. Do things our way and nobody gets hurt." And with that, Hawk started relentlessly beating Keirn all over the ring with really stiff punches and forearms.

Keirn's face was beet red, and it didn't take a genius to see how pissed and confused he was. All of a sudden, Keirn snapped and jumped out to the floor and got a chair, as Paul had predicted. He climbed back in and, while the referee called for the bell, he started wailing on Hawk with nasty shots like you wouldn't believe.

When I came running in to help, Keirn turned his attention to me. All I remember was covering my head and turning away as quickly as possible. He was swinging as hard as he could and yelling like a man possessed. It was about as real as things ever got inside a wrestling ring.

After a few more hits each, Hawk and I powdered[14] and started making our way to the back. The match was deemed a DQ, and we kept the belts.

When we got to the locker room, though, Verne and Greg Gagne were waiting for us—and, boy, were they piping hot.

Verne tore into us with his raspy voice: "Not in fifty years has somebody changed a finish to one of my matches. I can't believe this fucking shit. Who do you guys think you are?"

I answered, "Well, we did."

Then Paul, Hawk, and I turned and walked away.

Was it bold? Hell, yeah, it was, but at that time we really didn't care. We weren't interested in lying down and looking like idiots. Paul had always made it clear that we could go wherever we wanted, especially Japan, where he said our gimmick would be huge. We even told Verne if he wanted the belts back, he could have them. And you know what? He let us keep them.

Although we'd made up his mind for him by changing the finish, deep down Verne knew it was the best decision. He needed us, and we knew it. Greg Gagne knew it, too, but he didn't know when to stop running his mouth.

Two days later we were up at the Winnipeg Arena in Manitoba, Canada, in the TV room, where everyone was standing around waiting for interview time. Greg was holding court in front of all kinds of guys, including our old bouncing friend John Nord, Blackjack Lanza, Larry and Curt Hennig, Steve-O, and a new guy named Rick Steiner.

While Greg was busy flapping his yap about what had happened in St. Paul, I came walking in and looked at Greg. Normally, I got along great with Greg, but he was harping on the wrong subject. "Hey, if you've got something to say, tell me to my face or I'll knock you out in front of everybody." It was time for him to let it go, so I motivated him. That was the end of it.

Something else that happened around the same time we began feuding with the Fabulous Ones involved my old friend Scott Simpson from my Golden Valley Lutheran football days. I got a phone call from Jim Crockett, who was looking for some hot new talent for Mid-Atlantic Championship Wrestling.

MCW was now in the prime-time slot of 6:05 p.m. on TBS with *World Championship Wrestling*. Crockett, now at the helm, wanted to push harder than ever to make it the next big national wrestling show alongside the WWF. I told Crockett I'd see what I could do and get back to him.

I remembered Scott's impressive build and athletic talent. He was the first and only call I made. Scott, much like me, was never able to break through in football the way he'd wanted. Plagued by injuries since college, Scott had bailed out of the sports scene and was exploring career options. When I called and told him about Crockett's inquiry, he jumped at the chance and wanted to know when and where he'd begin.

After Crockett saw pictures of Scott, who was now 285 pounds, he was convinced. He told him to shave his head and report to Atlanta immediately. From there, Scott was given the Russian gimmick and name Nikita Koloff, the young nephew of Ivan Koloff. Scott took the role so seriously that not only did he legally change his name to Nikita Koloff, but he also learned the Russian language. Nikita never broke kayfabe in public and had everyone convinced of his Communist heritage.

Playing off of the Cold War sentiments, Nikita quickly gained prominence in the Crockett organization. His intimidating look, power, and delivery in the ring also brought Nikita another nickname, the Russian Road Warrior. Soon enough he'd become one of our great adversaries.

As 1985 rolled in, Hawk and I were in a rhythm we didn't even know was possible in the professional wrestling business. Wherever we went, we got huge reactions. We were having the time of our lives being the Road Warriors. We loved trying to create true mayhem in our matches, which wasn't hard to do in those days. In fact, inciting a total riot was easy if you played the audience right.

Take the people in Hammond, Indiana, for example. It was February and we were ready for a showdown with Baron von Raschke and Curt Hennig in Hammond. We always had great heat with Midwestern towns. They were blue collar and rowdy and, more importantly, believed every minute of the action. Baron and Curt valiantly tried to fend off our power, but we wore them down with a savage and unrelenting attack.

During the close of the match, we split Curt open and hung him by his neck from the top and second ropes while they were twisted over one another. As Curt's legs were dangling and he was struggling to free himself, Larry Hennig got involved and tried to help. We clubbed him off the side of the ring and kept punching Curt's bloody head. Finally, Baron and the refs ran us off to get to Curt.

As Hawk and I started to make our way to the dressing room, all hell broke loose around us. People were throwing garbage and drinks at us while we walked past. We didn't take it too seriously until someone got really carried away and threw a full-sized wooden folding chair and hit Hawk right on the head. That was it. We started throwing wild punches and shoving people as hard as we could before the police could help clear the way. For a few seconds, everything was legitimately out of control.

After we'd reached the back and caught our breath, we couldn't believe what had happened. It was one of the most amazing things we'd ever been involved in.

On the creative side of things in the AWA, when we weren't fighting off an entire arena of angry fans, Hawk and I also started perfecting our trademark Road Warriors interview style. For the first time, we found ourselves in a situation where we had to give interviews all the time—and now we were expected to actually speak. In Georgia, Ole had asked Paul to do all the talking and let us say only a word or two, literally, before cutting away. Now, we were given real mic time and wanted to deliver the goods.

We always had a basic structure to our promos. I would come in first and discuss our opponents; next, Hawk would come in and say something off the wall while flexing his dog collar off his neck with a shrug; then Paul would wrap it all up. While Paul summarized, Hawk and I usually walked off set, as if we were disgusted with everything around us.

Hawk always provided amazing comic relief when it was his turn. For example, I might start off an interview yelling about how the Fabulous Freebirds (Michael Hayes, Terry Gordy, and Buddy Roberts) tried to cheat us out of a win, and then I'd turn it over to Hawk. Then he'd go nuts. "Freebirds! You know what you are? You're a bunch of rats. And you know what that makes us? *D-CON*! Tell them, Paul." It was hilarious.

Many times I would start laughing on camera. I couldn't help it. Hawk definitely got into such a groove that people couldn't wait to see what he'd say next. I remember the camera guys telling us it was all they could do to not crack up and ruin the shot while taping us.

We got our style down to a real science, too, usually taking no more than the first try to nail it. The director and the crew even started referring to us as the One-Take Kids. It was about getting down to business and letting our opponents know how serious we were, while making the audience laugh, too.

From the fans to the other talent, everyone loved our promos. In essence, our Road Warriors gimmick was now totally complete. Now we could communicate perfectly, in true Hawk and Animal fashion, what we'd do in the ring. We were absolutely on fire, and Road Warrior fever was spreading everywhere, including faraway lands.

As I mentioned earlier, Paul told us all the time that we'd be perfect in Japan. He explained that our physical appearance and combination of power and athleticism were attributes the Japanese would clamor for. Everyone saw the potential of an impressive Road Warriors tour of AJPW.

It was a no-brainer and a win-win-win situation for the three parties involved. Verne would draw huge exposure for the AWA, as would Baba for AJPW. Baba would also be known as the first promoter to bring the Road Warriors to Japan. Of course, we won out in multiple ways. Aside from making great money and gaining a new place to work, we would get to test and fine-tune everything about our gimmick within a whole new world of professional wrestling.

To promote our arrival, we filmed a crazy video to freak out the Japanese audience even further. We ate raw chickens and drank Tabasco sauce while walking around the woods yelling nonsense. I even remember Hawk eating a dozen eggs complete with the shells. He was a total mess. At one point, we even scaled a twelve-foot wall with a running start. We were barely able to reach the top, but when we did we were strong enough to pull ourselves up and over. There's no question we didn't know what the hell we were doing, but we kept on doing it. We came off like a cross between aliens and Godzilla. It did the trick.

When we first touched down in Tokyo at the Narita Airport, we had to do a quick press conference right then and there. Hawk and I got off the plane, and media and fans swarmed around us. We were told that more people came to greet us than they did to greet Michael Jackson when he visited. No shit.

We went through customs and straight to the bathroom and put on our face paint. The bathroom smelled like an outhouse and had this big communal trough that everybody went in. It was horrendous, and we wanted to puke.

As we came back out, members of the press handed us 32-ounce beers and shouted, "Ike, ike."[15] I asked Paul what they were saying.

"It means chug the beers, Animal."

We were already a little hammered to begin with due to the drinking we'd done on the plane, but we were good sports and

15. Pronounced "ee-kay."

downed the beer. After some posing and hand shaking, Hawk and I were ready to leave when the same reporters started handing us bottles of Tabasco sauce.

"Ike, ike," they yelled again.

Ugh. I don't think we had a solid bowel movement the whole time we were there.

When we got to our hotel, we had the pleasure of finding out the All Japan office had booked us in the shittiest dump of a hotel you could imagine. I don't think we quite expected the Ritz-Carlton or anything, but we also didn't expect the Japanese version of a lousy roadside motel.

"You've got to be kidding me," Hawk said. Within a couple of days, he started complaining about being itchy all over and was scratching like crazy. It turned out he got crabs from the bed. That was it. Hawk marched right up to Joe Higuchi, an AJPW referee who happened to be our American liaison, before one of our matches and said, "I'm not staying another night in that fucking place."

That night Baba moved us to The Pacific, a much more suitable hotel where dignitaries always stayed. Now we could focus on the work we were there for.

In Japan, wrestling is like a fine art. For the most part, the crowd is subdued and stays seated. The action they were used to wasn't as swift and powerful as what we came in with. We were like giant cannons being secretly brought into a gunfight with an explosive display the Japanese had never seen in professional wrestling.

As soon as we kicked the door open with "Iron Man" blasting, the crowd parted like the Red Sea and collectively let out a huge gasp. They weren't prepared for our sprint to the ring either. We came out like bulldogs, and a sea of hands reached to touch

14. Ducked out of the ring.

us and grab our collars. Bulldozers couldn't have plowed through those people any better than we did. It was clear that Japan pretty much fell in love with the Road Warriors the very first moment we stormed the AJPW ring.

Wrestling in Japan was a real learning curve for us. There was a formality and respect to everything here, including wrestling. Hawk and I were used to running down the aisle, storming the ring, and starting the action upon immediate impact. In Japan, you'd get through the ropes and there'd be the announcer, maybe two or three company officials, and usually three or four girls dressed in gowns and holding bouquets of flowers.

The Japanese were used to these opening ceremonies and lengthy introductions for each match. We weren't. Sometimes we'd be respectful and subdue ourselves a little, but other times we went about our business and blitzed our opponents as usual. It was hilarious to see those girls run for their lives.

The audience was equally interesting. Most of the time when Hawk and I would jump into the ring, the fans would throw huge loads of confetti into the air from the upper seats and it went everywhere like the white flakes in a snow globe. It was a spectacle we'd never seen before.

During that first tour of Japan, we wrestled six matches in six nights and barely had time to catch our breath—and we loved every second of it. Here we were, just a couple of bumpkins from Minnesota with no worldly experience, and we were about to perform in front of a foreign audience. It was an epic platform of East versus West, and we were the big, badass Americans filled with piss and vinegar. At least that's the way I imagined it. We were sick to our stomachs for every show, but miraculously Hawk and

I kept things down.

Our very first match for AJPW was on March 8, 1985, in a city called Funabashi in Chiba, Japan, against the team of Killer Khan and Hiro "Animal" Hamaguchi.

I remember thinking, *Two Animals? Looks like I'm going to have to show these guys who the real Animal is.*

Khan and Hamaguchi were two strong and experienced wrestlers who were considered a monster tag team. Khan had some high profile matches against Andre the Giant in the WWF, and Hamaguchi was renowned for his great physical strength. Japanese fans couldn't wait to see how we stacked up against two of their most powerful performers.

Before the match, Hamaguchi, along with a translator who spoke broken English, approached me. "Um, Animal-san, Hamaguchi-san please request big honor in front of hometown." As it went, we were in Hamaguchi's home city, and he wanted to know if I'd take some bumps and help put him over.

"Sure, no problem," I said. "But when I get up, tell him to get ready for a big return."

They both bowed, shook my hand, and then left.

When it was time to storm the ring for the first time, we knew that all the flower girls and the announcer would be standing there for their usual presentation, but we didn't slow up for one second. We came barreling down at lightning speed and tore through the ropes, charging Khan and Hamaguchi with our usual blitzkrieg. The girls and the announcer went diving out to the floor to avoid being flattened like pancakes while Hawk and I hammered away at our opponents. Within seconds, we dumped them out to the floor as well.

I quickly jumped out, grabbed Hamaguchi, threw him into the steel ring post, and hopped back in. Hawk and I stomped around the ring looking at 4,500 people cheering and throwing long streamers into the air toward us. I flashed a big double biceps pose to one side of the ring. The audience erupted like thunder, and flashbulbs ignited.

The match itself was a four-minute squash, which basically served as a demonstration of our list of Road Warrior power moves. Hawk started off with Hamaguchi and slammed him, elbowed him off the ropes, gave him a shoulder-breaker, dropped about another four or five elbows, and then tagged me in.

I went right to the center of the ring and pressed Hamaguchi straight up over my head and threw him like a missile into the ropes. Without even thinking about it, I snatched him by the back of the head, whipped him into the ropes, and caught him for a huge powerslam that really popped the audience. Hamaguchi's pained expression indicated I'd knocked the wind out of him, but I didn't stop there. I hit the ropes and came back for a big splash, but Hamaguchi put his knees up and nailed me right across the rib cage. While I was doubled over in pain, Hamaguchi tucked and rolled over to the waiting Killer Khan and gave him the hot tag. *Whap!*

Khan, a six feet five, 300-pound Mongolian monster, was all over me in a heartbeat. He started giving me double judo chops to the sides of my neck and then backed me up against the ropes before sending me across the ring into the ropes. Khan bent down and tried for a sunset flip, but I kicked him in the chest and sent him flying. Then I tried to drop an elbow, and he rolled out of the way and jumped up to tag in Hamaguchi, who climbed to the top turnbuckle.

Khan grabbed me and flipped me on my back with a snap-mare, setting up a big splash from Hamaguchi from the top rope. Remember earlier in the night when Hamaguchi asked for the honor of getting in some offense against me during the match? Well, this was his big moment. Hamaguchi dove through the air with his arms and legs spread way out. *Bam!* He hit me hard, and I felt every bit of it. The crowd cheered as he went for the cover, but I kicked him off me at the count of two. Then Hamaguchi launched at me with two fast dropkicks.

That was enough for his moment. Now it was my turn. When Hamaguchi went for a third dropkick, I pushed him out of the way and then tagged Hawk for our big finish. For months now, Hawk and I had been working on developing a cool finishing move that involved both of us at the same time. What we planned in Japan for Hamaguchi was what I called the Guillotine.

I tagged in Hawk and then took Hamaguchi and threw him into the ropes. When he came back, I picked him up with a bear hug and held him there. Meanwhile Hawk charged into the ropes and came running up behind me and jumped up in the air for a huge decapitating clothesline on poor "Animal" Hamaguchi. He had been the first execution victim of the Road Warrior Guillotine.

After it was all over, Hamaguchi came up to me again with his translator. "'Animal' Hamaguchi-san wanted to thank you for big honor tonight."

I was floored. It was a huge sign of respect and a perfect example of how humble and gracious the Japanese people were. I took personal note of the moment. And that was how we started six days of wrestling action in Japan.

The next day, we woke up and saw ourselves on the front page of the *Tokyo Sports* newspaper, the most respected sporting periodical in Japan. The story featured all the details of this big American team that defeated the mighty Killer Khan and "Animal" Hamaguchi and how we were set to face off with the NWA International Tag Team champions, Jumbo Tsuruta and Genichiro Tenryu, that very night.

It was news to us. I kept thinking about the tension and drama we were creating in the wrestling world. It really was playing out as if we were these evil and unstoppable Americans sent over to destroy the Japanese. It was like something right out of the movies.

Our declared opponents, Tsuruta and Tenryu, were one of the most solid teams in all of professional wrestling. They were real-life athletes, too, which I respected. Tsuruta had been an Olympic basketball player and was even slightly bigger than Killer Khan at six feet five and 280 pounds. Tenryu was no slouch himself. At six feet two and 260 pounds, he was a former sumo wrestler and as tough as they come.

Our match was at the Ryogoku Kokugikan in Tokyo, one of Japan's historic sumo halls. In fact, this was the very first night professional wrestling was presented at the famous venue. A sell-out crowd of 11,000 people witnessed us wrestle Tsuruta and Tenryu in a best two-out-of-three falls series for the NWA International title, one of the two tag championships in AJPW along with the Pacific Wrestling Federation (PWF) World Tag Team belts.

This match, like the one with Khan and Hamaguchi, was also a platform for Giant Baba to show us off to the Japanese public on a much grander scale. All of the major news outlets came from around the world to cover our championship match and to see something they never had before. That night everybody got exactly what they wanted.

This time our entrance was a little more subdued to give Tsuruta and Tenryu the respect they deserved. We came running down as usual, but when we got inside the ring we didn't jump them. Instead, we paced back and forth during the announcements. Standing straight, arms folded, they didn't seem the slightest bit concerned about us. They wouldn't be bullied by anyone, and they were totally unconvinced by the Road Warrior hype machine, which had been busy at work for months before we'd even touched down in Tokyo.

The atmosphere was reminiscent of our AWA title match with Baron and Crusher in Vegas. It was youth against experience, only this had a much more obvious political tone to it due to our perceived American patriotism. In a lot of ways, Hawk and I symbolized what the Reagan era was all about in the United States: being the top superpower in the world and hotdogging it all the way with force, flash, and balls. For that fact alone, it was very interesting to see many of the Japanese waving American flags as we stormed down the aisle.

During the introductions of both teams, fans in the upper tiers were sailing paper streamers by the dozens into the ring. Even though it made a mess in the ring, I have to admit it was a pretty cool custom. The only things people in the United States usually threw at the ring were half-eaten snacks, cups of dip spit, and batteries. It was a nice change of pace.

When the bell rang, Hawk and Tenryu squared off and exchanged several tests of strength during their lock ups, which they worked evenly back and forth. Then Hawk grabbed a headlock and gave Tenryu a knee to the stomach before picking him up for a big press slam.

It was impressive as hell to witness from inside the ring, because the fans had never seen anything like this before. They were like little children jumping up and down, losing their minds. It was cool, too, because we were all making up everything as we went for the most part.

Backstage before we'd come out when we were working out the details of the match, communication had been very limited. Joe Higuchi did a good job of translating, but we still had a problem going over spots. We finally got the basics down, determining which team would win each fall, but other than that, we would all call the match as we went.

Back in the ring, Hawk threw Tenryu into the ropes and went for what looked like a powerslam attempt, but he was countered. After a continued struggle in the corner, Hawk came over and tagged me in. As I glared down the ring at Tenryu, he followed Hawk's lead and gave Tsuruta a tag into the match. The crowd started chanting in unison as the two big boys of each team stalked each other in the center of the ring.

When we finally locked horns, I had to show off a little by shoving Tsuruta off of me, sending him reeling backward into the ropes. While Tsuruta was trying to regain his bearings, I leaned out of the ring and acted like I was taking instructions from Paul. When we finally tied up again, Tsuruta moved behind me and got me into a full nelson. It was a classic show of strength as I slowly moved my arms down forcefully and broke the hold. I was yelling at the top of my lungs to show the intensity of the moment.

To take the whole show of strength angle even further, Tsuruta and I raised both of our arms and locked our hands in the strong man showdown. Whoever was forced down on his knees was always the outmatched man, and in the blink of an eye I had Tsuruta on his knees and then onto his back. I was flexing every muscle in my body and felt like King Kong himself.

But like any good strong man in wrestling, Tsuruta needed to shift the momentum and make his comeback. Tsuruta struggled with everything he had to get back up on his feet and push me back into the corner, but I grabbed a headlock on him and sent him into the ropes. I caught him with a gigantic powerslam. *Bam!* (Even I was impressed by that one. Tsuruta was one big dude.) I jumped up, posed for the crowd, and tagged in Hawk, who punched, then clotheslined, then pinned him.

As soon as Tsuruta got up from being pinned, he knew he had to save face in front of the Japanese fans and settle the score. He started overwhelming Hawk with big punches and kicks and then threw him into the ropes and charged at him with his own running clothesline, knocking the hell out of him. Tsuruta let out a big yell, picked Hawk up off of his feet with a belly-to-back suplex, and slammed him hard on his neck and back. It was as hard of a bump as I'd ever seen Hawk take. Tsuruta covered him and took the three count and the fall.

Now it was even, one to one. Paul, appearing disgusted by what he saw, ran over and got a steel chair, entered the ring, and started swinging at Tsuruta. By then Tenryu and I ran in and started beating each other all over the ring while Hawk took the chair and went after Tsuruta. The ref was completely incapacitated as he was getting thrown all over the place, so he signaled for the bell.

The announcer came over the speakers and said Tsuruta and Tenryu won the fall by disqualification, making them the majority winners, two to one. In a rush, we grabbed our AWA belts and stormed off to the back.

When Tsuruta and Tenryu finally made it back, we all congratulated each other for a great match. Personally, I had an even more profound respect for Tsuruta and Tenryu as workers. They could dish it out, take it with a smile, and always stand their ground. In that respect, they were a lot like us. It wouldn't be the only match we had with those guys.

The rest of the four-day tour we wrestled four more times in cities all around Tokyo: Yokosuka, Himeji, Yakkaichi, and Nagoya. We also met a lot of great new wrestlers, including Riki Choshu, Yoshiaki Yatsu, and Yuki Ishikawa, who became our lifelong friends. We were shuttled around at such a dizzying pace that everything sort of blended together and looked exactly the same. It also didn't help that we were still majorly jet-lagged from our fourteen-hour flight and the insane seventeen-hour time difference. Still, there was some downtime when we took to the streets to see what was going on.

Hawk and I couldn't believe we were in another country. Only two years earlier, we'd only been two punk kids throwing guys out of Gramma B's, and now we were in Japan performing before thousands. Talk about fish out of water! It was like being on Mars.

We must've looked like aliens, too. We were so much bigger than everyone that we got curious stares all day long. Kids would take turns running up to us to touch our arms and would sometimes give us little gifts. I thought it was adorable. We communicated with them sometimes in made-up sign language. It's funny how people can get along without saying a word.

Just as we were getting a foothold on our new surroundings and schedule, it was time to turn around and go back stateside. But that first trip to Japan was eye opening, and over the next phase of our career Japan became a second home to us. Our popularity there at one time in the mid-'80s may have even eclipsed our following in the United States.

Hawk and I were humbled by the loyalty of the Japanese fans. When we came in for that first run, we were built up to be a force and spectacle they had never seen before. We brought the best we could offer, allowing us to capture Japan's interest and imagination for the rest of our careers. It was simple. We showed up and performed at our best, and our bond with the Japanese grew stronger and stronger.

We were also very honored to have established such a sound business relationship with Giant Baba and All Japan Pro Wrestling. We knew we'd hit a home run with Baba and made him happy because Mrs. Baba was happy. That was the litmus test with him.

I remember Mrs. Baba giving us boxes of Road Warriors T-shirts they'd made to take home with us. In fact, we always left with interesting souvenirs. On my way out, I'd make sure to stock up on cool Japanese toys for Joey, like remote control cars and robots, so he could share in my experience. Once in a while other guys, including Ric Flair, would even ask me to grab toys for their kids, too. I was glad to help. It was always like Christmas when I came home from Japan.

7

THE BOOM OF PROFESSIONAL WRESTLING

When we got back from Japan, I thought we'd have some time off to recoup and decompress for a couple of days. Man, was I wrong! Not only did we get no rest, but on our very first day back on the road, Hawk and I wrestled two matches, in two cities, in one night. We'd just stepped off a flight from Japan that might as well have been a trip home from the moon. I was totally spent, and Hawk was hung over.

We started off in Denver at the Auditorium Arena for an afternoon match against Larry and Curt Hennig, which they won by DQ when Paul saved me from being pinned. Then without any time to breathe, we hauled ass to the airport and caught a flight to Minnesota for a rematch with the Hennigs, where we got the win thanks to some help from Paul.

I can't remember how many times Paul got involved in our matches when we were heels. Actually, I can't remember a time he didn't interfere in our matches when we were heels. That was the beauty of "Precious" Paul.

Whether he'd distract the referee, throw us a chair, or jump into the match and start brawling, Paul wasn't just the third Road Warrior; he was an integral part of our ring psychology. Nothing drove crowds crazier than when Hawk and I could start choking or hammering opponents because Paul had the ref's attention. To foil our Paul advantage and give the fans an answer to our cheating, Greg Gagne started pairing teams up with third partners to act as enforcers. You'd see matches like the Road Warriors versus the Fabulous Ones with Baron von Raschke or with the Crusher (each of whom dressed up like the Fabs with glitter suspenders and bow ties) in their corner, or six-man matches like the Road Warriors versus Larry and Curt Hennig with Jerry Blackwell or with Steve-O. We probably wrestled more six-man matches in 1985 than any other team in the business did.

After Denver and St. Paul, we made a few stops up in Winnipeg and Quebec, facing patchwork teams like Jim Brunzell and Greg Gagne and Dino Bravo and Rick Martel, the current AWA World champion. Rick and I had made friends since our little misunderstanding at The Gym a couple years back.

Anytime we wrestled against Rick in tag matches, which was rare and usually only in his native Canada, we always had to take the dive and DQ ourselves. No matter how popular the Road Warriors were, we weren't going to be booked to beat the company singles champion, let alone on his home turf. Most of the time, when you have champions of any kind facing each other, both sides need to come out looking strong regardless of the finish.

It was after those dates in Canada that I started hearing of some locker room grumblings about us. Apparently quite a few of the boys felt we not only didn't deserve our ongoing push in the AWA as champs but we also worked too stiff and never sold anybody else's moves. It was the same old story. We'd been getting that kind of shit since the early Georgia days when other teams routinely complained to Ole about us. Now we were hearing it in the AWA from some of the older guys.

One night in Milwaukee, Hawk and I finished a typical Road Warriors display against Dick the Bruiser and the hometown hero, the Crusher. You should've seen them go to the ring as the "Beer Barrel Polka" played. Afterward, Bobby Heenan was standing there in the back, staring at them, his arms folded.

Finally Crusher said, "What are you looking at?"

Without missing a beat, Bobby replied, "I was wondering why you didn't have nosebleeds from being up that high."

The look on Crusher's face said it all as he sat there silenced. He had to be humiliated. This was a man honored with his own statue in downtown Milwaukee and for decades one of the quintessential tough guys in wrestling. And now he was at the other end of the spectrum, running out his time putting younger wrestlers over.

But that's pretty much the way it goes in all businesses. Out with the old and in with the new. Hawk and I would experience the same thing later in our own careers, but let's not get too far ahead of ourselves.

Still at the height of our career, we were dealing with resentments for our relentless style. What could we do about that, though? It was the master plan from Dr. Frankenstein himself, Ole Anderson. Ole set us up, programmed us, and sent us out into the wrestling world with Paul to light the way.

Sure, it was easy as hell to get caught up in our own hype, but we never forgot the whole thing was a work. Backstage and after the shows, Hawk and I were everybody's friends, but when it was go time, it was like Hawk used to say: "In this world, there are two kinds of people—weasels and weasel slappers. And we're the weasel slappers." He was right. Weasel slapping was equal opportunity, had a great benefit plan, and was the steadiest employment we ever could've asked for.

A gimmick like the Road Warriors with pistons like us backing it up was something those guys had never seen. There's no doubt everyone, including us, had to make quick adjustments when that bell rang, because we dished it out and usually had no idea what the other guys were all about.

Hawk and I loved it most when guys, especially the Japanese and AWA old schoolers like Crusher, Baron, Jerry Blackwell, and Larry Hennig, dished right back at us with attitude. That's what it was all about. Every one of us was portraying a tough guy gimmick in one form or another, so why not go in there and make it look believable?

I'll tell you one thing: Larry Hennig knows what I'm talking about. In April, we faced Larry and Curt at the Meadowlands and had a funny encounter. The arena was shoehorned with 10,000 people for an eleven-match card featuring us in the main event. What was great about wrestling Larry that night was his attitude.

I think he'd had enough of being a Road Warriors punching bag during the last few months and decided to vent some steam in Jersey. When Larry and I locked up, I could feel him using all of his 275 pounds to muscle me into a corner. Then, as he let go, he smiled and gave me an open-handed slap in the face. *Crack!*

That got my attention *really* fast. I looked at him as he was backing up, and Larry was smirking. *Okay, you son of a bitch*, I thought. *Let's see you try that again.*

As we tied up for the second time, I'll be damned if he didn't back me into a corner again. *Smack!*

Aw, shit. With the speed of light, I reached out and whacked Larry right back in his big-bearded face. *Pow!*

He looked at me and put his dukes up for real.

I shouted out, "Let's end this shit and fight right now 'cause I ain't taking another one of those slaps."

We squared off for a couple of seconds with only referee Scott LeDoux keeping us separated.

I looked over at Hawk, who was chomping at the bit in the corner like a rabid dog with his tongue hanging out. "Yeah, Animal, knock his block off."

Then I shot a quick glance over at Curt, who was standing there shaking his head. You could tell he wanted no part in a potential throw down. Truthfully, neither did I. Larry was actually a good friend of mine and Hawk's by that time. I think he just got a little carried away with his frustration. Even though wrestling's a work, it can be really easy to blow a gasket in the ring and lose control.

Fortunately, our little standoff ended abruptly when Larry snapped out of the moment and resumed working our match. Afterward, we had a laugh about it and squashed the tension—or so I thought. But later that same night, I was told Larry had mentioned something on the way out about still needing to "teach the Road Warriors a lesson."

It's funny because a month or two later when Larry was finished with his leg of the tour and went home, I heard an interesting rumor. According to local legend, during a match in Madison,

Wisconsin, only a few days after our showdown at the Meadow-lands, Larry Hennig and Jerry Blackwell roughed us up pretty good and taught us some manners.

They did? I almost asked the news bearer what planet he was from.

We definitely wrestled those guys in a really stiff and heated match, but aside from my body slam of the 470-pound Blackwell, there's nothing memorable about that night at all.

But there it was. Once rumors in pro wrestling start floating around, they take on a life of their own. Larry and Blackwell probably wanted to make it sound as if the old big dogs had shown the new guys how it was done. And you know what? Fine. We had nothing but respect for them, and I still do.

I remember how good it felt to be back home in the groove of the AWA travel loop and seeing the guys. But when Hawk and I went to tell everyone about our overseas exploits, nobody seemed interested. Instead, something else buzzing around the locker room had everyone's attention. Something called WrestleMania.

Apparently while we were away, the WWF had begun heavily promoting WrestleMania as the Super Bowl of pro wrestling. It was the next big step in the evolution of both Vince McMahon and the entire professional wrestling industry. A couple of years earlier, on November 24, 1983, Jim Crockett Promotions had presented the first major closed-circuit television event called Starrcade. The show was a huge financial success and featured all of the top stars of the NWA, including Ric Flair and Harley Race, who wrestled in a historic cage match for the World Heavyweight Championship.

Vince took one look at Starrcade and knew he had to do something even bigger. He had already been hard at work trying to market the WWF to a broader audience and eventually found the perfect face to make a push into the mainstream when he lured Hulk Hogan from the AWA.

Hogan was hot off of his appearance as Thunderlips, a hyped-up version of himself, in the movie *Rocky III*, and Vince knew he had a star on his hands. On January 23, 1984, Hogan defeated the Iron Sheik for the WWF Championship, giving birth to the campaign that Vince would build an empire around: Hulkamania.

All of a sudden, WWF faces like Hogan, Captain Lou Albano, the Iron Sheik, and Roddy Piper were being seen on Cyndi Lauper music videos. MTV even held a couple of highly rated wrestling specials called *The Brawl to End It All* and *The War to Settle the Score*. Those shows did so well that a new special called *Saturday Night's Main Event* (SNME) started showing every couple of months at 11:30 p.m. on NBC. SNME blew everything else away those nights, even the ratings for the show it bumped when it aired: *Saturday Night Live*. The WWF had really penetrated the mainstream. I saw it for myself when I picked up a *Sports Illustrated* magazine at an airport during that time and saw Hulk Hogan staring back at me.

The WWF wasted no time capitalizing on the boom, as action figures, lunch boxes, cartoons, record albums, and even WWF Popsicles began appearing all over the world. What had once been seen as a carnivalesque attraction in dark, smoky arenas filled with drunken old men was suddenly a colorful and bright spectacle that was a hit even with women and kids.

The WWF wasn't the only company seeing an explosion of popularity. I remember the first time I saw the AWA Remco Toys line of wrestling figures featuring Hawk and me. The figures had little cloth chaps, plastic title belts, and dog collars. They were even rereleased later with a "Precious" Paul character. You can imagine the feeling I had when I handed my son, Joey, a Road Warrior Animal action figure. Pretty damn cool.

When WrestleMania finally happened at Madison Square Garden on March 31, it came off big-time. Vince pulled out all the stops by bringing in major celebrities to attract the mainstream media, including Cyndi Lauper, Muhammad Ali, Mr. T, and Liberace, who danced with the Radio City Rockettes. It worked. Over one million viewers saw WrestleMania, making it the largest closed-circuit TV event to date.

Sure, 'Mania was huge and deserved all of the hype on the streets, but honest to God, at the time, as when Black Saturday was going on, Hawk and I really didn't care. We were caught up with what we were doing and focused on the road. Our heads were spinning all day long with travel schedules, personal appearances, interviews, and main event matches. We knew we had a great payday in the AWA as the main attraction, and that was all that mattered.

One thing I definitely did start to take notice of after Wrestle-Mania, however, was the growing trend of "the body." With so many eyes now focused on the wrestling product, a lot of wrestlers felt the pressure to stack up to bigger, more muscular physiques. Hogan, Hawk, and I, and other guys like us, were having such success with our massive physical presence that everyone started to look at themselves and think, *I need to be competitive with these guys, or I won't be around long.*

Before you knew it, steroids seemed to be running rampant and 250-pound guys started sprouting up out of the woodwork. I could see it all happening a mile away. With the wrestling industry heating up as it was, there was no time to waste in making a level playing field. That was why I'd discovered them in the first place back in my powerlifting days. Who wants to get run over by someone with an edge? Not me. Not anyone. When livelihoods and millions of dollars are at stake, that decision pretty much makes itself.

There's no need for me to get preachy about the steroid issue. There's enough of that already out there. In 1985, steroids weren't illegal to use for nonmedical reasons. (That didn't happen until the Anabolic Steroid Control Act of 1990, when steroids were placed on the federal controlled dangerous substance list.) Not only were we not criminals for having and using them, but we were also completely unaware of their potential health hazards. By the time they passed the law in 1990, I had already stopped using them altogether. I hate to say it, but '80s professional wrestling wasn't the era of "the body"; it was the golden era of steroid use.

By all accounts, Hawk and I were slamming through the spring of 1985. By the end of May, we had wrestled makeshift teams of my old buddy Sgt. Slaughter, Jerry Blackwell, and the Hennigs all over the West Coast. On May 21, we had a match up in Portland for promoter Don Owen's 60th Anniversary Wrestling Extravaganza for Pacific Northwest Wrestling (PNW).

We loved working for Don every time we went up there. PNW was one of the great NWA territories because of Don's traditional sense of doing good business. He put on great events, knew how to treat (and pay) the talent well, and had a phenomenal following in Oregon and Washington for his locally syndicated *Big Time Wrestling* TV show. A lot of top guys got their start with Don, including Roddy Piper, Jimmy Snuka, "Mad Dog" Vachon, and even the legendary Gorgeous George.

That night in Portland we lost a match by DQ to none other than Larry and Curt Hennig. Ric Flair and Portland favorite Billy Jack Haynes wrestled to a sixty-minute draw for the NWA World title in a hell of a match that had people, including me, on our feet the entire time. At six feet three and 250 pounds, Billy Jack was another big, young stud coming up in the business with a ton of promise. When we'd first met backstage, he really made me laugh when he pointed at me and said, "Holy shit, this guy's got arms as big as legs."

Right after Portland, Hawk and I hit another quick run over in Japan for Giant Baba. That's how it went our entire careers: whenever we wanted a quick getaway and some great money, we took off for All Japan Pro Wrestling. While there this time, we once again faced off with Jumbo Tsuruta and Tenryu. I remember that match on June 6 in particular because it was the first time Hawk and I double press slammed Jumbo and Tenryu the second we hit the ring.

When we slid under the ropes, Hawk ran up on Tenryu while I took Jumbo. We kicked them in their stomachs and in perfect sync pressed them over our heads. As Hawk and I stood there holding the NWA International Tag Team champs in the air, all we could hear was the astonishment of the fans: "Oooooh!" It sounded like a tornado was sucking all the air out of the place. Then we slammed them down. *Boom!* That spot became the match opener whenever we wrestled Jumbo and Tenryu from then on.

We got back to the United States just in time for Jim Crockett Promotions' first annual Great American Bash on July 6 at American Legion Memorial Stadium in Charlotte, North Carolina. Verne and Crockett had a great relationship and knew we should participate, so they made it happen. With 27,000 screaming lunatics crammed in with almost standing room only in an old outdoor football stadium, we were brought in to face off against the NWA World Tag Team champions Ivan Koloff and Krusher Khruschev (more familiar to me as Barry Darsow). What happened that night is Road Warriors history.

One thing you have to remember is that back in 1985, we were still in the Cold War with the Soviet Union. To say the overall American sentiment was "Fuck the Commies" is the understatement of the century. Under President Ronald Reagan the United States was charged with huge national pride, and *far* be it from professional wrestling to fail to cash in on the pulse of the nation. Even Hulk Hogan went to the ring holding a big United States flag, while his theme song, "Real American," unified the crowd into a rally.

The anti-Soviet tension in the crowd was extra hot that night in Charlotte, too, because the main event was Ric Flair versus none other than Nikita Koloff. I did find it interesting that two of my closest friends (Barry and Nikita) who made it in the business were both Russian heels in the same company.

The program Flair and Nikita had going into the Bash was a pressure cooker on the verge of exploding. When it finally did, Hawk and I got to ride right in on the political tidal wave they had caused. But we never anticipated the magnitude of the reaction we'd get against Ivan and Barry (Krusher).

Ivan Koloff, the Russian Bear, was a longtime veteran in the business who even famously defeated Bruno Sammartino in 1971 for the World Wide Wrestling Federation[16] (WWWF) title. Now, in 1985, Ivan was teamed with Barry's gimmick of Krusher

---

16. The previous name of the WWF.

Khruschev, an American-born Soviet sympathizer who rejected his citizenship in favor of Communism. Ivan and Krusher had the kind of heat most heel teams dreamed of and worked entire careers trying to achieve.

Although we'd been getting some babyface reactions here and there since our debut in St. Paul against Curt Hennig and Steve-O, nothing ever could have prepared us for the ovation we'd receive this time as we ran toward the ring with the AWA belts in our hands. As "Iron Man" pumped behind us, it might as well have been the national anthem. The Road Warriors, the new American heroes, were coming to bust some Soviet heads.

When we dove under the ropes and ran up on Ivan and Krusher, they took a powder to the ground as the stadium erupted in chants of "USA, USA." The whole thing was odd and completely overwhelming. It was one thing adjusting to cheers, but USA chants? That was a new one.

I remember Paul leaning over and saying, "Boys, tonight you guys are the biggest babyfaces in wrestling."

There was no argument from me on that one. At that moment, the Road Warriors turned babyface forever.

Because our match was another example of champion versus champion and no titles were being dropped, the four of us gave the fans an evenly battled DQ. The finish came when Hawk and I were setting Ivan up for my new powerslam from the second rope. Hawk hoisted Ivan up heels-over-head and helped position him on my shoulder as I was sitting perched on the turnbuckle.

Just as I was poised to dive down for the big slam, Krusher jumped up onto the side of the ring with a chair. I let go of Ivan while Hawk grabbed the chair away from Krusher and smashed them both. *Bam!* Then Hawk tossed referee Earl Hebner across the ring onto his ass, and that was it. Disqualification.

We couldn't have been more thrilled by what happened that night. And I'm not talking about the match. Those Charlotte fans, who had Crockett Promotions/NWA Mid-Atlantic in their blood, fell in love with us right then and there. More importantly, so did Jimmy Crockett.

What transpired at the Great American Bash was similar to the Japanese fans' response to us during that first tour. Once we had that North Carolina face turn, you couldn't book us as heels if you tried. Our tide had completely turned, and the people were behind us for life. Jimmy Crockett saw the bond we made with the fans that night and couldn't get it out of his head. Now he, too, had Road Warriors fever. It was an epidemic.

To start luring us into thinking about hopping over from the AWA, Crockett started booking us to do big money shots throughout the rest of the summer in all of his big towns, such as Charleston, Greensboro, Raleigh, Roanoke, Baltimore, and Philadelphia. Taking our cue from what had happened in Charlotte, we took on various formations of Ivan and Nikita Koloff and Krusher, sometimes making six-man tag matches with Paul joining us in the ring.

That summer especially was when Crockett really started mounting his big push into the national spotlight like Vince McMahon and the WWF. Jimmy had recently been reelected as the president of the National Wrestling Alliance board, comprised of all the other NWA territory owners, further solidifying his role as the most powerful figure in the entire organization. In the time following Black Saturday when Vince had sold the Saturday night time slot on Superstation WTBS to Crockett, he consumed the scattered remains of Georgia Championship Wrestling and consolidated all its talent and championship titles.

Although Jimmy still operated under the Mid-Atlantic Championship Wrestling name on the books, he repackaged the promotion to reflect a less regional-sounding name, giving birth to the World Championship Wrestling moniker. World Championship Wrestling (WCW) emerged as the center stage of the NWA, which was now on the heels of the WWF. The AWA was becoming more and more an afterthought as one of the Big Three.

Even though Verne had worked diligently on his national TV deal on ESPN for the joint AWA/NWA experiment, *Pro Wrestling USA*, the whole thing tanked in less than a year. Now Verne was doing a new, exclusively AWA program on ESPN called *AWA Championship Wrestling*, but it still didn't stand a chance against *World Championship Wrestling* on the Superstation at 6:05 p.m. Hawk and I were getting that sinking feeling again, as we had in Georgia when things had gotten sticky. That proved it: Hawk and I were becoming Rhodes scholars at reading writing on the wall everywhere we went.

We'd been in the AWA for well over a year and had no complaints about anything. Verne brought us aboard and unleashed us full steam ahead into the next stage of our evolution. We made more money with Verne than we'd ever had before and were exposed to Japan thanks to his relationship with Baba. Having said all of that, after a year of working so closely with Verne, we realized he wasn't getting with the times. It's not that the AWA wasn't still doing well, because it was. It was Verne himself. All of the drive he'd had seemed gone.

Unlike Verne, his son Greg Gagne understood the absolute

necessity to expand the AWA product through better branding, as Crockett and the WWF were doing. Greg wanted to strengthen their TV presentation and was even friends with corporate executives in the NFL who were interested in investing. But with Verne, it all fell on deaf ears. He thought he knew best and wouldn't budge. It was frustrating to see a powerhouse like the AWA start driving around in circles, while in Charlotte and Atlanta Jimmy Crockett was kicking ass and taking names. I realized that between Verne and Crockett, there was no comparison.

While Hawk and I mulled these business issues over, we jumped headfirst into our new wrestling lifestyle as babyfaces. Being cheered on as good guys was an awesome change of pace. It turned the whole concept of our gimmick upside down and made it feel completely new. The villains in black were now the heroes in black. That was the thing. We may have been faces in the sense of being legit fan favorites, but we had more attitude than ever. What did change was our audience dynamic.

Hawk and I used to have hostile attitudes toward the fans in the arenas and civic centers, making it totally clear that we were the ones not to fuck with. We'd invite people to step up and fight us all the time and never hesitated to throw punches if the need arose, as it had in the riot back in Hammond, Indiana.

Now the rug had been pulled out, and the people were more than allies; they were our lifelines. During our matches we came to depend and thrive upon the crowd interaction, fueling ourselves with the energy exchange. When we stormed the ring, we could triumphantly raise our hands, pose, and get an "LOD, LOD" chant going instead of getting pelted with batteries and nickels. Now when an opponent had us down and out, the people stomped their feet and clapped their hands for us to rally.

Being a babyface even made me feel better as a person. I didn't have to frown so much in public anymore, for one thing. No shit. I felt like a town sheriff or something, being seen out shaking hands and kissing babies (just kidding). People in public everywhere would pat me on the back and give me thumbs-up or slap me five. Yes, sir, babyface living was my kind of style; just call me Joe Public.

I knew I'd kind of miss being a heel, though. It seemed only yesterday that we'd first come into the AWA and cut one of our first interviews in the ring. I'd taken the mic and said, "Hey, all you people at home getting fat, watching *Happy Days,* and eating potato chips, take a good look at us." Now, instead of belittling the fans, we were their defenders.

The reaction from the fans now was getting out of hand, in a great way. With each successive show, the pop grew more intense than at the previous event. Eventually the eruption of the crowd during our "Iron Man" entrance became so distinct that some of the other boys started referring to it as the "Road Warrior pop," a term known throughout the industry to this day.

Another fine benefit of turning face was watching our typical DQ win/loss ratio turn into a landslide of wins by definitive, destructive pinfalls. Even Paul, who was once our world champion of outside interference, was now the purveyor of truth, justice, and the Road Warriors way. Now he was the one countering any heel managers looking to stick their noses where they didn't belong.

The spin took a little time to get used to, but it sure was fun as hell. And because the dates we worked throughout August and September for Crockett turned out to be so profitable, we decided to sit down for a face-to-face with him to see what he had in mind.

Since we were each already doing somewhere in the neighborhood of a couple hundred grand for the year with Verne's payouts, I decided to highball the figure a few bucks to nearly a million for negotiation leverage with Crockett. I also wanted a guaranteed contract. It was going around town that both Ric Flair and my bud Nikita Koloff had signed exclusive, multiyear deals with Crockett Promotions. When I heard that, I wouldn't accept anything less. Paul said we had the drawing power to respectfully ask for what we thought we were worth.

As it turned out, Crockett was an even bigger proponent of ours than I realized. He may have been the president of the NWA, but for our meeting he came off more like the president of a Road Warriors fan club. Jimmy was nothing but smiles and compliments and even asked us for our autographs for some friends and family members.

I found it all especially funny because Paul had prepared a whole spiel extolling the virtues of the Road Warriors and how much Crockett Promotions would benefit from an exclusive deal with us. It would've been preaching to the choir.

After dispensing of all the pleasantries, Jimmy jumped straight to the money issue with a gleaming smile and wide eyes. "Boys, just to let you know, it won't be any problem at all to immediately start making more than you are with Verne. Hell, with the piece of the gate I'll be giving you, there's no reason you shouldn't be pulling in half a million a year each."

I almost fell out of my chair. *Half a million dollars!*

As soon as I heard Crockett say it, I flashed back to my first run in Georgia as the Road Warrior. Night after night, I had sat in some fleabag hotel, broke and starving, with a baby boy sitting in Minnesota counting on my every move. I knew I needed the security of a full-time job and came to terms with sucking it up and giving the drudgery of Honeywell another try. When that didn't work out for the second time, I swore I'd never go back to a tie and a desk.

But now things had worked out. After struggling and busting my ass night in and night out along with Hawk and Paul, we'd finally carved ourselves a prime spot in this granite business. And now it was time to find the rock-solid security in a contract to match it. I'd earned it. My son needed it. I was going to get it.

"Jimmy," I began, "we want to come in here and do great things with you, but we need a commitment that we can trust in. We want to make Crockett Promotions our home." Crockett didn't blink as I continued. "You know you need to lock us in like the other top guys if you want to build this company right."

I could see Jimmy's face start to drop and realized right then and there we weren't getting guarantees.

"Joe," he said, "I'd love to be able to offer you contracts like you want. If it was within the realm of possibility, I'd be signing them with you right now." Then he went into various explanations of why guaranteed contracts were a scourge to the wrestling business and could ruin a company, sending it careening into bankruptcy.

Crockett said he'd keep an open mind in the future about giving us guarantees but that for now we should keep working any and all dates for him that we could and keep our star rising in the NWA. We could start pulling double duty as main eventers in both companies and even triple duty for that matter with our trips to Giant Baba and All Japan. For the time being, I agreed, but under protest.

When we all stood up and shook hands, I pulled Jimmy in close and said, "You realize you'll be changing your mind before you know it, right?"

He winked and replied, "We'll see, Joe. We'll see."

As soon as we were out of the building and hitting the streets, I told Paul to call Vince McMahon and schedule a sit-down. We needed to see what was going on with the one place we didn't know anything about, the World Wrestling Federation. One way or another, one company or the other, I was getting my guaranteed contract.

RECEIVING THE *PRO WRESTLING ILLUSTRATED* TAG TEAM OF THE YEAR AWARD YET AGAIN. 1985.

8

FACE-TO-FACE WITH VINCE

In 1985 virtually nobody in professional wrestling had guaranteed money. Everybody's paydays were based on percentages of viewers. With the advent of annual and then quarterly PPV events, top performers could count on big paydays based on the live gate as well as home viewing subscriptions. The basic adage was "If you put asses in the seats, you're putting money in your pocket."

It wasn't outrageous at all to hear about guys like Hogan or Flair getting million-dollar payoffs from WrestleMania and Starrcade even back then. We had nothing but respect for those guys. I'd see guys approach Flair (and later Hogan) all the time to shake his hand as if he was a made man in the Mafia, thanking him for helping put food on their tables at home. It was well-deserved respect.

But what performers like Flair and Hogan had that I admired most was their business experience. They knew they were prized commodities and had the negotiating experience to play the game accordingly, bringing promoters like Crockett and McMahon to terms they couldn't refuse for fear that the talent would jump over to the other guy.

And that's why I knew we had to go see Vince McMahon for ourselves. A few days after our meeting with Jimmy Crockett in early September, the three of us boarded a flight from Minneapolis to New York City.

I remember we flew first class and had some cocktails on the way. As we approached JFK Airport in the distance, as corny as it might sound, I stared out of my window at the Manhattan skyline with the awe and wonder of a kid. It was the first time I'd ever flown directly into New York City and seen the Statue of Liberty from above. They were doing heavy renovations at the time for the Statue's upcoming hundredth anniversary, even replacing the original torch, so there was heavy scaffolding surrounding every inch. Still, I had a weird, humbling moment when she first came into view up close. Like so many thousands of hopeful travelers before me, I took pause and thought of the great opportunity at hand.

It was time to see what might be in store for us when we landed. After we picked up our luggage, our limo driver held up a sign with the words "Hawk, Animal, and Paul" on it. I elbowed Hawk, who walked over to the driver, pointed at the sign, and said, "That's *Mr.* Hawk and *Mr.* Animal to you. Got it?" Then he started cracking up and put his arm around the guy. We even autographed the sign for him so he could have a good story for later.

During the thirty-mile drive up to Stamford, the three of us didn't really say much, choosing instead to watch the landscape pass by. Without a word, I knew we were all wondering what to expect from the man behind the magic curtain at the World Wrestling Federation.

Finally we were off the main highway and going down a long

private driveway in the woods, which opened up to a sprawling estate. When we pulled up to the main house, I saw two Great Danes lying beside each other like the royal dogs of Castle McMahon. As I was stretching my legs and looking out at the front yard, the main door swung open and out came Vince himself.

Smiling, he welcomed us to his house and shook our hands. When I said, "Nice to meet you, Mr. McMahon," he immediately corrected me. "No, no, none of that 'Mr. McMahon' stuff while you're at my house. Call me Vince."

I was surprised how big he was. Not that he was huge or anything, but I'd say he was my height and around 230 pounds, an obvious gym rat.

"Been following the Hulkster's advice, huh, Vince?" Hawk asked.

Vince looked at him and smiled. "What's that, Mike?"

Hawk leaned over. "It looks to me like you've been saying your prayers and taking *vitamins.*"

Vince's smile grew as he put his arm around Hawk and looked over at Paul and me. "Well, Mike, aren't we all?"

As we walked to the front door, I noticed Vince's clothes. He looked as if he'd popped right out of an L.L.Bean catalog. Not only was he wearing penny loafers and khakis, but he actually had a sweater tied around his neck like a model in a Doublemint gum commercial or something.

He took us on a quick tour of the house, a very traditional colonial type. In the main sitting room, a large, hokey painting of Vince himself in a green suit hung above a grand stone fireplace. What struck me about the portrait was that the Vince on the canvas looked way too thin to be the guy standing next to me.

I couldn't resist commenting. "That was pre-Deca, right, Vince?"

Vince just looked at me with a smile and again we all burst into laughter.

After walking through the rest of the house, we all sat down and had an incredible lunch prepared by Vince's personal chef.

When it was time to get down to business, Vince took us all into his office. "I can't begin to tell you how surprised I was when I got the message that Paul Ellering called. And I couldn't be more delighted that you're in my home right now."

Then he leaned forward in his chair and folded his hands on the desktop. "So what can Vince McMahon do for the Road Warriors?" All of a sudden, he'd turned into a Mafia don or something.

Paul took center stage and spoke on our behalf, getting straight to the point. "Vince, I wanted to let you know that Mike and Joe here have been offered guaranteed contracts with Crockett for close to a million dollars a year." Paul knew that in the art of salary negotiations, it's important to start off big. After all, if you aim for the stars and come up a little short, you're still high in the sky. "Before we committed to a deal that's going to give Crockett the advantage of being the home of the Road Warriors, we thought we should give you a gentleman's chance to weigh in. Maybe there's another opportunity we might be able to explore in the WWF."

Vince looked amused. I'd like to say that the rest of our talk with Vince was a keystone moment in my life and I learned amazing things about the inner workings of professional wrestling contract negotiations, but none of that's the case.

Paul had only begun his pitch for guaranteed contracts when Vince interjected his own theory of how we'd fare in the WWF. "Boys, I can't give you guarantees. That's not the way I conduct business. In the WWF, we do things with a verbal agreement and a handshake. What I can offer you is the opportunity to make every bit of the amount you can make with Crockett." He went on to explain that unlike any other company, the WWF stressed the earning potential of merchandising. He said guys like Hogan and Roddy Piper were going to be multimillionaires from royalty checks alone.

As he spoke, he walked around the room with spreadsheets in his hand. Before excusing himself for a trip to the bathroom, he strategically placed the papers on his desk right in front of us.

We took the bait and looked at the sheets. We could see they were for Piper, but none of it made any sense. Personally I think Vince screwed up and left the wrong pages out. All of the numbers and percentages were out of context, making it impossible to decipher. I've wondered if Vince put those papers there just to have some fun with us. It's not hard to picture him on the other side of the door standing in the hall laughing to himself and looking at his watch.

None of it really mattered anyway. My ulterior motive was clear from the get-go, and that was to put pressure on Crockett and get our contracts. If by some shot in the dark Vince would've wanted to scoop us up for a similar deal, all the merrier. Any way you sliced it, being at Vince's for our little powwow was something I wouldn't have missed for the world.

When Vince finally came back in, we knew things wouldn't work out for us in the WWF for the time being.

"I figured as much, Joe. No worries. After all, you've got guaranteed deals waiting for you down in Charlotte, right?"

Right. Well, not really. But we all shook hands, and I told Vince we'd be back someday to take over his tag team division.

He let out one last laugh as we walked out the door.

When we got back from Vince's, word got out quickly about our meeting, which was the perfect way to let Crockett know we weren't fooling around. Now that Hawk and I were pulling our load for both him and Verne, Jimmy would have to "shit or get off the pot" in regards to signing us to contracts. Meanwhile, Hawk and I knew our run as champions in the AWA was over and we needed to drop the titles before taking off.

At thirteen months, our reign as the AWA World Tag Team champions was the longest in company history. We could have kept on going for as long as we wanted to, really, but it was time. Aside from the fact that we weren't going to be focusing on the AWA anymore, our recent breakthrough as babyfaces helped force the issue. When we'd been monster heels, people had always wanted to see if anybody would be able to step up and dethrone us. It never happened. Like us, everybody from the fans to the other guys in the AWA got used to us always being the champs.

As in Georgia, the reason we were given the tag belts in the first place was to get us over with the new AWA audience. Now, a year later, we were one of the hottest tickets in the United States, Canada, and Japan. Not only did we not need the titles, but having them was anticlimactic. Verne asked us to suggest who should have the belts, and we knew right away it should be "Gorgeous" Jimmy Garvin and "Mr. Electricity" Steve Regal (not to be confused with Steven William Regal from the WWE).

We'd wrestled those guys countless times, and they would fly all over the ring selling our moves. Besides that, Hawk and I really liked them personally. To set up Garvin and Regal's title win, we came up with a two-part plan involving the Fabulous Freebirds. Now that Hawk and I were faces, the Freebirds rotated directly into our old position as the top heel team in the AWA. Our con-frontation had been coming for a long time.

The Fabulous Freebirds consisted of Michael "P.S." Hayes, Terry Gordy, and Buddy Roberts, one of the most successful heel teams of all time. They were like a cool gang of Dixie rebels from Atlanta. Hayes was their long-haired, moonwalking front man who did all the talking—and singing. Hayes recorded the Freebirds' entrance song, "Badstreet USA."

While Hayes brought all the flamboyance to the Freebirds, six feet four, 290-pound Terry Gordy supplied the brawn, and Buddy Roberts, a bushy-haired Harpo Marx lookalike, was a scrappy little presence you always had to watch for. In regular tag matches with the Freebirds, Roberts usually was odd man out because he was older and smaller. While Hawk and I would be focusing on the action in the ring, Paul had to keep a sharp eye out for Buddy.

The first match we ever had with the Freebirds in the AWA was during a super card show at the Meadowlands on August 16 in Jersey. Because the Meadowlands complex was across the Hudson River from New York City, it was considered WWF country, and that's why Verne always pulled out all the stops when he rolled into town. He'd call Jim Crockett, and the two of them would pool their rosters and stack the event with the best stars each company had to offer. They figured if you're going to be in Vince McMahon's backyard, you might as well have a party at his expense for a change.

With Paul as our partner, we took on all three of the Freebirds in a chaotic whirlwind of a match. The whole thing was mostly out of control with all six of us constantly in the ring brawling. I'd always go right for Gordy because he was the biggest and I wanted to get my hands on him for a press slam.

That slippery son of a gun kept avoiding it until I finally had my chance. Near the end of the match, Hawk and Paul were on the floor with Hayes and Roberts on various sides of the ring while I was all alone with Gordy in the middle of the ring. I had Gordy in a headlock and whispered, "You're going up, big boy." Then I grabbed him by his crotch with one hand and his neck with the other and sent him up on his way. He went up quickly. It was probably the only time he'd ever been picked up like that. I could tell by the look on his face when he hit the mat how surprised he was at my ease in pressing his big ass. After all, he was 300 pounds.

The thing about the press slam as a move is its usual reliance on the person being pressed. He has to know how to properly go with the move, keeping his body as stiff as possible to help distribute the weight evenly. But once I'd get someone rested on my collarbone, even if he was 400 pounds, he was going up.

During my powerlifting days, pressing movements had always been my suit. Who'd have ever thought I could translate my lifting into a practical profession? I was made for press slamming. And I don't care who came before or after me; nobody press slammed or powerslammed with as much strength and finesse as I did. If there's nothing else I'm remembered for in pro wrestling, that would be perfectly fine with me.

I've got a strong man's pride and can honestly say that throughout my entire career I never failed on a press slam attempt, and that includes lifting the likes of wrestlers over 300 pounds including Jumbo Tsuruta, Killer Khan, Hulk Hogan, and Terry Gordy.

That night at the Meadowlands, Gordy came down so hard on his back that he yelled for Buddy Roberts to help him. Roberts climbed into the ring and brought a chair with him. He started whacking me across the back. *Bam, bam, bam!* The DQ was called.

The Freebirds' loss by disqualification that night in Jersey gave buildup for a co-main event AWA World Tag Team Championship rematch at SuperClash on September 28 at Comiskey Park in Chicago, our kayfabe hometown. Twenty-one thousand wild fans filed into that old baseball stadium for Verne's super card extravaganza, an answer of sorts to the success of recent shows like WrestleMania and the Great American Bash.

Collaborating with Crockett, Verne was able to feature both Ric Flair versus Magnum T.A. for the NWA World title and Rick Martel versus Stan Hansen for the AWA World title. Even Giant Baba himself as well as Jumbo and Tenryu flew over from Japan to compete together in a six-man tag match.

When it was time for our match, the Freebirds came out first to the field through the visitors' dugout, and would you believe it? Hayes, Gordy, and Roberts all had their faces painted like the Dixie flag to mock us. They did their faces up completely red, with two white diagonal stripes with stars intersecting right at the bridge of the nose.

I had to give it to them; it was pretty funny. We didn't even know they were doing it until right before they were set to go out and passed by our dressing room. Hayes poked his head in and waved, saying, "See you out there, motherfuckers."

I looked at Hawk and about died laughing. It was a first-class rib.

After Hayes was done moonwalking in the ring, we made our way down with a huge throng of security guards surrounding us on all sides. Fans were running to us in droves, trying to see us up close as we made our way down the field. As Hawk and I dove under the ropes and jumped to our feet to run down Hayes and Gordy, they met us head on, beating us to the punch, literally.

They were all over us with forearms and kicks, but it was short-lived. We quickly reversed the situation and dumped the Freebirds out of the ring, at which point Hayes and Gordy walked back toward the dugout like chickenshits, a classic cowardly heel move. (Ric Flair used to do it all the time, too.) The Chicago crowd really let them have it, sending waves of booing and jeering that echoed from one side of Comiskey to the other.

While we circled the ring and awaited the Freebirds' return, Hawk came up and gave me a big double pat on the chest. "Are you ready for this, big man? Listen to those people." Hawk was in one of his extra pumped-up moods that night and even flexed for the crowd a few times, pushing down on the top rope and sticking out his tongue. That pose became a Hawk trademark.

Hawk had some fun getting in some moves and then tagged me in for some of the hijinx. Hayes hammed it up by bailing onto the floor to stall things up. I paced back and forth with my hands on my hips waiting for him to come back. Outside I saw a fan right in Hayes' face screaming, "Get the fuck back in there, you redneck pussy!" Ahhh, it was like music to my ears. You had to love the Chicago fans. There ain't nothing like 'em anywhere else in the world.

When Hayes did mount an effort back to the ring he immediately tagged in Gordy, who cautiously stepped through the ropes. Gordy was a fantastic heel, who loved playing everything up and making his opponents look like a million dollars. Hayes was equally entertaining to watch. The two of them were right out of a cartoon or something.

After I tagged in Hawk and he was getting to work on Gordy

and then Hayes, out on the ground I noticed Paul and Buddy Roberts having some words and putting up their fists to fight. I turned and faced the altercation like I might jump down, but they broke it up.

Back inside the ring, Hawk and Hayes were mixing it up pretty well with Hawk taking the advantage of the exchange. After Hawk nailed him with an uppercut, Hayes came over to our corner like he thought it was his, so I hit him. Hayes then turned back around and let Hawk hit him again, which turned him around one more time so that I could knock him down to the ground. It was like in a *Tom and Jerry* cartoon or something, when Tom runs into a yard full of gardening tools and steps onto the rake, smashing himself in the face with the handle and then stumbling forward onto a bunch of nails, causing him to step back onto the rake again. It was pure comedy.

When Gordy and Hayes finally got an offensive opportunity, they took every advantage they could to double-team Hawk. At one point Gordy gave Hawk a big suplex after which he started maniacally barking like a dog in my face. It was just a strategy, though, because when I tried to get into the ring to smack the shit out of him, the referee would start pushing me back, warning that he'd stop the match with a disqualification. While the ref's back was to the ring, that's when Hayes and Gordy would pummel Hawk into oblivion. Gordy even caught Hawk with a piledriver that left him clinging onto one of the ropes for dear life.

For the next minute or two, Hawk kept getting closer and closer to my outstretched hand only to be driven down time after time. I was going crazy on the outside cheering Hawk on the best that I could. Finally after a collision from the ropes that left both

Gordy and Hawk laid out, Hawk was able to recuperate and make a diving tag to me just as Terry was about to stop him. *Boom!* I got the hot tag and it was time to clear house as 21,000 Chicago die-hards cheered me on like I was Carlton Fisk after hitting a game-winning home run for the White Sox!

I must've elbowed Gordy five or six times before giving him an atomic drop. Then I picked him up and whipped him into the ropes, catching Terry for my powerslam, *whom!* I could feel all of the air collapse out of his lungs as I heard a faint grunt come from his mouth. As I went for the cover, in came Hayes with a kick to my head as Hawk ran in to help. All four men were in the ring slugging it out in total chaos.

While we were wrecking Hayes and Gordy, Roberts jumped onto the side of the ring like he was going to get involved, but Paul grabbed him down and clobbered him. When Paul turned around, Roberts got a folding chair and hit him over the head with it, knocking him down and out. When Hawk saw what Roberts was doing, he jumped out to kick his ass, leaving me alone with Hayes and Gordy.

They tried to double-team me but I ducked a punch while being held back, and Hayes was the one knocked silly. Then my big moment came as Hayes was on the mat and I grabbed Gordy and proceeded to press him high over my head before dropping him for a slam. *Pow!* Considering how late in the match it was, I was surprised at how easily I got the big guy up, but I was running on pure adrenaline.

The fans in the front row were jumping up and down chanting my name. Out of nowhere, Hayes came up on me, but I threw him into the ropes and caught his ass with one of the most fluid powerslams I ever had the privilege of executing.

It was a great moment to level both Gordy and Hayes with my two strongest displays of power. Then, just as I was celebrating, Gordy came charging back at me and again I threw him into the ropes, this time charging straight at him and jumping up in the air for a flying shoulder tackle.

Finally, the finish came. Hayes had climbed on the second turnbuckle and jumped down, hitting me in the head with a pair of brass knuckles he'd gotten from Roberts. Gordy had enough wherewithal to roll over on top of me for a cover. One, two, three! The Freebirds beat us and took the titles.

Or did they? Although they did get the pin and walked away with the belts, did the Fabulous Freebirds do what few teams in the history of the Road Warriors' career had accomplished?

Well, in a word, no.

After careful review of video instant replay, the AWA officials determined that the Freebirds did indeed cheat in order to win. Therefore, the Freebirds were stripped of their win and our belts. Hayes and Gordy threw a tantrum and stormed off, vowing revenge. It was all part of the angle setting up our loss to Garvin and Regal the next night at the Saint Paul Civic Center.

The match on September 29 wasn't anything spectacular. Like so many matches we had with the same teams repeatedly, like Larry and Curt Hennig, for example, we developed a basic routine that we'd do twenty or thirty times around the country in a year. Sure, we knew we were going to drop the titles, but we really didn't care at that point.

We knew it was a necessary step in moving forward with our dual presence in both the AWA and Crockett Promotions until

Crockett would come around and give us contracts, which we knew was only a matter of time. The wrestling wars were really heating up at that point, and we knew Jimmy Crockett would come tapping us on the shoulder for our guarantees at any time. We knew he needed us for his battle with the WWF.

The match came off without a hitch, with both teams getting in enough offensive action to keep the unsuspecting fans off guard for what was about to happen. Near the end of the match, I was in the ring with Garvin and had given him a flying clothesline when Regal came in to help. Hawk came surging in and, like so many times, we had all four men in the ring, which almost always meant the end was coming. When that many guys were in the ring, there was plenty of opportunity for the ref to get distracted and not see somebody cheat.

Hawk and I had Garvin and Regal each backed into opposite corners and pulled them both out at the same time, running toward each other, meeting in the middle with an unavoidable double crash. We tried to pin them both at the same time, but they kicked out at the count of two. Then the crowd started going crazy outside of the ring. The Freebirds came down and had started beating Paul down. Hawk scrambled out and started taking care of business while I was still inside with both Garvin and Regal.

I was in the midst of destroying Garvin first with a devastating powerslam, and the second he was down I streamrolled right over Regal with a nasty clothesline. The fans were in a complete frenzy as it seemed I was nearing victory. Then as I was going back to get Garvin again, the referee was focusing on the action outside. Michael Hayes got up on the top turnbuckle and jumped down, hitting me in the head with the same brass knuckles from the previous night and rolling the laid-out Garvin over me for the cover. One, two, three!

That was it. Jimmy Garvin and Steve Regal were the new World Tag Team champions, and the era of the Road Warriors in Verne Gagne's AWA was winding down. We had bigger (and better-paying) fish to fry.

JULIE AND I WERE GLOWING IN WHITE FOR OUR WEDDING ON NOVEMBER 1, 1985.

9

GETTING HITCHED, BEING CLONED, AND SPIKING OUR IMAGE

As soon as Hawk and I dropped the AWA titles to Jimmy Garvin and Steve Regal, we hopped on the first flight to Japan to enter the last couple of weeks of the monthlong 1985 AJPW World Champion's Carnival tour. Leaving right after that loss was definitely a feeling of severance from the AWA.

I mean, we still planned on working a ton of dates there all the way into 1986, but our concentration for the future had shifted toward the NWA and Jim Crockett Promotions. We knew it was only a matter of time before Crockett would make us a counteroffer and get our contracts, so for the time being we wanted a change of pace and some different scenery. And no place can provide those things like Japan can.

I'm telling you, having Baba as an ally with his open-door policy to the Road Warriors was an asset we took full advantage of. We were having big fun developing a classic international rivalry with Jumbo and Tenryu. We were set to collide with them yet again on October 21 on a card that featured Ric Flair and Rick Martel in an NWA/AWA battle of world champions.

But the night before we could get our hands on Jumbo and Tenryu, we had a long overdue first encounter at the Industrial Hall in Shizuoka against another fabled American team, the Funks.

Dory Funk Jr. and Terry Funk were two of the rowdiest Texan cowboys to enter the professional wrestling business and had been legends in Japan since before we were out of diapers. Billed from The Double Cross Ranch in Texas, Dory and Terry had both been in the business since the mid-'60s and were both former NWA World Heavyweight champions. For years they'd teamed on and off, winning every tag team championship available in the territories.

The Funks versus the Road Warriors was yet another showdown of the old regime against the new, only this had the additional appeal of being on foreign soil. All of the American wrestling journalists were on the first flight over to make sure they had it covered for magazines like *Pro Wrestling Illustrated*, *The Wrestler*, and *Inside Wrestling*.

Although we had nothing but respect for Dory and Terry outside of the ring, when we came shooting down the aisle like locomotives on the verge of derailment, we dove under the ropes and treated them as we did everybody else: total blast load. Hawk chopped Terry right out of the ring, while I pushed Dory back into the corner, letting him go in favor of a better idea that popped into my head.

I bailed out and ran around the other side to where Terry was still getting up from Hawk's chop over the top. I grabbed him by the head and whispered, "Press," then shot him straight up over my head. Then I walked him right over to the bottom and second ropes, inserting him neatly inside the ring like he was a quarter for a vending machine. It was the first time I ever did that spot, and it became a permanent go-to from that moment on.

As soon as he landed on his ass, Hawk was there to greet him. Their whole exchange ended with Hawk's favorite piledriver spot from Lawler/Idol where Terry picked him upside down, drove him onto his head only to see Hawk bounce one time before no-selling it and standing right back up.

In hilarious *Three Stooges* fashion, Hawk started slapping the top of his own head with both hands over and over to show Terry and Dory that it would take more than a mere piledriver to faze him. Dory stared at Hawk in disbelief.

The end of the match came as I was in the ring with Terry after Dory and Hawk decided to take their brawl outside on the floor. My back was against the ropes, and as Terry came toward me, I dropped down and grabbed both of his legs, pulled them out from underneath him, and cradled myself on top for a quick three count.

Unfortunately, the referee saw that Paul had reached in from outside and helped hold Terry down from kicking out. The match immediately resumed, and Terry hooked my head and rolled me over for a small package, but I kicked out at two. The next thing I knew, Terry picked me up, threw me into a corner, and then ran me to the side and dumped me out of the ring.

With all four men out on the floor, it was total bedlam as we swung folding chairs at each other until the ref called a double count-out. The finish was set up so neither team had to lose face in front of the Japanese, but there was no question that the Funks had given the Road Warriors the upper hand for the whole match.

The main objective of entertaining the AJPW crowd with nonstop action was achieved, and a decisive winner wasn't even needed. In a match like that one, everybody came out shining.

And that night, I was shining particularly brightly. Earlier, before the match that day, I had taken a huge step in my life by asking Julie to marry me.

During the course of the last year, Julie and I had been gaining momentum in our relationship until we'd finally moved in together in a town house in Maple Grove, Minnesota. Not only was she totally cool with my travel schedule and not only did she know how to pamper me during the short periods we had together, but she was awesome with my son, Joey, too. Whenever I'd bring him over, Julie was the perfect play partner and found all kinds of things for him to do. I'll tell you, with the three of us together under one roof, we felt like a real family. It felt right.

So for months, all of this had been building up inside of me until I was about to burst. I finally gave in and called her that afternoon from Japan. As the phone started ringing, my heart was pounding and almost skipped a couple of beats when she picked up. I knew it was now or never, so I didn't mince words with a big drawn-out buildup. "Hey, this has been a long time coming, sweetheart, so let's do this. Let's get married as soon as I get back."

There was a deafening silence on the other side for a split second, which made me panic, but then a tiny little "Of course I'll marry you, sweetheart" came from the other side.

A wave of relief rushed over me. I told her to arrange a justice of the peace, call our parents, and make sure Joey was there. She said she'd take care of everything and told me she loved me.

"I love you too, Julie." I was a happy man.

Later that night when I told some of the other boys the big news, they unanimously decided to throw me an impromptu bachelor party. So right after the show, Ric Flair, Paul, Hawk, and a Japanese rep from AJPW named Wally Yamaguchi went to a restaurant known as the Hama Steakhouse, one of the most exclusive in Tokyo.

Usually closed on Sundays, Hama Steakhouse opened up just for us thanks to a phone call from Baba. That night was the first time I ever experienced Kobe beef, which, for those of you who haven't had the pleasure, is the most tender and juiciest meat in all of Japan. Legend has it that Kobe beef cows are fed a beer per day with their grain and also get daily massages with sake.

While we stuffed ourselves with every entrée and piece of sushi Hama could offer, we also got hammered off our rockers on mugs of beer and flask after flask of piping hot sake.

The big kicker of the evening came when we got back to the hotel and Flair wanted to wake up Terry Funk, who was passed out in his room from a long day. Ric started pounding on the door while laughing. "Open up, Terry. We know you're in there, and we won't take no for an answer."

Terry never answered.

That wasn't good enough for Flair, so he kept on pounding. "This won't do, Animal. This won't do," he shouted. "Animal, three point stance."

I knew where he was going with this, so I got down in a football position and waited for my orders. Ric raised his arm and then dropped it like a firing squad captain, yelling, "Go," at which point I launched at the door, smashing right through the flimsy lock mechanism. The door was literally hanging off the hinges.

When we got inside, there was Funk, naked and passed out with ice bags wrapped around both knees. It was hilarious. What was even funnier was that he was so trashed himself that he never woke up the entire time we were in there. He must've had a great time trying to explain what the hell happened to the door to management, let alone remembering for himself.

The next day when I was arriving at the Ryogoku Kokugikan, our arena in Tokyo, Wally Yamaguchi came strolling in, excitedly shoving an open magazine in my face.

"What the hell is this?" I asked.

"Oh, Animal-san, there's much humor. You and Hawk-san, very funny."

When I looked at the page, I saw a crazy-looking Japanese cartoon featuring Hawk and me. Right off the bat I noticed Hawk wearing an apron and standing over a stove, which definitely called for an immediate explanation. Wally said it was an advertisement for a popular instant noodle soup.

The concept was that this instant soup took only four minutes to cook, which was related to the amount of time we took to defeat our opponents in the ring. So if you put your soup on the stove at the beginning of a Road Warriors match, it was ready by the time we were finished.

You have to picture Hawk in a kitchen wearing an apron and preparing boiling water, while at the same time I'm in the ring with an opponent. By the time the soup was finished, so was I, and the next panel showed a bowl on the table while Hawk yelled, "Animal, soup's on!" You know you've made it in Japan when you're being used for instant soup ads.

That night we wrestled Jumbo and Tenryu in front of 10,900

people to a ten-minute DQ when Hawk and Jumbo started swinging chairs at each other, which was probably fueled by real mounting tensions between the two. According to Hawk, Jumbo kept botching certain spots whenever they were in the ring together, and it was starting to piss off Hawk. He felt Jumbo was intentionally doing it to make him look bad.

After the match, Hawk said, "I'm telling you right now, Animal. If that motherfucker keeps testing me, we're going to have a problem."

I tried to calm him down, assuring him that it probably wouldn't happen again.

Another funny little milestone about that tour was that because we'd now been over to Japan for three different tours, we were granted permission to upgrade our seats on the bus. You see, there was a pecking order on the bus from front to back. The front seats had extra leg room, and only the most established guys in All Japan were allowed to take these seats.

You'd see Baba sitting up there with guys like Ric Flair and Harley Race. I wasted no time in hopping right up there with Baba, happy to be coming along so far in the world. Hawk didn't care. Sitting in the back with the two Terrys (Gordy and Funk) and getting drunk on beer and sake was good enough for him.

One other thing I remember about those bus rides was that the great masked Mexican wrestler Mil Máscaras never took his mask off. He sat for three-hour rides staring out the window with that mask on. He even ate and drank wearing it.

When the tour finally came to an end on Halloween, I knew the real adventure still awaited me back home, at the altar. Even though I was battered, bruised, and jet-lagged out of my mind, I pretty much stepped right off of the plane and into the church.

On November 1, 1985, I married Julie in an intimate ceremony in front of our parents, my little Joey, who was the ring boy, and Nikita Koloff, who flew in to surprise me as best man. I was so happy to look into the eyes of my beautiful new bride, Julie. We had so much ahead of us to accomplish together as a wedded couple, and I couldn't wait to start. My new family had begun.

Unfortunately, as was usually the case, I had to cut my stay at home short to get back on the road and bring home the bacon, Animal style. I promised Julie we'd have a honeymoon vacation at a later time, which she understood, as she always did when it came to my crazy schedule.

Hawk, Paul, and I knew we had a serious load ahead of us, starting the day after my wedding. I wouldn't have had it any other way. Since our debut two years before, I had been riding on an amazing high, never wanting it to end. I also knew our hard work was about to pay off with contracts from Crockett. That motivated me more than anything, especially now that I had a son and a wife to take care of at home.

After having been gone from the United States wrestling scene for over a month, Hawk, Paul, and I knew it was time to turn things up a notch. On November 3, we beat the Freebirds in Rosemont, Illinois, working for both the AWA and the NWA.

November of 1985 was an interesting month for a couple more reasons, too. The first was that Hawk and I decided it was time to add a little something extra to our wrestling wardrobe. I was always impressed with the way Ric Flair seemed to have a new $5,000 robe for all of the big shows. He'd make an event out of himself by giving the people a true spectacle that would help take them out of reality, if only for a few minutes.

The escape that pro wrestling offers people is undoubtedly one of the main reasons they spend their hard-earned money on a ticket or PPV in the first place. Wrestlers like Flair respected the fans for their patronage and in turn delivered for them every night, both in flash and performance. I knew the Road Warriors should follow the same philosophy.

I had a friend named Steve Raitt, a singer and sound engineer in Minneapolis (and brother of country singer Bonnie Raitt) whose wife, Lonnie, made outfits for famous performers like Tina Turner. Hawk and I sat for about ten different fitting and design sessions for what would become a badass pair of heavily spiked chain mail leather vests. Lonnie also made matching spiked leather wristbands that covered our entire forearms all the way up to the elbow.

When the finished vests were unveiled, Hawk and I looked at each other, rubbing our hands together like little kids on their birthday. We immediately suited up and looked in the mirror. I'd say we looked more like gladiators at the Colosseum in Rome than wrestlers ready for a match at the Meadowlands in New Jersey. The costumes were perfect.

Hawk's vest had rows of four-inch polished stainless steel spikes in sections near his chest and on his shoulders, giving the appearance of a bed of nails or the inside of an iron maiden. My vest had a single row of fatter five-inch spikes going up each side of the front, both of which were attached to the back section with chain mail. Even bigger seven-inch spikes were screwed onto the shoulders, but these were only used for special shows.

The best thing ever was when we debuted them at the annual AWA Christmas night show at the Saint Paul Civic Center. When we came out from our dressing room with the vests on, it was déjà vu. It felt like our first arrival with our haircuts and face paint at the Georgia Championship Wrestling studio. Nick Bockwinkel, Baron von Raschke, and Marty Janetty were all staring, mouths hanging wide open. Mission accomplished.

That month also marked the first of the Road Warrior clones hitting the wrestling scene. I think I was in the dressing room at the Salt Palace in Salt Lake City when someone threw a wrestling magazine at me and said I should check out the article. I couldn't believe my eyes. Pictured were two bodybuilders in tights, boots, and painted faces. When I read their names, I laughed out loud: Rock and Sting, the Blade Runners. Not only was the name taken from a science fiction movie (*Blade Runner* with Harrison Ford), but it kind of sounded like ours, too. I showed Hawk. "Hey, check this out."

He grabbed the magazine, took one look, and tossed it back over his head, saying, "Fuck 'em. It was bound to happen eventually. I bet they're the shits."

I picked up the issue from the floor to see where they were from, and when I saw Mid-South Wrestling, it all came together. "It was Bill Watts."

Hawk corrected me. "You mean Bill Farts." Hawk didn't really care for Watts anymore.

Neither did I, honestly. We didn't like the way Watts did business and took advantage of his wrestlers. But I couldn't help wondering if Watts took one look at those two guys' muscular builds and thought of the time he and Ole had given us advice on our face paint. Maybe he thought lightning could strike twice.

Well, it didn't. The Blade Runners dried up and blew away within a few months, but it wouldn't be the last we'd see of Rock and Sting. Rock broke off and migrated to World Class Championship

Wrestling in Dallas, where he became known as the Dingo Warrior, a precursor to the Ultimate Warrior gimmick he'd use later in the WWF. As for Sting? Well, he stayed on with Mid-South for the next couple of years until fate would intervene and put him directly in our path, but that's a story for a later time.

The entrance of the Blade Runners was an inevitable part of the business that Hawk and I had never considered. Sure, it's true that imitation is the sincerest form of flattery, but it's a bizarre feeling when you're the one being imitated. I remember seeing a guy wrestling throughout the Mid-Atlantic and GCW regions named "Nature Boy" Buddy Landel, who was a complete carbon copy of "Nature Boy™" Ric Flair®. It was the craziest thing I ever saw. Buddy Landel imitated every aspect of Flair's gimmick down to the blond hair and robes and even came out on national TV claiming to be the one and only real Nature Boy. What's even funnier is that Ric Flair couldn't really say too much because he had, in fact, molded himself after "Nature Boy" Buddy Rogers from the '60s.

I took the Blade Runners thing in stride and accepted it as a pat on the back for a gimmick well done. Besides, the Blade Runners may have been the first, but they certainly wouldn't be the last of the Road Warriors clones. Not by a long shot.

Now that Hawk and I were top attractions for the AWA, NWA, and AJPW, as well as the inspiration behind a spawning of imitators, we eagerly looked ahead to 1986. We couldn't have imagined how big of a year it would turn out to be. From winning the inaugural NWA Jim Crockett Sr. Memorial Cup to Hawk and I each taking on Ric Flair in singles matches for the NWA World Heavyweight Championship to even wrestling twenty-five feet above the ring on a scaffold at Starrcade '86, the Road Warriors stepped up to the plate and smashed every ball out of the park. Of course, that's what we always did.

When it was time to ring in 1986, Hawk and I celebrated the best way we knew how: performing in front of a sold-out crowd for an NWA/Crockett Promotions New Year's Day show at the Omni in Atlanta. Because of our insane babyface status in the NWA, it was only natural that we'd be paired up with the most popular wrestler in the company: "The American Dream" Dusty Rhodes.

In the main event of the night, the three of us defeated the stable of the NWA World champion Ric Flair and his kayfabe Uncle Ole and cousin Arn Anderson in a six-man tag match. I'll tell you what: being put in the spotlight like that with Dusty, Flair, and the Andersons not only was a testament to the level of respect we were getting from the company, but it was the seed of what I consider to be the greatest alliance in Hawk's and my entire career.

Once we teamed up with Dusty, we were permanently sculpted into pro wrestling heroes for all time. Along with Dusty, Magnum T.A., and the Rock 'n' Roll Express (Ricky Morton and Robert Gibson), we were like the Mount Rushmore of NWA babyfaces. Naturally, we were still badasses, but now we were badass vigilantes. We still stayed to ourselves exclusively, but whenever we were called upon to stand next to Dusty or any of his friends in battle, the fans knew the Warriors would be there in a flash. Dusty was like our personal beacon of the NWA babyfaces and bridged the gap between the Road Warriors and the other allies.

Adding Hawk and me to the roster brought some serious additional clout to the already booming lineup of money-drawing talent. We were thrown into the mix and happy to start making great Crockett paydays, but still we were waiting for Jimmy to step up to the plate with our contracts. Until such time, however, we ran the gauntlet by working for both the NWA and the AWA. One night we'd be in Charlotte wrestling the Koloffs for NWA/Crockett, and the next night we'd be in Rosemont, Illinois, teaming with Jerry Blackwell against the Freebirds for the AWA.

Simply put, for the next couple of months, Hawk and I were double agents. We didn't mind being pulled in every direction around the country by two of the Big Three, especially considering the increased exposure and great payoffs. We definitely weren't complaining. My patience was rewarded sooner than I imagined, twofold.

March is a month of transition and growth, and I'll be damned if that wasn't the case for me to a tee in 1986. One day about midmonth, Julie broke the news to me that she was pregnant. I was overjoyed. As important as wrestling was to me in every way, knowing I was up for round two with fatherhood helped keep me rooted in reality. In the wrestling business, the grind of the road can chew and spit a guy out if he's not grounded in the right ways. In my case, the endless merry-go-round of planes, rental cars, hotels, and arenas only made me want to get home to Julie and Joey that much sooner.

Julie was absolutely glowing as a mother-to-be, and I was excited to see how great of a brother Joey would become. To make things even more interesting, Julie and I opted to keep the gender of our new gift a surprise until "D-Day," which we projected to be in December.

When I thought my hands were pleasantly full, Jimmy Crockett figured he'd add another little surprise. I got the call from Paul that Crockett wanted to meet with Hawk, Paul, and me to discuss some business at his office in Charlotte. My stomach started churning. Was this finally it? Would our long-anticipated contracts be sitting on Jimmy's desk?

When we finally got there, Crockett delivered the goods like a pro. "Boys, I've been thinking about your future here with us in the Crockett Promotions family. I also want you to know of the respect I have for you coming to me like businessmen and asking for what you want. The bottom line is that I can't match the number you asked for back in September, but I think you'll be interested in what we came up with."

When he told us the amount of the contracts, which was in the mid-six figures, I couldn't help but crack a smile from ear to ear. My perseverance had paid off, literally. There's something to be said about the satisfaction of bustin' your tail chasing the American dream and then actually snaring it. It was like reeling in the moon.

Hawk and I were offered three-year guarantees in exchange for our exclusivity to Crockett's unified NWA powerhouse, which was on the fast track to the big time. With us taking center stage with the likes of Dusty, Flair, the Andersons, Magnum, and the Rock 'n' Roll Express, Jimmy had more than the necessary artillery to evenly take the battlefield against Vince and the WWF for the top dog position in American professional wrestling.

I couldn't have been happier putting pen to paper in Crockett's office that day. When we signed those first big deals, it put us among the very elite in the business. We knew we had to turn things up to a new level of intensity and really make everyone in the NWA from the fans to the other wrestlers wonder what the hell had hit them. We told Jimmy to give us the ball and watch what happened. He nodded and even suggested we come up with an event that would showcase us and symbolize the mutual commitment between Crockett and us.

When it came time for Paul's contract negotiation, Hawk and I excused ourselves from the room. Paul took care of his affairs on his own. I can only imagine the skillful display Paul put on for Jimmy because in the end that crafty genius actually got almost as much as Hawk and I did, a fact that would prove to seriously disgruntle some of the other talent.

The bottom line is that Paul was worth every penny and more, and we knew it. Hey, if you have the ability to go into the office of a powerful man and get what you want, God bless you. If you don't, well, the world needs ditch diggers, too, right?

So it was official. The Road Warriors were contracted hit men for Jimmy Crockett and the NWA. We still had a schedule of shows to finish out for the AWA, which we were happy to do for Verne. After all, he'd given us a great break in the company and essentially carte blanche with our tag team title run, even when things had gotten interesting (as they had in our little situation with the Fabulous Ones back in St. Paul). We'd do anything for old Verne. We went out and had drinks that night to celebrate the signing of our contracts, and Hawk got completely shitfaced.

Hawk loved to party; we all did. After a hard night's work, it was time for everyone to get together at the bars and clubs to blow off some steam. It was a clockwork ritual. With Hawk, though, I slowly but surely started to notice the recreational activities becoming a liability—for both of us.

On many occasions, Hawk missed a flight and couldn't make it to a show. Paul and I would then have to improvise. Sometimes he and I tagged together or I'd do a two-on-one handicap match.

Everyone started asking me, "Hey, Animal, where's Hawk?" When Hawk and I would meet back up, we'd laugh it off, but I wondered how long I'd be able to look the other way. Personally, I thought if people paid for a ticket expecting to see the Road Warriors, they should get the Road Warriors, right?

Only a few days to a week after we officially became NWA talent, we got some big news. Dusty called to tell us he and Crockett had come up with a huge event to be held at the end of April at the Superdome in New Orleans called The Jim Crockett Sr. Memorial Cup Tag Team Tournament, a single elimination tag team tournament featuring twenty-four teams from every NWA territory in the country and Japan. The main prize was one million dollars (kayfabe) and the Crockett Cup itself, which kind of looked like the Stanley Cup.

The tournament would be held all day long with two different sessions, one in the early afternoon and then the finals in the evening. The final match for the Crockett Cup was the actual main event, taking place right after the NWA World Championship match between the ever-feuding Ric Flair and Dusty Rhodes.

"Sounds good to me, Dust," I said.

"Oh, I didn't tell you the best part," he replied. "You and Hawk are winning this thing. You know you're my babies, right?" It was his favorite term for us.

Crockett was putting us in front of the entire roster of the best teams in the world and saying, "The Road Warriors are my show-case team. Get used to seeing big things from them." The only thing crazier was the fact that we were scheduled the very next day in Minneapolis for the AWA's WrestleRock '86 event in a cage match against the Freebirds. It was my kind of schedule.

In the first round of the tournament, we faced Wahoo McDaniel and Mark Youngblood. It was a fairly standard Road Warriors squash match and didn't take long. Youngblood took most of the punishment and went down for the three count after Hawk clotheslined him from the second rope.

The second round was a little more interesting because it was the first time we ever worked against the current NWA World Tag Team champions, the Midnight Express, "Loverboy" Dennis Condrey and "Beautiful" Bobby Eaton, with their manager Jim Cornette. Much as Paul was the third Road Warrior, Cornette was the third Midnight.

All three of them were awesome together. I've always felt Bobby was one of the best workers in the business, and Cornette was a quick wit with the gift of gab like no one else. But the most important aspect of Cornette's heel manager gimmick was his trusty tennis racket. He had it with him at all times, and most any team facing the Midnight Express knew they had to watch out for the devious, racket-swinging Cornette.

Because the Midnights were the champs and we were obviously advancing to the finals, the match had to result in a DQ finish in our favor. It all came down to me and Dennis in the final seconds as I powerslammed him. Then as I went to finish him with a big running clothesline, Jim Cornette hit me in the back with his tennis racket. *Crack!* I remember being instantly surprised at how much it hurt. It felt far more like a crowbar than a measly racket.

Of course, the ref saw Cornette's interference and called for the bell and the end of the match. With the DQ win, our mission to make it to the final round of the show was accomplished as we advanced to the final round of the tournament. It was also a picture-perfect beginning to a much-storied rivalry with the Midnight Express that would really heat up in the months ahead.

For now, though, we had a main event showdown with the team of Magnum T.A. and Ronnie Garvin for the Crockett Cup.

As I've mentioned, Magnum and Garvin were two tough sons of bitches who didn't take crap from anyone, and the fans loved them for their gritty, common-man gimmicks. Garvin especially was notorious for his extra hard punches and chops and was even known then as The Man With the Hands of Stone, often winning his matches with a single right-hand punch.

Prior to the Crockett Cup Tournament, during a match with Arn Anderson for the NWA World Television Championship, Tully Blanchard and J.J. Dillon jumped in on Anderson's behalf and kayfabe broke Ronnie's hand. So for our match together that night in New Orleans, Garvin was in full kayfabe with his hand heavily taped from wrist to fingertips. When we entered the ring, we showed both Magnum and Garvin respect by not rushing the ring as usual. Even when we casually stepped through the ropes, though, the fans exploded into cheers for the Road Warriors.

The match wasn't a long one, but it was a real barn burner. One thing I really remember is Garvin biting Hawk on the head. That's the way Ronnie was: scrappy as hell, tougher than five Hollywood stuntmen, and relentlessly going toe-to-toe with anybody willing. He used every form of biting and stretching a guy out until you damn sure never forgot what a match with him was like. Years later, I think I still feel sore from some of my matches with Ronnie.

When it was time to take the match home, believe it or not, Magnum hit a powerslam on yours truly, and Hawk ran in to break up the pin. When Garvin stepped in and all four of us were in the ring beating the hell out of each other, I had a clear shot at Ronnie with a running clothesline. I nailed him, got the pin, and that was it. We won the first ever Jim Crockett Sr. Memorial Cup and were handed a fake check for one million dollars. Man, I wished it was real.

But again, who was I to complain? I had my contract from Crockett, my beautiful wife, Julie, was pregnant with our new baby, and Paul, Hawk, and I were standing head and shoulders above the rest in tag team wrestling and were leaving a giant Road Warriors footprint everywhere we went. If ever there was a feeling of a golden age in my life, it was right then and there in early 1986.

SERVING UP ANOTHER BIG PRESS SLAM IN JAPAN. 1986.

10

SNACKING ON DANGER
AND DINING ON DEATH

After winning the Crockett Cup, Hawk and I didn't have much time for celebrating as we had to make a mad dash to catch a red-eye flight to Minneapolis for WrestleRock. Verne had been heavily promoting the event on TV during the last couple of months and really wanted to be competitive with the big shows that the WWF and NWA were pulling off.

WrestleMania II had happened on April 7 and was another resounding success, sending ripples of pressure out to guys like Verne and Jimmy Crockett to step up to the plate or die off and go away. Verne's answer was WrestleRock, and he brought us in for the main event: a tag team cage match with the Freebirds.

Even though Hawk and I were happily committed to our new home in the NWA, we were more than willing to help Verne out one more time. When we arrived at the Metrodome that Sunday afternoon, we were excited to hear the place was jammed with 23,000 fans ready to see some great action. In the back, we saw so many guys we hadn't in a while, like Harley Race, the Fabulous Ones, Mike Rotunda, Barry Windham, and even good old Sgt. Slaughter.

Another guy who was there that Hawk and I hadn't really met before was Jimmy "Superfly" Snuka, who was booked in a tag match with Greg Gagne against Bruiser Brody and my old Gramma B's bouncing colleague John Nord. I remember being right next to Greg near the bathrooms when he started complaining to Verne about Snuka, who may or may not have been drinking can after can of beer and dabbling in a certain substance while getting ready. "How in the hell is Snuka going to work tonight?" Greg asked. "He's all fucked up."

Right after the words left Greg's mouth, Snuka, who was probably about ten beers in, stepped around the corner with a look of rage. He'd heard everything. "Fucked up? *Fucked up?*" Snuka said to both Greg and Verne. "Wait right here. I'll show you fucked up."

Snuka disappeared into the bathroom. We heard some familiar animal noises, and a second or two later, he came out rubbing his nose—I guess he had a bad cold or something. He went straight up to Greg with an even more deranged look on his face than before. "Now. *Now* I'm *fucked up*, brother." And then he stormed off.

That evening at WrestleRock '86, the legendary "Superfly" Snuka still went out and wrestled without a hitch, even doing his trademark splash from the top of the cage.

After the entertainment of Snuka and Greg was over, I started to settle into full Animal mode. The switch was flicked in my head, taking me from mild-mannered Joe Laurinaitis to the intense, butt-kicking Road Warrior Animal. A lot of guys in the wrestling business didn't have the luxury of a gimmick like mine and Hawk's that allowed us to separate ourselves from our characters. Guys like Flair and Nikita, for example, lived their alter egos all the time and were, in a sense, trapped for life. Hawk and I were able to walk around as Mike and Joe, without our paint jobs and spikes, and we didn't have as much of an outside recognition factor with the fans, especially if we were at a bar or the mall. Man, it was great to be a Road Warrior.

That night we entered the cage for our match with the Freebirds. Knowing full well it was going to be our last event with the AWA, we went all out. The same was true for Michael Hayes and Jimmy Garvin (an on-and-off Freebird since 1983), who were both moving on to different companies following the match: Hayes to WCCW in Texas and Garvin to Crockett's NWA. The fans were totally hot for our match, and their cheers could be heard bouncing and booming off of every square inch of the enormous domed ceiling.

Hawk started off first with Hayes, and the two of them ignited the match perfectly. Hayes caught Hawk with a flurry of punches, then got him up for a piledriver. *Bam!* As only he could, Hawk bounced over and, while Hayes was celebrating with his back turned, got right up and delivered a high standing dropkick. Then Hawk sent Hayes into the ropes across the ring, bounced off his own set, and collided with Hayes courtesy of a flying shoulder block. The second Hayes hit the mat, Hawk picked him right back up by his long and flowing golden mop of hair and pressed him high above his head before slamming him hard. *Boom!*

Man, I could not wait to get in there and dish out some moves of my own. When I finally got the tag, it was Jimmy Garvin in the ring. I threw him into the ropes and caught him right off the bat for a graceful powerslam. *Boom!*

The crowd exploded with cheers as if it were the first time they'd ever seen such a display, but they were about to get more. As soon as I got up, I knew it was time for my own press slam—but not an ordinary version. I pressed Jimmy up, held him there, then proceeded to pivot around in a circle so all of the people on each side could watch as I lifted him up and down for six full reps before dropping him face-first to the canvas. Jimmy crawled as fast as he could over to Hayes for a tag, but Michael wanted no part of it and walked away from him. The entire Metrodome roared with laughter, and even Hawk and I had to contain ourselves. Those guys were great together!

The big finish of the match came as all four men were in the ring in a chaotic storm of punching and kicking. When the referee made Hawk go back to the outside, all of a sudden Garvin grabbed me from behind and positioned me in front of one of the corners, where Hayes was standing on the top turnbuckle. As Hayes jumped down to clobber me, I broke free from Garvin and he wound up hitting Jimmy instead. I covered Garvin, and that was all she wrote: the Road Warriors had won their last match for the AWA.

Although WrestleRock was a big success, outdrawing the Crockett Cup by over 7,000 people, the AWA was now tilted at a steady decline. With teams like us and the Freebirds leaving for greener pastures, it would only be a matter of a couple years before Verne's company would take the ultimate nosedive into the wrestling graveyard.

After back-to-back performances at the Crockett Cup and WrestleRock, we spent the next two and a half weeks wrestling alongside Dusty Rhodes in six-man tag matches against the NWA World Six-Man champions, Ivan and Nikita Koloff and Baron von Raschke. By this point, Krusher Krushchev (Barry) had legitimately and severely injured one of his knees in a match with Sam Houston and was out of the picture for the next few months, so Baron had stepped into his spot.

Being booked with Dusty against those guys was about as good as it got. We were more than a team; we were a superteam. It was like Captain America teaming up with Superman and the Hulk. The fans couldn't get enough of the three of us together, and on May 17 in Baltimore, we defeated the Koloffs and Raschke to become the new World Six-Man champs.

Our momentum kept on growing, too. Adding a little cherry on top of our NWA success sundae, we decided to hit Japan for a little business and represent our new company for the first time. Dusty liked the idea of me and Hawk heading over to Japan and even urged us to take the Crockett Cup and our Six-Man belts along to show off our NWA pride, which was cool with us.

We only wrestled a couple of times during that short trip, but it was more about showing off our American triumphs. Each time we launched down the aisle, Paul was right behind us holding the Crockett Cup high as a symbol of what the Road Warriors were all about: winning.

During this particular trip in Japan, on June 7, we faced Jumbo and Tenryu for the last time in 1986, and the match ended with a bang. The mounting tension between Jumbo and Hawk finally hit the fan. As I mentioned, Hawk was convinced Jumbo was botching crucial high spots whenever he had the chance. After about the third or fourth time we faced them, Hawk made it abundantly clear that he'd knock "that motherfucker" out if he did it one more time. Well, this was one more time.

I don't even remember exactly what happened, but I think Jumbo may have forgotten Hawk was going to give him a running clothesline off the ropes followed by a jumping horizontal punch, and it looked like a mess.

When the match was over, Hawk breezed right past me, muttering, "That's fucking it. I've had it. I'll show that motherfucker not to botch my moves."

I thought, *Oh, shit. Animal, you better get your ass back there before someone gets killed.* I had to haul ass to catch up to Hawk, who was charging like a bull past the fans to get to the back.

Once we were in the locker room, Hawk went straight for the room Jumbo was in, which had its own glass door. I could see the unsuspecting Tsuruta taking a seat on a bench when Hawk raised his right foot and kicked the whole fucking door in. *Crash!* Flying glass went everywhere as Hawk continued right in and started screaming at the top of his lungs at Jumbo. "All right, motherfucker. Get up. You think you're gonna fuck with my matches? *No fucking way.*"

Though shocked, Tsuruta jumped up and started yelling back in Japanese.

By that time, I already had my arms around Hawk. Our AJPW rep, Wally Yamguchi, wedged himself between the two. I remember he looked like a baby sapling in the middle of two great oaks.

I managed to pull Hawk out of there and get him into our room, where he was able to calm down. Giant Baba came down to see what had happened and was rightfully upset about the door. I apologized for Hawk and told him it would never happen again and even offered to pay for the door.

In the end, Tsuruta denied any wrongdoing and claimed there

was never any problem to begin with. From that point forward, the two of them never raised another issue with each other and the whole thing wasn't brought up again.

We got back to the United States just in time for the Great American Bash, which only a year before had been the event responsible for catapulting the Road Warriors into the spotlight in the NWA as monster babyfaces. This year's Bash wasn't going to be a one-night event but a fourteen-city tour starting on July 1, hitting the biggest and best cities in the NWA's fold. Even greater news came our way when Hawk and I were told we'd each get a shot at wrestling Ric Flair for the World Heavyweight Championship. I was floored.

Apparently Flair would be wrestling with his title on the line every date of the tour, and Dusty thought it would be interesting to give him a diverse cavalcade of opponents, like Ricky Morton, Robert Gibson, Nikita Koloff, Ronnie Garvin, Magnum T.A., Hawk, and me. I thought having Flair booked against guys he normally wouldn't face in singles matches was a stroke of genius. It not only gave the fans many dream matches they never thought they'd see, but it really mixed things up creatively, especially for Flair, to help make the Bash one of the hottest tickets the business ever saw.

We had a great buildup for our matches with Flair each week on *World Championship Wrestling*. I think it all started off during one of our interviews when at the end Hawk mentioned the fact that he'd be facing Flair in a few weeks on July 1 in Philadelphia at Veterans Stadium for the kickoff of the Bash. He suggested to the champ that he'd better get in the gym because it sure didn't look like he had been lately.

Then the following week, Flair came out and addressed

Hawk's comments and said that if he had the guts he'd come out and get his face slapped on national television by the world champion. I'll give you a few guesses as to what happened when Flair went to the ring for a rare TV match against jobber Tony Zane.

No sooner did the bell ring for the match to begin than "Iron Man" started playing. The fans got up and started screaming as Hawk suddenly entered on camera and headed toward the ring. The second he got up onto the apron, Flair ran and landed a flying knee and pulled him inside.

Flair attempted a couple of chops, but Hawk no-sold them and shoved Ric so hard that he flipped all the way into the opposite corner. From there, it was a murder scene. After nailing Flair with a flying shoulder block, Hawk pressed him high over his head and walked to the edge of the ring and threw him over the ropes into the awaiting arms of Arn Anderson and Tully Blanchard, who had come out to interfere. While Hawk stood in the ring surveying his work, I guess he got sick of referee Randy Anderson and quickly tossed him to the outside floor.

None other than Ole Anderson came sliding into the ring from behind and started pummeling Hawk with knees into the corner. Then all of the Four Horsemen, as they were known, swarmed Hawk and were totally leveling him.

Of course, I came running out for the save, but instead of helping out and stomping some Horsemen tail, I was knocked to the floor by Flair and Blanchard. From there, Hawk and I received the worst professional wrestling beating of our careers. I was given a piledriver on the concrete floor, Paul was knocked out by manager J.J. Dillon's shoe, and Hawk was flattened by an Arn Anderson gourdbuster. Nobody had ever manhandled the Road Warriors like that, and it made a big statement, even if we were outnumbered. But if anyone could've been booked into a believable position to smash us like that, it was the Horsemen.

For my money (as well as the fans'), the Horsemen, named by Arn Anderson in reference to the Four Horsemen of the Apocalypse from the Bible, was the most legitimate clique in the business. Not only were they four of the most reputable workers in the ring, but the Horsemen were masters of the interview promo.

Flair and Blanchard especially always bragged about their Rolex watches, four-star hotels, custom suits, and high-class ladies, all of which were the creed. Tons of fans caught on, and at the shows you'd see college guys dressed up in suits and sunglasses putting up the four-finger sign of the Horsemen and yelling out Ric's trademark, "Whoooooooo!" The Four Horsemen were crass, vilified, totally over with the fans, and among our personal favorite rivals of all time, no question about it.

Needless to say, Hawk and I were chomping at the bit to wrestle Flair one-on-one. We knew we'd learn so much from Ric in the ring and that he'd give us the rub, making us look like a million bucks. That's the way Flair operated. The better he made you look, the better it made him look as a resilient champion who could take all you had for up to sixty minutes and then still pull it out in the end. Hawk and I were both honored with the opportunity to step into the ring with The Man.

When July 1 rolled around, it was time for the kickoff of the Great American Bash, and everyone on the entire roster was pumped up for the big show. Even Hawk was so pumped up for his match with Flair that his vomit reflex from the nervous early days came back hard. "Joe," he said, "I'm wrestling Flair, man.

This is fucking intense." Then he turned and ran for the garbage can.

As much as I was at Hawk's side for support, I was also a little nervous for my own match with Dusty against Ole and Arn in a cage. Between Hawk and me, we were clashing with three of the Four Horsemen, and we had serious axes to grind for what they'd done to us on TV. Dusty and I brutalized the Andersons and came away with a dominating win in front of an almost sold-out crowd at Veterans Stadium.

Hawk's match against Flair was an instant classic that came off perfectly. Ric bumped and sold as if Hawk were superhuman. He also must've press slammed Flair ten times in the match, which will tire out a person quicker than you'd think.

The end of the match, which was a formula used for almost every one of Flair's Bash title defenses, saw Hawk getting in some offense with a flying shoulder block. However, as Hawk launched at Flair, he ducked out of the way, resulting in referee Tommy Young getting knocked out of the ring instead. Then Hawk grabbed Flair and gave him a giant standing backbreaker, knocking Ric cold.

When Hawk went for the cover, Tommy rolled back in, made a three count, and called for the bell. Hawk won the title!

Or did he? Tommy grabbed the belt and gave it to Flair, citing a DQ against Hawk for hitting him with the shoulder tackle. You should have heard that crowd and seen the shit they were throwing into the ring. They were so passionate for Hawk; it was incredible to see.

I remember Hawk coming up to me after the match huffing and puffing, saying, "That motherfucker wanted me to press slam him all night. I couldn't take it." His chest was also beet red from all of Flair's chops, with bruising already taking nasty shape. I wondered if I'd be in for the same treatment when it was my turn.

My little date with Flair came eight days later, on July 9, in Cincinnati at Riverfront Stadium. We worked a match almost identical to the one Ric had wrestled against Hawk, and I absolutely loved every second of it. I press slammed Ric until I think he'd finally had enough. I knew my arms and shoulders had. Man, they were burning.

The crowd was so hot that night that it seemed to be my time to take the World Heavyweight Championship, but of course I didn't. The end was like Hawk's match: I threw Flair into the ropes and accidentally knocked Tommy Young out of the ring, getting myself a nice DQ. It didn't matter, though. Having that exclusive experience with Flair was as good as winning the title as far as I was concerned. Ric is a class act and, in my mind, will always be the one and only World Heavyweight champion in professional wrestling.

The rest of the Great American Bash tour saw Hawk and me involved in random matches against various combinations of the Four Horsemen as well as several matches against the Koloffs and Krusher (Barry), who had recently returned after successfully rehabilitating his injured knee. One of the more memorable meetings with Ivan and Nikita during the Bash was a Russian Chain match in Charlotte at Memorial Stadium, the exact venue of Hawk's and my face turn against Ivan and Krusher a year before at the Bash '85.

I don't mind gimmick matches like the Double Russian Chain match, but I don't prefer them by a long shot. Gimmick matches were always limiting when it came to what spots you could perform. I liked to make sure I got in my press slam and powerslam during each match for the fans, but with my wrist linked to a ten-foot chain, which was attached to an opponent's wrist, I didn't have the luxury of doing much more than punches, kicks, clotheslines, and chokes.

Within the first few minutes of the match, Ivan was busted wide open. In general, the contest was chaotic and all over the place. We beat the Koloffs that night with help from Paul, who pushed Ivan off of the top rope, allowing me to get the pin. As different as the Russian Chain match may have been, I couldn't help but feel the crowd deserved more.

Gimmick matches are a part of the business that at one time or another most workers will be booked into. All you can do is put your best foot forward, try not to get hurt, and put on one hell of a show. Little did I know that over the course of the next year Hawk and I would be involved in two of the most historic gimmick matches in wrestling history.

For the rest of the summer and into September, Hawk and I ran around the country wrestling the Koloffs and Krusher. I was having an amazing time working with my great friends Nikita, Barry, and Hawk. We had a ton of laughs thinking about how far we'd come since our punk days in Minnesota, when we never would've imagined we'd all be professional wrestlers in the same company.

It was funny, man. I looked at Nikita, especially, and thought about how random his entrance into the business was. Even though I'd certainly helped him out, it was ultimately his look and his desire that broke him into a prime spot. I was glad to have been able to assist Scott Simpson along his journey into the persona of Nikita Koloff, but not everyone shared my enthusiasm.

Believe it or not, Hawk actually didn't care much for Nikita at all, and each of them never considered the other a real friend. They never came to blows or had words or anything, but they had an obvious indifference toward each other. In some ways, I think it was a simple case of Hawk feeling slightly threatened by my closer friendship with Nikita.

There's no question Hawk and I were inseparable brothers as the Road Warriors, but Nikita and I also had a special bond that had taken root back in my football days at Golden Valley Lutheran. Nikita took me under his wing back then, and I never forgot it. Now that Nikita was injected into the wrestling business and we were all working for the NWA at the same time, Hawk might've felt slighted by my divided attention.

But also, Hawk and I led very different lifestyles by that point. I definitely liked to have my share of partying after a show, but everything had its limits. With Hawk, there were no limits and there was no sunrise. He'd party all day and all night, burning the candle at both ends. Eventually, as I've mentioned, it started spilling over into serious matters, like being late or absent for flights and shows and sometimes showing up to wrestle in a less-than-capable mind-set.

But, no matter how much of a brotherly role I'd try to assume with Hawk, I still had to tiptoe around addressing how serious his behavior was becoming. I put it off to a later time.

In the meantime, I spent more time with Nikita, who was a little more reserved when it came to the after-hours scene like me. I'm sure there are a lot of you reading this right now who think of the long time Hawk and I worked with Nikita as teammates and would've assumed we were all great friends behind the scenes. It simply wasn't the case.

Sure, the two of them worked with each other and had no issues, but you wouldn't find them sharing a booth at Denny's on any given night. In the end, minor problems aside, I was just happy to have some of my closest friends working in the business with me.

As it came to be, I had the chance to help yet another friend from Minnesota step into the wrestling industry. Terry Szopinski was a six feet five, 320-pound freak of a guy I noticed working out at The Gym back home one day. Terry was so big that I had to approach him and introduce myself. After a little chat, being the savvy wrestling scout that I was, I asked him if he'd ever consider getting into the business.

"I know a guy who could train you if you're interested," I told him. Of course, that guy I was talking about was Eddie Sharkey.

Terry took me up on the offer and did, in fact, start working out with Eddie in the old church basement ring. Eventually Terry's dad saw the potential in his son's efforts and realized his connection with me could very well land him a lucrative new career. Within a few weeks, Mr. Szopinski opted to shell out a couple grand and build Terry a full-scale wrestling ring in the backyard. From that point forward, I donated as much time as possible when I was home from the road to personally train him.

For a guy his size, Terry had made good enough progress that I could take some pictures to Dusty and show him my latest protégé. Before I left, snapshots in tow, I asked Terry what his gimmick name was.

"The Warlord," he said. "Tell Dusty I'm The Warlord."

I laughed and told him it was perfect.

When I reconnected with Dusty and showed him the shots of Terry, he went for it hook, line, and sinker. "Give him a call, Joe," he said. "Tell Terry to pack his bags and meet me in Atlanta in a couple of weeks. We'll put him to work."

I was so thrilled to tell Terry, you'd have thought I was the one getting the call. Man, it's an incredible feeling to be able to tell a friend his dreams have come true.

Terry couldn't believe it. "What? No way, man. Are you shitting me?"

I told him it was the real deal and to get himself ready for a real change of pace.

And like that, Terry Szopinski became The Warlord and was put on the road for Crockett Promotions as a brand-new monster heel under the management of Paul Jones. I began to think I was getting pretty good at spotting new talent and always kept my eyes wide open for the next big thing.

When September rolled around, we booked ourselves onto a three-week tour in Japan for the latter part of October and early November. When Dusty found out about our little trip, I guess his creative juices started flowing because he approached us with an interesting angle: "I'm going to book you boys in the main event of Starrcade '86 on Thanksgiving night against the Midnight Express in a scaffold match. We're going to call it Night of the Skywalkers."

We had heard of scaffold matches but had never actually seen one before. Basically, two 25-foot columns of scaffolding are erected outside opposite sides of the ring so that a thin catwalk can be suspended between the two over the ring. From there, in our case, two teams would climb up their respective sides and try to win the match by throwing both members of the opposing team off of the scaffold. Simple, right? Wrong. But as always, we were team players and said we'd do it. The only thing we had left to do before we took off for Japan was to set up the feud with the Midnight Express.

The whole thing went down on the September 20 episode of *World Championship Wrestling* when Midnight Express manager Jim Cornette, along with his bodyguard, six feet five, 300-pound Big Bubba Rogers called us out. (Big Bubba, up until recently, was just another poor jobber using his real name, Ray Traylor.) He said we were a bunch of muscle-bound idiots who couldn't compete with the skilled mastery of Dennis and Bobby in the ring. Never backing down from a challenge, "Precious" Paul decided to go and answer the call.

When he got in Cornette's face and the two exchanged insults, Paul reached back and slapped the taste out of his mouth. The second Paul landed the slap, Big Bubba and the Midnights started beating him down, prompting Hawk and me to run down. We didn't have a chance to do much to help Paul because Dennis and Bobby got a hold of Cornette's "loaded" tennis racket and worked us with it. I took the brunt of it when they got me into the ring, threw me against the ropes, and gave me a nasty gutshot. Cornette pranced around like a sissy little bandleader, cheering and whooping it up about destroying the mighty Road Warriors.

The injuries we had to sell for the feud gave us the necessary time off to work our dates in Japan and let the buildup of Starrcade '86 work. Before we left, we shot one of our most memorable promos for the event. We decided to find some abandoned scaffolding in downtown Atlanta and show the people at home exactly what the Midnight Express could expect on Thanksgiving night. We climbed up about 30 feet and took along two big pumpkins bearing the names Loverboy and Bobby in black marker.

"This is what happens when you fall off a scaffold," Hawk said before launching the "Loverboy" Dennis pumpkin over the side.

Then there was this long, slow-motion shot of the pumpkin plunging to the ground, where it exploded into a thousand pieces.

It was my turn. "This is what your head's gonna do when it hits the ground." I shot the Bobby pumpkin straight down for a nice messy impact.

All the boys in the locker room loved those vignettes, especially Cornette, Dennis, and Bobby.

When we were all set up to head off to Japan, I checked in with Julie at home. By early October, she was now seven months pregnant and looked ready to pop. Our doctor said it was likely she would deliver in the first week of December, so she was getting close.

Even though she was late in the timeline of her pregnancy, Julie stayed as fit and active as ever. Sure, she might've had her various food cravings, but she definitely didn't sit around eating pickles and ice cream all day. She took care of the house and visited Joey, as she always had.

When we got to Japan, our first match was another all-out brawl with the Funks on October 10, but it was the match on October 21 against Baba and Tenryu that threw a little monkey wrench into the rest of the tour and threatened to cancel our main event at Starrcade.

It all happened so fast. Right at the beginning of the match, Hawk was thrown into the ropes for a simple backdrop, but when he took the move and flipped, he landed awkwardly on his left leg and snapped his lower fibula. *Crack!* Hawk got up and immediately started hobbling over to the corner. "Fuck, Joe, I broke my leg. I felt it. I *heard* it."

I could tell by the look on his face how much pain he was in, so I told him I'd finish the match, which I did, taking the victory after powerslamming Tenryu almost through the mat.

Afterward, we took Hawk to the emergency room and found out it was indeed a break. His leg was wrapped in a cast, and we were sent on our way.

Hawk knew Paul and I were concerned about Starrcade. "Don't worry, guys. I'll be up on that scaffold if it's the last thing I do."

Even though he tried to reassure us, I still had my doubts. In the meantime, I had to pick up the slack for my fallen partner. Although most of our matches for the next couple of weeks were cancelled, I did have a couple of handicap matches where I wrestled two guys by myself.

By the time we got back to Minnesota in early November, I started thinking Hawk's situation wasn't as bad as I'd initially thought. Hawk was getting around pretty well and was even back in the gym training, and he was still intent on working our match in three weeks. As relieved as I was about our situation for Starrcade, something else had developed while we were in Japan that was far worse than the possibility of not performing.

On October 14, while Hawk and I were competing in the Far East, our dear friend and fellow NWA babyface superstar Magnum T.A. had been terribly injured in a car accident. Apparently Magnum had lost control of his Porsche while driving in the rain and struck a telephone pole. It was over two hours before anyone discovered the scene and called 911. He sustained two broken vertebrae, paralyzing his right side for months. Doctors thought he'd never walk again, but eventually with the aid of a cane, he did. Magnum would never wrestle again.

Losing Magnum was a huge tragedy, both personally and professionally. He was the next big star on the rise, having been groomed for a run as the World Heavyweight champion. In fact, it was Magnum who was supposed to face Ric Flair at Starrcade for the title. Dusty, who was absolutely devastated by what had happened to his dear friend, came up with an amazing idea that showed how much of a genius he was in the business.

Dusty decided to take Magnum's most hated and fierce rival and put him in Magnum's place. Nikita Koloff, my best man and the dreaded Russian heel whom Magnum helped rise to another level during their blistering feuds for the NWA US Championship, was about to get one of the most dramatic face turns in professional wrestling.

The week following Magnum's accident, Dusty found himself getting a huge beat down on *World Championship Wrestling* by all of the Four Horsemen. As the fans were going insane for someone to run out and help, none other than Nikita came sliding into the ring to clear house. The people couldn't believe it and were jumping up and down.

Dusty played it cautious at first but then shook Nikita's hand and gave him a hug. As the story line went, Nikita, upon hearing about his fallen adversary Magnum, was so moved with compassion that he felt compelled to "fight the good fight."

The union of "The American Dream" Dusty Rhodes and "The Russian Nightmare" Nikita Koloff became known as The Superpowers, in reference to the United States and the Soviet Union. With Nikita now a strong ally with Dusty (and us as well), he was booked in Magnum's place against Ric Flair at Starrcade. Between Hawk's broken leg and Nikita's face turn, Starrcade '86 was shaping up to be one interesting event.

HAWK AND I ALWAYS KEPT OUR GAME FACES ON, EVEN WHEN OUR WAR PAINT WORE OFF. 1986.

11

SCALING DIZZYING HEIGHTS

When Thanksgiving finally arrived on November 27, 1986, I was as ready as I'd ever be. As for Hawk's leg? Well, let's say that when we arrived at the Omni in Atlanta earlier in the day, Hawk decided to perform a little cast removal. With a pair of scissors and a knife, he cut into that thing until he had a perfect line sliced from top to bottom. He grabbed both sides of the cast and tore it off, revealing one hell of a pale and atrophied calf muscle. He started laughing. "Damn, Joe, as if my legs weren't skinny enough already!" He got up and lightly walked on it, and although he winced in pain a little, he said he could manage it.

Since I'd taken a class on athletic injuries in college, Hawk asked me to tape his ankle and leg for him. Back in those days, the boys didn't have the luxury of trainers in the locker room, so anytime someone hurt an ankle, it was always, "Animal, we need a tape job." I should've charged money.

So after Hawk's cast came off, I looked at it and proceeded to go to work taping the old basket weave formation with a heel lock for total stability. I'm telling you, by the time I was finished taping Hawk up, it may as well have been a cast on his leg. I was proud of my work, and it was no wonder I'd passed the college class (though few others).

When we were both done, we decided to go out to the arena floor and check out the scaffold. As we walked out from behind the curtain into the Omni and saw the scaffolding structure, I wondered if we'd made a big mistake. The thing looked ominous. When we arrived at the very bottom of the base where the side ladder rungs were, I looked straight up at the catwalk suspended over the ring and then straight down to the mat. Then I did it again. Holy shit, was it a long way down! We were told the distance to the bottom was 25 feet, but I'm telling you it made me dizzy the second I looked at it.

To get a better feel for it, Hawk and I climbed up to the top. As I grabbed each rung and pulled myself up, I saw the arena seats get smaller and smaller until I was finally at the top. Hawk didn't seem to be having any problem on his way up, so all was well. When we were both standing on the top of the structure, I started to get a little vertigo and held on to the railing. I swear I could feel the scaffold swaying a little.

The only thing keeping the entire thing steady were a couple of safety cables attached to each side and bolted in the flooring. I also noticed how narrow the catwalk to the other side was. It couldn't have been more than two and a half to three feet at the most. There definitely wasn't a large margin for error on that structure. One fuckup and there'd be casualties, no doubt about it.

Back in the dressing room, we talked things over a bit with Dennis, Bobby, and Jimmy, setting up certain spots and making sure we'd look out for each other while up there. This would have to be the greatest of team efforts, not only for the sake of entertaining the fans, but to maintain our safety at all times. Jimmy Cornette even insisted on taking a bump off of the scaffold at the very end, where Big Bubba would be waiting in the ring to catch his drop. Well, like a lot of things in life, it sure sounded good in theory.

When it was time for us to go on, my heart was beating like a jackhammer. There was so much that could go wrong, so little room for error. And yet I knew that once our music hit, it was going to be nonstop until the match was over, for better or worse, in life or death. No shit, man, it could have happened.

Boom! Our music hit, and it was time for the Night of the Skywalkers. When we came through the curtains, Hawk and I nodded at one another and patted each other's back. Then off we went. Crockett had sprung for these cool pyrotechnic cannons to go off as we went by, shooting off giant Roman-candle-style fireballs. *Bam, bam, bam!* The smell of smoke and the roar of the people are all I remember as I made my way to the scaffold.

In true Road Warriors style, Hawk and I knew exactly how to handle our entrance: storming to the top of the scaffold as we'd always stormed the ring. We launched up the small side ladders built into the structure and made it up there in a matter of seconds. Again, I had a sense of vertigo, but this time I was scanning the 20,000 people standing and screaming for us. We were exactly eye level with the fans in the upper tiers. The lighting rig was really hot, something I would never have noticed down in the ring.

The Midnight Express had come out before us, but they were really playing up their fear factor for the 25-foot scaffold. Cornette was hilarious as he shared Dennis' and Bobby's anxiety and was hugging both of them and yelling, "This is insane. This is ludicrous."

Hawk and I stood on the catwalk, shouting for them to start their climb. I kept making chicken wing motions to show the fans what I thought about the Midnights.

After a few more minutes of comedic cowardly stalling, they finally made their way to the ladder rungs. As you can imagine, Dennis and Bobby took forever to climb to the top, which was probably due to a combination of shtick and real fear.

When they finally got to the top, we thought it'd be funny to shake the skinny little guard rails and scare the hell out of them. It worked like a charm. I remember being shocked and a little worried about how flimsy the rails were. They felt like they were held together with tape instead of screws.

In fact, when we started shaking them a second time, one of the rails on Hawk's side broke and swung down toward the ground. He immediately looked at me. "Holy shit. Did you see that?"

Across the catwalk, Bobby was pointing over to the rail and saying something to Dennis, which I'd guess was something along the lines of "Oh God, we're going to die."

And with that, while the two of them were on their knees, Hawk and I made our way across the catwalk to start the match. I led the way as we walked carefully in little shuffle steps until we were about halfway across. I was praying the whole time and trying not to look down. As I got close to Dennis, I yelled out to him, "C'mon, Loverboy, let's do this."

He crawled toward me and then ducked between my legs.

I spanked Loverboy's ass as he went through and made my way to Bobby by the rails, and *bam!* I started throwing punches and kicks at Bobby while Hawk was headbutting and kicking Dennis. As we stomped on the catwalk, it made the loudest, most shrill noise I'd ever heard, like hitting a tin roof with a frying pan.

For the first couple of minutes, the four of us carefully paced ourselves, trading shots slowly and deliberately. Then it was time for the Midnights to take control, which they did by pulling little bags of baby powder out of their trunks and throwing it into our faces. The big explosion of powder kayfabe blinded us and allowed Dennis and Bobby to take the upper hand of the match.

Hawk was doing an amazing job of dangling his legs off of the side of the scaffold, really looking like he could've spilled to the concrete floor below at any second. It also didn't help that another one of the guard rails disconnected and swung to the side. The entire audience (and Dennis, who was right next to it) gasped. The Night of the Skywalkers was truly living up to the hype of being a life-or-death situation.

Hawk and I weathered the storm and let the Midnights have their way for a minute before turning the tide back in our favor. On the other side, I could see Hawk slamming Dennis' head into the steel repeatedly until he drew blood. On my end, I followed suit and busted Bobby open, too, which put us in the position to take the match home.

Both Hawk and I, on opposite ends of the catwalk, eventually moved Bobby and Dennis onto their stomachs and off of the side of the scaffold. They were both holding on to the inside of the structure, facing the ring. The catwalk was underlined from end to end with two parallel sets of ladder rungs exactly like a set of monkey bars in a jungle gym.

Dennis was holding on to a rung and lost his footing so that he was only hanging by his arms. Hawk, too, was hanging from one of the catwalk rungs and started to barrage Dennis with swinging kicks. Dennis couldn't hang on any longer and, just like that, he let go and fell like a ton of bricks into the canvas. *Boom!* At the same time, Bobby decided to monkey bar all the way out to the middle of the catwalk, 20 feet above the ring. I was right behind him and started to swing and kick his lower back with my right foot. *Boom, boom, boom!*

Bobby swung wildly back and forth maybe five times before losing his grip and taking a full-out crash onto his ribs and hip in one of the nastiest bumps I've ever seen in the business. Both Dennis and Bobby looked like two dead bodies lying in the ring, battered and bleeding. We won the match and got our revenge on the Midnight Express.

But the action wasn't over yet. Jimmy Cornette still had a date with the top of the scaffold. With Dennis and Bobby in a crumpled mess in the ring, Cornette thought he'd sneak attack Paul with his tennis racket. Just as he was about to swing, Paul turned around, blocked the shot, and chased Cornette into the ring and up one of the sides of the scaffold. He climbed all the way to the top and found himself all alone with me.

In a great performance, Cornette shuffled his way cautiously out to the middle of the catwalk, got down onto his stomach, and started to reach underneath the platform to the monkey bars. I crawled right down on top of him and assisted him over the edge. In a flash, Cornette swung off and was hanging completely vertical from the catwalk, yelling, "Bubba, Bubba, catch me."

Well, either the lights were in Bubba's eyes or he was terrible at playing catch, because when Jimmy let go, he plummeted straight down and landed flatfooted, blowing out one of his knees. He was lying in the ring, crying out, "Oh, Bubba, my knee. I hurt my knee."

He wasn't kidding, either. Cornette wound up being gone from the business for a few months until he could rehab the injury.

In the meantime, lucky us, we got to tour the entire country until early 1987 doing Skywalker rematches with Dennis and Bobby. That little stretch couldn't have ended soon enough for all four of us. But I'll tell you what, as exciting and climactic as Starrcade was, the biggest excitement of the year had yet to arrive.

Not even a week after climbing up the scaffold in Atlanta, I got the call on December 2 that Julie's water had broken. Shit, I was going to be a father again, and here I was in the middle of a TV taping in Greenville, North Carolina. I didn't even take my gear with me as I scrambled to make the first flight out of there to Charlotte and then to Minneapolis. I'm telling you, it was nothing like the convenience of today's airline travel.

I finally got back at about 10:30 a.m. on December 3 and made it to the hospital about a half hour before Julie delivered. As I mentioned earlier, Julie and I decided to keep the baby's gender a surprise, so when the big moment came, we had no idea what to expect. And what did we get? A baby boy, whom we named James.

We were both overwhelmed with joy at our new gift from God and, man, you should've see James' size. He was huge. All of the nurses were betting each other on how much he weighed, which I said would be at least ten pounds. He came out at 10.4 pounds— and with a full head of black hair, which eventually turned blond.

There he was, my son, screaming and hungry. As I held him, I also looked at Julie, who'd put in the greatest effort for nine months carrying a kid this size. I said, "James, you're going to be one amazing athlete someday, bud." With the genes he'd inherited from Julie and me, our son was loaded with potential. We both knew great things were ahead for our baby James.

By late February of 1987, Hawk and I finally wrestled the last of our scaffold matches with the Midnight Express, although our long-term feud with them was far from over. The Road Warriors' popularity had risen to such a height that Giant Baba gave us a call. He wanted Hawk and me to come to Japan and go over Jumbo and Tenryu for the NWA International Tag Team titles. It was a huge honor.

Usually guys from America who were privileged enough to be given those belts had been in the business for years and had legendary reputations. Sure, the whole wrestling business is a work and titles are given, not won, but when you're on a short list of respected American workers with the likes of Abdullah the Butcher, Dory and Terry Funk, and even Dick the Bruiser and the Crusher, it was clear how much respect the Japanese truly had for us. With only three and a half years of experience, Hawk and Animal were among the very elite ranks.

Fortunately, by the time we arrived at the Tokyo Dome on March 12, 1987, Hawk and Jumbo had long since laid their problems to rest. When it came down to it, both teams respected the hell out of each other and wanted to do great business for Baba by putting on a phenomenal show. And, believe me, we definitely outdid ourselves.

I particularly enjoyed the opening of the match. I started off with Jumbo, and the crowd let out a mixture of chants for both of us. It was electric. After locking up and pushing off each other a couple times, we locked horns a third time and Jumbo snapped me over with a fast arm drag. *Whoom! Bam!* I hit hard and skidded sideways before jumping up like a startled lion.

I thought we needed to pick up the pace a bit, so I looked at the crowd, started screaming, and launched at Tsuruta with a big boot to the stomach. *Boom!* Then I whipped him into the ropes, bounced back, and smashed him with a flying shoulder block. As soon as I landed, I ran to Jumbo, picked him up off the mat, and then pressed the big man high over my head as the Japanese people stood in amazement. That was my official Animalized opening for our championship night.

The rest of the match was a smooth and successful demonstration of two seasoned teams working their craft. After two years of being in and out of the All Japan trenches with Jumbo and Tenryu, we had definitely reached an instinctual level of understanding and communication in the ring.

The way we won the match was interesting because it was by count-out due to giving Tenryu a piledriver on the concrete floor and running back into the ring at the last second. Now, in the United States, a title could never change hands by count-out. The only way a challenger could win a belt in the United States was by pinfall or submission, period. But in Japan, they didn't have the same stipulations we did, so the finish allowed us to capture the NWA International Tag Team Championship and also allowed Jumbo and Tenryu to save face by not being clearly beaten in the middle of the ring. Nevertheless, Hawk and I did it.

We were given the ultimate recognition from Baba as highly respected entities in Japanese professional wrestling. You should've seen the giant four-foot-tall trophies we were given. I'd never seen anything like them.

In fact, championships were handled very differently in Japan. In America, the referee raised your hand and the announcer made the call and it was over with little fanfare. In Japan, it was a much different, more reverent scenario. The procession was serious, and we were as humble as possible for the duration. After all, we were still just oversized kids in another country following the leaders, excited and grateful to be there. We were also given the International title belts, which we actually gave back to Baba after the show was over.

About a month before we had left for Japan, Jimmy Crockett had been so proud of us going over to AJPW and winning the championships that he'd had brand-new American belts made for us, but we used Baba's belts whenever we wrestled in Japan. Now we were the NWA Six-Man Tag Team champions (with Dusty) and the NWA International Tag Team champions.

As it would turn out, that night proved to be the very last time we would face Jumbo and Tenryu as a tag team. Not long after, they would split up. In a lot of ways, I guess winning the titles from those guys kind of ceremoniously ended the classic rivalry altogether. In fact, just a couple of years later, we'd invite Tenryu to be our six-man tag partner in WCW. But Hawk and I had some business to attend to first.

When we touched back down in the United States, we started getting ourselves prepared for the upcoming 2nd Annual Jim Crockett Sr. Memorial Cup in Baltimore in April. Although Hawk and I were the defending Crockett Cup winners and were on one hell of a team in the business, we were told by Dusty that he and Nikita were going to win the Cup. At that point, Dusty was still intent on getting Nikita as over as possible with the fans, who were still reeling from the loss of Magnum T.A. back in October.

It was also around this time that yet another set of Road Warriors clones were brought to my attention. A few months earlier in January, the WWF debuted a team by the name of Demolition, which was nothing more than a slightly different approach to our Road Warriors gimmick. Ax and Smash came to the ring wearing black spray-painted hockey masks along with black spider-strapped singlets studded with little spikes.

When the masks came off, Ax and Smash were both revealed to be completely made up in bizarre mixtures of silver, black, red, and yellow face paint. To be honest with you, I felt their look and posturing looked a little more like the rock band KISS than like us, but the overall tone was definitely based on us.

I wasn't too upset about Demolition, though, because the guys behind the Ax and Smash gimmicks were our old friend Bill "Masked Superstar" Eadie and fellow partner in crime Barry Darsow. You see, Barry's contract with Crockett had recently expired and he was looking for any and all new opportunities.

Meanwhile, Randy Colley, the original Smash, was removed from the role after starting it up. Apparently, Randy had been too recognizable as Moondog Rex, half of the former tag team the Moondogs, and needed to be replaced by an unknown. As fate would have it, that unknown had turned out to be Barry.

In all honesty, I feel Demolition originated directly out of Hawk's and my meeting with Vince the year before. I think his wheels started turning the minute he realized we weren't signing with the WWF, and he must have thought, *If I can't have the Road Warriors, I'll make my own.* Had Hawk and I agreed to terms with Vince, there's no doubt in my mind Demolition never would've come to be.

The Demolition gimmick provided both Bill and Barry with a new life in the business, and God bless 'em, they took full advantage of it. Managed by Mr. Fuji, Demolition destroyed every team in the company (in true Road Warriors fashion) and became the un-beatable WWF Tag Team champions.

The wrestling magazines had a field day with the rivalry, con-stantly theorizing who would win in a dream match if both teams ever faced each other. Fans used to ask me on the street all the time. Shit, even I was starting to wonder who'd win. In time, everyone would get their answer.

When the Crockett Cup weekend rolled around on April 10 and 11 at the Baltimore Arena, honestly I was a little disinterested in the tournament. I guess I got a little too used to winning every-thing and was a little put off when we were told we wouldn't take this year's Cup. But I quickly got over it. I had to.

At the end of the day, as hard as it was, I always had to remind myself that the wrestling business was a work and I couldn't feed into all the bullshit about wins and losses. The second a guy takes championship belts and himself too seriously, he becomes a mark. Sure, it's easy to be swept up in the hype, but we had to maintain a separation between ourselves and our gimmick.

To keep grounded in this industry, all I had to do was remember that the most important word in the phrase "wrestling business" was "business." Everything else was details. As cliché as it may sound, above and beyond everything was the commitment I felt to being a consummate professional and giving the fans what they paid for.

I never forgot what it was like toiling at my dead-end job: when it was time to get off work, it was time to unload and escape. And there were definitely times I looked forward for months for the AWA to come to town. Now I was on the flip side of the equation, and I took that perspective with me into every match. The fans who came to our shows had probably waited excitedly for months with their tickets tacked onto their corkboards for the big night when the NWA and the Road Warriors finally came to town. We owed those people what they wanted to see: something special and unforgettable.

In our first match of the tournament, we quickly flattened the team Paul Jones managed: Shaska Whatley (the former "Pistol" Pez Whatley) and a guy named Teijho Khan. In our second and last match of the event, we faced the Midnight Express, but it wasn't the team of "Loverboy" Dennis and "Beautiful" Bobby. Dennis Condrey had abruptly left the company a month or two before and, needing an immediate replacement, Cornette and Bobby had hired Stan Lane, our old rival with the Fabulous Ones.

"Sweet" Stan Lane fit into the spot vacated by Dennis almost seamlessly and breathed new life into the Midnight Express. Since I'd seen him last, Stan now fancied himself a martial artist and was including side body kicks and 360-degree spin kicks in his arsenal. All the other boys, including us, thought those kicks were laughably bad. For most of the match, the Road Warriors dominated (except for Stan's vicious kicks), leading to the controversial ending.

I was in the ring with Stan and came off the ropes with a flying shoulder block and, in classic fashion, knocked the referee right out of the ring. In the mayhem of not having an official to witness any interference, Jim Cornette quickly jumped into the ring. Immediately when I turned to face him, he lit and threw a handful of flash paper into my face. *Whoom!*

All I remember was blistering heat and the smell of my singed eyebrows. I grabbed my face and rolled around as if it were melting off. In the meantime, Paul got a hold of Cornette's tennis racket and took a good shot at Jimmy's back. Then I recovered enough to grab the racket, and as I started whacking away on Stan and Bobby, the referee saw me and called for the bell. We lost by DQ. Rats.

In May we flew down to St. Petersburg, Florida, to wrestle at the Eddie Graham Memorial Show in honor of Eddie, a great guy and promoter who had shot and killed himself on January 21, 1985, after years of serious alcoholism. In front of a sold-out crowd at the Bayfront Center, Hawk and I wrestled NWA World Tag Team champions Manny Fernandez and some guy named Ravishing Rick Rude.

Yeah, tell me about it. It seemed like every time I turned my head, I was in a match with one of my old hometown buddies. Not only that, but between Hawk, Barry, Rude, and myself, we had held or were holding every major tag team championship from around the world. Eddie Sharkey had to have felt like a proud father.

By now, Rude had real swagger as the robe-wearing, narcissistic, egomaniacal heel who went to the ring to the tune of Sade's "Smooth Operator." I had to give it to him, after struggling for quite some time to come into his own, Rick had developed one smooth gimmick, and I couldn't have been prouder. Now he was half of the NWA World Tag Team champs. Hell, that was a title Hawk and I had yet to win.

Manny Fernandez was an interesting guy, too. He'd spread the funny rumor that he was in fact the same Manny Fernandez who'd played for the Miami Dolphins in the 1970s. I knew he was full of shit and told him so, but he sure pulled that rib on everybody else. They just didn't know their football like I did.

We had a great match that night with a double DQ finish when manager Paul Jones came into the ring and broke up the pin I was about to score after powerslamming Manny. Then "Precious"

Paul ran in and started beating Jones down, and the ref called for the bell. That didn't stop Hawk and me from getting one last lick in on Rude. We picked him up from the mat, threw him into the ropes, and double clotheslined his head off. What else are friends for?

Funny enough, also that month, the entire wrestling industry got a little black eye when Jim Duggan and the Iron Sheik got arrested together in New Jersey. On May 26, Duggan and Sheik got pulled over on the NJ Turnpike and were both found under the influence of drugs. But forget about all that, because the kicker is that those two were currently in a hot feud in the WWF. Talk about breaking kayfabe, brother!

There they were, hateful enemies on TV, caught being the best of buddies. As you can imagine, the WWF wasn't very happy about Duggan and Sheik exposing part of the business and drawing negative publicity to the company. They were both released shortly after.

So, after finishing up in St. Petersburg with Rude and Manny, we had a few dates to hit in the Southwest, where we suffered a big hit to our gimmick—and our wallets. We were staying at a hotel in Weslaco, Texas, slightly above the Rio Grande River from Mexico and west of the Gulf of Mexico. I guess somebody had been watching us during our stay. All I know is that the next morning when Hawk and I went outside to our van, one of the side windows was smashed in. When we opened up the van and took a look inside, it was as I feared: they'd taken our spiked vests. I could've killed somebody.

Hawk was livid. "Fuck, man. That's bullshit."

I felt violated in the worst way and cursed the fact that we had spent $3000 each on them, including big, custom foam carrying cases. *Poof!* Gone. It makes me sick to think that today, somewhere out there, Hawk's and my prized vests are probably sitting in a pawnshop collecting dust.

But you know what? Maybe it was all meant to be because the loss made me think even bigger. I decided to give a call to a buddy who worked at Riddell, makers of collegiate and professional grade football shoulder pads, and ran some ideas past him. He sent me a couple pairs of the pads, and I went to work on the vision I had for the Road Warriors' newest piece of artillery.

I called an old coworker from my days at Honeywell and asked him if he could fabricate a few nickel-plated spikes in various sizes. He said it would be no problem and got to work right away. The next step was drilling holes in the tops of the pads and then spray-painting the entire sets with a flat black.

When the spikes were ready, I simply popped them in place like rivets into the holes. After clamping some chains between the breastplates, I tried them on. They were even better than I'd hoped. Like an excited little kid, I called up Hawk and told him to get his ass over and check out my newest creation.

"Holy shit, Animal, those are badass," he said.

We both put our pads on and looked at each other in the mirror. It was love at first sight. The Road Warriors had been supersized.

Inspired by the new addition to our gimmick, I also started to experiment with a new Road Warrior Animal paint job. Sketching out some ideas, I began to draw a web with a spider in the middle. That was it! I drew the webbing onto my face in the same general shape as my standard devil horn look, only I didn't fill it in with solid colors. I simply connected a series of lines into a point between my eyes and then painted a little black spider hanging right in the center.

It gave me chills looking at it. I thought, *Don't get caught in the web.* Hell, yeah. Being stuck in Animal's web meant certain doom for all unfortunate prey.

My Road Warriors inventiveness didn't stop with the pads and the paint job. During another trip back to Japan in early June, after watching a match with the British Bulldogs, I was inspired to develop a new finisher to captivate audiences. Davey Boy Smith and Dynamite Kid were one of the most innovative and exciting teams I'd ever seen, and one spot Dynamite did in particular caught my attention.

The move was called the electric chair drop, which involved Dynamite bending over and scooping an opponent onto his shoulders in an upright seated position, as if to give him a piggyback ride. From there, Dynamite pushed backward as hard as he could, giving his opponent a back-bump from hell. *Boom!*

I wondered what it would be like if I put somebody up for the electric chair and Hawk clotheslined them from the top rope. Hmmmm. Only one way to find out.

A few days later we were doing TV tapings for AJPW against a couple of jobbers, and I thought we'd take my new idea for a test run. When we got to the end of the match, I told Hawk to climb to the top. I walked up behind one of our dazed opponents, stuck my head between his legs, and raised him high up on my shoulders. When I'd adjusted to the additional weight, I pivoted around to face Hawk, who launched off and clotheslined the guy with a ton of force, knocking him for a full backflip. *Whoom!*

The resulting carnage was incredible and perfectly Road Warrioresque. The move was like a decapitation and a graceful trapeze act all at the same time. Hawk and I knew we had a winner the second we watched it back on tape. No one was doing anything like what we had executed. The only thing we were missing was a name, which we quickly came up with: the Double Impact. But when we went back to the States, we eventually settled on a new, permanent name for our finisher: the Doomsday Device.

When we came back to the United States and used the Doomsday on our first TV taping, the guys in the back were less than thrilled. "Oh, great," Arn Anderson said. "Now we get to do that? What's next, a firing squad?"

12

THE GOLDEN AGE OF JIM CROCKETT PROMOTIONS AND THE NWA

We'd just revamped our Road Warrior gimmick with the addition of the shoulder pads and the Doomsday Device when the time came yet again for the Great American Bash, another monthlong tour in July of 1987. But this year the Bash itself would be a mere backdrop for the event Hawk and I felt was the defining moment of each of our careers—War Games: The Match Beyond.

War Games was another brilliant invention of Dusty Rhodes, who'd been thinking of a way to get all Four Horsemen in the ring with himself, Nikita, and us in a super match. I don't know how he came up with it, but Dusty envisioned two rings, side by side, enclosed by one giant, ceilinged cage. The resulting concept would become the uncontested king of the gimmick matches.

I remember arriving with Hawk at the Omni for the match on the Fourth of July, the kickoff night of the Bash. We couldn't wait to go out on the floor and see what this thing was all about.

I couldn't believe what I saw. There in the empty arena, hanging ominously about 70 feet in the air above the two rings, was the giant War Games cage. It's an image I'll never forget.

Like little kids in awe, Hawk and I walked to the rings and checked them out. Right away I noticed there was about a five-foot gap between the ropes where the rings were side by side, and got big ideas. "I got it, man," I said to Hawk. "We hit a set of double flying shoulder blocks." With a new playground like this, the possibilities were endless.

The match was in two parts: the War Games and then the Match Beyond. The way it all worked was so simple that it was brilliant. War Games started off with two men, one from each team. After two minutes of no-rules combat, a coin toss decided which team got to send in another member for a two-on-one advantage. Then after two more minutes, the opposite team was able to even up the score with another entrant. This sequence went back and forth every two minutes until both teams were completely in the ring at the same time, at which point the War Games became the Match Beyond. The Match Beyond itself had an even simpler premise than the War Games: the first person to submit or surrender lost the match for his team.

I thought the whole idea was amazing and couldn't wait to get painted and geared up. In a lot of ways, the War Games meant so much more than being a wrestling spectacle; it was a symbol of the heights the NWA and Jimmy Crockett had scaled in the industry. At that time, the company was in the midst of a golden era of popularity and profits, and it was because of our loaded roster of top guys.

In all seriousness, the Road Warriors, Dusty Rhodes, Nikita Koloff, and the Four Horsemen's stable—NWA World Heavyweight champion Ric Flair, NWA World Television champion Tully Blanchard, Arn Anderson, and Lex Luger (who had recently replaced Ole)—were the hottest ticket in the company. Any combinations of singles, tag team, six-man or even eight-man tag matches drew sellout business wherever we went. With that in mind, it was a no-brainer for Dusty to figure out how to take all of us and do something the world had never seen before. Crockett hyped the coming of the War Games for months on TV, too, with cool commercials for the Bash showing pieces of the cage being welded together.

I'll never forget how excited and nervous I was for the match to start, and when our music hit and it was time to go, my mind went blank. Hawk and I looked like full-scale monsters in our giant shoulder pads as we plowed down the aisle with Nikita, Dusty, and Paul. That night, not only was Paul involved in the match as our fifth member, but so was Tully Blanchard's manager, J.J. Dillon, the Fifth Horseman in the match.

With the lights out and spotlights scanning the screaming audience, a loud voice announced over the PA, "Let the War Games begin." It was like something out of the movies, and I had chills up and down my arms. It was so loud in the Omni that it was hard to hear anything.

When it all finally started, it was Dusty and Arn first and then Tully, me, Flair, Nikita, Luger, Hawk, J.J., and then Paul. The event was total chaos, and I absolutely loved it. Everyone was hurt, exhausted, and bleeding by the end.

When I first jumped into the cage, I leveled Arn and Flair and then took Tully and launched him like an arrow over the ropes and into the second ring. I raced over there and, with my back to the cage, hooked his legs under my arms and picked him up sit-up style into the cage. After five or six face-first cage smashes, Tully was pulverized, and I dropped him like a big bag of bones.

Tully also served as cannon fodder for Hawk when he first tore into the War Games like a starving tiger. After climbing into the ring and knocking Lex Luger half unconscious, he grabbed Tully and yelled, "Press. Spear."

I wasn't sure what he meant until I saw him press Tully over his head, then throw him like a human spear into the corner, where he landed in a crumpled heap.

Because everyone, especially Dusty, had been so impressed with our new Doomsday Device finisher, we'd been told we had the honor of bringing the match home. It was also decided that J.J. Dillon would have the distinct pleasure of receiving our fine little maneuver.

The plan was to be extra careful. Well, sometimes things don't go quite as planned.

Referee Tommy Young started frantically yelling over to us, "Wrap it up. Wrap it up. Let's take it home."

We knew there were time constraints, so we hastily got ourselves into position. The ceiling on the cage complicated the whole Doomsday dynamic. When I had J.J. up on my shoulders, he had to kind of hunch over to the side in order to fit upright. When Hawk clotheslined him, he jumped off the top a little before I was ready and poor J.J. fell awkwardly on his side and separated his shoulder.

As soon as he landed, I knew there was a problem.

"Oh, shit. I'm hurt." J.J. groaned. "I popped my shoulder out."

To end the match, we quickly made J.J. submit and the bell was rung. I have to admit, winning the War Games was bittersweet because of the injury. Rule number one in the code of professional wrestling is to protect each other at all times.

When we got to the back, Flair, Tully, and Arn weren't happy at all. They said we were careless, but J.J. spoke up and came to our defense. "It wasn't their fault. There wasn't enough room between me and the top of the cage. I couldn't take the bump right."

Although I felt horrible about J.J. and appreciated that he defended us, I personally didn't think it was anybody's fault. The War Games were too fast-paced and out of control. Hawk, J.J., and I rushed the Doomsday together and, far beyond our control, J.J. took the fall. It was just one of those things. One thing is for sure, though: the ten of us made professional wrestling history that night. Over twenty-three years later and counting, I get asked more about the War Games than anything else I ever did.

War Games was such a huge success, in fact, that Dusty decided immediately to have a sequel. War Games II took place at the final show of the Bash on July 31 in Miami at the Orange Bowl. All of us returned for the big sequel, except of course J.J., who was replaced by War Machine, who was actually Big Bubba Rogers under a mask.

Our team again won the Match Beyond, but in my opinion it didn't compare to the first one. Sure, all of the key players were back, but like many part twos, the magic wasn't the same. A lot of people don't know that we actually had two more War Games that August: one in Chicago at the Pavilion and one in Long Island at the Nassau Coliseum. We won both of those as well.

The Great American Bash '87 was another success for the NWA and Jim Crockett Promotions, and Jimmy sure wasn't shy about spreading the wealth to his main players (us, Dusty, Nikita, and the Horsemen). Not only did Jimmy start treating us to

Caribbean vacations, city-to-city limousine rides, and four-star hotels and restaurants, but he even reached in really deep and sprung for a company Falcon 50, one of the most exclusive private jets money could buy. Honestly, there was nothing cooler than leaving a show and being chauffeured directly to our own plane.

We were all having so much fun that no one ever stopped to wonder how long it would last. When business is booming like it was in 1987 in the NWA, no one ever imagines a day when things might take a different turn. Right then and there, the only things we were all concerned with were making sure the jet was fueled up and the champagne was on ice. There were others, however, in the business who weren't faring as well.

Bill Watts' Mid-South Wrestling, now called the Universal Wrestling Federation (UWF) for a more global marketing appeal, was starting to tank. As a result, Jimmy Crockett figured it would be a great idea to buy out Watts and absorb the UWF, which he'd done around the same time as the Crockett Cup back in April.

When the Bash rolled around in July, several UWF talents, such as announcer Jim Ross and wrestlers like Dr. Death Steve Williams, "Hot Stuff" Eddie Gilbert, Rick Steiner, and Sting (the former Blade Runner) were able to successfully make the transition into the NWA over the months leading up to Starrcade '87 in November.

Usually the premier event for the NWA and Jim Crockett Promotions, Starrcade proved to be a monumental disaster in 1987. First, Jimmy decided to hold Starrcade in Chicago instead of Atlanta or Greensboro, removing the event's traditional territorial Southern roots for the first time.

It was also Crockett's first attempt at doing a PPV, a market

Vince McMahon and the WWF had firmly monopolized since the first WrestleMania back in '85. When the WWF discovered Crockett's bold ambition to host the Starrcade '87 PPV on Thanksgiving night, they decided to step in and squash it.

In retaliation to Starrcade, Vince developed the first ever Survivor Series PPV to air opposite our show on the same night. He then called up all of the major cable companies he normally did business with, the same ones that had already intended to commit to Starrcade, and informed them that if they didn't exclusively run Survivor Series instead of Crockett's show, then they'd lose out on all future WWF PPVs, including WrestleMania.

One thing you have to understand is that earlier, in April, WrestleMania III had featured Andre the Giant against Hulk Hogan at the Pontiac Silverdome. The show had become the biggest indoor sporting event of all time, with a live attendance of almost 94,000 people. It crushed all buy rate projections with revenue in the ten-million-dollar range. It was record business.

With that fact still fresh in the minds of cable executives, the thought of losing out on a guaranteed moneymaker like the WWF caused many of them to quake and opt to heed Vince's ultimatum. The outcome? The WWF outsold Starrcade by more than a two-to-one ratio and really stuck it to Jimmy, killing profits and stirring up a lot of uneasiness within the company.

It was a shame, too, because Starrcade '87 was a damn good show. Hawk and I wrestled a hell of a match in front of our kay-fabe hometown of Chicago against Tully and Arn for the tag team titles. We didn't go over that night, but rest assured that crowd was ours from beginning to end.

The competitive war between Jim Crockett Promotions and

Vince McMahon was really getting out of control by that point. The two of them were hell-bent on beating each other and emerging as the clear victor, but at what cost? What happened with Starrcade caused Jimmy to kick into overdrive to develop an answer to Vince's tactics. Should he have slowed down and focused on the strong points of his NWA franchise? Probably. But there was no hitting the brakes. With Jimmy Crockett, it was all or nothing.

By early 1988 Hawk's and my attention was once again directed into the path of a new feud. This time it was against our newest set of clones. The Powers of Pain (POP) was Paul Jones' freshly formed tag team of his two biggest and baddest clients, the Barbarian and Warlord, my old student. Barbarian, or Barb, had been in and around the business about the same amount of time as we had and his gimmick looked very similar to mine.

He had a Mohawk, face paint, and the exact same tights and boots as we did. Not to mention, at six feet two and near 300 pounds, Barb was about my equal in size and strength. When Warlord was brought into the picture, he was given Hawk's reverse Mohawk, face paint, and the same gear as Barb's. Together, the POP looked almost exactly like us and had their own conniving manager in Paul Jones, who spoke exclusively for them just as Paul Ellering had for us in the early days. They were immediately booked into a program with us.

The angle was pretty simple. Jones came out on TV and announced that he had this new monster tag team and started making claims that Barb and Warlord were stronger than the Road Warriors. From there, we started working against the POP in house shows throughout early January, which warmed us up for Jim Crockett Promotions' second attempt at a PPV, the Bunk-

49 Street Station
Downtown & B'klyn

N RR

Photo courtesy of Pro Wrestling Illustrated

For some reason whenever Hawk and I went to NYC, little old ladies tossed us their purses and cried for the cops. 1986.

Posing for our PWI Tag Team of the Year issue as the
NWA National champs. Winter 1984.

Photo courtesy of Pro Wrestling Illustrated

MORE COLOR THAN EVER BEFORE!

INCREDIBLE FULL-COLOR CENTERFOLD: JIMMY SNUKA & HULK HOGAN—TOGETHER!!!

March 1984
$1.75

DELL 04683

T.V. SPORTS

PRO Wrestling ILUSTRATED

SPECIAL YEAR-END AWARDS ISSUE!

THE ROAD WARRIORS
Tag Team Of The Year

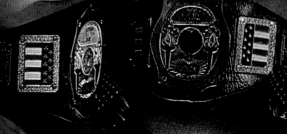

HARLEY RACE ● Wrestler Of The Year
GREG VALENTINE ● Most Hated Wrestler
BRETT WAYNE ● Most Improved Wrestler
HULK HOGAN ● Inspirational Wrestler
JIMMY SNUKA ● Most Popular Wrestler

0 71572 04683

03

The finished PWI cover for our 1983 Tag Team of the Year issue.
Not bad, huh?

THE ROAD WARRIORS

Photos by Bob Mulrenin

Top: Hawk, Paul, and I waiting for the music to hit during our brief NWA World Tag Team title reign. Fall '88.
Bottom: Time to bring home the bacon.

Photo courtesy of Pro Wrestling Illustrated

Getting ready to defend the NWA World Six-Man Championship with Dusty Rhodes. Summer '88.

Photo courtesy of Pro Wrestling Illustrated

Photo courtesy of the Laurinaitis family.

Top: Once I grabbed onto Julie, I never let her go! 1986.
Bottom: With my father (left), brothers, and mother at John's wedding in Clearwater, Florida.

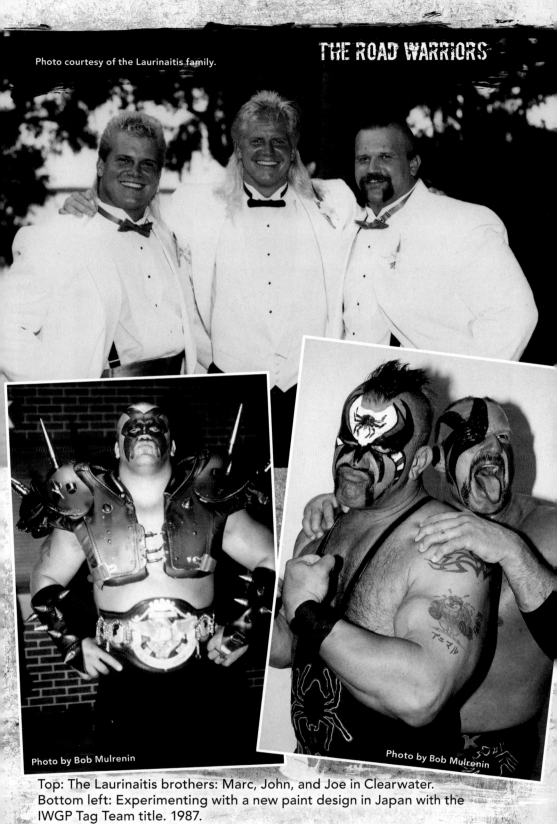

Photo courtesy of the Laurinaitis family.

Photo by Bob Mulrenin

Photo by Bob Mulrenin

Top: The Laurinaitis brothers: Marc, John, and Joe in Clearwater.
Bottom left: Experimenting with a new paint design in Japan with the
IWGP Tag Team title. 1987.
Bottom right: Hawk and I were still going strong in 2002.

Photo courtesy of Pro Wrestling Illustrated

Broken orbital bone at the hands of the Warlord. I thought my eyeball popped out! February '88.

house Stampede.

The Bunkhouse Stampede was another Dusty invention and another ambitious move by Jimmy Crockett to compete with the WWF. Dusty and Crockett even decided to take the show up to Long Island at the Nassau Coliseum. It was a bold statement. It would've been like Vince taking the WWF to North Carolina at the Greensboro Coliseum and thumbing his nose at Jimmy.

Well, history repeated itself in the form of the Starrcade/Survivor Series scenario from the previous November. As soon as the Stampede PPV was announced, the WWF decided to create the first annual Royal Rumble and offer it for PPV on the same date. Man, it was getting ugly. Not only were the gloves off, but there were brass knuckles.

Hawk and I and the majority of the locker room had zero idea how bad things were actually getting. All I knew was that I had a great time in the Bunkhouse match itself, which was basically an every-man-for-himself, no-rules battle royal in a cage.

Six thousand fans watched as the POP, Dusty, Ivan Koloff, Arn, Tully, Lex Luger, and I kicked the crap out of each other for a kayfabe $500,000 prize and a big bronze statue of a cowboy boot. After personally eliminating Ivan and Warlord, I took a boot to the back of the head from Barb, which sent me through the cage door and out of the match. When it was all over, Dusty emerged as the winner of his own main event.

Hawk, on the other hand, got another chance to wrestle Ric Flair for the World title. He was really amped for that match. He always loved working with Flair, so when the rare opportunity popped up for him to step into the spotlight with the Nature Boy, Hawk soared to the occasion. It was essentially the same match as their Bash '86 encounter, only this time it was Flair who DQ'd himself by hitting Hawk over the head with a steel chair.

Unfortunately, as solid of a show as the Bunkhouse Stampede might've been, it was blown out of the water by the inaugural Royal Rumble, which also featured a huge battle royal for its main event. Jimmy Crockett was against the ropes and needed to come up with an answer to the WWF and try to stop the bleeding.

When the Stampede was over and Hawk and I resumed our tag team rivalry with Barb and Warlord, wouldn't you know it? I got injured for real. On January 28, we were in a six-man tag match with Paul against the POP and Ivan Koloff in Hammond, Indiana, when things went very wrong. During an attempted Samoan Slam, in which the 330-pound Warlord would prop me laterally behind his back and slam himself and me down to the mat, he landed on the side of my head. *Bam!* When we first impacted, I swear my left eyeball popped out of and back into the socket like a jack-in-the-box, and it completely freaked me out. All I knew was that I was in a ton of pain and couldn't see out of my eye. I grabbed my face, rolled out of the ring, and yelled to Hawk, "Aw, shit, man. I think my eyeball's hanging out of my head." Fortunately, it wasn't, but I knew something was wrong. The pain was excruciating, and my whole head and face were pounding. It was agony.

But Hawk thought I was kidding. He hadn't noticed the fall. "Yeah, your eyeball's hanging out. And your head's off of its shoulders, too." And then he pushed me back into the ring.

When I slowly got to my feet, Ivan was coming at me, and I told him, "Ivan, I'm messed up. Let's take it home."

We quickly finished the match with me getting a super quick, weak clothesline off on Ivan and grabbing the pin. As soon as it was all over, Paul and Hawk drove me to the emergency room.

On our way out, Warlord ran up and apologized, asking if there was anything he could do, but it wasn't necessary.

"Haven't you done enough already?" I joked.

Just like J.J.'s injury at the War Games, this was an accident. Anytime you're performing a high-risk maneuver that involves a 330-pound behemoth falling onto your face, all bets are completely off.

When we went to the medical center in Hammond, the X-ray machine they had was outdated to the point that it wasn't strong enough to read through my thick head. No kidding.

"Nothing but rocks in there," Hawk quipped. "I've been saying it for years."

So we hopped in a car and drove twenty-five miles to a Chicago hospital, where the injury was diagnosed. "Mr. Laurinaitis," the doctor said matter-of-factly, "your nose is broken, your cheekbone is fractured, you have a hairline fracture in the back of your skull, and your orbital bone is completely smashed."

I looked at him, thinking, *No shit it's smashed!*

I remember sitting there holding my nose and feeling like I had to blow out all of the resulting congestion that was building up. Big mistake. As soon as I went to blow my nose, all of the skin under my left eye started puffing out, indicating that my sinuses were all messed up, too. It was horrendous.

Even worse was the fact that I had to put off the necessary surgical repair until after the TV tapings in Greensboro two days later. We had a highly anticipated little bench press contest to attend. Because Paul Jones had been mouthing off for so long about how much stronger Barb and Warlord were than us, I'd suggested to Dusty that we have a bench press contest for $10,000 (kayfabe). The event would also serve as the perfect chance to have the POP attack us, kayfabe injuring my orbital bone. It was a rare example of incorporating a legit injury into a story line as a way to explain its origin.

So, with my face literally needing reconstructive surgery and my mind half out of it due to the pain medication, I walked out into the Greensboro Coliseum to put on one hell of a show. Only one person from each team was selected to compete: Barb and I.

The bench was set up right next to the ring on a large piece of plywood, with various sizes of weight plates lying all around. They even had a bin of chalk powder so we could secure our grip on the bar. We opened with a legit starting weight of 475 pounds, and I went first and banged it right up. My eye didn't even hurt. The crowd gave me a big ovation, chanting my name, *"Animal, Animal, Animal."* It was music to my ears.

In response to my lift, Barb sat down to the bench, got a tight grip, and pressed the weight up as if it were 135 pounds. Barb was one strong dude.

After our first lifts were officially completed, we added another plate, bringing the real weight to 500 pounds. For extra drama, Hawk and I acted like we were strategizing off to the side and finally announced we wanted no part of 500 pounds; we wanted 600 pounds.

Again, the crowd went insane and gasped as an additional two more plates were added to the bar, which was starting to bend in the middle. Paul Jones, who didn't want anything to do with such big weight so early in the contest, told Ellering that he only wanted 500 pounds and then poked him in the chest.

In an instant, "Precious" Paul smacked Jones across the face.

Whack! We ran to his side and got into a stare down with the POP and their cohort Ivan Koloff. The slap would prove to be the spark that would light the impending powder keg of tension. With the 600 pounds loaded onto the bar, I paced back and forth like a snorting bull, turned to the audience and posed with a big roar, and sat down to take position for the lift. And that's when all hell broke loose.

As Hawk, my spotter, was about to help lift the bar from the rack, Ivan grabbed the pin of chalk powder and dumped the whole thing into his and my faces. While we were both blinded, the POP, Ivan, and Paul Jones attacked us, taking me in particular and ramming my face into the bar. *Boom!* Now everyone had a kayfabe explanation for my very real injury.

The funny thing about the attack is that after I was thrown into the bar, it fell backward. *Bam!* I yelled to Hawk to get out of the way, and it landed two inches from his arm, which would've been crushed on impact. The bar started rolling toward the audience. Finally, at the very last second, two of the officials ran over and stopped it from flattening the ringside fans. When it was all over, Hawk, Paul, and I were laid out on the floor in shambles.

The whole scenario gave me the proper amount of time to sell my "new" injury and get the overdue surgery. When I did have the procedure, as high of a threshold of pain as I may have, it was beyond brutal. In order to gain the proper access to the damaged orbital, the surgeon had to cut through the roof of my mouth while simultaneously slicing through the bottom of my eye. In order to reconstruct my orbit, bone had to shaved off of the side of my nose for building materials. Then the doctors actually used a sort of superglue to painstakingly adhere tiny bone fragment to tiny bone fragment until the shape and structural integrity of the orbit had been restored.

After the surgery, I was out of commission for almost the entire month of February. In my absence, Hawk and Paul wrestled against the POP all around the country. By the end of the month, I had healed enough to make run-ins during matches where Paul Jones or Ivan Koloff decided to get involved. To protect my face and ensure I didn't suffer any accidental shots, I wore a custom white hockey mask, which I painted in a cool black variation of my spider and webbing face paint.

I thought my mask was the coolest thing. When I came running down wearing it for the first time, I felt like Jason Voorhees from *Friday the 13th*, ready to hack my victims to pieces. I got plenty of time to live out my Jason fantasy, too, as I wound up wearing the mask for the next six weeks or so. As a matter of fact, I wore it for our match at Crockett's latest entry into the professional wrestling wars with the WWF, the Clash of the Champions.

In direct retaliation to what the WWF did to both Starrcade '87 and the Bunkhouse Stampede by promoting new PPVs on the same night, Dusty and Crockett came up with a last-ditch trump card in time for WrestleMania IV on March 27. Clash of the Champions was an NWA/Jim Crockett Promotions wrestling card from the Greensboro Coliseum of PPV magnitude that was broadcast for free on Superstation WTBS, opposite WrestleMania.

For that show, Dusty joined Hawk and me, hockey mask and all, in a no-holds-barred barbed wire match against the POP and Ivan. What a fucking mess. I guess because we'd done it all by that point, everyone figured, *Hell, let's put the Road Warriors in a match with barbed wire surrounding the ropes. That'll work.* Great idea.

I'm pretty sure I speak for everyone involved when I say barbed wire matches are the most useless and dreaded in the business. Seriously, I'd take the Russian Chain, the scaffold, or the War Games over the barbed wire match any day of the year. There simply wasn't any room to negotiate with, and most of the time even if you didn't intend to get cut or to bleed, you did. How could you not? There was barbed wire at every turn, twist, and bump. No, thanks.

Fortunately the match wasn't booked for more than five minutes, and I scored the pin on Warlord at the hands of a personally auto-graphed Road Warrior Animal powerslam. After the match, the three of them attacked me and pried my mask off, but at the last second Dusty came running back in for the save.

The main event of the Clash was a twenty-minute time limit draw for the World Heavyweight Championship between Ric Flair and the rising new star carried over from the defunct UWF, Sting. The match, a lightning-fast barnburner between Flair and the young rookie, made both of them shine brighter than they ever had. When it was over, Sting was a bona fide superstar. And to think, only two years earlier Sting was a Road Warrior clone as one of the Blade Runners.

Watts' selling out the UWF to Crockett was the best thing that could've happened to Sting's career. He had the look, the charisma, and the desire to learn and improve: traits that were music to Dusty and Crockett's ears. In Sting, they saw the future of the NWA for years to come.

The emergence of Sting as one of the company's brightest new talents wasn't the only good news to come out of the night. When the numbers came back, Clash of the Champions had successfully destroyed WrestleMania's PPV buy rate. Compared to 'Mania III's monster profit yield, 'Mania IV was a flop. The war battled on.

I have to admit, though, being a part of such a huge, free-roaming business enterprise like Crockett Promotions had really gotten me thinking during the last few months. Here I was making a great living and raising a new family, but I hadn't been planning for the future. What I needed to do was find a sound investment and start making my money work for me in the long run. But what could I find to invest in? Sure, I'd recently put some money toward financing and partnering with Hawk and our old pal Jim Yungner for a new fitness facility called the Twin Cities Gym, but now I was thinking bigger. Little did I know that the answer was right in front of my face the whole time. Literally.

13

AND IT ALL COMES CRUMBLING DOWN

I'd been thinking of how I wanted to invest my money for quite some time and still had no idea what to do, until one fateful afternoon at the Twin Cities Gym. Wearing a big, baggy pair of body-building pants I'd picked up on tour somewhere, I went strolling in for a quick workout. When I got there, Hawk and two of the sales guys, Dan Stock and Bob Truax, took notice of my pants and asked about them.

After I told them, I mentioned how I was sick and tired of trying to find comfortable clothes that could actually fit guys like me. Whenever I went to a big and tall store, the pants I'd find that would fit over my legs would have something ridiculous like a forty-eight-inch waist. The only places I found pants that really fit well and were active enough for my lifestyle were at the gym. As I was explaining the background of the pants, it was like a lightbulb went off over all of our heads at the same time. "Why don't we make our own versions of these things?" I asked.

Hawk said, "Yeah, why don't we?"

As it turned out, a girl who worked at Twin Cities had experience in stitching and pattern work. We loaded her up with a bunch of different fabrics and my original pair of pants and had her go to work. She deconstructed the pair and took notice of everything from the style of the fabric to the type of stitch used. By examining my pair of pants, we developed our own interlock stitch pattern on a custom nylon, polyester, and cotton blend. I know, I know, it sounds like I was turning into one of the Fruit of the Loom guys or something, but this is one Animal who takes business seriously, powerslam and sewing machine alike.

The bottom line was that Hawk and I liked what we saw with the first few prototypes of our new pants so much that we agreed to invest $75,000 each into opening up Warrior Distributing Corp. We also came up with a great name for the pants themselves, Zubaz, which was gym lingo for "in your face."

Because Hawk and I knew nothing about the garment industry, we partnered up with Bob and Dan and put them in charge of Warrior Distributing. They would oversee all aspects of production and secure retail distribution. To their credit, those two stepped up and immersed themselves in learning the ins and outs of the textile business, giving Hawk and me the breakdown when we came back from the road.

When we finally tested the first line of Zubaz pants in Twin Cities Gym, the response was overwhelming. In the first month alone, selling exclusively out of our own pro shop, we totaled over $13,000 in revenue. Not bad, but it was only the beginning.

Although we had started out with solid colors, it was when we started experimenting with zebra print designs in wild colors that things really took off. Smelling big success at hand, we got all of the other top gyms in Greater Minneapolis to carry Zubaz and even started placing mail order ads in the back of *Muscle and Fitness* magazine. Six months later, the Zubaz clothing line was available for purchase in national clothing store chains like JCPenney, Macy's, and Foot Locker. It was far beyond our expectations.

Hawk and I were so proud of Zubaz that for the next couple of years we were rarely seen not wearing them. We knew better. Being on the road as much as we were made us the perfect traveling advertisement. Basically, all of our fans took one look at the new pants the Road Warriors were wearing and climbed all over themselves to be the first on the block to have a pair.

All of a sudden, Zubaz was everywhere. Love them or hate them, they became an instantly recognizable part of the late 1980s, like us. No doubt about it, Hawk and I had become damn fine entrepreneurs. Within a couple more years, Zubaz would gross over twenty million dollars in wholesale orders to retailers and become an official clothing brand for the NFL. Everyone from Jim McMahon of the Chicago Bears to the soccer mom across the street was wearing Zubaz. It was a beautiful thing.

While Bob and Dan knocked down deal after deal for Zubaz, Hawk and I were kept plenty busy on the road with the POP until the end of April, which was Crockett Cup season. Yep, it was time for the third annual Jim Crockett Sr. Memorial Cup Tag Team Tournament, and even though Hawk and I weren't slated to go over for the kayfabe check and the trophy, I had a very different interest than usual in the two-day event.

If you looked up the Crockett Cup '88 and saw the list of team entries, at first you most likely wouldn't notice anything out of the ordinary. However, when I first scanned the names on the sheet Dusty gave us, I saw two names: Johnny Ace and The Terminator, who were part of different teams. I cracked a big smile. "Holy shit, Mike. Would you look at that?"

Hawk looked at the sheet for a second and started laughing. "Ha! There they are. I'll be damned. Your brothers made it."

That's right. Johnny Ace and The Terminator were none other than John and Marc Laurinaitis, my little bros—only they weren't so little anymore. About a year and a half before, after John and Marc had both graduated from Minnesota State University at Mankato, they'd come a knockin'. "Joe, we want to wrestle. Will you help us out?"

Of course I would. After all, athletics were strong in the Laurinaitis blood, and I guess seeing me become famous as Road Warrior Animal had a bigger effect on them than I imagined. I couldn't blame my brothers at all for wanting to give it a go. Shit, if our roles were reversed, you'd better believe I would've come to check it all out myself. Who wouldn't?

John had actually gotten into the business a few months before Marc when I'd put him in touch with Nelson Royal. Nelson was a longtime wrestler and former NWA Junior Heavyweight champion who was running his own training school down in North Carolina. While John had learned the business down South, Barry Darsow had let him stay at his Charlotte home, where at the very least I knew John was being well fed. Barry's wife, Theresa, cooked one mean country fried steak. Mmm.

Before long, John started wrestling on his own in late 1986 as Johnny Ace down in Mike Graham's NWA territory in Tampa at Florida Championship Wrestling (FCW). FCW was actually the old Championship Wrestling from Florida (CWF) run by Mike's late brother Eddie. It was renamed after the company briefly closed in 1987. Shortly after John's debut, Marc joined him down in Tampa, where he developed a gimmick called The Terminator based on the Arnold Schwarzenegger movie. By the time the Crockett Cup came around, both John and Marc were experienced enough to get into the action with the big boys.

I was proud to show my brothers to everyone, letting all the boys know that the Laurinaitis name was now a triple threat. In fact, a few months later, in September, John and Marc would team up and win the NWA Florida Tag Team Championship. At the 1988 Crockett Cup, however, they were on different teams, which were each defeated in the first round.

Hawk and I didn't fare much better, losing by DQ to the Powers of Pain in the quarterfinals. To be honest with you, aside from seeing John and Marc, the whole thing was pretty forgettable. When the show was over, Hawk and I took off on a six-week tour of the Southeast, facing a random onslaught of the POP, the Midnight Express, and Tully and Arn.

In early June, we took off for Japan for the first time in 1988 and learned we were going to drop the NWA International Tag Team titles to Jumbo Tsuruta and his new partner, Yoshiaki Yatsu, a former Olympic wrestler. Baba decided he wanted to unify our International titles with the Pacific Wrestling Federation (PWF) World Tag Team belts, which Jumbo and Yatsu held, and establish the AJPW Unified World Tag Team Championship. On June 10, 1988, in front of 11,800 people at the Budokan Hall in Tokyo, we dropped the titles to Tsuruta and Yatsu the same way we'd won them, by count-out.

I remember arriving home from Japan and getting a call from Warlord, who had some serious concerns to discuss. "They want me and Barb to wrestle a series of scaffold matches with you during the Great American Bash tour in July, and they want us to take the big bumps off the thing."

I didn't hesitate for a second to respond. "I wouldn't do it. You and Barb are over 300 pounds each and could get seriously fucked up taking a fall like that."

Warlord told me he was afraid of that and needed advice from someone who'd been on the scaffold before.

What happened next was surprising but perfectly understandable. Warlord and Barbarian decided to tell Dusty they had no intention of going up on the scaffold, and I guess they all got in a disagreement over the whole situation. Next thing I knew, the Powers of Pain walked out of Jim Crockett Promotions and headed for the open doors of the WWF.

Once Barb and Warlord made the jump over, they were introduced as babyfaces and started a successful feud with Demolition. Even with the POP out of the picture, Hawk and I weren't off the hook. We were given replacement opponents, Ivan Koloff and the Russian Assassin.

Because Ivan was in his forties and the Assassin was another big guy around six feet five, 300 pounds, we ended those Skywalker matches as quickly as possible, in the five-minute range, to avoid the likelihood of serious injury to any of us.

Wouldn't you know it? Aside from the scaffold matches, Dusty still had another card up his sleeve for the Great American Bash. In retrospect, I think he should've left it up there.

Taking a cue from the groundbreaking event that the first

War Games proved to be, I think Dusty felt he had to top his previous blockbuster ideas. What he came up with was a mess called the Tower of Doom, a disastrous three-story, triple-cage match that was a classic case of someone going to the well too often. I thought the whole thing was complete bullshit.

The Tower of Doom featured three different-sized cages stacked on top of each other, from largest to smallest (bottom to top). Like War Games, the Tower had two teams of five members, with entrants starting out in the small cage at the top trying to make their way to the bottom and out of the large cage. Once all five team members exited the Tower of Doom, the match was over. Man, I'm telling you, that whole thing was an overcooked disaster.

On July 10 at the Baltimore Arena, Hawk and I teamed up with Steve Williams and Ronnie and Jimmy Garvin against Kevin Sullivan, Mike Rotunda (with his healed-up penis after that drunken swim incident), Al Perez, Russian Assassin, and Ivan Koloff. From the minute the Tower match started, I wanted it to end.

To begin with, I can't exactly say I approved of the caliber of guys in the match. I mean, come on. Al Perez? The Russian Assassin? Who the hell were these guys, and why were they in a match of this magnitude with us? It was beyond me. Now, in regards to the actual Tower itself, the word "clusterfuck" comes to mind right off the bat.

Because the flooring of the top and middle cages was regular fencing attached to the corner supports, it felt like you could fall through it at any second. There was no way to balance, and there was nothing to hold on to. By the time I got in there, I couldn't even focus on the action with the other guys because my footing was so shaky on the bending metal.

I also remember the production guys not finishing the Tower

itself until a day or two before the show. The black paint they sprayed all over the cages wasn't even dry, and we were all coated in it by the end of the match.

After the event, pretty much all of the boys told Dusty the horrors of the Tower of Doom. Fortunately, he took it off the road, except for a date or two in early August.

To recoup all of the other events originally scheduled to feature the Tower, Dusty brought back the War Games, which was sure to please the masses. But in hindsight, creative booking catastrophes like the Tower of Doom were the least of everybody's problems in Jim Crockett Promotions.

Like Georgia Championship Wrestling in '84 and then the AWA in '85, by September '88, the Crockett Promotions' faction of the NWA was starting to billow smoke from every crack, nook, and cranny. And where there's smoke, especially in the wrestling business, you can rest assured there's fire. I was starting to wonder if Hawk and I were cursed.

Seriously, though, between Jim Crockett's careless spending habits and vain attempts at competing with the WWF, rumors were swirling that the company was bottoming out. It was all bound to happen, especially considering the recent financial disasters of Starrcade '87 and the Bunkhouse Stampede and the fruitless purchase of the UWF.

In the midst of all that shit, Dusty started flying the Falcon 50 back and forth to Texas. He had a vision of expanding the Crockett/NWA franchise out West, where he had already taken over Bill Watts' old UWF office in Dallas. As it turned out, that valuable and dwindling Crockett Promotions money could've gone to much better purposes, such as keeping our top guys fairly paid and therefore in the company.

Aside from the Powers of Pain leaving us for the WWF because of the booking conflict with the Skywalkers matches, other top drawing names in the NWA, like Tully Blanchard, Arn Anderson, and even fan favorite Robert Gibson (half of the Rock 'n' Roll Express) left after payday disputes. Gibson actually left the company first during the middle of the Great American Bash '88 after allegedly receiving an $1100 check for a full week of shows, which he took as an insult.

In my opinion, the worst of the walkouts at that time were Tully and Arn leaving for the WWF. Apparently, following the Great American Bash, they both found out that they were making significantly less than quite a few others, including a couple of managers, like "Precious" Paul. When they went to Dusty and Crockett for an immediate raise and were told no, they jumped up North to the WWF.

It's always a shitty feeling when your peers, especially good friends, leave the company you're in. Being a part of Jim Crockett Promotions during the previous two years had bonded all of the main players like a big family. And now it was like some of our brothers were running away from abusive parents and leaving the rest of us in a soon-to-be foreclosed house. My stomach was turning on a regular basis because of the turmoil and stress. I knew right then and there that the golden era of the NWA was over.

Sometimes in chaos there lies opportunity. With all of the shifting and pulling within the company, Hawk and I got a knock on the door for something new. For three and a half years, we had been among the top babyfaces in the promotion, along with Dusty, Nikita, and the Rock 'n' Rolls. Dusty suggested it was time for us to turn heel. We'd also get the World titles.

It sounded fine to us. It's not like we had a real choice anyway, but I honestly didn't think the people would accept us as heels anyway. We had way too much momentum on our side as super-heroes with the new generation of young fans. But, hey, business is business and if that meant we had to betray some allies, win the straps, and have a nastier mean streak than usual, who were we to argue?

It all went down in a specific three-step process.

The first step was Tully and Arn dropping the World Tag Team titles to the Midnight Express in a match on September 10 that also helped turn Bobby and Stan into bona fide babyfaces. After that, on October 7 at the Richmond Coliseum, Hawk and I turned on our six-man tag partner and "brother in paint," Sting, in a match against the Varsity Club of Mike Rotunda, Kevin Sullivan, and Rick Steiner.

We worked it as if Sting was trying to steal the win against Rotunda after we did all the work. As he tried to put Rotunda in his Scorpion Deathlock submission hold, we interrupted Sting and cut him in half with a double clothesline.

As soon as Sting landed, I ran over, picked him up, and pressed him over my head. As soon as I had him up, Hawk jumped off the top rope with a big elbow to the back of his head. *Crack!* As if that weren't enough, we followed all of that up with a Doomsday Device that knocked Sting for a perfect backflip. *Bam!* The hot Richmond fans were jumping and screaming their heads off—only they weren't booing like they were supposed to. They were cheering.

The carnage continued when Lex Luger, who was now a fan-friendly babyface and personal buddy of Sting, came running down to help. I personally laid his ass out with a nasty clothesline.

Finally as Nikita and a bunch of other guys arrived to chase us off, we scattered out and tromped back to the dressing room, where Hawk summed it all up at the end of a scathing interview for commentator Tony Schiavone.

"We did what we're best at, and that's bustin' face. If it's Sting, if it's anybody. He was in there trying to make us look bad, and we don't need any of that. We're tired of carrying people. We're tired of making everybody else look good at our cost. Well, now it's just us, the way it used to be. Forget about the rest, 'cause we don't need 'em and we never did."

After announcing to the world that the Road Warriors were back in business for ourselves the way we preferred, we were sent on a collision course with the World champs, the Midnight Express. On October 29, 1988, in New Orleans at the Municipal Auditorium, Hawk and I destroyed Stan and Bobby in less than five minutes for the NWA World Tag Team Championships. Even though we were coming in with heel personas and we brutalized Bobby outside of the ring, busting him wide open, the fans were still cheering for us. I'm telling you, man, the only way we could've successfully gotten over as heels would've been if we went to the WWF and jumped Hulk Hogan. And even then, I'm not too sure.

Over the course of the next month, we brutalized both the Midnight Express and the team of Sting and Luger. By November 21, however, I found out that Jimmy Crockett was the one who had suffered the greatest beating of all. Bankruptcy.

In a panic, Crockett called upon the mighty Ted Turner, owner of WTBS and CNN, to bail him out. In an unprecedented move, Turner bought the flagging Jim Crockett Promotions and all of its assets, laying to rest the fifty-seven-year-old tradition of

Mid-Atlantic Championship Wrestling. In an effort to rebrand the product, Turner renamed his new organization after its flagship show, *World Championship Wrestling*, and hence WCW was born.

To his credit, though, for the most part, Turner came on board to maintain the NWA product as it already was, and nobody lost their jobs. Aside from some basic aesthetic changes, like ring and logo redesigns, the company seamlessly kept doing business as usual.

WCW was now the consolidated effort of Ted Turner himself, who always enjoyed the high ratings *World Championship Wrestling* brought to TBS for such a low production cost. Turner also had it out for Vince McMahon ever since the Black Saturday fiasco when the Briscos had sold out their majority share of GCW stock to him back in '84.

However, with the purchase of Crockett Promotions, Turner himself handed down some regulations to make the show more family friendly. When the new WCW rule book came down the pike into the hands of Dusty, I think he got frustrated with the corporate interference. In response, Rhodes decided to make a statement the best way he personally knew how, and for our old friend and trusted booker, it proved to be a fatal move.

On November 24, during a *World Championship Wrestling* taping at the WTBS studio in Atlanta, Hawk and I were recruited by Dusty himself to participate in a now infamous TV angle that would lead to his removal as booker and subsequent firing. It all started off when Hawk and I cut promos about our newfound antipathy toward Sting, Luger, and Rhodes. I personally put the exclamation on the interview to commentator David Crockett that ignited the fuse for the upcoming explosion.

"You know, David Crockett, I heard I've got a match December 7 against Dusty Rhodes, right? Dusty Rhodes, you seem to forget we ain't new in this sport. Just like us, your credentials speak for themselves. You have a long history of wins against great opponents, but we made a name for ourselves beating legends. Legends just like you. You're gonna find out what I'm made of December 7, and you ain't gonna like it one bit."

Just as Hawk and I left the interview, Dusty entered and challenged me to come out right then and there to take him on. He climbed into the ring, and I came right back out with Hawk and Paul to answer his challenge. I jumped through the ropes and pushed Dusty back into a corner to start dishing out some kicks to the gut. *Bam, bam, bam!* Then I whipped him across the ring into the opposite corner and charged with a clothesline only to miss when Dusty ducked out of the way. He turned and ran straight back at me with a big clothesline of his own and took me off my feet. *Whoom!*

At that point, Hawk was already plowing into the ring to batter Rhodes into kingdom come while I recovered. While Hawk was taking care of business, I reached over for my shoulder pads, which Paul had set in the corner, and unscrewed one of the big seven-inch spikes.

As soon as the spike was free, I ran over with a double-over-handed thrust to Dusty's forehead. Then the big drama came as I carefully made it look like I was trying to stab Dusty's eye out of the socket.

Jim Ross, one of the commentators back at the podium, was going crazy. "He put it in his eye. He put the spike in his eye!"

While Dusty was rolling around bleeding like a stuck pig,

Sting, Luger, Bam Bam Bigelow, and a bunch of other guys ran in for the save.

Oh, did I forget to mention that one of the most important new rules handed down from Turner was no bloodletting on TV? Oh yeah, it sure was. WTBS was flooded with hundreds of angry callers complaining about what they and their children had seen. Before Dusty even had time to wonder what management thought of his little stunt, he was swiftly relieved of his booking duties. But the worst for Dusty was still to come.

On December 7 in Chattanooga, I went over Dusty in a singles match by DQ after Rhodes bashed me with a chair as retribution for his heavily bandaged eye. Then, a few weeks later we met on December 26 at Starrcade '88 (moved up a month from its traditional Thanksgiving night slot to avoid competing with WWF's Survivor Series). Hawk and I lost to Dusty and Sting by DQ due to Paul's interference.

Right after the match, Dusty Rhodes, the former World Heavyweight champion and creator of some of the greatest wrestling events in NWA history, was fired due to backlash from the spike incident. From beginning to end, 1988 was a turbulent year of big changes, some good and some bad.

The great moments, like my brothers making their debuts in the business and Hawk and I finally winning the NWA World Tag titles, were unfortunately counterbalanced by the bullshit of losing Tully and Arn, Jim Crockett going bankrupt, and, of course, Dusty's firing. It was all part of the insanity that is professional wrestling.

Aside from all of the high drama at the workplace, though, the biggest news for me personally came before the 1989 New Year, when Julie told me little Joey and James were going to get another playmate. That's right! My amazing wife was expecting our second child together and the third addition to the Laurinaitis clan.

To prepare for the newest little bundle, I decided it was time to build our own house, one with plenty of room. And that's what I did. We bought a good-sized lot in a really nice neighborhood in Hamel, Minnesota, and had a contractor go to work on Casa de Laurinaitis. It would take the better part of nine months to finish and would be ready in time for Julie's expected delivery. Good planning, right?

With Jim Crockett and Dusty removed from the picture of Turner's WCW, there were some huge voids left to fill. Turner's answer was to put a guy named Jim Herd in charge of the company. Herd was a former Pizza Hut executive from St. Louis who had once been the station manager of KPLR-TV, which aired the very popular NWA show *Wrestling at the Chase*. Everyone in the locker room was very skeptical of what the "pizza man" would deliver to WCW.

One of the first decisions Herd made at Turner (after firing Dusty) was to place Ric Flair in the role of booker. It was welcome news to us. Ric was one of Hawk's and my most trusted friends in the company, and we were relieved to see someone of his credibility step up and be the man calling the creative shots.

Flair got right to work and immediately pushed for one of his greatest former rivals, Ricky Steamboat, to come to WCW. Back in the late '70s and early '80s, Flair and Steamboat had a legendary feud in Crockett's old Mid-Atlantic territory that helped propel both of them into superstardom. When the WWF started luring top names from the NWA around '83 to '85, Steamboat was one of the guys who made the jump. Now, a few years later, Ricky

"The Dragon" Steamboat left the WWF, giving Flair an opportunity he was happy to seize.

Steamboat debuted in January on *World Championship Wrestling* in a tag team match with Eddie Gilbert against Flair and Barry Windham. In a big moment on national TV, Flair the World champ was pinned by Steamboat, reigniting their old feud for the next four months.

During that time, Steamboat defeated Flair for the NWA World Heavyweight Championship at the Chi-Town Rumble in February, successfully defended the title against Flair at Clash of the Champions VI in April, then finally lost the belt back to the Nature Boy at Music City Showdown in May. That little run of Steamboat and Flair's really brought a lot of excitement to WCW and was a much needed morale booster. It sure seemed like things with Herd and Flair were going to work out fine. Yeah, *seemed like*.

At the same time as Flair and Steamboat's wars, Hawk and I remained the NWA World Tag Team and World Six-Man Tag Team champions by having a few battles of our own. Because Dusty had long been our six-man partner and was now gone, we needed a replacement. We asked Flair if we could bring in Tenryu from Japan, and he liked the idea. By this time, the experiment of turning us heel had pretty much disappeared without a trace. The fans just wouldn't boo us.

At Clash of the Champions V in Cleveland on February 15, we defeated the entire Varsity Club (Steve Williams, Mike Rotunda, and Kevin Sullivan) by DQ after Sting, Michael Hayes, and Junkyard Dog ran in for a nine-man brawl. After the win, Tenryu went back to Japan to focus on winning the Triple Crown, the consolidation of the all-singles titles in AJPW. When Tenryu left, the company decided to shelf the World Six-Man Tag Team Championship permanently.

Five days later, on February 20, we successfully defended our World Tag Team titles at Chi-Town Rumble against Williams and Sullivan. After that, Ric came to us and said he wanted us to drop the titles to Williams and Rotunda at Clash of the Champions VI in New Orleans on April 2 (same day as WrestleMania V, which was once again offered as a free WCW alternative).

We said, "No problem, Ric."

At the end of the match, Williams pinned Hawk, and referee Teddy Long gave a blatant fast count of only two but rang the bell and awarded the Varsity Club our titles. Easy come, easy go.

Just like anytime we dropped championship belts, it didn't matter to us. We didn't need them for credibility any more than Hulk Hogan or Flair himself needed their respective World titles. Once you reach a certain level of success and popularity, everything else is secondary. Championships are really meant to establish new guys and give them the rub as emerging main players. That's the way it had happened for us six years earlier when Ole dropped the NWA National tag belts on our shoulders and said, "There you go! Now let's see what you two can do from here."

With all of the change and transition, Hawk and I were experiencing by that February in 1989, we still weren't out of the woods yet. The WWF, in a successful bid to bypass the New Jersey State Athletic Control Board's 10 percent surtax on all televised sporting events, released a statement admitting that professional wrestling was staged. Part of the document declared that wrestling was "an activity in which participants struggle hand-in-hand primarily for the purpose of providing entertainment to spectators rather than conducting a bona fide athletic contest."

And there it was. A few keystrokes on a WWF typewriter and some Xerox copies later, the oldest and most important tradition of professional wrestling was wiped off the face of the earth.

From a business point of view, I easily understood why Vince did what he did, but his modernization of the wrestling industry as "sports entertainment" forced the deliberate exposure of kay-fabe on all of us. Wrestlers who had been laboring over their kay-fabe gimmicks, injuries, and rivalries at all costs for the sake of protecting themselves and the business were now left out in the wind. You can see why more than a few guys weren't happy about the WWF's revelation. Nobody was ever supposed to pull the mask off of the Lone Ranger.

The first few months of '89 also saw a ton of new talent come into WCW. With the last of the other competitive promotions like the AWA and World Class Championship Wrestling fading away from the forefront, a lot of workers were running for the hills and found sanctuary in the NWA.

Along with guys like Sting and Rick and Scott Steiner, who were acquired during the Crockett Promotions' dismantling of the UWF, the talent roster in WCW now boasted great prospects like Scott Hall, the Great Muta, "Flyin'" Brian Pillman, Tom "Z-Man" Zenk, the Samoan Swat Team, Sid Vicious, Cactus Jack (Mick Foley), and "Mean" Mark Callous. There were also two new tag teams on the scene in WCW that I'd helped along the way, The Terminators and the Dynamic Dudes.

The Terminators were the team of Al Greene and my brother Marc, while the Dynamic Dudes consisted of Shane Douglas and my brother John (Johnny Ace). Although The Terminators saw a lot of action in the ring, they didn't see too many wins. Down the road a couple years, Marc and Al created a Road Warriors-inspired gimmick known as the Wrecking Crew and would become WCW World Tag Team champions.

The Dynamic Dudes, two bleach-blond skateboarders, came onto the scene in early '89 and were managed by Jim Cornette. Although initially put into a successful feud with the Midnight Express, the Dudes were dumped by Cornette and eventually decided to part ways. Johnny had been successful over in Japan, where he was doing his big brother—and the fans—proud. Shortly afterward, John went to Japan, where he caught on and did damn well for himself.

By May, our suspicions about Jim Herd were proving to be true. After Flair was put in charge of booking, things went spiraling out of control like you wouldn't believe. For starters, Herd didn't know how to negotiate with the talent. After Ric went through hell to bring in Ricky Steamboat and wound up having a critically acclaimed series of matches, Herd failed to come to a contractual agreement with him and he walked. Just like that, Steamboat was gone and it ruined the planned program between him and Lex Luger, which had already started.

As big of a blunder as the Steamboat debacle was, it didn't compare to the revolving cavalcade of horrible ideas Herd kept trying to introduce. The WWF had a heavily cartoonish roster of popular characters—Brutus "The Barber" Beefcake, the Honky Tonk Man, and the Big Bossman (Big Bubba repackaged as a corrections officer)—all with elaborate costuming and props. Herd thought he could mimic Vince McMahon's product and get the same results. Boy, was he wrong.

This guy Herd actually introduced gimmicks like the Ding Dongs (a pair of masked wrestlers who rang bells during their matches), the Hunchbacks (a tag team that couldn't be pinned due to their costume humps), and Big Josh (Matt Borne in a ridiculous lumberjack outfit with dancing bears). He even famously tried to convince Ric Flair to cut off his trademark blond hair and change his Nature Boy persona into a Spartacus gladiator gimmick.

God, I wish I could tell you I'm kidding, but I'm not. Herd was trying to erase the classic, very distinct line between the WWF's product of over-the-top spectacle and showmanship and the NWA/WCW product of gritty, realistic professional wrestling.

Hawk summed it up eloquently one night during one of our on-air interviews in a jab at Herd. "Some of us should stick with what we're good at. For some, that means wrestling. For others, it means making pizza."

All the boys in the back popped huge for that one.

I'm pretty sure I can safely speak on behalf of my brothers Hawk and "Precious" Paul when I say that the second half of 1989 and into the spring of 1990 simply wasn't fun at all. That's the best way I can explain it. From the day we started back in '83 in GCW up till around the time Crockett had to sell in late '88, we were having a great time. But now, as the turmoil between Ric and Jim Herd started to escalate, I looked forward less and less to showing up for work.

Even now when I think back over my career, as great as our opponents were at that time—the SST, the Steiners, The Skyscrapers (Sid Vicious and "Dangerous" Danny Spivey), and Doom (Ron Simmons and Butch Reed), for example—I can barely remember a thing about our matches. It's all a blur.

Things had gotten stale, and Hawk and I were getting bored. What more did we have left to do in WCW, anyway? Maybe we should pick up the phone and give Vince a call up at the WWF. We didn't know.

It was decided that we'd stay as long as Flair was booker. We hoped he could turn things around.

In the meantime, since my interest in WCW was waning, I was able to put some long overdue focus on my family. In the summer of '89, my little Joey was eight years old, James was climbing along at two and a half, and on August 8 I got the call that Julie was ready to burst. I got my ass to the hospital with Joey and James in tow.

As we had with James, we'd kept the gender of our new baby a surprise, and I had my catcher's mitt ready for the big reveal. With one big, final push, Julie unveiled our beautiful new daughter, the first Laurinaitis girl born in fifty years. Keeping our letter *J* theme intact, we named our little sunshine Jessica. Now we were Joe, Julie, Joey, James, and Jessica Laurinaitis. What a crew!

Now with Jessica and Julie, I had my two girls and my two boys. It was funny with Joey and James. All they knew was that one day we went to the hospital with Mommy and then, like magic, they had a baby sister of their very own. Those two lit up when they saw Jessica. In an instant, Joey and James became protective big brothers. I have pictures of them holding her tiny hands. I gotta tell you, moments like those are the ones that burn into your memory forever. No matter how old my babies continue to grow or how far away they may travel from me, I will still see them all together as they were that August day when Jessica was born.

Soon Julie and I would make another big decision to bring

our family closer together. We decided to take full custody of Joey and bring him home full-time. Julie and I could offer Joey a home where he had his little bro and sis always looking up to him, following his every move. It was the right thing to do, and everyone was excited to have him permanently under our roof.

We got Joey started out in youth hockey, which he loved. The little guy fit right in, and none of us ever looked back. As always, Julie didn't miss a beat. She made sure Joey's transition was smooth and tenderly cared for him.

It was also around this time that my parents had decided to retreat from the harsh Minnesota winters for a more favorable climate in Florida. My mom suffered from lupus, a disease that causes the immune system to treat the body's own tissue as a foreign substance and produces antibodies to fight it. It was literally wearing her down with each passing day, but she never complained and kept as busy as ever.

I returned to the road in September for Clash of the Champions VIII: Fall Brawl, where the Road Warriors defeated the Samoan Swat Team of six feet four, 260-pound Samu and six feet one, 375-pound Fatu. Those guys had great chemistry with us, and much later, in the late '90s, I was happy to see Fatu get another run in the WWF as the dancing, "big ass in your face" character Rikishi. The other guys we faced in the closing months of 1989 worth mentioning were Doom and the Steiners—at Starrcade '89.

On December 13 in Atlanta, we were put in the Iron Team tournament with the Steiners, SST, and Doom at Starrcade '89: Future Shock. The team with the best two-out-of-three match record won the title of Iron Team. Well, by the name of the tournament, everyone should've guessed who'd emerge on top.

In the first round of the tournament, we easily dispatched of Doom, who were for all intents and purposes another variation of our Road Warriors gimmick. Ron Simmons and Butch Reed were two big, tough, masked brawlers who were assembled by referee-turned-manager Teddy Long. Simmons was a six feet two, 270-pound two-time all-American defensive nose guard at Florida State University and former Cleveland Brown, while Reed was a six feet two, 260-pound former Kansas City Chief and an eleven-year wrestling veteran. They were a brand-new team with a ton of potential, but that night at the Omni in front of 6,000 people, they were just another couple of Road Warriors victims.

The most dangerous team we faced that night (and maybe in our careers) were the current NWA World Tag Team champions, the Steiners. Rick and Scott Steiner, legitimate brothers and former collegiate wrestlers from the University of Michigan, were two of the greatest, most innovative workers. With Rick's brazen, smash-mouth style of power moves combined with his younger brother Scott's reckless and unorthodox array of suplexes and aerial maneuvers, they were among the greatest teams in wrestling history.

At Starrcade with the Steiners, we put on a tremendous show, with both teams doing the majority of their trademark moves. In the end, though, the Steiners stole the win. After Hawk and I delivered a Doomsday Device to Scott, I fell back with him in a sort of belly-to-back bear hug so my arms were wrapped around his midsection.

When we landed, both his and my shoulders were on the mat so that when the referee made the three count, Scott picked his right arm up at the last second and was credited with the pin. Damn, screwed again, wouldn't you know?

Well, not really. In the end, we went on to win the Iron Team tournament with a final victory over the Samoans, proving once and for all who the true Iron Team was. Did you ever doubt us?

Starrcade '89 also saw the return of Arn Anderson to the newly reformed Four Horsemen along with Sting and Ole Anderson. It was great to see Arn come back from the WWF, but he was originally supposed to arrive with teammate and original Horseman Tully Blanchard. After Tully and Arn spent the better part of a year as The Brain Busters under the management of Bobby "The Brain" Heenan in the WWF (even becoming the World Tag Team champions by defeating Demolition), things fell apart.

In November, before the WWF PPV Survivor Series, Tully failed a drug test for cocaine, which proved to be a double-edged sword. Not only did the WWF release Tully for the violation, but then WCW decided not to take him back because of it as well. Arn had no choice but to return without his longtime partner, even though the two of them had looked forward to reuniting with Flair and Ole. Left with nowhere else to go, Tully spent the next year or so making random appearances for the AWA and other independent promotions before ultimately retiring for good.

It was a shitty end for one of the best workers I ever stepped inside the ring with. I saw that whole thing as another example of Jim Herd dropping the damn ball. Sure, Tully made a bad choice, but bringing him back into the mix with the original Four Horsemen would've been big business. Maybe even big enough to prevent the disaster looming on the WCW horizon.

14

WHEN ONE DOOR CLOSES, SMASH YOURSELF A NEW ONE

Even though Hawk and I approached the beginning of 1990 with a positive outlook and concentrating on doing good business, there were too many distractions. Ric and his creative team of Jim Cornette and Kevin Sullivan were under fire from Jim Herd for their booking decisions. According to Herd and some of the other boys, Flair was being self-serving by putting himself and the other Four Horsemen over in major angles. It was also thought that Flair was refusing to drop the NWA World title, which was bullshit because Ric had been carefully building up a feud with Sting for that very purpose. Unfortunately, it all went wrong for both of them.

At the Clash of the Champions X on February 6 in Corpus Christi, Texas, Flair and the Andersons were in a main event cage match against Muta, the Dragonmaster (a new masked Japanese wrestler), and none other than old Buzz Sawyer, who was crazy as ever.

The angle was that Sting had been kicked out of the Four Horsemen and was looking for revenge, especially against Flair. Near the end of the match, the plan was for Sting to come running down, climb the cage, and get his payback, thus setting up the feud with Flair for the impending title change.

As Sting came running down the aisle and started to make his way up the cage, we heard a loud *snap*. Sting's left patella tendon ruptured; his kneecap was shoved up into his thigh. The injury would keep him out of the WCW for six months. Even though the accident was no fault of Ric's, Herd looked to make some changes to the booking committee.

Hawk's and my match at the Clash was completely unremarkable but distinctly memorable only because of one of our opponents. We were facing The Skyscrapers, only Sid Vicious had been replaced after suffering a legit broken rib during a match with the Steiners. His replacement was a six feet ten, 300-pound, redheaded Texan named "Mean" Mark Callous.

Mark was only twenty-five years old at the time and had only recently started in the business, but he performed and carried himself with the maturity of an old pro. In about nine months, the rest of the world would take notice of Mark when he emerged on the scene in the WWF as the Undertaker.

For the rest of February and into March, we went through the motions of a few dozen haphazardly thrown together matches against Doom (who lost their masks in a match against the Steiners at Clash X) and The Skyscrapers, but burnout was setting in. In a move that would prove to hammer the final nail in the WCW coffin, Ric, under insurmountable pressure from Jim Herd, resigned as head booker.

With Flair out of the creative picture, Herd decided to put Ole Anderson in charge of the booking committee, which also featured guys like Jim Ross, Terry Funk, "Wahoo" McDaniel,

Kevin Sullivan, Jim Cornette, and even Jim Crockett (who was given a job as part of the sale to Turner). During the course of the last few weeks, Ole had been forced out of the Four Horsemen and active duty as a wrestler due to his age. He was seen as an experienced and viable candidate to take Flair's place, which he was, until the disagreements began.

Within no time at all, Ole and Herd started butting heads over the direction of WCW, and everything went straight into the toilet. Ole thought the guaranteed contracts Herd was giving out to all the new talent undermined his ability to control their story lines. If someone had a guarantee with Herd, where was the motivation or urgency to follow Ole's direction? A guy feeling slighted by Ole could go over his head and appeal to Herd directly and get what he wanted. In response, Ole figured he'd roll the clock back to the early 1980s and recruit many of his trusted, loyal old talents from the GCW days.

All of a sudden, it was like a time warp back to 1983 as Hawk and I saw Paul Orndorff, Iron Sheik, Thunderbolt Patterson, Tommy Rich, Stan Hansen, Tim Horner, and even Mr. Wrestling II walking around in the dressing room. Ever heard the expression "Take one step forward and two steps back"? Well, what we were seeing in WCW with the pissing match between Herd and Ole was more like two thousand steps back. There was a hostile divide, and nobody knew what the hell was going on.

"Precious" Paul, in all of his infinite wisdom, decided he'd finally had enough and decided to quit. Paul was such a concise and calculated businessman that he marched right into the office and talked them into paying him the rest of the balance for the year on his contract. As I've said before, pure genius.

I'll never forget Hawk's reaction to Paul's leaving, which was completely directed at Herd and WCW.

We were at the UIC Pavilion in Chicago when Paul broke the news to us. "I've had enough, boys. This shit with Herd has me burnt out. I'm leaving."

Hawk flipped out. "What the fuck? That motherfucker Herd has no clue what he's doing to this company."

As I leaned over to put my boots on, I felt something fly by my head, missing me by mere inches. In his rage, Hawk had picked up a chair and thrown it as hard as he could at the wall, smashing the thermostat into a few dozen pieces.

We couldn't believe Paul was leaving, but we couldn't blame him either. If Herd was hell-bent on unwittingly destroying WCW, great, but now he was fucking with the Road Warriors equation. I was sad beyond words to see my trusted friend leave. Paul had overseen everything we'd done since day one and was as responsible for the success of the Road Warriors as we were.

Forcing Paul out was the last straw. We had to weigh our options, and if there was one thing the Road Warriors always had, it was options. We knew we could hop over to Japan or pick up the phone and call the WWF, or both. We decided to get out while the gettin' was good.

"Fuck this shit, Animal," Hawk said one day. "We're way beyond a place like this. Let's get the hell out of here and give Vince a call."

We decided our match at Capital Combat on May 19 in Washington, DC, would be our last for WCW. Considering what we witnessed that night, Hawk, Paul, and I couldn't have made a wiser choice.

First of all, one look at the match we were booked in at

Capital Combat told the entire story of where our WCW career was going: nowhere. Hawk and I were teamed with a 400-pound guy named Norman the Lunatic against Bam Bam Bigelow, Cactus Jack, and Kevin Sullivan. I mean, absolutely no disrespect to any of those guys, but at that time in our career as the Road Warriors, we were used to being in main events with a purpose. That night in Washington, DC, I felt drained of all desire to step into the ring, but the capper for the event was still to come.

You see, because Turner had a film distribution division and was about to release *RoboCop 2*, Herd and everybody else thought it would be a stroke of genius to cross-promote the movie on WCW programming. However, rather than simply putting *Robocop* promos on during the Capital Combat PPV, they came up with an even better idea: they'd have Robocop himself make an appearance. Not only would the science fiction movie character show up in person; he'd play an important role in the most pivotal story line of the whole PPV.

Man, I'm telling you, Hawk and I watched in amazement with our mouths agape as Robocop made his way down to the ringside area. After arriving next to a small cage that Sid Vicious and Barry Windham of the regrouped Four Horsemen had thrown Sting into, Robocop ripped the iron door off its hinges. Can you believe it? Neither could we, but he sure did.

There they were, Sting and Robocop side by side, making the Horsemen back off. The whole thing was spectacularly bad, and we had a hearty laugh at Herd's expense as we grabbed our stuff and headed to the armory doors.

"Let's get out of this dump," I said, referring to WCW. And that's exactly what we did.

We weren't alone. As the months dragged on, Flair and Herd would reach such an unprecedented level of dissension that Ric would eventually defect to the WWF as the reigning NWA World Heavyweight champion, taking the belt with him to use against WCW.

The resulting fallout from Herd's lack of foresight to prevent such a nightmare not only cost him his job, but WCW wound up falling into its darkest era, yielding the worst ratings in company history. It would take several years and many more personnel changes than you can imagine to turn things around.

After we unceremoniously left WCW in the dust, we called Vince McMahon to see if his offer still stood.

"Of course," Vince said. "We'd love to have you in the World Wrestling Federation. When can you fly up to Stamford to go over the details?"

This was it. Hawk and I were finally going to the big show of the WWF. It was the last place we had yet to conquer. The excitement of wrestling started to pulse throughout my body for the first time in a long time.

When we went up to the WWF headquarters in early June, first we met with Vince to go over the business part of our deal. Even though I insisted on guaranteed contracts like we had in WCW, Vince basically offered us the exact same scenario he did when we'd sat down with him back in '85.

"I can't give you guaranteed money, but what you will have is the opportunity to make as much if not more than you were earning in WCW."

We didn't really have a choice, so after being sold on the great payoffs from PPVs and merchandise sales, Hawk and I shook Vince's hand and agreed to a three-year deal. The next step was an unanticipated creative session concerning the direction of our Road Warriors gimmick.

"We'd like you guys to grow your hair out and take the paint off," Vince declared. "We'd also like you to change your team name from the Road Warriors to something else."

Hawk and I looked at each other like, *What the fuck is this guy talking about?*

I spoke right up. "You're shitting us, right, Vince?"

It turned out that he was shitting us, about the hair and paint, but he still wanted us to change our name from the Road Warriors to something that "wouldn't confuse the public."

I didn't get it. Confuse the public? Did I miss something? Everybody who watched professional wrestling knew who the Road Warriors were, regardless of what organization they favored. Hawk and I had been on the front cover of every wrestling magazine known to mankind for the last seven years. Even if you lived under a rock, I'll bet you still heard of us. I asked Vince to please explain.

"I've already got the Ultimate Warrior as my World Heavyweight champion," he said. "Adding the Road Warriors to the mix is too much. Too many Warriors in one company."

Too many Warriors? What a joke. We *were* the Warriors.

As I explained before, the Ultimate Warrior (along with Sting) was one of the Blade Runners, an amusing attempt by Bill Watts at re-creating the Road Warriors. After the Blade Runners disbanded, Warrior went to World Class Championship Wrestling in Texas, where he became the Dingo Warrior. After taking one look at his picture at the time, there was absolutely no doubt in my mind that the Dingo Warrior was one of our estranged offspring. Even his face paint design bore a strong resemblance to Hawk's full-faced version. We were even told not to use the press slam because Warrior used it. Neither Hawk nor I knew the Warrior from a hole in the wall, so we were more than annoyed. It was frustrating to compromise our gimmick because of someone obviously influenced by us in the first place.

After I got to know Jim, in time, I found him to be a pretty good guy who was just trying to make good business for himself, as we were for ourselves. Like Warlord, Barbarian, and Demolition, who all used Road Warrior-like concepts, it was hard to fault someone for finding and using something that works in the wrestling industry. When guys like Warrior identified with what Hawk and I were doing because of our size, strength, and unrelenting style in the ring, he was able to combine his own colorful eccentricities into the Ultimate Warrior.

In the end, our initial conflict with Warrior was nothing more than a timing issue. Had we landed in the WWF before Jim, I'm sure the Ultimate Warrior would've been the Ultimate Something-Other-Than-Warrior. However, when we came to the company, Warrior was right in the middle of his WWF Championship reign after beating Hulk Hogan, and the Road Warriors needed to find an alternate name.

Fortunately, because we had always been known as the Legion of Doom synonymously with the Road Warriors, we suggested it as our new moniker.

"Hmmm, the Legion of Doom," Vince said as he looked around the room, "I love it."

Soon enough, the WWF fans would, too.

It was also decided that we would add a little color to our gear, which was a Vince standard for all talent. Our completely black shoulder pads and boots were changed to mostly red with black accents. We even painted our chrome spikes black to go along with the new theme. It was different and a little cartoonish, but that could've been said about the entire WWF product at the time.

A few weeks before joining the WWF, Hawk and I had been offered a big money deal to make a three-day tour of New Japan Pro Wrestling (NJPW) at the end of July. NJPW was the other major promotion next to Baba's AJPW and was run by another Japanese wrestling legend, Antonio Inoki. Basically, New Japan boasted a younger talent roster than All Japan, which was seen as more of the old guard of veteran wrestlers.

Because we had always been exclusive to Baba, Inoki respectfully asked him if he could use us, probably in exchange for a monetary kickback. After we signed with Vince, who let us meet our New Japan obligation, he said we needed to tape a couple of matches for TV to help build our introduction to the WWF fans.

In those days, it wasn't uncommon for the WWF to tape several weeks' worth of programming in a single day and air them over the course of the next month or two. Vince was famous back then for scripting story lines almost an entire year in advance. Even WrestleMania for the following year would be booked match for match, and then the WWF creative team would work backward, building the angles to the present day.

Crazy, right? Try living it.

Those tapings were memorable for so many reasons, including the fact that Vince was pissed about our new red boots and entrance music not being ready. Even though it was Vince's idea for us to update our gear and used his guys to make everything (except the shoulder pads, which I made myself), it was somehow our fault that they weren't ready for the tapings.

The music issue sucked because we could no longer use "Iron Man" due to copyright laws. While we waited for WWF music composer Jim Johnston to come up with something, we used some generic rock song he must've had lying around. To his credit, though, Jim came up with a cool track influenced by "Iron Man" that perfectly complemented us.

To customize the new entrance theme even more, Jim had Hawk record one of his trademark interview lines to kick off the music. When we sat down to listen to it for the first time and Jim pressed play, Hawk and I heard, *Oooooooohhhhh, what a rush!"* And when the music kicked in with a hanging guitar chord followed by a nice heavy drumbeat, we both knew it was the perfect fit.

On June 25 in Dayton, we made our official WWF debut for the July 21 episode of *WWF Superstars*. In front of seventy-five hundred LOD faithful, we defeated Black Bart and Tom Stone in about ninety seconds with the Doomsday. Tom Stone worked the entire match by himself after Bart was knocked to the floor at the opening bell. We were like the Mike Tysons of professional wrestling, making people think twice about blinking because they just might miss our match.

We also made an appearance on *The Brother Love Show*, one of many mock interview programs (like *Piper's Pit* with Roddy Piper) inserted into the many WWF TV shows. This one aired on the July 28 *Superstars*. Brother Love himself, portrayed by producer Bruce Prichard, was a loud, red-faced, heel parody of a TV evangelist. On the show, Love accused us of being Demolition imposters. We laughed, said it was the other way around, and walked offstage.

Earlier in the day, when we'd arrived in the locker room at the

Hara Arena, it had been like an old high school reunion. Barry Darsow (Demolition Smash), Dusty Rhodes, Curt Hennig, Rick Rude, Ronnie Garvin, Big Bossman, Warlord, Jake Roberts, and even Sgt. Slaughter immediately welcomed us. Those guys really helped make the WWF feel like home.

The next night on June 26 at the Civic Center in Huntington, West Virginia, we annihilated Al Burke and Bob Bradley (for the July 15 WWF *Wrestling Challenge*) in under two minutes. Because the WWF wanted to set up our first feud with Demolition, they inserted pretaped interviews with Ax, Smash (Barry Darsow), and Crush (six feet five Brian Adams, their newest member) into our match at the bottom of the screen. It was funny to see Demolition calling us out for copying their gimmick, as Brother Love had said to us. *Their* gimmick?

"The Legion of Doom," Ax yelled in his deep, gravelly voice, "or should we say Demolition imposters with spikes and paint all over their faces? Well, we're gonna kick the paint right off their faces."

It was a great, natural way to set up the obvious rivalry between the two teams. (The funny thing is that we didn't even get to see this until we came back from Japan, which is where we were when our TV debut aired. Just like that, after two days of light work, we were good for an entire month of WWF programming while we were in Japan.)

After the show, I got to catch up on things with quite a few of my old pals, especially Rude. We stayed up all night at a bar called Robby's in Huntington and talked about the last three years in the business since we'd parted ways in '87. We told him all about the downfall of Crockett, the horrors of Jim Herd, and being burnt the hell out in the new WCW. Interestingly enough, Rude confided that he was feeling the same way in the WWF and was seriously considering checking out WCW.

That's the thing about wrestling. Guys are always stricken with a "grass is greener in the other promotion" syndrome and constantly flip-flop.

Rude was particularly sick of his almost two-year feud with the Ultimate Warrior. Earlier that night, he'd lost in a big main event cage match to Warrior for the WWF Championship and was less than thrilled. "I'm tired of leading that guy every night for nothing," Rude said. "I was hoping they'd eventually give me the strap or bigger paydays."

He got neither. By November, Rude was back in WCW.

Meanwhile, in Japan, we wrestled what would prove to be our last match there together for about six years. While working for the WWF, we had to be exclusive to them, which meant no more moonlighting for Baba, Inoki, or anyone for that matter. On July 22, Hawk and I faced the team of Masahiro Chono and Keiji Mutoh and lost by DQ.

Chono and Mutoh were two of the fastest-rising, most popular stars on the Japanese scene. Mutoh in particular was interesting because he was equally well-known for his alter ego, the face-painted, mist-spraying acrobat, the Great Muta. Mutoh wrestled (and still does, as of this writing) full-time as both himself and Muta, even working different matches on the same show as each character.

When we got back to the United States, we started preparing for our first official PPV appearance for the WWF at Summer-Slam '90 in August. Our new black and red outfits were finally ready, and when we suited up, I had mixed feelings about our new image. The red and black kind of softened our usually dangerous solid black-and-chrome appearance, but Hawk and I knew it was business, plain and simple. Being on WWF television and getting pushed into the spotlight with Vince's promotional machine of home videos, toys, T-shirts, and video games was the last frontier for us to explore. For better or for worse, sink or swim, we jumped in with both feet and never looked back.

SummerSlam '90 was on August 27 at the Spectrum in Philadelphia, and Hawk and I were booked to interfere during Demolition's World Tag Team title defense against Bret "The Hitman" Hart and Jim "The Anvil" Neidhart, better known as the Hart Foundation.

After gearing and painting up, I had a chance encounter with none other than Rowdy Roddy Piper, the same Roddy Piper who had told me I wasn't going to make it in the wrestling business when I was a nobody.

"Hey, Roddy." I approached him in full gear and paint. "Whaddya think of my chances at making it now?"

Piper looked at me with a big, funny Piper smile and clapped his hands. "Not bad, kid. Not bad at all."

Oh, man, I'd been waiting to run into him again for a long time.

So for our SummerSlam angle that night, we ran down and exposed Demolition's cheating during the match. Smash and Crush (who was added to assist and eventually replace the ailing Bill "Ax" Eadie) were scheduled to face the Hart Foundation, while Ax was banned from coming to ringside. Well, that didn't stop Ax from running down and switching places with Smash two different times as the referee was distracted by Crush.

Being the new sheriffs in town, Hawk and I came out to a huge ovation as we made our way to the ring and dragged Ax from underneath the ring. With the Harts' disadvantage removed from the match, they scored the win and the belts. The Legion of Doom had made their presence known in the WWF as the new force to be reckoned with.

The next day, we started our first run of WWF house shows in Wheeling, West Virginia, being paired up with none other than the Ultimate Warrior for a three-month series of six-man tag matches against Demolition. I guess Vince thought teaming us up with the Warrior was a natural way to put his three biggest baby-faces (with undeniably related gimmicks) together, so that Hawk and I were evenly pitted against the three members of Demolition.

To be honest with you, although I got along great with both Warrior and Crush, I was a little disappointed we didn't get to face the original Demolition team of just Ax and Smash by themselves. I think the fans were, too.

When Demolition first came on the scene in '87 and all of the comparisons between us were made, they were made between us and Bill and Barry. Unfortunately, Bill had gotten sick after an allergic reaction to shellfish and was hospitalized for enough time to worry Vince about the longevity of the Demolition gimmick.

When that happened, Vince brought in Brian Adams to fill the void as Demolition Crush and to eventually replace Ax, who started taking a less physically demanding role in the team. Our arrival into the WWF combined with Demolition being scaled down from their earlier heights meant they weren't booked to win even once out of the hundred or so times we faced them.

Not to mention, we had the Warrior on our team. Jim was still the WWF World champion at the time and in the middle of the hottest run in his career. With Jim in the mix, we were guaranteed to win but not to score the pinfall of the match with the Doomsday Device. It was always understood from the get-go that it would be Hawk and Animal building up the heat of the match in order to give Warrior the hot tag to take it all home. Once he was tagged in, it was tackle, tackle, tackle, clothesline, clothesline, clothesline, splash, splash, splash, and the pin. Always.

When it all went down with Jim, you had to steer clear because he ran in like a hurricane, huffing and puffing and charging wildly. It's funny how so many people used to complain about his "stiff" or "dangerous" style in the ring. Hawk and I would look at each other and shrug. That's exactly what guys used to say about us!

I got to know Jim fairly well at that time. We weren't the best of friends or anything, but he'd occasionally let me ride in his limo or we'd grab some dinner and a beer. I actually found him to be a pretty funny (and loud!) guy.

Sure, he was being chauffeured in a limousine and had his own Winnebago dressing room, but you know what? Neither Hawk nor I ever had a problem with Jim in or out of the ring. Any of the amenities he had were obviously spoils that went along with having the WWF Championship and his working agreement with Vince.

Within a few weeks on the road, I got used to the WWF routine, which was definitely different than other companies' routines. Hawk and I were on what was referred to as the A team (no, not the Mr. T show from the '80s), which was one of three teams of talent in the promotion. Back then, to cover different areas of the country at the same time, Vince divided the roster into three simultaneously traveling teams of talent.

The A and B teams featured a constantly shifting lineup of the very top drawing talent in the company, such as Hulk Hogan, Warrior, Rude, Jake, Hennig, and us. The rest of the guys, especially new talent that would be tested before audiences in smaller market towns, were placed on the C team. We were all dispatched into different travel schedules. About once or twice a week, all three teams would reunite for TV tapings, where we'd be sequestered at the arena all day.

I'm telling you, man, it was totally brutal. We'd have back-to-back tapings, and whether we wrestled once or three times during the course of the day, everyone had to stay put. Between the flying, driving, working out, wrestling, and all-out waiting around in our travel schedule, I was always beat. I'd be hunched over catching a few Zs wherever and whenever I could at those venues.

Hawk and some of the others would just say, "Fuck it," and snort lines of coke to stay up all day and night long, a habit of his I was completely sick and tired of. I was letting it slide for the time being, keeping my mouth shut and hoping for the best. But Hawk was like a brother to me, and I didn't want anything bad to happen to him. It wouldn't be too much longer before I'd officially address it.

While we were burning down the house all over the country with Warrior against Demolition, we rolled into Toledo, Ohio, on September 18 for TV tapings, including our first edition of *Saturday Night's Main Event*, to air on October 13. True to our current road tour, it was another six-man match against Ax, Smash, and Crush, and it was the first time a national audience got a chance to see the LOD and the Ultimate Warrior team together. Demolition claimed they were going to expose us for the phonies we were, and even their manager Mr. Fuji was wearing face paint, looking like the fourth member of the team.

In short, the six of us delivered a bombastic performance and gave the fans at the Sports Arena an unforgettable time. That night also marked the return of Hulk Hogan, who had taken some time off before Hawk and I came into the WWF. I have to admit, I was a little curious to get to know Hogan on some level.

For the last three or four years, our names were always included along with his in the magazines among the biggest stars in wrestling. But you know what? Hogan was the biggest star in wrestling and was the undeniable centerpiece of the WWF boom in the '80s. One of the greatest compliments Jimmy Hart used to give us back then was "Man, you two are the Hulk Hogan of tag teams."

I guess I wondered if Hogan was down-to-earth or some egomaniac. When I eventually got to find out, I was pleasantly surprised to see how cool he was. But you're going to have to wait for that one, just like I did. In the meantime, after the Toledo tapings were over, we took off with Warrior and Demolition to resume our cross-country feud. It all culminated on Thanksgiving Day in Hartford.

Survivor Series had become the WWF's Thanksgiving tradition after being introduced as the company solution to the NWA/Crockett Promotions annual Starrcade extravaganza. On November 22 at the Hartford Civic Center, Hawk and I teamed with Warrior and "The Texas Tornado" Kerry Von Erich as The Warriors (Kerry actually used to be known as The Modern Day Warrior during his earlier career in World Class Championship Wrestling) against The Perfect Team of Mr. Perfect and Demolition.

A Survivor Series match was a four-on-four, single elimination match until there was only one team member left. Of course, our team won with Warrior getting the pin, but what I remember most about that night was the debut of one of my fellow WCW defectors, Mark Calaway, the former "Mean" Mark Callous of The

Skyscrapers. When he came over to the WWF, the creative team came up with a gimmick that would make Mark a huge star: the Undertaker ('Taker for short), or "Kane the Undertaker" as he was first called.

'Taker's first appearance made a big impression on the live audience and an even bigger one on the boys watching the locker room monitors. I loved it. 'Taker played the slow, ominous moves of a reanimated dead man perfectly. He was invincible, emotionless, and didn't say a word. And when he picked up Koko B. Ware for his very first tombstone piledriver, everyone knew the Undertaker was going places.

I also remember it was great to team with Kerry Von Erich at Survivor Series. I had known Kerry for years ever since Hawk and I saw him wrestle Flair at one of Bill Watts' Superdome Extravaganza shows in the spring of '85. Kerry was a huge star even then and, aside from having Hollywood good looks and a great physique, was a former NWA World Heavyweight champion after beating Flair in Texas Stadium in '84.

I remember one night when Kerry was really messed up on something (or everything) and gave a memorable performance if ever there was one. Ric whipped Kerry into the ropes to set up a back drop/sunset flip combo, but when Kerry came running back off the ropes he completely missed the mark and didn't even realize it. I mean, you had to see Kerry do the front flip somersault about a foot to the right of Flair instead of directly over him.

I leaned over to Hawk. "Did he really just do that?"

The bottom line was that Kerry was a down-to-earth Texan who was a lot of fun to hang out with. Occasionally I'd ride and room with him on the road. It was during one of those trips that

I was let in on a little secret. Back in '86, Kerry had a bad motorcycle accident and severely injured his right leg, eventually resulting in the amputation of most of his right foot.

When we started to room together, I guess he got comfortable enough to reveal the prosthetic foot he used to wear inside of his boots. To watch him walk, let alone wrestle, you'd never have known at all. Kerry kept his foot covered up in the locker room all the time, even though I think most of the boys already knew.

Around this time I suffered a great personal tragedy. My mom, Lorna Laurinaitis, passed away on December 6, 1990. For the previous year or so, Mom and Dad had been living in Tampa to help relieve the symptoms of my mother's lupus. I was devastated to think I'd never see Mom's glowing smile or hear her infectious laugh again. Vince gave me a few days off so I could try to pick up the pieces and make sense of it all. Years later, I'm still trying.

WE WERE ALWAYS A TICKING TIME BOMB BEFORE OUR MATCHES. 2001.

15
THE LEGION OF DOOM DOMINATES THE WWF

The conclusion of Survivor Series marked the end of our feud against Demolition alongside the Ultimate Warrior. Demolition was pretty much dismantled and shelved by the late winter of 1991. I guess after the genuine article came into the company, Vince and the writing team lost interest. After floundering around the Federation without any real purpose for the better part of six months, Bill (Ax) outright left the company, Barry (Smash) was repackaged into a new gimmick known as the Repo Man, and Crush was moved into a singles career.

It was also around this time that I finally realized Hawk was losing control of himself. For about seven or eight months after joining the WWF, a noticeable divide had started to form between Hawk and me in our ways of life. It was simple when I looked at it. While I had some grounding, because Julie and the kids depended on me, Hawk didn't. He was unleashed and free flying in an environment where it was easy to find like-minded individuals and keep the party going all the time. It's not like I was an angel or anything myself, but the many years of Hawk's excessive use of cocaine, muscle relaxers, and painkillers had started to take their toll on my partner's reliability.

It got to the point that some of the boys would come up to me before the show and ask, "How's your partner tonight? Is he all fucked up? Will he be on time?"

I'd always cover for Hawk when I could, but the truth of the matter was that management knew exactly what was going on. Once in a while, the WWF would conduct random drug testing and Hawk would get nabbed. For the most part, they'd turn the other cheek and let him off the hook with a warning or a fine, but I wondered for how long.

The thing about Hawk was that he was easily influenced if he had people in his ear, which he did. Jake Roberts was the worst, and none of the guys Hawk gravitated toward had each other's best interests at heart.

Any random night that I'd stop by Hawk's hotel room, there'd be any number of people cheering him on. "Holy shit, Hawk," I'd hear, "I've never seen anybody do that many lines in a row." Then someone else would chime in. "I can't believe how much you can drink, Hawk." Those were the worst kinds of things you could say to someone like him. It only served to fuel Hawk's fire, and in the professional wrestling business, the devil's playground is always right around the corner if you're looking for it.

On any random night as I'd be lying down to sleep at 2:30 a.m., which was bad enough, I'd look out of my hotel window and see Hawk and Beefcake getting a cab to find the next bar. I'd shake my head and hope he'd show up on time the next day, and if he didn't, guess who was always left alone holding the bag when Vince would come walking around?

"Animal, where's Hawk?"

"He's okay, Vince. Just running a little late; that's all."

It got old really quickly. Jake Roberts used to see me from across the locker room having those moments with Vince and tried to claim to Hawk that I was ratting him out.

At one point in the early Georgia days Jake was a good friend of mine. We'd even shared an apartment for a time. But now he was the one scumbag trying to corrupt my relationship with Hawk.

I'd try to reason with Hawk all the time. "Man, I'm your real friend. I've been through it all with you, and I'm not going anywhere. Where will guys like Jake or these other jokers be next year? Or even next month?"

It all fell on deaf ears.

And you know what? It wasn't only when he was on the road with Jake and the rest of his crew that all the craziness went down. One time when we had a few days off, Hawk went up to a small cabin he had up at Leech Lake in northern Minnesota. He was up there with a buddy of his, and the two of them decided to take Hawk's little fishing boat out on the water for a late-night ride. Now keep in mind, it was the middle of the winter, so Hawk was dressed up in a big, heavy goose down parka along with his usual bandana, jeans, and cowboy boots. Did I mention that Hawk was also out of his mind on Somas (muscle relaxers)? Well, he was.

I guess they went about 100 yards out when Hawk fell backward into the lake and completely disappeared. Hawk's friend Matty ran over and started yelling for him, using a spotlight to look on all sides of the boat and out in the water. He saw a huge pocket of air bubbles coming from the area Hawk had fallen into and put the light under the water.

After waiting and staring down at the water for about a solid minute, Hawk suddenly popped up in a big rush. He was gasping for air and swinging his arms and then went back under. He later told me that he went up and down like that about five times before Matty could help pull him over the side of the boat.

"I sank all the way to the fucking bottom, man," Hawk told me. "My coat filled up with water and dragged me down. I couldn't see a fucking thing except that light Matty was shining. I don't even know how I made it back."

But that was Hawk, facing death and seeing his life constantly flashing before his very eyes. Whether he was tearing ass on a motorcycle throughout a graveyard in Japan or rolling his Cadillac off the side of a mountain road in Minnesota to avoid a logging truck, Hawk was pushing impossible limits. Somehow he always managed to come out on the other side okay, but for me, stories like that had lost their humor.

I looked at Hawk's escapades and felt increasingly disrespected that he'd take risks that could affect our livelihood. My livelihood. It was great if Hawk didn't want to grow up and follow the rules, but all that I asked of him was to consider where I was coming from. I wanted to do what we always did, and that was have fun and do good business. That's what wrestling's all about.

All bullshit aside, Hawk and I knew we were still getting warmed up in the WWF and had a lot of big accomplishments lined up to look forward to. Although I kept my eye on him as much as possible and helped steer us back on track from time to time, I left Hawk to live the way he saw fit with no barking from me. I hoped he'd make the right decisions for himself, our employer, and me. In the meantime, I made steady road companions with Davey Boy Smith and Warlord, with whom I shared similar eating and workout habits.

For the next few months, things between Hawk and me were going really great, and I'll tell you what, I was definitely having fun again. On January 19 we competed in our first ever Royal Rumble in Florida at Miami Arena. Out of the thirty entrants, I think Hawk was like the sixteenth and I was the eighteenth to enter the ring.

One of the highlights was Hawk and I eliminating the Undertaker with a double clothesline that flipped him perfectly over the top rope and onto his feet on the floor below. *Whoom!* After that, Hawk was eliminated by Hercules Hernandez and Paul Roma, known as Power & Glory, while I was dumped over the top when Earthquake ducked one of my running charges.

None other than Sgt. Slaughter, who was now playing the role of a Saudi Arabian sympathizer in the wake of Desert Storm, ended Warrior's WWF World title run and became the champ. It was weird because the Sarge had always been a hero to the public for the last fifteen years, even being a popular character in the G.I. Joe toy line. Now the once-hailed American patriot had become a traitorous heel in a turn so convincing that he even started receiving death threats.

Nine days after the Rumble, we went to Macon, Georgia, for another *Saturday Night's Main Event* TV taping, which aired on February 1, 1991. We faced the team of Pat Tanaka and Kato, The Orient Express. Tanaka and Kato were absolutely phenomenal together and, now that Demolition was disbanded, they were even managed by Mr. Fuji. Working with those guys was a dream. They knew their roles so well against a team like us that Hawk and I barely ever said a word in the ring; it was all Tanaka and Kato.

I'm telling you, those two would constantly suggest the best spots to put us over and throw themselves into every move in the LOD handbook. Press slams, powerslams, flying tackles, clotheslines, and finally the Doomsday—they gladly did them all and looked like a million bucks doing it.

I particularly remember a spot when we gave Tanaka a double back drop and he told us to throw him up as hard and high as we could. I think Pat got more than he bargained for, though, because we'd launch his ass about 15 feet in the air before he came crashing down. *Boom!* Hands down, Tanaka and Kato were one of the best heel teams I ever worked with.

One funny fact about Kato was that under the mask was actually a Croation-born former professional soccer player I knew as Paul Diamond. Kato the Japanese wrestler was actually no more Japanese than I was. Along with Tanaka and Diamond, I thought Mr. Fuji was phenomenal, too. With his perfect timing and intuition as a venomous heel, Fuji was definitely one of the greatest meddling managers of all time.

No doubt about it, going on the road with the three of them for the next month and a half was an absolute pleasure, and if I could've wrestled them for another ten years straight and then retired, I would've.

It was a good thing Hawk and I were polishing up our skills with guys as solid as The Orient Express. As it turned out, the coming month of March brought three of the biggest moments of our entire WWF career. It all started at the TV tapings on March 12.

We were in Biloxi, Mississippi, at the Coast Coliseum, booked to win a nontitle, babyface versus babyface match against WWF World Tag Team champions, the Hart Foundation. What's interesting about the whole thing was that the top two teams in the WWF were meeting for the first time, but it was like a weird little secret.

There was no previous announcement for it. There was absolutely no story line or angle for it. And overall, there was no reason for it. But then it hit me: it was Vince testing us out against his top guys. He wanted to see how the audience would react to the Legion of Doom, grooming them for our climb to the top.

When we first came in, Vince used to love to mess with me and claim the WWF fans didn't know who the Road Warriors were, and one of the reasons he paired us with Warrior in our first tour against Demolition was to make sure we'd get over.

Hawk and I would just roll our eyes.

"Oh, brother. Come on, Vince," I'd say. "You put us in there with anybody, anywhere, anytime and you'll see what happens."

It looked as if he was finally ready to take me up on my offer.

As our music hit and we came out, we were greeted with a Road Warrior pop that probably knocked McMahon off his feet.

Well, Vince, I remember thinking, *that pop's for you.* I also noticed little kids and teenagers everywhere wearing pairs of our WWF toy shoulder pads, which was pretty damn cool. Three years earlier when I'd made the first real set out of Ryder football pads, I'd never imagined they'd be mass produced for children's toys.

The match was a classic scenario of Bret and Neidhart assuming a somewhat heel role, but only in the sense that they kept the pace and the heat slowly building by keeping Hawk away from my outstretched hand. When it was time to bring it all home, Hawk finally got away from Neidhart and made the hot tag. I came smashing in, knocking Anvil to the floor and acknowledged the audience with two big thumbs raised high, signaling that it was time for the Doomsday. As I had Bret up on my shoulders, Neidhart interfered by pushing Hawk down to the floor, leaving me at the mercy of the Hart Foundation. Or was it the other way around?

Just as they had me down, Neidhart ran over to rocket launch Bret from the top turnbuckle with an assisted press and throw, but I was ready. I leapt to my feet, caught Bret in the air, and power-slammed him. *Bam!* While Hawk tripped Neidhart from the outside, I covered Bret for the three count. In a true gesture of baby-face sportsmanship, we tried to help Bret to his feet and offered our hands in friendship. It was an awesome moment, and it was exactly as I'd expected: the Biloxi crowd was ours.

Could there have been any question that Vince, who undoubtedly saw every second from the back, was impressed with our perfor-mance? Hell, no.

That match, in every element, was one of the key steps in our path toward an eventual shot at the tag titles. Though it wasn't taped for the purpose of a TV airing, it was packaged as part of the *WWF Wrestle Fest '91* home video.

As amazing as Biloxi was that night, it still didn't compare to what was still to come twelve days later: WrestleMania VII. After hearing all of the stories about how spectacular and over-the-top "The Super Bowl of Professional Wrestling" was, we were about to find out for ourselves.

The seventh WrestleMania was conducted in Los Angeles, of all places, so I expected to see famous people everywhere I turned. I wasn't disappointed. When we were walking around the back of the LA Memorial Sports Arena, I remember seeing Willie Nelson, Lou Ferrigno, Henry Winkler (Fonzie from *Happy Days*), Alex Trebek, and Donald Trump, just to name a few of the stars who showed up to be part of 'Mania. I even saw little Macaulay Culkin, the star of *Home Alone*, walking around meeting the wrestlers.

There was also extra security in full force that evening, as it was rumored that Sgt. Slaughter's life had been threatened due to his continued anti-American gimmick. It looked like kayfabe wasn't dead and buried just yet!

Hawk and I were going to be booked into a title run feud with the Nasty Boys, Brian Knobbs and Jerry Sags, who were slated to win the WWF tag titles that very night against the Harts. We were given Power & Glory as opponents. Hercules and Paul Roma were a fantastic, recently formed heel team, but they wouldn't get a chance to shine just yet.

You see, Vince had a WrestleMania agenda to showcase the Legion of Doom in front of the world as his team of the future. Unfortunately for Power & Glory, this was translated best in Hawk's prematch interview: "Power & Glory? When we get through with you, you'll be Sour & Gory."

In vintage Road Warriors fashion, Hawk and I proceeded to smash through Herc and Roma in a fifty-nine-second squash match from hell. When Hawk clotheslined Roma for the Doomsday, Roma flipped and crashed hard with a bit of a corkscrew landing. *Crack!* Roma sold it like a true pro, lying there like a slug and holding his stomach. With his hands on his hips, Herc stared at us while the 16,000 LA faithful gave us a standing ovation.

As I stared around the arena, I thought, *Wow! WrestleMania. This is what it's all about.* And it really was. After having wrestled in every company in the world, there was simply no comparison to the WWF.

The airtight cohesion between Vince's dream and his team of employees was evident. Everything about the production and execution of the WWF's product screamed "big time." To be in the company at that point in time and to have Vince's respect for our gimmick on display at 'Mania made everything feel perfect. A mere six days later, I'd get even further proof of how over the Legion of Doom was in Vince's eyes.

Back in October of 1990, Vince signed a promotional deal with a new Japanese wrestling company called Super World of Sports (SWS). The deal called for the WWF and SWS to copromote huge super cards in Japan featuring many of their top stars, such as Tenryu, Great Kabuki, and Yoskiaki Yatsu, in matches against our roster. When it was announced that we were doing a WWF/SWS super card at the Tokyo dome, we figured we'd be natural main players in the show, but I was floored when I found out what our match would be: the LOD against Genichiro Tenryu and Hulk Hogan.

The prospect of working against Hogan at the first ever WWF show in Japan felt like a crowning achievement if ever there was one. Hulk was the biggest thing in wrestling and had recently won the WWF World title from the Sarge at 'Mania VII. Getting a crack at Hogan in his prime before almost 65,000 Japanese fans was a dream come true.

As I thought about what was about to go down, it was a real "top of the world" feeling for me. We had Tenryu, long established as one of Japan's premier superstars; Hogan, who'd had famous battles with Antonio Inoki and Andre the Giant in Japan during the early 1980s; and then there was Hawk and I, former NWA/ AJPW International Tag Team champions whom the Japanese had more or less adopted as two of their own. The Japanese knew they were getting their yen's worth on March 30.

But it didn't go down with at least a little controversy in the locker room before the match. I'll never forget when WWF road agent Jack Lanza came to us right before the match with Hogan and Tenryu and said, "Okay, guys, here's the way Vince wants the finish."

I was listening very casually, wholeheartedly thinking it was going to be a double count-out or a double DQ of some variety.

"Hogan's going to put Hawk up on his shoulders, and Tenryu's going to clothesline him from the top turnbuckle."

I almost fell over when he said it. Beat us in Japan with our own Doomsday Device?

I spoke right up. "What? Abso-fucking-lutely not." It would've totally wrecked our hard-earned Japanese credibility and then some. I looked at Hogan, whom I still didn't really know from a hole in the wall, and Tenryu.

"No offense to you guys, but this is my one safe haven. Letting you guys humiliate us like that would be career suicide for us."

The truth of the matter was that our contract with Vince was only for the United States. His joint venture with SWS to copromote wrestling events in Japan was a completely separate deal for us with its own payday. I mean, sure, I understood it was smart business for the WWF to expand into the Japanese market, but it wasn't going to be at our reputation's expense.

We were even originally told we didn't have to work the show if we didn't want to, but Hawk and I thought it was a smart move, being right in the middle of our big push toward the titles and all.

Now I knew why we weren't told the finish before we got on the plane. Underneath it all, I didn't like being ambushed like that and found myself struggling to wrap my mind around the whole situation.

In a rare show of unselfish diplomacy, Hawk thought about compromising and taking the Doomsday.

"Mike, don't do it, man. I'm telling you, it's a bad move."

"Well, what are we gonna do?" he said.

I had no idea.

All of a sudden, Tenryu put his arms on my shoulders. "Animal-san, you beat me. Get win. Better?"

Man, Tenryu should've been a politician, because he amicably resolved what could've been a serious international conflict. I humbly and respectfully accepted his offer, and Jack Lanza reported back to Vince. It was a go. We'd get the win by count-out.

One of the most interesting details about the match, aside from the finish, was that because Hawk and I weren't familiar to the Japanese as the Legion of Doom, we were billed once again as the Road Warriors. SWS even recognized the value of having our original theme song and actually paid the necessary $10,000 licensing fee (the reason we'd stopped using it around 1988 for all WCW programming) so that we could once again make our way to the ring while "Iron Man" blasted throughout the Tokyo Dome.

While we stood on the giant stage platform waiting for our entrance, the Black Sabbath bass drum started kicking. I said to Hawk, "Just like old times, huh?"

He nodded and smacked me on the shoulder.

During one great moment during the match, I finally got a chance to press slam Hogan. From the time we were asked to be in the match with him, I knew I was going to get my hands on him first thing and put him up. Because Tenryu was in the match, we decided to go for the double press slam spot we always did with him and Jumbo Tsuruta.

When the bell rang, it was Tenryu and I in the ring, and he quickly placed me into a side headlock. I picked him straight up and threw him over to Hogan, who tagged himself in by reaching down and slapping Tenryu's chest. You should've heard the impact of the crowd cheer for Hogan as he stepped into the ring. *Whoom!* It was like the concussion of a sonic boom you could feel right in your chest. So there he was, Hulk Hogan, all six feet five and 302 pounds of him, staring right at me. I was having an *Oh, shit!* moment if ever there was one.

We locked up, and Hogan pulled me toward him before launching me back into the corner with a big push. I was surprised how tall he was when we locked up for the second time, and I felt myself getting on my tippy toes to get a good tie-up with him. Again, he pushed me back. This time I jumped right at him with a big boot to the stomach and started throwing wild punches while Hawk jumped in and joined me.

When Tenryu ran in, Hawk grabbed him and looked at me for the signal. Then I pulled Hogan to the center of the ring and nodded at Hawk, and we both yelled, "Press."

Now, I knew Hogan was a big boy, but I figured he'd go up about the same as Terry Gordy or Killer Khan had, but it wasn't the case. When I had him up on my chest and collarbone, I started having trouble balancing Hogan's long legs. It also felt like he was deadweighting me a bit. I remember feeling slightly bad for Hawk because after pressing Tenryu, he had to stand there holding him up until I was ready.

After wobbling slightly and adjusting, I pressed Hogan straight up for a lockout and slammed him down. I almost passed out after letting him go and was thankful I hadn't failed on the lift.

The entire match continued with stiff exchanges in and out of the ring until Hawk and I finally picked up the victory by count-out. I always wondered if Hogan was a little pissed off about the original finish conflict, because he came into the match really aggressively and pumped up. He even had a scowl on his face and was kicking Japanese cameramen out of the way during his entrance.

If I didn't know any better (and I don't), I would've sworn Hogan turned heel for that match. Maybe he did toward us that night to show he could dish it out to the Road Warriors. Who knows? He never said a word about it or ever acted any differently toward Hawk or me past the fact. But any way you sliced it, between defeating the Harts in Biloxi, destroying Power & Glory at 'Mania, and having scored a landmark victory over Hulk Hogan and Tenryu in Japan, our March of 1991 was one of the greatest months of my professional life.

16
HAWK SOARS TOO CLOSE TO THE SUN

It's funny how sometimes you can be at a place in life where everything is going great and you're just sailing along and then, *bam*, something comes along and screws everything up. After coming off a huge month of accomplishments in March and then running around the country with the Nasty Boys throughout April, I got a crushing blow in May.

"Joe, I've got some shitty news," Hawk told me. "I failed a drug test, and they're suspending me for sixty days."

I couldn't believe it. "Mike, you've gotta be kidding me. What the fuck?" I felt like all of our hard work in the WWF was for nothing.

As mad as I was, Hawk was equally remorseful. "I'm sorry, man. I'll get help and do whatever it takes to make things better. It won't happen again."

I wanted to believe him and just make the problem go away, so I let it go. Hawk had also chosen a really poor time to get in trouble with substance abuse. For the last year, a steroid scandal had been rocking the WWF, and particularly Vince, to the core.

Apparently, one of the WWF staff physicians by the name of Dr. George Zahorian III, had gotten a little too friendly with some of the boys and sold them steroids. Well, to make a long story short, Zahorian was found guilty on July 4, 1991, of selling steroids and named not only Hogan and Piper as among those he sold to but Vince as well. By the time Hawk had his little mishap, the whole company roster was under a microscope, and he got nailed.

It really sucked to see Vince kind of transform over the last year from the confident, in-your-face businessman to someone under federal investigation with his back against the wall. He'd also been spreading himself a little thin by focusing too much of his energy on the ill-fated World Bodybuilding Federation (WBF). Vince, an avid bodybuilding fan, decided to create his own WWF-style version of the sport. By the time the whole steroid thing was being aired out in public in mid-1991, the WBF was a multimillion-dollar disaster and was shut down.

As you'd imagine, it was like walking on eggshells at the shows. Everyone in the locker room was also now on high alert about their own extracurricular activities and didn't want to find themselves in the spotlight. They'd be toast for sure. Actually, Hawk's punishment of sixty days could've been much worse, all things considered. He could've been used as an example and out-right released. Thank God that wasn't the case.

Although he told the office he was going to rehab, Hawk actually just went home to Tampa and hung out for two months. On the other end of the reality spectrum, I was left alone to fulfill all of our bookings against the Nasty Boys until late July. I didn't mind working singles matches against Sags and Knobbs, but I did feel bad for all of the people who had looked forward to seeing both Animal and Hawk, as advertised.

To add insult to injury, I was also disappointed to learn that I was taken off all TV tapings, including a big show in NYC at Madison Square Garden on July 1, because both members of the Legion of Doom weren't available to face the Nasties.

When Hawk did finally return, we basically picked up right where we'd left off, and neither Vince nor I said a word about the suspension or warnings for the future. In fact, I was completely surprised (but relieved as hell) when we were told we would still win the tag titles at SummerSlam '91 on August 26.

Vince must have figured too much investment had been made during our long-running feud with the Nasties and wanted to see how it would all play out. I also think he was interested in testing us under the pressure of being champs and dealing with Hawk's drug issue. He was feeding us enough rope to see if we'd hang ourselves.

When the big day arrived for SummerSlam in NYC, both Hawk and I were able to show Vince exactly what the LOD was capable of at its best.[17]

With the WWF World Tag titles firmly around our waists after SummerSlam, we hit the road for a couple months of obligatory rematches with Sags and Knobbs. In October, we went over to London, England, for a series of shows, one of which was against Power & Glory at the famous Royal Albert Hall near Hyde Park in Westminster.

Before the match, Paul Roma came up to me and said he wanted to have a quick word. "Animal, it's about the Doomsday Device." He looked worried. "I don't mind taking a finish that everyone will be happy with, but I don't want to go up for that thing again."

17. To remember the details of our SummerSlam '91 match, you can flip back to my prologue at the front of the book.

Paul continued to explain that when he took the Doomsday back at WrestleMania VII he landed awkwardly and it scared the shit out of him. I perfectly understood.

Many guys were afraid of our finish, and in most of the cases, as with Paul, we came up with an alternative. Nine times out of ten, if you saw us taking a victory in those days without using the Doomsday Device, it was to cater to someone's fear. When the time came for us to win this match, I simply caught Paul from a dive off the top and flipped him over for a powerslam.

When we got back to the United States, I was happy to see another show scheduled at Madison Square Garden. New York City was the absolute pinnacle of wrestling for the WWF, and whenever you went there it was electricity beyond belief. This time, though, the electricity wasn't provided by our match, the crowd, or Con Ed.

You see, around the time of SummerSlam, none other than "Nature Boy" Ric Flair joined us in the WWF after finally being fired from WCW by Jim Herd. When Ric came in, it was like a breath of fresh air, and I couldn't wait to see how he'd shake things up. Well, after the show at MSG, Flair indeed got right into the mix the old-fashioned way.

Anyone who knew Ric knew he was the twenty-four-hour life of the party. Whether in the club, restaurant, hotel room, yacht, or airplane at 30,000 feet, you could rest assured that Flair was dancing with a drink in his hand, sometimes clothed and sometimes completely Nature Boy under one of his $5000 sequined robes. Sometimes when he'd had a few too many cocktails, which was often, Ric would get into fights, too.

After the MSG show was over, a bunch of the boys, including me, went to the China Club on West 47th Street. I was quietly hanging out in a booth with Mike Enos (Blake Beverly from the Beverly Brothers) when, out of nowhere, a big commotion broke out and a crowd formed near the bar. It was Flair and the Nasty Boys.

Ric had slapped Knobbs across the face. When Sags saw what was going on, he ran right over and socked Flair in the eye. All I knew was that I was never one for getting my ass in trouble with the cops, so Enos and I bailed and got a cab. The next day, all the boys were talking about Flair and the Nasties; it was classic pro wrestling bedlam. Man, was it ever good to have the Nature Boy back into the "swing" of things.

In November at Survivor Series '91 in Detroit, we teamed with our old buddy Big Bossman against I.R.S. (the guy I knew better as the accident-prone Mike Rotunda) and the Natural Disasters, Earthquake and Typhoon. Earthquake was actually a guy named John Tenta, and Hawk and I had actually wrestled him a couple of times in Japan back in the '80s. Tenta was a legit six feet five, weighed around 450 pounds, and was a Japanese trained sumo wrestler. One look at Earthquake in the locker room and I knew he'd been eating his Wheaties. And everything else, for that matter. He was huge.

Hawk and I scored the pin and the victory of the match by welcoming Rotunda into the WWF with the Doomsday Device, a move he was more than familiar with from our days together in WCW.

The match was actually a setup for our new tag feud with the Natural Disasters, which we'd be involved with for the next few months into 1992. But before all of that, the entire WWF roster converged upon the state of Texas for a series of TV tapings in early December.

After the show we did in San Antonio on the third, I

finally got a chance to hang out with none other than Vince McMahon, who decided to check out what we were all up to. We were at a strip club in San Antonio called The Yellow Rose having a bite and unwinding in privacy. Davey Boy Smith, Warlord, and I always ate at strip joints after the shows because they filtered out the majority of crazed autograph seekers, who were mostly under twenty-one. I don't care who you are, from the president to a janitor, everyone needs their downtime away from the elements of the job. I guess I wasn't the only one who felt that way that night, because we all had an unexpected visitor share the bar with us.

I remember being midbite into a chunk of prime rib when my eyes caught Vince himself casually walking through the doors. We all stopped to watch as he made his way past all of us to the bar to grab a beer. I'll tell you what, within about thirty minutes Vince was like one of the boys. He was holding court and telling big stories while all of us, including Hogan himself, listened and laughed.

At one point we were all standing around, and out of nowhere Hulk came up to me and put his thumbs in the air. "Hey, Animal. Why don't you get Vince up for your finish? Give him the Doomsday."

Hawk and I looked at each other and smiled. In a flash, Hawk took off across the room over to the dancing platform while I came up behind Vince and proceeded to pick him up onto my shoulders.

He was crying out for help. "Hey, what the hell are you guys doing? Let me down." He wasn't up there two seconds before Hawk came running off the platform with a jumping clothesline right between two dancing strippers.

Before Vince knew it, he was gently caught by Hogan, who'd been standing there the whole time. When McMahon got up, he started celebrating. He said to Davey Boy Smith and Warlord, "I did it. I took the Warriors' finish. What do you think of that?"

Everyone was laughing and cheering for the guy. We all knew what Vince had been going through with the whole investigation, which was far from over, and we were happy to let him have the moment. He deserved a break from the monotony. When someone at the club called the cops on us for rowdiness, everyone, even Vince, dove into Sgt. Slaughter's camouflage limo for the getaway. As always, thank God for the Sarge.

That was the first time I was able to say to myself, *You know what? I really like that guy.* Vince had such a mystique about him and was always such a walking gimmick that it was nearly impossible to get a handle on the guy. That's just the way he had to operate, you know? He had to place a distinct line between him and us in order to run the company. After all, you can't get too close to the inmates, right? But in San Antonio at The Yellow Rose that night, Vince finally opened himself up in front of me for the first time, and I liked what I saw.

After San Antonio, it was business as usual as we continued our new rivalry with the Disasters, even facing each other in another WWF/SWS show in Japan on December 12. I even got Typhoon up for a modified bear hug so we could hit him with the Doomsday Device. We pretty much duplicated the match for the Royal Rumble with 'Quake and Typhoon on January 19, except they got the count-out win. We still kept the titles but not for long.

A couple of days after our triumphant title defense at the Royal Rumble, I got the call that Hawk failed another drug test and we were forfeiting the belts. At that point, I didn't have a clue how to even approach my partner about what his latest infraction with the company meant for us, or my family. He was well aware on his own, especially considering that he was suspended without pay for another sixty days.

Hawk was completely defiant about the situation. "Fuck this shit, Joe. I'm not going to let somebody tell me how to live my life."

Hawk wasn't as apologetic as he'd been before, and suddenly I realized our career was in more serious jeopardy than I'd thought.

At the January 27 TV taping in Lubbock, Texas, for WWF Wrestling Challenge, which aired March 1, it was announced that we lost the titles to the team of I.R.S. and the Million Dollar Man, Ted Dibiase (known as Money Inc.) in Denver. The truth is, that match never happened. After years of building up to winning the WWF Tag Team Championships, it was all taken away in a matter of seconds without our ever stepping into the ring.

After sitting on the sidelines and sulking for the better part of ninety days, we were invited to come to WrestleMania VIII in April at the Indianapolis Hoosier Dome, and we brought a surprise along. During our time off, I had been talking to "Precious" Paul Ellering about working with us again. After having been away from the wrestling business for about two years, Paul was interested in checking out the WWF and cut a deal with Vince to return.

Unfortunately, the angle under which Ellering was repackaged turned out to be a half-baked disaster. During his time off, Paul had taken up the hobby of ventriloquism to entertain his three young children and had made mention of it to Vince and me. Because the LOD was now being heavily marketed toward the ever-blooming children's fan base, it was decided that Paul would introduce a ventriloquist dummy named Rocco. Before I knew it, we were brought in for WrestleMania to tell the fans we were returning to our roots by reuniting with a very important figure from our past, Paul Ellering.

Slowly but surely over the course of the next couple of months leading into SummerSlam '92, Paul began bringing out Rocco during interviews, claiming it was Hawk's and my long lost childhood toy from Chicago. The story line with Rocco implied that we had a sentimental attachment to the doll and that we could draw strength and motivation from him the same way Undertaker did from the urn his manager Paul Bearer tightly clutched.

Maybe in the grand scheme of things Vince saw a possible product line launch of Rocco dolls and Rocco T-shirts, but the whole thing never really left the starting gate. Thankfully.

I've got to give it to Vince, though. Even with the couple of drug test suspensions that sidelined us, McMahon never gave up on trying to push us to the top of the WWF. More than likely, we were given additional chances that other guys probably wouldn't have gotten.

When Hawk finally came back in the spring and we feuded with the Beverly Brothers and Money Inc., I think we were able to earn a little trust back with the office. We got the word from Jack Lanza that we were booked to go over Money Inc. at SummerSlam '92 in England. I was hoping we'd finally be back on the fast track to the top and retrieve our titles from the Natural Disasters.

When the big day finally came on August 29 at Wembley Stadium in London, I approached my partner with some words of inspiration. "Mike, this is a big one. We really need this match against Dibiase and Rotunda to show Vince and everyone else we're back to stay."

Hawk agreed and said not to worry. "We're gonna knock 'em all dead, Joe." Little did I know that Hawk had already been drug tested before we'd left for the UK and was anticipating yet another suspension or his outright release at any time.

So with that information swimming around in Hawk's mind, and my complete ignorance to it, he proceeded to take several sedatives in plain view of pretty much everyone in the Wembley dressing room. By the time we were gearing and painting up, he was lethargic, leaving little doubt in my mind that our appearance was in serious trouble.

I also knew that we had a huge entrance planned in which Hawk, Paul, and I would each be riding down the 500-foot walkway on custom Harley-Davidsons. When it was time to make our entrance for the first match of the night, Paul took off (with Rocco sitting on the handlebars), followed by Hawk and then me. The whole time we were riding down, I was hoping Hawk wouldn't fall or crash, but I was treated to something much better.

When all three of us began to park our bikes, Hawk accidentally stopped and docked his Harley down too close to me. When I tried to get off my motorcycle, I was so close to Hawk's exhaust pipe that my right boot and tights melted right onto the metal, frying my skin. As soon as I felt the heat and subsequent pain, I had to contain myself from letting anyone notice something had happened. I'll tell you what, man, when I got in the ring and heard 80,000 fans chanting, "LOD, LOD," I forgot all about my leg and felt like a wrestling rookie all over again.

SummerSlam '92 was the first big WWF PPV to ever come to England, and the people came out in droves. The huge outdoor Wembley Stadium was sold out. It was the biggest audience I'd ever seen, and it was pure pandemonium. We even debuted our brand-new shiny gold shoulder pads and gold-accented tights, which had all been designed to complement our gold WWF Tag Team Championship belts. (Of course, by the time our new gear was ready, we didn't even have the belts anymore.)

When it came time to wrestle the match, I was relieved to see Hawk manage himself pretty well against Dibiase and Rotunda. I clearly remember his stupor having a negative impact only when we realized it might be a mistake to attempt the Doomsday Device. If Hawk climbed to the top turnbuckle and fell, it would've been a total disaster, so I decided to take matters into my own hands and finish off Rotunda with a powerslam.

Funny thing is, when I threw I.R.S. into the ropes, Hawk was standing in my path. "Mike," I hollered, *get out of the way.*" He barely made an effort to move, and I had to pull back on how big the slam was so he wasn't kicked in the head.

As our hands were being raised, I glanced down at the announcer's table, where Vince was, shaking his head.

I put it all out of my mind and thought, *All right, we had an acceptable showing, the fans love us more than ever, and everything's looking up to another title run.* It sure sounded good in theory.

After the show, Heenan came up to me and said Vince had been cursing Mike off camera the entire match.

Great.

The reality of what happened post-SummerSlam was that while Paul and I were on our flight back to the United States (during which I told Paul to permanently "lose" Rocco) for a TV taping in Hershey, Pennsylvania, Hawk was hanging out with the London chapter of the Hells Angels with no intention of joining me. It wasn't until I was painted up and waiting with Paul at the Hershey Park Arena for him to show up that I knew something was wrong.

Vince came in looking grim and told me Hawk quit.

He what?

"Mike called the office today looking for me but only got my secretary," Vince said. "He told her to relay the message that he'd had enough and was quitting the company."

I was hoping it was a joke, but Vince wasn't even slightly smiling. Hawk had no interest in owning up to his latest drug test failure and figured he'd take off on his own without letting me know. Man, I was pissed beyond belief and probably more confused than anything. I never imagined the end of the Road Warriors/Legion of Doom would go down this way.

Then I started wondering what Hawk's quitting meant for Paul's and my future with the WWF.

"Well, Joe," Vince said, "our deal was for both Road Warriors, not Road Warrior Animal. I'll have to see what we can come up with."

Great. It sounded like the kiss of death. In the meantime, I went home without work and Paul quietly semiretired from the business yet again.

Finally, after about two weeks without hearing from Hawk, I got the long-awaited call.

"Hey, Joe, what's going on?"

It was a little too casual for my liking, and I let him know it. "What the fuck do you think's going on? I'm sitting at home wondering where my next check's going to come from to take care of my family."

Hawk apologized, as he always did, and went on to explain how he was a grown man and wasn't going to let anyone (Vince) tell him how to live his life. He also said he'd been talking with Masa Saito and Brad Reinghans for some time about having the

Road Warriors come and work exclusively for NJPW. "Our money in the WWF never panned out like Vince said it would. We made less and less money each year there than we did with Crockett. That wasn't the deal."

Hawk was right about the money part not being what we'd hoped for, but I was still committed to finishing up our scheduled bookings in the WWF. "I can't go with you, Mike. I've got work to finish up for the both of us here first, and then I'll think about it. But I'm really fucking upset with the way you handled this."

He said he knew and that he'd make it up to me in the long run, and we hung up.

I wouldn't talk to him again for almost six months.

Coincidentally, the next day after my phone call with Hawk, I took off for Japan myself to wrestle a couple of singles matches, including a handicap match against both Beverly Brothers on September 15 in Yokohama. Right in the middle of the match I was given a double-suplex and didn't land right. I knew I was in trouble the second I hit. Pain shot through my lower back, and I quickly told Mike Enos (Blake Beverly) we needed to take the match home.

When I got to the back, all I could do was lie down on a bench and wonder why things were going the way they were. Not only was I dealing with the emotional hurt of Hawk's desertion, but now to complicate things even more, I had a herniated C5 and C6 vertebrae.

After loading up on pillows, ice packs, and painkillers, I endured the most insufferable series of plane rides in my life to reach Minneapolis. When I finally got home and walked through the door to be attacked with hugs from Joey, James, and Jessica, I knew it was going to be a loooong time before Road Warrior Animal would see the light of day. Now it was time to rest, think things over, and enjoy being Joe the family guy.

After I had been officially diagnosed with my back injury, not only did I immediately schedule the necessary surgery to fix it, but I filed a significant insurance claim with my policy carrier, Lloyd's of London. Being a professional entertainer in such a high-risk environment like a wrestling ring, I'd known it was a smart move to take out a personal injury policy with Lloyd's a few years back. Now, my wise decision was literally paying off.

It was during this time, around mid-December of 1992, while being laid up after my successful spinal fusion surgery that I got a call from a wrestling magazine reporter looking for my opinion on the Hell Raisers.

Huh? I had no idea what the guy was talking about. My mood started to plummet from groggy and grouchy to completely livid as I learned that Hawk had formed a new team in NJPW based completely on our Road Warriors gimmick.

I knew he'd been running around the world doing indie shots for various promotions, but I guess he'd also promised Masa Saito and Brad Reinghans at NJPW that both he and I were coming over as a package deal. When Hawk explained he was coming without me, they decided to pair him with an up-and-coming rookie named Kensuke Sasaki (Kenskee for short) and form a new version of the Road Warriors. Thus, the Hell Raisers were born. They took Kenskee, painted his face, named him Power Warrior, and gave him a set of gear and shoulder pads identical to ours, except in green.

Hawk, or Hawk Warrior as he was called, kept the red and black theme from the WWF. They even went so far as to use another Ozzy Osbourne song, "Hellraiser," as their entrance music. I was even told that the Hell Raisers had won the IWGP Tag Team titles from Tony Halme and our old friend Scott Norton.

The news made me sick. I told the reporter to get his pen ready. "You can tell the people that even if Hawk has Power Warrior as his new partner, he'll never replace Road Warrior Animal and my rightful place as one-half of the Road Warriors. It's disrespectful to put someone else into a spot I worked my ass off to establish."

I think my point was made. A couple months later, I got a call that confirmed it.

"Hey, Joe." It was Hawk. "I heard what you said about Kenski, and the office at New Japan ain't happy. They think you're burying him."

Like so many times in the recent past, I couldn't believe what I was hearing, and I responded accordingly. "How is this my fault, Mike? You're the one who abandoned me and decided to disrespect everything about our gimmick. You didn't even discuss it with me first."

Hawk went on to explain that with me out of the picture, Inoki suggested he team up with Kenski to establish instant credibility with the Japanese fans. He also said the Hell Raisers were temporary until I healed up enough to make my official comeback and reunite the Road Warriors.

Honestly, maybe it's me, but I felt Hawk had a lot of nerve to call and complain about my totally justified thoughts. He was the one I felt put me in the whole situation to begin with. It had nothing to do with me trying to throw Kenski under the bus. Personally, I liked him just fine. The heat I vented to the reporter was strictly between Hawk and Animal or, more to the point, Mike and Joe.

Well, needless to say, the call didn't end on a high note. Hawk dial-toned me at the last second.

It would be the better part of a year before we'd talk again.

Embittered by Hawk and the whole Hell Raisers situation, I completely withdrew from the pulse of professional wrestling altogether. I tossed my gear bag into the closet to collect some dust and turned all of my attention to my family and to coming back bigger, stronger, and better than ever before.

During my long sabbatical, I was able to reflect on where I was in life and what made me tick. It was my family. There was nothing better than coming home in those days. I would be so beat and in need of serious decompression, and the minute I'd come in the door, Joey, James, and Jessica would be all over me. Right then and there, the fatigue and pain would wash away. There wasn't any therapy in the world a doctor could prescribe that matched the healing powers of being with my babies.

I remember coming home from Japan and being so jet-lagged that it would take days to recover from it all. My mind would be in another world while I'd be lying on the floor in the family room watching TV. I'd be propped up with a pillow against the family room steps, almost falling asleep, when all of a sudden I'd hear the sound of running feet coming down the hall behind me. *Bam. Bam! BAM!* Then it would get quiet. Too quiet.

BOOM! All of a sudden, James would land on my chest laughing and tickling me while Joey would be attacking my legs. I was being double-teamed by my own sons, the Legion of Laurinaitis. Little Jessica, never one to be outdone by the boys, would join in and try to hang with her big brothers.

Joey, James, and Jessica got along great while growing up. They all really hit it off with one another. Before Jessica was old enough to really get involved in the scheme of things, my boys had been quite the duo. Even though Joey was five years older, James was the same size by around age six, so there was a lot of wrestling going on in the house.

Also, there was a lot of "monkey see, monkey do" with the moves the kids saw me performing on TV. Before I knew it, Joey and James were as good as their old man at delivering clotheslines and powerslams into the couch or swimming pool. They'd even put Jessica up on James' shoulders so Joey could dive off the springboard and Doomsday Device her right into the water. They had such great chemistry together, a parent's greatest blessing, and boy did they have a ton of fun.

One time when James was three, he was chasing Joey and fell chin-first into our sliding glass door. That wasn't fun. But even less fun was the wet bar incident. We had a sunken living room area with a nice wet bar, the kind with the overhead wineglass racks where we'd hang each glass upside down by the base.

I remember laying down the law. "Guys, no hard hockey balls in the house." Famous last words. Thirty seconds later, I heard breaking glass. *Crash, crash, crash!* There went three glasses. *Smash, smash, smash!* There went another two. By the end of the week, only two of the original set remained. We threw them out and forgot about having wine altogether. (It made my stomach hurt anyway.)

Something most families don't have to worry about with their children is "the talk." Of course, I'm not referring to the old birds-and-bees routine but something much more complicated: professional wrestling. For Julie and me, it was important to explain to our kids the true nature of the business and that what they saw happen to me in the ring wasn't exactly what it seemed. The concept wasn't easy for them because I would sustain legit injuries once in a while and come home all banged and stitched up.

Take it from me, it's nearly impossible to convince little children that wrestling's a work, but they eventually got the idea that I was an entertainer. Joey and James in particular loved pro wrestling and would have sleepover parties for every WWF PPV. With Road Warrior Animal as their daddy, they had a pretty popular household in the neighborhood.

Parenting Jessica was obviously a little different than parenting the boys. Of course there was more huggy and kissy time with Jessica, but come on, that's a given. In general, though, I treated her the same way I treated my boys. Even Joey and James would kid with her to toughen her up. They'd walk by her in the hall and shoulder block her against the wall or take her down and tickle torture her. It was all in fun, and Jessica loved it. She'd go right after them and show everyone she wasn't scared of messing with the boys. Even more priceless than Jessica's bravery was her in-your-face attitude.

Once, when she was about three years old, I was on the phone taking care of a Japanese booking or something. Well, Jessica wanted Daddy's attention, and I guess I wasn't giving it to her, so she took matters into her own hands. Literally.

Before I knew it, a little hand was pushing my right cheek and another little hand was pushing my left cheek until I was being stared at straight in the eyes. Then I heard, "Daddy? Do you hear me, Daddy? Do you hear me?" I lost it and started laughing. It was hysterical. To this day, Jessica and I still joke about it. If she's trying to talk to me and I'm distracted, I'll hear, "Daddy, do you hear me?"

When I was wrestling, I wanted to create a home life with as much normalcy as possible. Whether it was Julie reading bedtime stories and tucking in the kids every night, or everyone sitting together for dinner when I was in town, the little things made the most difference.

The pride I have in my family knows no boundaries. Like anything that's important, you have to work at family all the time. We always kept open and clear lines of communication and worked out any and all problems right on the spot. Now that I think about it, the work's never done, and maybe that's what makes it so rewarding.

But while my family bloomed all around me in so many fantastic ways, far in the back of my mind, there was a rumbling in the cage. Animal wanted back out.

HAWK LOVED BEATING PEOPLE UP IN JAPAN AND EVERYWHERE ELSE FOR THAT MATTER. 1985.

17

THE RESURRECTION OF
THE ROAD WARRIORS

It had been about two years since Hawk had taken off for Japan and formed the Hell Raisers with Kenski in New Japan. Meanwhile, my spinal fusion surgery had been so successful that I was back in the gym sooner than expected. I started off lightly with cardio and machines, but after getting my hands on the weights, the pounds packed right back on. I was 300 pounds before I knew it. And I didn't just rehab my back; I supercharged it. Man, my hands were getting itchy for press slams and Doomsday Devices like you just don't know.

I was also finally able to reconnect with Mike from 1993 through 1995 with a series of phone calls he made to check in on me and let me know what was going on. It was a big step in the right direction for both of us. Letting go of all the unresolved bitterness I personally harbored was as important to my healing process as the fusion surgery had been.

It was during one of those calls that Mike revealed he'd

recently contracted hepatitis C from using dirty needles for various reasons. For those of you not familiar with it, hep C is a serious viral disease that will destroy your liver and lead to a whole world of problems no one wants. Mike went on to tell me about these nasty interferon shots he'd had to take during the last year.

"They wiped me out, Joe," he said. "I've never experienced anything like it in my life. You feel like you have the flu for weeks. I haven't felt like training or doing anything but resting. It's been totally fucking brutal."

But then he told me he'd recently met someone. While hanging out with Hulk and Linda one night down in Tampa where Mike and many of the other guys lived, too, he was introduced to a girl named Dale. The two of them really hit it off and quickly became a serious item. He told me they were engaged.

"Holy shit, bro," I said. "That's great news. Anything else you want to tell me while you're at it? You're on a hell of a roll as it is."

In fact, there was something else on his mind. "I can't wait for you to come back, Animal. There's a lot of unfinished business in the world for the Road Warriors."

After that phone call, I had quite a lot to think about. My head was spinning. Hawk had hepatitis, was engaged, and couldn't wait for me to come back. My mind kept drifting to the part about returning. Mike was right, of course. We did have unfinished business. But I still needed to be cleared by my doctors and Lloyd's of London, so for the time being, Hawk would have to go back to work without me.

During my little hiatus on the wrestling sidelines, Hawk and Kenski actually did great things together, even holding the IWGP Tag Team Championships on two separate occasions. By January of '95, however, the Hell Raisers started winding down as a team. As planned, Kenski was starting to branch off into a singles career.

I think everybody, from the fans to the office, was curious where Road Warrior Animal was and how he was doing. So I figured I'd show them. On January 4, 1995, during a singles match between Hawk and big Scotty Norton in Tokyo, I nervously made my way to the ring in my paint and street clothes. I was thinking crazy shit, like, *Maybe they won't remember me*, and *Maybe they didn't even notice I was gone*. But that train of thought ended the second I came stomping down to the NJPW ramp in my cowboy boots and jeans and everyone saw who it was.

Blasting me with the first Road Warrior pop I'd heard in two and a half years, the fans erupted and gave me the confidence booster of my life. They made me feel as if not a second had passed since the last time I'd stood in front of a crowd, and with my 22-inch arms bursting from the seams, it sure didn't look like it either. The message was perfectly delivered: Animal was on his way back and badder than ever.

After my little hello to the wrestling world in Japan, I went back home to finish all the therapy necessary for Lloyd's of London to clear me. Although it would be nearly a year before I was ready, it didn't stop us from making plans with WCW to bring the Road Warriors back to the company for the first time in almost six years.

Boy, I'll tell you, quite a lot happened to the world of professional wrestling in the few short years I was off. Around the time Hawk and I had split back in September of '92, I heard that the pizza man Jim Herd had been fired from WCW. It was during Herd's brief tenure that one of the top wrestling companies in the world was run straight into the ground. Jim Crockett Sr. was probably spinning in his grave down in Charlotte. It was also during his tenure that there was an exodus of top guys like Flair (who went right back to WCW after Herd's firing), Sid Vicious, and us, but also of up-and-coming guys like Mark Calaway (Undertaker), Steve Austin, Mick Foley (Cactus Jack), and even Scott Hall and Kevin Nash. Hell, even commentators Tony Schiavone and Jim Ross left.

WCW's product was completely in the toilet with the worst TV ratings in WTBS history, and Ted Turner wasn't happy about it. After making several more unsuccessful personnel shifts to try to turn things around, Turner finally landed on a young guy named Eric Bischoff.

Bischoff had been hired for light duties, including conducting backstage interviews, when we were still there. I guess Eric was able to put himself in the right places at the right times and say all the right things, because he curried enough favor with the upper management of TBS to land himself the role of executive vice president. Once that happened, Bischoff was able to open up Turner's deep pockets and completely rebuild and rebrand WCW.

During all of the WCW's disastrous follies, the WWF hadn't been faring too well either. Vince wound up taking huge financial hits on all sides not only because of failed business ventures like the WBF and subsequent ICOPRO vitamin supplement line but also due to his own federal steroid trial. McMahon, like Dr. Zahorian before him, was in the fight of his life to avoid conviction for anabolic steroid distribution to some of the boys.

It was a nasty period not only for Vince but also for Hulk Hogan, who took the stand to testify and admitted to his own steroid use. Talk about a black eye for the business. Hogan's wholesome image of "Say your prayers and take your vitamins" was dead in the water, and the WWF along with it. As with WCW, WWF TV ratings and live event attendance virtually disappeared.

Vince even decided to take a leave of absence from the WWF and put his wife, Linda, in charge until the legal drama blew over. I remember receiving a subpoena of my own to come and testify, but I had nothing to say of any value. I never saw anything, never knew Dr. Zahorian. When I conveyed as much to the prosecutor, they excused me from the whole proceeding.

In 1994, Vince was finally acquitted of all charges, but the damage had been done. The once unstoppable WWF/Hulkamania machine of the '80s was broken down on the side of the pop culture road and needed a major overhaul. And this is where things got really interesting. Sensing a huge opportunity to take advantage of Vince's less-than-favorable situation, Eric Bischoff made a huge power play that changed everything.

Much as Vince had done in the '80s, Bischoff started offering big money deals and a fresh start for almost everyone still working in the WWF. Ted Turner's financial backing and WCW's restructuring all of a sudden gave a new lease on life to guys like Randy Savage, Roddy Piper, Bobby Heenan, "Mean Gene" Okerlund, and, of course, Hulk Hogan. Bischoff was so convinced that Hulk was going to be the savior of the company that he gave him open access to creative decisions and talent acquisitions.

The Nasty Boys, Jimmy Hart, Brutus Beefcake, Honky Tonk Man, and even John Tenta (Earthquake) and Fred Ottman (Typhoon) were all guys from the WWF glory days who were given deals and put on the WCW roster.

Back in Stamford in his office, Vince was reeling from the diminishing talent ranks of his company, but instead of rolling over and dying, Vince decided to get to work. If Bischoff was going to decimate his pool of main eventers, he would establish new ones. Instead of spending money he didn't have on recruiting too many new faces, he focused on who he already had. Within a year or two, midcard-level guys like Shawn Michaels, Yokozuna (a six feet four, 550-pound Samoan under a Japanese sumo gimmick), Scott Hall (as Razor Ramon), and Kevin Nash (as Diesel) took center stage in the WWF Championship scene along with the likes of Bret Hart and 'Taker.

As if the brand rivalry between the WWF and WCW wasn't heated enough already, Vince and Bischoff unwittingly put themselves into a new pressure cooker that would ultimately destroy one of them in the end: the Monday Night Wars.

Looking for a way to give the people a side-by-side comparison of WCW and the WWF, Bischoff convinced Turner to give him a cable slot on TNT (Turner Network Television) against Vince's *Monday Night Raw* on the USA Network. *Raw*, which debuted in '93, had been established as a very successful and innovative approach to wrestling on TV every Monday night. On September 4, 1995, however, *WCW Monday Nitro* premiered on TNT opposite *Raw* and ignited a frenzy between McMahon and Bischoff to outshock and outscore each other every Monday night in front of the world for the next 284 weeks.

This was when we happened to come into the picture. Hawk was really good friends with Eric Bischoff's right-hand man Sonny Onoo, who had earlier worked in NJPW as WCW's liaison, and got us in for a good "pay-per-shot" money deal until we could work out a long-term contract. In preparation for our WCW debut, I had blue shoulder pads and gear made up for our first match.

I imagined the whole new approach as the Road Warriors' Black 'n' Blue era (as in, the way all of our opponents were going to end up). I had such high hopes then.

On January 29, 1996, Hawk and I made our *WCW Monday Nitro* debut with a victory over the Faces of Fear, which was the team of our old bud the Barbarian and his new partner Haku, or Meng, as he was now known. When we came walking down the ramp to the ring, it was the first time we'd been in front of a WCW audience in five and a half years, and the people made us feel as if it were 1986 again.

When I started off with Barb and exchanged a couple of push-offs, I threw him into the ropes and picked him up for my first powerslam. *Bam!* I followed up with one of my trademark vertical jumping elbow smashes. *Crack!* I got up, let out a huge scream, and flexed my arms out to the side to show what it felt like to be back. I hadn't even so much as stepped into a ring to fight since my injury, and if there was ever any question about my status, it was erased from the board with a sledgehammer.

But that would be about the only notable highlight from our "big" WCW return. Right after our debut match on *Nitro*, we entered into a half-assed feud with the WCW World Tag Team champions, Sting and Lex Luger, but we weren't booked to take the titles. By February of 1996, Sting and Luger were top contracted company guys and there was no way Bischoff was going to uproot their championship run with a couple of freelancers like us.

I also got the weird feeling that Sting and Luger were less than thrilled when we came back. Let's face it. Hawk and I were always used to being the big boys everywhere we went to work, so when those two saw that the Road Warriors were back, I'm sure they felt like our spot had faded years ago. Although I felt the unspoken tension, I focused on being a good businessman and finally tracking down Eric Bischoff so we could get our contracts squared away.

One night around mid-March, I saw Eric with Sonny Onoo at a bar in Atlanta and made my approach with Hawk to have a chat.

In short, Eric became our new best friend for the night. "Hey, bartender," he yelled across the bar, "these are my new best friends, the Road Warriors. Get them whatever they want." During that night, Bischoff promised us the moon and the stars. "I'm going to make you guys the highest paid team in WCW, and I'm going to make you the champs."

Unfortunately, a deal couldn't be reached.

The long and short of how the rest of our time in WCW went was, in a word, frustrating. Throughout the late winter and into spring, we aimlessly wrestled against all of our old rivals, such as the Nasty Boys and the Steiners, and actually did have a few great matches with new guys like Booker T and Stevie Ray, or Harlem Heat, as they were called.

Man, we could've had a long and really memorable feud with Harlem Heat if Bischoff would've green-lit the idea. Booker and Stevie were talented and tough black inner-city kids (and real brothers) from Texas. To me, pitting them against inner-city Chicago badasses like Hawk and Animal was a natural moneymaker. Oh well.

In the end, Bischoff kept dodging our contract requests, so we decided to call it a day in WCW and book some dates in Japan for the summer and fall. It was probably just as well that we left when we did, because as obsessed as Bischoff was with beating the WWF when we were there, things were about to get even crazier.

While Hawk and I wrestled our last WCW PPV match at

Slamboree Lethal Lottery on May 19 in Baton Rouge, about 800 miles north in NYC at Madison Square Garden, Scott Hall and Kevin Nash had coincidentally finished their last match for the WWF. Over the course of the next couple months, Hall and Nash were seen invading WCW live during PPVs as well as *Nitro*.

Calling themselves the Outsiders, Hall and Nash actually pulled off a phenomenal angle where it seemed as if they were sent from the WWF to destroy WCW from the inside out. When they claimed to have a third partner already in WCW waiting to lead them to victory and revealed him to be Hulk Hogan, it was the birth of the New World Order, NWO, and the biggest boom in the professional wrestling industry since Vince and Hogan had created Hulkamania thirteen years before.

When Bischoff convinced Hogan to turn heel and become "Hollywood" Hogan, the NWO became the hottest angle in wrestling. The antihero/counterculture appeal of the NWO wasn't at all unlike what Hawk and I had experienced in our early days when our raw image and style had made us unexpected fan favorites.

The ensuing NWO versus WCW story line that pitted the growing renegade faction of Hogan and his cronies against the babyface grouping of Sting, Luger, Randy Savage, and the Steiners proved to be the tipping point for Eric Bischoff. As a result of the hugely successful NWO story line, *WCW Monday Nitro* finally beat *Monday Night Raw* in the ratings for the first time that summer and would hold the definitive lead as the most watched cable program on TV for eighty-four more consecutive weeks.

Although we were finished with WCW while all of the developments of the NWO were taking place, we did join them for some joint WCW/NJPW shows in Japan. I remember one show in particular on July 16 at the Nakajima Sports Center in Sapporo, Hokkaido, for its incredible fireworks show—and I'm not talking about bottle rockets and Roman candles. No, sir, the bombastic display I'm talking about was a little altercation between my own partner and "Macho Man" Randy Savage.

The story goes that while at a Japanese hibachi dinner (you know, the kind where they cook in front of you) a couple years earlier in Tampa, Hawk and his fiancée, Dale, and Savage were all seated at the same table.

When Hawk got up to use the bathroom, Savage leaned over to Dale and said, "Hey, how'd you like for me to take you under the table and show you what a real man's like?"

Startled, Dale ignored the Slim Jim spokesman and opted to keep the incident quiet from Hawk for about two years. When she finally did open up, his reaction was something along the lines of "What? He said what? I'll kill that motherfucker next time I see him."

Well, that next time was right there in Japan that night. The whole time we were getting ready, Hawk kept saying, "I can't stand it. I'm going to confront that motherfucker when we're done."

Randy was wrestling Ric Flair for the WCW World Heavyweight Championship and was actually all geared up and literally about to walk through the curtain when he got a very angry Mike Hegstrand right in his face. "Heard about what you said to my old lady at the restaurant, motherfucker."

Savage denied it.

"Oh," Hawk said, "so you're calling her a liar?" And with that, Hawk leaned over the railing and smashed Savage right in the face with a powerful bitch slap. *Crack!*

Macho's trademark neon sunglasses and little cowboy hat

went flying. I saw Tatsumi Fujinami grab and hold up the stunned Savage as I grabbed Hawk to prevent him from following up with anything more. Sting and Keiji Mutoh were there watching the whole thing.

Hawk was still raging. "That's what you get for messing with my girl, asshole. If you want more, I'll be in the parking lot after the show."

Randy was steaming to get his hands on Hawk, but he had to get to the ring. Flair was literally waiting for him. There's no doubt in my mind that Savage was seeing red that entire match from thinking about Hawk. Evidently he never forgot or forgave Hawk for the incident, either, because a few years down the road, they had a rematch at a Kid Rock concert.

In the meantime, however, when the craziness of Japan was all over, we found ourselves sitting at home on our asses again. What Hawk and I needed was full-time work in the United States for a major company. With WCW no longer an option, it meant there was only one place to turn or, more to the point, one man to turn to. I decided to pick up the phone and see if Vince McMahon was interested in doing business again with the Legion of Doom.

For obvious reasons, I was a little concerned Vince was going to hold the past against us and not be interested in bringing us back to the WWF. I was glad it wasn't the case. At that point in time, Vince was being soundly defeated one battle at a time in the Monday Night Wars and probably figured he could use all the help he could get. Naturally, he wanted to know how Hawk was doing.

"Mike's doing great," I said. "He's found himself a good girl, and he's been staying out of trouble." I hoped I wasn't saying anything that would come back to haunt me later.

We agreed to a three-year deal that was fairly similar to our old one. I was just happy to have a job again. Vince said he was going to come up with something special to reintroduce the LOD to the WWF fans and told us to show up for *Raw* in NYC on February 24, 1997.

When we arrived at the Manhattan Center and found the dressing room for the Grand ballroom, it was interesting to say the least. Gone was "the house that Hogan built" and guys like Andre the Giant, Mr. Perfect, Big Bossman, Earthquake, and Ultimate Warrior. Long gone.

Now when I looked around, I saw tons of new gimmicks like Goldust, Mankind, and Yokozuna. There was also still Undertaker with Paul Bearer and other guys we knew from Japan like Big Van Vader. When you took all of those guys and threw us into the mix, the whole scene looked like a cross between Halloween and Mardi Gras.

It was really good to see a lot of the old WWF guard still holding down the fort while we were gone. Bret and Owen Hart, Davey Boy, and Neidhart were all still deep in the trenches while some familiar faces from the old WCW had joined them with new WWF names like "The Time Bomb" Brian Pillman, Sycho Sid Vicious, and Ron "Farooq" Simmons.

I imagine a lot of the young guys who'd never met us before could've been pretty intimidated by our arrival, but Hawk and I couldn't have been more humble. All I wanted to do, as always, was have fun and make good money. Sitting there gearing up, I had to chuckle. I was feeling nervous as if we were starting all over again.

A few minutes later, while we were waiting for the call, our old pal Jerry Brisco, one of Vince's top agents now, told us McMahon wanted to have a quick hello.

"I wanted to wish you guys luck out there tonight," Vince told us. "This will be a fresh beginning for all of us."

It was music to our ears.

Vince told us none other than Jake Roberts, who was also working as a WWF agent, would go over our match details, and then he barreled out of the room.

Jake looked at us with a big, creepy grin and said, "Boys, I want you to meet somebody." Then he led us over to another part of the locker room.

"These are The Headbangers, Mosh and Thrasher. They're kind of like the new Road Warriors."

The new Road Warriors? Was Jake on crack? Oh yeah, I forgot, *he was.* I looked at Mosh and Thrasher, and they seemed like nice enough kids with a little face paint, shaved heads, and combat boots, but these were the kind of guys we'd expect to be jobbing that night, not being compared to.

"The four of you are going to wrestle a quick match to a double count-out. Sound good?"

A double what-out?

As Jake tried to slither away, I caught up to him to verify the finish. "Are you sure that's the way our return's supposed to go? That doesn't really make any sense, Jake."

"Don't worry. You'll make it up. There's big plans coming for you and Hawk. This is the way Vince wants it."

And you know what I did? I ignored my better judgment and let it all go. If I'd come this far to get back into the WWF, I figured I might as well see where this little path would take us.

As I'd predicted, when our music hit and we came out, the fans went ape shit. You see, we were an unannounced surprise sent in to face The Headbangers, who made an open challenge to any team in the back. So when we came out, that packed little theater of about 5,000 turned into a vintage Marietta, Georgia, crowd circa 1985. Those New Yorkers were literally hanging over the balconies and going insane as we hit the ring.

Unfortunately, as I'd also predicted, the whole thing took a shit when the match turned into a ridiculous outside brawl and double count-out. The fans booed. They'd expected us to win. They'd expected to see the Doomsday Device. How the company could blow our big return with that finish I'll never know, but my guard was up now. With an opening like that, I realized two things: (1) Vince still didn't give a crap about the tag team division, and (2) the Legion of Doom that everybody in the stands and at home wanted wouldn't always be the Legion of Doom they were going to get.

I think part of it was that, just as in WCW, we came into the WWF right in the middle of some serious transitional points and got lost in the creative shuffle. Vince was killing himself in order to counter the gritty, black-and-white realism of what Bischoff was doing with the NWO and decided to rebrand the WWF product with what he called "Attitude."

During the Attitude Era, as it became known, Vince took desperate measures and began to push the envelope of whatever family decency the wrestling business had left. Using his own company rebels like D-Generation X (the clique of Shawn Michaels, Hunter Hearst Helmsley, and 225-pound female enforcer Chyna) and fan-favorite antihero "Stone Cold" Steve Austin, Vince countered WCW's dominant programming with his own brand of edgy sports entertainment. Vince even injected himself into the story lines as "Mr. McMahon" to provide the perfect corporate antagonist for DX and Stone Cold.

Actual professional wrestling took a huge backseat to toilet humor, cursing, half-naked chicks, and more middle fingers than there are stars in the galaxy. I don't want to sound like the old man who's not in on the joke or anything, but every Monday night at home, front and center, my Joey, James, and Jessica were waiting to see their daddy wrestle on *Raw*. Between Julie watching at home and me watching from a monitor in the back, I knew there were at least two parents cringing every time Shawn and Hunter yelled, "Suck it!" to the crowd while jerking off with Super Soaker water guns.

More often than not, I'd come home and catch Joey or James yelling, "Suck it!" all over the house, and I'd want to put my head through a wall. What do you do when your own company is responsible for putting that kind of crap out there? Julie and I would again have to try to explain the many differences between real life and what was on Daddy's TV show.

It was frustrating to watch professional wrestling deteriorate into unrecognizable tripe. And still I pressed on to see if we could somehow fit into Vince's new vision.

On March 23 at WrestleMania XIII in Chicago, we competed in a six-man Chicago Street Fight (no rules) with Ahmed Johnson against Farooq, Savio Vega, and Crush, who'd been completely repackaged since the Demolition days. In fact, it was Crush who ate the first Doomsday Device since our return.

In April we all went on tour to Kuwait City (one of the friendliest and pro-American places I could imagine). For whatever terrible reason, Hawk decided to get good and annihilated on booze and Somas. His eyes were rolling back in his head, and he looked like he could fall on his face at any second. This was all happening as we pulled into the sheik's quarters, where we were all invited to stay as guests.

Oh no, I thought. *This is not fucking good.*

There we were—docked at the base of a plush red carpet that stretched all the way inside the palace, where there were huge marble columns and dozens of 15-foot-tall paintings featuring the sheik's family—about to make an embarrassing international scene. One by one, we came walking off the plane waving and smiling in front of all the guards, and there was Hawk, being helped arm-in-arm by Henry and Phineas Godwinn, our chief rivals at the time.

As Hawk's feet limply dragged across the carpet, Jerry Brisco looked ready to pop a gasket. Fifteen minutes later, as usual, Hawk was the life of the party again, as though nothing had happened. He was flying around from person to person with a drink in his hand and a cigar in his mouth. Brisco pulled him aside and seriously reamed him out.

Hawk was lucky to have kept his job, which of course meant *I* was lucky he kept his job. Isn't being in a tag team fun? I'm pretty sure when the news got back to Vince he shook his head and thought we were hopeless.

When we came back home from overseas, we entered into feuds with the WWF Tag Team champions Owen Hart and Davey Boy and the Godwinns. We even had a match against the Godwinns in which six feet five Henry sustained a cracked vertebra in his neck after landing on his head during the Doomsday Device. The doctors told Henry he'd have to stay out for fifteen weeks. (He was back in eight.)

For the next few months, we looped around the entire United States and Canada plugging away toward our promised push to the titles and hoping for the best. Even though it was taxing as hell, I tried to look after Hawk as much as I could, but sometimes it wasn't enough.

During a stop in Cincinnati on September 8, we were staying at the Drawbridge Hotel and were all down in the bar putting a few back. I'd kept my eye on Hawk all night long and saw he was about to hit the floor, so I helped him up to his room, put him to bed, and told him to stay put. Fifteen minutes later, someone pointed over to the foyer and steps leading down to the bar, and there was Hawk laid out in a crooked heap.

I ran over, picked him up, and once again took him upstairs. This time I put my hands on his shoulders and told him to stay put. "Mike, listen to me. You have to stay here. The security guys are getting pissed, and it's not cool."

He stared at me blankly. This time he did manage to stay put, but not without bringing the party to his own room. Brian Pillman told me that later that night he and Henry Godwinn and anyone else who happened to walk by Hawk's room had a wild time. It turned out to be at Hawk's expense far more than he would've ever bargained for.

The next day on the plane, Hawk was in a shitty mood. "I lost my fucking jewelry, or someone stole it. I don't fucking know."

See, he had a really expensive gold watch and a $4,000 gold nugget bracelet with *Hawk* imprinted on it in diamonds. Whenever Hawk partied, he would hide his jewelry to protect it from being lost or stolen.

Well, I guess when he woke up in the morning with no recollection of the night before, he tore the room apart in a panic trying to find his jewelry. In the end, defeated and without his prized bracelet and watch, Hawk had to leave and catch our flight. I have a feeling that somewhere behind a ceiling tile in his old room at the Drawbridge is a very expensive Hawk bracelet.

In October we had one of the craziest and most memorable months of our entire careers beginning in Minneapolis on the fourth at the Saint Paul Civic Center. The day started out great with me bringing Joey, James, and a bunch of their friends to the show hours before the match so they could look around and maybe meet some of the guys. They wound up getting the thrill of their lives.

We were there early in the day, when the only people around the arena were security guards and the tech crew. The ring was set up, so I let the boys get in there and bump around. I was standing way up on the entrance ramp watching when I heard someone call my name.

"Hey, Joe, hit that button right there." It was Stone Cold. He was telling me to press the button if I really wanted to freak the boys out.

The next thing you know, Joey, James, and their friends heard the familiar sound of glass breaking followed by Austin's music as the man himself stormed down to the ring for some action. The boys didn't know what to do. James was a really brave little boy, though, never moving an inch when Austin charged in and delivered a perfect Stone Cold Stunner on him. When he got in there, they jumped all over him and he went with it. It was hilarious.

As much fun as the show was later that night, the biggest shock of the year came early the next morning when we were told Brian Pillman was found dead. Brian was another guy who'd lived a tough and troubled life with drugs and alcohol and struggled to keep basic composure.

I remember when Ken "The World's Most Dangerous Man" Shamrock had first come into the company a few months earlier and had no clue about the levels of excess going on all around him. We'd all been at Denny's near the Philadelphia airport after one of Ken's first shows, and he couldn't understand why Brian was facedown in his cereal.

"What's wrong with this guy?" he asked. "Is he always like this?"

Pillman died at only thirty-five years old.

I'VE ALWAYS APPRECIATED THE RESPECT THE FANS HAVE GIVEN ME. 1999.

18
OUR CONTINUING JOURNEY INTO THE UNKNOWN

Two days after Brian Pillman's death, we were in Topeka for an episode of *Raw* (which was dedicated to Brian). It looked as if things were finally on the upswing.

"You guys are going over the Godwinns tonight for the belts," Vince said. "You deserve it."

Was there fine print on his forehead? I thought maybe I was in the twilight zone or something. Twenty minutes later, though, when Hawk pinned Phineas for the WWF titles, I knew I was right where we should've been all along: on top.

It lasted all of six weeks. We dropped the championships to another faction of DX, the New Age Outlaws. Badass Billy Gunn and "The Road Dogg" Jesse James were also the latest part of Vince's answer to the NWO, which meant we were in for a few months of humiliation and losses the likes of which I never knew possible. We lost more matches in the first few months of 1998 than we did in the entire fifteen years prior. When Hawk came up positive for whatever (just pick one substance) at the end of February, we sat out for thirty days while Vince and his team of creative writers literally planned the rest of our miserable fate in the WWF.

When we came back, we were immediately subjected to a gimmick overhaul into the LOD 2000, which included Hawk and me growing out our hair into regular flattops, completely changing our shoulder pads and intro music, wearing ridiculous airbrushed motorcycle helmets, and getting a little piece of eye candy named Sunny as our new female manager.

Sunny was great, and the fans loved her for her undeniable charisma and sizzle, but man, I remember thinking, *What the hell happened to the Road Warriors?* We were getting further and further away from our roots, which was the worst thing that could've happened to us.

Well, *almost* the worst. By June, Sunny started getting phased out of the LOD 2000 picture in favor of adding a third member to the team. Now things were completely out of control, and I hated every second of it.

Adding Darren Drozdov (Droz) to the dynamic of Hawk and Animal was like saying, "The Road Warriors need help. They can't cut it on their own." The truth, which bothered me most of all, was Vince's message to me that Hawk's unreliability had to be dealt with any way he saw fit.

But he wasn't finished yet. "Animal," Vince said to me during a creative meeting, "I'm thinking about going very dark with the Legion of Doom. I want you to personally take on an angle where you're staggering around drunk and high on TV, constantly causing the LOD to blow winning opportunities in the ring." So that was Vince's plan: to play off our real-life situation.

I felt the same as I had when Jack Lanza said Hawk would take a Doomsday in Japan against Hogan and Tenryu. "Absolutely not," I said. "I'm not touching anything like that. It's a terrible business decision for us."

The echo from my voice didn't even silence when Hawk spoke right up. "I'll do it. I don't give a fuck."

Vince smiled. "That's the spirit, Mike. I like a team player."

The irony of it all made me sick. Now Hawk was given an open excuse to justify his substance issues.

"I have to do it for the gimmick, Animal."

Great. *Just great.*

Week after week, Hawk would come out and either fall off of the stage, stumble off of the walking ramp, trip through the ropes, or lose his balance on the top rope. On a good night, he'd do all four. And what no one realizes is that Hawk wasn't merely working his new story line. He really was blasted all of those times. It was method acting at its drunken best.

The whole angle came to an embarrassing climax when a drunk and frustrated Hawk pretended to fall off the top of the 25-foot-tall Titantron video screen during *Raw* as I pleaded with him to be careful from the stage below. And that was it.

Shortly afterward, life imitated art, as Hawk gave his very last dirty urine in the WWF. We were told there was nothing left for us creatively and were sent home.

So there we were, excused from our duties with the WWF. Honestly, that whole second run in the company left a terrible taste in my mouth (and I'm not talking about the Godwinns' slop). Although I was still collecting a guaranteed check, it wasn't as much as I would've made with the now monthly PPV schedule. Everyone always got kickbacks from those shows, especially Wrestle-Mania, when you could always count on an extra big payday.

As far as my relationship with Mike at the time, it was pretty nonexistent. There's no question I was frustrated beyond belief when my career with Mike kept stalling out due to his lifestyle decisions. We rarely spoke, but when we did it was short, sweet, and usually about business. Truth was, I'd never give up on our partnership as the Road Warriors. We were brothers in paint and had been through way too much to just smother it out and go our separate ways. Hawk and Animal were bigger than Mike and Joe. Whether or not we wanted to acknowledge it, our alter egos had taken on lives of their own since we'd created them back in '83.

By the spring of '99, I started becoming aware that everywhere I went, people were referring to the Road Warriors as legends and the greatest tag team of all time. When you hear stuff like that, it's easy to get embarrassed and quickly shrug it off with a "Thank you very much," but at the heart of the wrestling business, money aside, gaining the respect of your fans and peers is what it's all about. That was around the time it really hit me how amazing of a run Mike and I had and were still on.

We had also been around long enough that we had to face our own share of tragedies. I got a call from a friend on April 20 that Rick Rude had died in the middle of the night in his hotel room due to drug-related heart failure. Rude and I, along with Mike and Barry, had started out together all those years before in Eddie Sharkey's crappy basement ring with no clue what the hell we were getting ourselves into. We were bonded for life by that experience.

In that time, the four of us saw the very best and the very

worst of the professional wrestling business, and not one of us was ever completely immune to the dark elements of it all. It was no secret that Rude had partied hard and, in a lot of ways, was actually very much like Mike, except that he had a wife and three kids at home. Richard Rood, known to the world as Ravishing Rick Rude, was only forty years old.

About a month later, on May 23, the entire world was shocked when Owen Hart fell 78 feet from the ceiling of the Kemper Arena to his death during a WWF PPV in Kansas City. I was sitting at home when James came running in saying something horrible had just happened during the show, which he was watching downstairs.

"Dad, Owen Hart just died on TV. Come quick."

What? I couldn't believe it. I ran down and watched as Jim Ross and Jerry Lawler confirmed what James had said. It made me sick to my stomach thinking about it. Owen, in his sparsely used Blue Blazer gimmick, had this big entrance to the ring where he would drop from the rafters strapped into a small harness and cable, which he'd always told everyone how much he hated.

As the story goes, thinking he had been hooked to the cable properly and was ready to suspend down, Owen stepped off the catwalk and free-fell to the ring, where he hit one of the corners with his chest and face. He died almost instantly due to the severe trauma. Like the rest of the wrestling community, and anyone who ever had the pleasure of knowing Owen, I was heartbroken.

In a great show of compassion and human understanding, Vince McMahon paid for everyone who'd ever worked in the WWF past and present to attend the funeral in Calgary. I took James with me. You see, because Minnesota is one of the gateway states to Canada, Owen used to stop by our house all the time and became a family friend. He'd come with me to watch Jessica play hockey and told me about his two little babies and post-wrestling plans.

Few people knew Owen had earned a teaching degree earlier in his life. "Joe, I want to teach," he'd said. "I can't wait for my days in the ring to be over. They're numbered." Owen was truly one of the good guys. He was thirty-four.

With great friends like Rude and Owen dying so suddenly and leaving behind families, man, it really hit home. I couldn't imagine what it would be like if I, too, met with an untimely accident and Julie was left alone to raise Joey, James, and Jessica. As burned as I may have felt being made to sit out a year from working, being able to get even that much closer to my Laurinaitis clan made me quickly forget all about it. After all, I had coaching duties to attend to.

That's right. From the day Joey, James, and Jessica were all able to walk, you can rest assured I had my coaching hat (or Zubaz bandana) firmly on. When Joey started getting to be around six years old, he gravitated straight toward hockey and stayed with it all the way through high school. I'm telling you, man, the kid had no quit in his heart, ever.

Joey wasn't as big as some of the other players, but you never would've noticed because of his good, old-fashioned hustle. Whenever I came home, we'd go over his slap shots and passing in the driveway with a little net. Even with 300-pound Road Warrior Daddy completely blocking out the sun on the tiny little goal cage, Joey would nail shot after shot.

By 1999, Joey was a man of eighteen and had really filled out after finding a passion for weight lifting, as I had, in high school. He weighed about 185 pounds and stood at five feet nine. I'll never forget the day he made me respect him man-to-man when he came in and announced to Julie and me that he was going into the military. And I was even prouder when his boot camp physical training scores came back as the highest in his company. Within another year or so, during the political turbulence after 9-11, Joey would enter the National Guard and go overseas to defend our country in Iraq.

Because Joey was now eighteen, the age difference between James and Jessica was a much bigger factor than it had been only a few years earlier. While he was busy departing for the big, waiting world outside our front door, he was also completely leaving behind the childhood stage that his younger brother and sister were still smack in the middle of.

From the moment James had started crawling around the house, I could tell how coordinated and sports-oriented he already was. In T-ball, he'd hit home runs every single time he was at bat. I kid you not. Whether it was a grounder and he ran all four bases before they could throw it home or he smashed it over the fence, the kid was a natural. He grew so rapidly that he was the same size as his eleven-year-old brother Joey by the time he was six.

After years of hearing him say, "Can I play football yet? Can I play football yet?" we finally enrolled him. He was a nine-year-old terror on the football field—and every other arena, for that matter, including baseball and hockey. But it was on the Pop Warner football field that James emerged as a definitive leader and I got to become Coach Animal.

I'll never forget when James was only nine or ten years old and I had him and the other most advanced player on his team, Blake Wheeler (now a center on the Boston Bruins hockey team), running passing plays all day long. You would've thought those two were junior high varsity starters the way they instinctively picked up on what I showed them. At the actual games, I'd be laughing out loud with the other parents as James and Blake schooled every one of those other teams during the season.

Only a few years behind James was ten-year-old Jessica. When she wasn't doing all of the regular girl things, like playing with her Barbie and Easy-Bake Oven, Jessica was doing amazing things on her hockey and softball teams. From day one, there was nothing she couldn't do as well as my boys. From throwing the baseball to swinging the bat, Jessica had pure talent.

With Joey not around as much anymore, James didn't hesitate to take Jessica over to our huge trampoline, which I called Thunderdome, and would never get tired of chokeslamming and power-bombing his little sister until the cows came home. And you know what? Jessica loved it. She was a tough cookie by now and, even according to James himself, was "the best natural athlete in the whole family." My boy knows what he's talking about.

When she first started grade school, all of the kids were required to run around the whole school. Man, Jessica smoked everyone (including the boys) by a couple hundred yards. No doubt about it, my little baby girl was another fine charter member of the Laurinaitis and Co. Super Athlete's Club. It's quite exclusive, you know.

Now, of course, behind any squadron of well-behaved, well-juice-boxed young athletes is a dedicated team mom. That's where Julie came in. Already the center of the universe for our own children, Julie devoted herself to making sure all of the kids on Joey's, James's, and Jessica's teams were always looked after. Whether it was rides to and from the field or taking the time to slice up a few dozen orange wedges for the team's midgame replenishment, Julie was the mom other moms looked up to, wondering, *How does she do it all?* Simple. She's the real Supergirl. I pulled her out of the crater myself back in '84.

At the end of the day, it was Julie who had to take up the role of both mom and dad in my absence, which was over two hundred days a year when I was on the road. I missed PTA meetings, school pageants, and birthday parties, but Julie was there, front and center, taking me along in spirit. There's no question my family wouldn't have turned out as brilliantly without her planted in the center. Like my own mother before her, Julie was the glue holding the Laurinaitis family together.

Before I knew it, not only was I completely rejuvenated by my time away from wrestling, but our WWF contracts had recently expired so we were free to go to work again. My long-term goal was to land us back in WCW by the end of the year, but those talks were yet to come. So at the end of July, the Road Warriors hopped on a plane for a series of shows Down Under with nothing but high hopes. Sadly, the whole experience would turn into a total nightmare.

The first two shows started off great in Wollongong, New South Wales, on July 28, when we defeated Public Enemy, Rocco Rock, and Johnny Grunge for the i-Generation Tag Team Championships. Two days later, we retained the titles against Rocco and Johnny at the Superstars of Wrestling PPV at the SuperDome in Sydney. Hawk was in great spirits and telling everybody crazy stories from his recent time off, including one about running into Randy Savage at a concert in Tampa. (Remember the rematch I mentioned?)

As the story goes, Hawk took Dale to the Sun Dome for a Kid

Rock concert and was hanging out backstage when none other than Savage and his girlfriend came walking by. Hawk said he extended his hand in friendship only to be punched right in the face by the Macho Man. *Crack!*

Mike smiled and asked, "Is that all you got?" He was about to grab Savage's head and "give that son of a bitch a swirlie right there in the bathroom," he later told me, but security grabbed them and put the whole thing to an end. (In case you're wondering, a swirlie is when you stick someone's head in a toilet and flush.) We were all dying laughing at that one.

It was right after our triumphant championship defense on the thirtieth that things took a hard left turn for the worse. We had a couple days off before our next show and stopped for a break in the city of Adelaide down in South Australia. The worst thing you could do with professional wrestlers was give them a few days of downtime in a foreign country; it was like giving them a license to party. No harm done. It's just what they did. As always, Hawk and I split ways and agreed to meet at the show, which left him to run off with some buddies and see what kind of trouble he could get himself into.

Days later in Melbourne, Hawk and I painted up. When it was time to go into the ring, I looked around and saw a crowd gathering around someone lying on the ground. It was Hawk! He looked panic-stricken as I'd never seen him before. His chest was pounding so hard I could actually see his left pectoral muscle spasming out of control.

"Joe, don't let me die, man," Mike pleaded.

I was in one hell of a spot. We were about to go out for our match, and the place was sold out. There was no way I could just leave with Hawk and screw the promoter and fans. Thinking quickly, I grabbed a couple of guys and asked if they would take Hawk to the hospital and I'd be there as soon as the match was over. They agreed, and I found this giant Aboriginal Australian in the back to be my substitute partner. He had no idea what he'd do out there in the ring, but I reassured him. "Don't worry about it. Just get in there with me, and I'll do everything."

After the show, I went to the back and called Hawk at the hospital in Adelaide.

"Animal," he said, "you've got to come and get me. Where I'm at right now, three people just died with the same heart condition I've got. I'm freaking out."

When I got there, Hawk was arguing with the staff about letting him go. He had a resting heart rate of 188, and they wouldn't let him leave. I remember hearing him say, "I've got a 300-pound partner who says I'm gonna leave."

And that's what I did. The joke was on me: you've got to picture me in my do-rag wheeling my 275-pound partner out of there, through the Melbourne terminal, onto our flight, through the LAX International and US terminals, and to his gate in Tampa.

I cancelled the remaining dates we had scheduled in New Zealand and took a flight back to Minneapolis. With Mike's latest escape from the icy fingers of death, I wondered how much longer his luck would last.

About a week after returning home, Mike gave me a call to let me know what was going on. He had been diagnosed with cardiomyopathy, a condition in which one of the valves leading into the heart becomes stretched out and can't pump blood as it should. Due to his limited diet and the uppers and downers he'd been taking, his body had crashed. Thankfully, once home in the States, he'd been able to get the right kind of medication that would keep him alive.

The bottom line, though, was that Hawk was going to be sidelined with rest and recovery for the next solid year, so I decided to get back in touch with WCW, which had now burnt out in the Monday Night Wars and was a distant second to the WWF once again. I asked Eric Bischoff if they had a place for me until Hawk was ready to come back and reform the Road Warriors, and he said in fact there was.

In January 2001 Bischoff brought me back in a solo capacity as the "Enforcer" of The Magnificent Seven, created to protect WCW World champion Scott Steiner. Since the last time I had seen Steiner, he'd completely reinvented himself during the NWO craze as the crude and platinum heel Big Poppa Pump. Scott now had an ongoing feud with Sid Vicious, which Eric and none other than my own brother John injected me into.

John had retired from active wrestling and was brought into WCW as an agent to work out matches with the talent. It was explained to me that I would make my debut at the Sin PPV during a four-way match with Sid, Scott, and Jeff Jarrett as the fourth man and help take out Vicious with his own powerbomb finisher.

Minutes before the match, John went up to Sid and said that near the end, to cue my run in, he was to go on the second turnbuckle and take a high boot to the face from Steiner on his way down. Sid didn't want to do it. At six feet nine with long, slender legs, he simply wasn't meant for those kinds of spots. John wouldn't listen and told him everything would be fine.

Far from it. When the time came for Sid to jump off the rope, he came down and landed at an awkward angle and completely broke his lower left leg in half.

When I came running down for my spot to powerbomb Sid, Steiner was screaming, "Powerbomb him. Powerbomb his ass!"

When I turned to Sid and saw his leg, I wanted to puke. It was completely broken at a right angle away from his body, exactly in the shape of the letter *L*. If it weren't for his boot being on, Sid's leg might've been completely severed from his body. Meanwhile, the poor guy was hollering and writhing in agony, and to this day I don't know how he managed to stay conscious.

I looked at Steiner and pointed. "Holy shit, Scott. Look at his fucking leg!"

Steiner was so hopped up on the adrenaline of the match that he didn't notice anything and was actually stomping Sid, making his leg dangle back and forth. It was the worst thing I've ever seen in a professional wrestling ring. Period.

After they wheeled Sid to the back and put him in the ambulance, I went up to him and asked him how he was.

"Tell your brother thanks a lot," he said. "I told him it was a bad idea."

After that match, I wrestled a couple more times in tag matches with Chavo Guerrero, of all people, against other cruiser-weights. I think they were also in the midst of pairing me up with Rick Steiner for a while until Hawk could return, but boy did all of *that* get permanently interrupted.

To make a very long and complicated story short and simple, back in 1996 Turner merged with Time Warner and stayed on as the chief stockholder, thus giving Eric Bischoff the financial backing he needed. With Turner in that supportive role, Warner might've dropped WCW entirely, but Ted was loyal to the show that had once helped him build a broadcasting empire back in the '70s and '80s, the classic *World Championship Wrestling* at 6:05 p.m. on Saturday nights.

All of that would change in January, though, right when I came in as Time Warner merged with America Online (AOL) in a multi-billion-dollar deal to form AOL Time Warner. The deal effectively removed Ted Turner from being in charge of his networks.

Without Ted Turner's protection, WCW was left at the mercy of corporate wolves who wanted no part of the money-losing ($60 million in 2000 alone) disaster. So AOL Time Warner put a for-sale sign up in the front yard of WCW headquarters and waited to see who came calling. I'll give you one guess who wasn't about to pass up an opportunity this good.

For a mere $5 million, Vince McMahon swooped in like a vulture, only too happy to take advantage of the WCW carcass, and after an eighteen-year battle, bought his competition. Even though WCW had been formed back in '88 when Jim Crockett sold the combined assets of both his company, Mid-Atlantic Championship Wrestling, and the remnants of GCW, it was still more or less the same entity that had entertained millions of people for more than seventy years. Now it was all gone.

My prediction that the Monday Night Wars would doom either Bischoff or Vince turned out to be true. If Eric had left well enough alone back in '95 and stayed on Saturday nights instead of running himself and WCW into the ground with the Monday Night Wars, none of it would've gone down like that. There was room enough for both WCW and the WWF to coexist and do great business for years and years to come, but now it's a waste of

Photo courtesy of Pro Wrestling Illustrated

I was ready for action when we made our WWF return in 1997.

Photo courtesy of the Laurinaitis family.

During my first run in the WWF, the only person who could really take me off my feet was Jessica! September 1991.

Photos courtesy of the Laurinaitis family

Top: Merry Christmas 1990 from the Laurinaitis family! James on my right, Joey on my left, and Julie with little Jessica on her lap. Check out my Zubaz bow tie! Bottom: Sometimes James wouldn't even go to eat with Joey and me unless I painted him up like Daddy first! Fall '90.

Photos by Bob Mulrenin

Presto! My game face is on in a few easy steps for all occasions. Don't get caught in the web!

Photos this page courtesy of the Laurinaitis family.

Top: A little brotherly love as James practices his powerbombs on Jessica. Summer '94.
Bottom: Coaching Joey's Legion of Doom little league team was another favorite role.

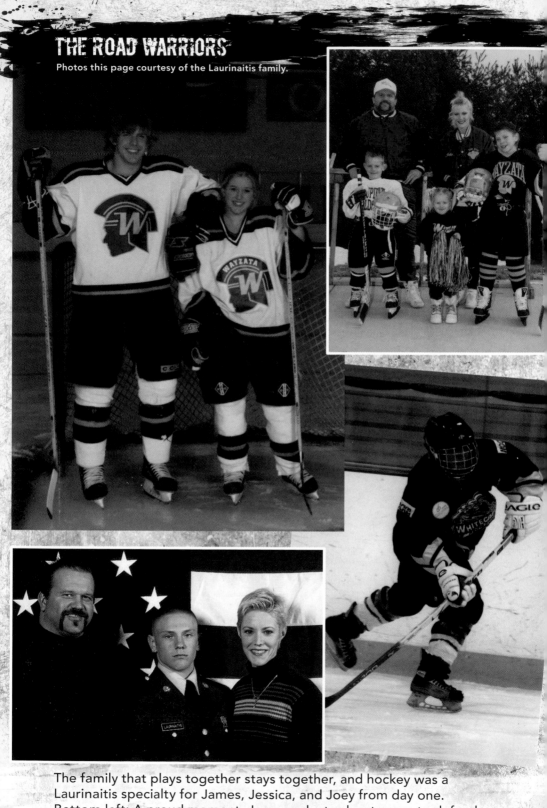

THE ROAD WARRIORS

Photos this page courtesy of the Laurinaitis family.

The family that plays together stays together, and hockey was a Laurinaitis specialty for James, Jessica, and Joey from day one. Bottom left: A proud moment. Joey graduates boot camp to defend the USA in Iraq. January '00.

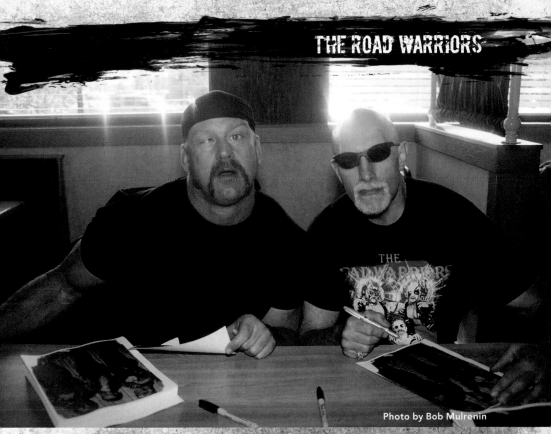

Photo by Bob Mulrenin

2006-07

Family photos courtesy of the Laurinaitis family.

Top: Hawk hamming it up with Paul at an autograph signing during the summer of 2003.
Bottom: James and Jessica flashing their bright smiles during their high school years.

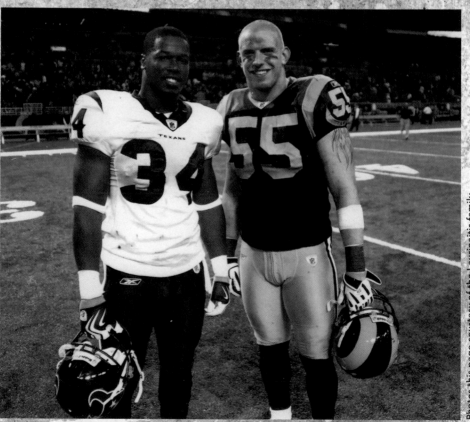

Photos this page courtesy of the Laurinaitis family.

Top: Julie, Jessica, and I visiting James during his sophomore year at Ohio State. Fall '06.
Bottom: James as a St. Louis Ram visiting with Houston Texan and fellow Wayzata High School graduate Dominique Barber.

breath to theorize about any of it.

I'll never forget standing next to Rick Steiner in the back at what turned out to be the very last *Nitro* on March 26. We were in Panama City Beach, Florida, and nobody had a clue what was going on when out of nowhere Shane McMahon came in and cut a promo about the sale and purchase of WCW. It reminded me a lot of Black Saturday back in '84 when Vince appeared on *World Championship Wrestling*.

I nudged Steiner. "Well," I said, "there goes the neighborhood."

HAWK LOVED TO WREAK HAVOC. 2003.

19

SPIRITUAL REBIRTH AND THE END OF AN ERA

When Vince shocked everybody in the wrestling world by purchasing his longtime rival, WCW (with me in it), no one knew what to expect. Maybe Vince was going to maintain it as a separate company and everyone would get to keep their jobs as rumored.

Maybe not. WCW, with the exception of a piss-poor and short-lived invasion angle into the WWF, was dismantled and gone forever.

It was starting to feel as if a lifetime had passed since I'd had a full-time gig with a guarantee. Trying to pick up the pieces of a dying wrestling career, I started taking indie bookings for appearances. I was feeling really tired about that time. My morale was down, my mood was bad, and my temper was being tested. There was no doubt in my mind or my heart that I needed something to help anchor me. It wasn't something I could put my finger on, until a sign was actually put into my hand.

After doing a shot for some small promotion somewhere in Albuquerque, I ran into Nikita Koloff. In the early '90s, my old buddy had semiretired from the wrestling business and was now an ordained pastor. He'd wrestle during the week and preach on the weekends. I remember him giving me a copy of his autobiography, *Breaking the Chains*, which dealt with his personal issues as a young man and how finding Jesus Christ had changed his life forever.

Although Nikita had given me his book in the past, I'd never looked at it. This time, for whatever reason, I read it from cover to cover in one night at the hotel, and it made a huge impression on me. Nikita stopped me after a match the next night and said, "Hey, last night you were yelling, 'I'll kick your ass,' and tonight you were yelling, 'I'll kick your butt.' What changed?"

It took me off guard. "I don't know, man."

"That's the Holy Spirit, brother," he said. "He's knocking at your door."

I know what you're thinking. I was thinking the same thing, too. *Oh no, here we go again. Another athlete talking about God.* Well, those of you who know me personally or from TV know that I say it like it is—no BS. The events following would prove to me that God has a sense of humor. I mean, think about it. If He could hunt down a 300-pound, Mohawked wrestler with face paint and spikes, He could hunt down anybody.

After that, I started trying to work through everything I'd read and known about Christianity. I knew a lot of guys in the business had used religion to get a second chance with the wrestling executives after making a mess of themselves, but then they'd just turn right back around and make another mess. I didn't want anything to do with that. It had to mean something to me to give my heart up like that.

A couple days later when Julie picked me up from the airport,

I told her about Nikita's book and that maybe there was something to this spirituality thing. I asked her to drop me off at The Gym so I could clear my mind with a good workout.

After finishing a set of lat pulldowns, I went for a drink of water. When I turned around, five of the biggest guys I'd ever seen were staring right at me. It was the Christian group The Power Team. One of them, a former Hells Angel from Texas named Big Russ, asked me a question: "Hey, Animal, do you have Jesus in your life?"

I looked at him blankly. "Bro, I don't know what's going on." It was true. I couldn't process everything rolling around in my head lately.

Then the guys from The Power Team invited me to their event in town at the Living Word Christian Center. With an open mind, I decided to go with my whole family.

Sitting in the front row of this 10,000-seat facility, where the guys from the team had given us seats, we watched all of their typical strong man exhibitions: tearing phone books in half and bending frying pans and stuff. It was funny because I was sitting there saying, "Oh, I could do that."

Looking back, though, all of it was God knocking at my door. The moment of truth came when they did what the Christian faith calls the altar call. Let me explain. An altar call is when a preacher invites you to come up in front of the congregation and invite the Lord as your Savior. Responding to an altar call means you have to decide to check your ego at the door and say, "Do I really want a relationship with God?" You admit you're a sinner and say the sinner's prayer.

For me, this was where the rubber met the road. I was having an internal struggle. *Do I go? Do I not go?*

Then a miracle happened. I'm convinced the Holy Spirit worked through my boy James, because he took me by the hand and said, "Daddy, let's go."

How do you say no to that? So we went up, all of us, and together accepted Jesus Christ into our lives.

Keep in mind that Julie was baptized Presbyterian but didn't ever go to church growing up, and I was raised Catholic (I still have ruler scars on my fingers from Catholic school to prove it), but by then we were disenchanted with it all. Becoming "born again" meant we could accept the Lord into our lives and have a true relationship with Him.

That moment at the Living Word really hit James. Since that night, he's read a chapter of his Bible almost every night, and so have I. My daughter, Jessica, was too young at the time to really understand what was going on, but now she does. To this day, even though they're separated by a few hundred miles, James still makes a point of sending Jessica passages of scripture through e-mails. It's really inspiring how strong James has become in his faith.

As I look back on my life, I am so thankful to the Lord because I know that He protected Joey through his years serving in the Army, He's protected James and Jessica through their years of intensely competitive athletics, and He's protected me and Julie. Today, I travel telling people about what God has done in my life, and I know He guards me as I fly through the airways and when I'm bringing His saving grace into the devil's neighborhood. God had His hand on me all along. I'm far from perfect. I lived a crazy life, but after giving me an opportunity to get my own name out there on every major television network over the years, God turned my life around to make His own name great. I have Him to thank for everything, especially for leading me and my family to the Living Word that night.

About a year after my family and I turned our lives over to Christ, Hawk, who had recovered enough to take some light bookings, called and said he had a show for us in June.

"I can't, bro," I told him. "I'm meeting with Nikita and Ted Dibiase (also born again) in Phoenix for the Athletes in Ministry Conference (AIMC)."

By this time, Mike was more than familiar with my faith and respected it. "Really?" he said. "Let me call you right back." A minute or two later, the phone rang. "Hey, Joe, can Dale and I come, too, if we want?"

Wow. I was surprised as hell at Mike's request but quickly said it was okay by me but to call the pastor in charge with Nikita and get all the details. And you know what? That's exactly what Mike did.

But before any of us had a chance to get really excited about the trip, I got word of even more tragedy. On May 18, at a resort somewhere in Canada, Davey Boy Smith died of heart failure caused by drug usage. I remembered seeing Davey Boy a few years back at Owen's funeral, and he looked as if he'd lost about 30 pounds of muscle, but he'd been battling a really bad pill addiction for years. In the end, all of Davey's abuse finally caught up with him, and his heart couldn't take it anymore. He didn't make it to forty, dying just shy at the age of thirty-nine.

When I did arrive with the whole family (except Joey, who was in Iraq) at the Phoenix First Assembly, guess who was the first one to greet me. Mike, with an ear-to-ear smile. He was so excited to be there with everyone. You could feel the positive energy.

When I looked around the room, I saw all kinds of guys,

including Sting, Terry Taylor, and Shawn Michaels, who were all newcomers to the faith as well. It was like a big family. And it was before the members of that family that Julie, James, Jessica, and I were baptized into our new faith by Nikita, Pastor Larry Kerychuk, and Phoenix First director Tommy Barnett right there in the congregation wading pool. At one point, Tommy Barnett told me he'd been a closet wrestling fan, but not anymore. He's a fan and unashamed. You know, there was a time when believers were closet Christians, but the time for closet Christianity is over. Wrestling is cool now, and so is Christianity.

Later, when we divided into groups and it was time for the altar call like I'd been a part of at Living Word the year before, I got the surprise of my life when Hawk and Shawn both got up, hugged, and turned their lives over to Christ in front of the whole place.

It didn't stop there for them. The great thing about being a Christian is that it's not about going to church. It's about having a personal relationship with the Lord, and that is what changes people. Those guys were a great example. They used to hate each other. I had a quick flashback to a time in Germany during our first WWF run, when Hawk, Shawn, the Nasty Boys, and I were going to this really high-class strip club. I think Knobbs was being too loud as we were walking into the building. I hadn't even started down the stairs when Hawk and Knobbs came barreling back up. Hawk had grabbed him and smacked the taste out of his mouth and then turned to Shawn, who was also mouthing off, and picked him up against a garage door and, just before decking him, let go and walked away, laughing it off. Later that night, I found Shawn passed out in the hotel lobby and holding a wrapped up pillowcase filled with bottles, rocks, and all kinds of stuff. He had been waiting all night for Hawk to come back to do God-knows-what.

And now, ten years later, you should've seen those two crying in each other's arms like babies. It was one of the most touching and enduring moments between two human beings I've ever seen in my life. It was something I think was long overdue for Mike. I could see some of those heavy personal burdens lift right off of his shoulders in that room.

When Hawk accepted Jesus into his life, there was such a change in him. He cleaned up a lot and became the true partner I remembered from the early days. When we'd talk on the phone, which was much more often than usual, he'd always end with "Hey, Joe. I love you, man."

From that point forward, Mike really did become a much more lovable guy and, even more so, a dependable Road Warrior. We got back into action doing some independent stuff here and there, even doing a couple of shots at the end of the year into 2003 with Dusty Rhodes working for Jerry and Jeff Jarrett's new NWA/ TNA (Total Nonstop Action) Wrestling out of Nashville.

Hawk and I felt we were truly climbing back on top of our game together in the ring. Our timing was right on, and the fans were making us feel like old friends. Things were really starting to look up, and then they crashed right back down again.

The phone rang. Another wrestling death. This time it was Curt Hennig. Picking up the phone those days was really starting to become a risky proposition.

I don't want to start sounding cliché, but the sad reality of the situation is that Curt was found dead in his Florida hotel room on February 10 due to a combination of cocaine and Somas. That was the deadly game some guys used to play. They'd stay up all night doing certain substances only to take a bunch of something else to bring them down.

After years and years of spinning the wheel of chance, my buddy Curt, the fantastic Mr. Perfect, one of the most talented workers wrestling this side of Ric Flair, bottomed out at forty-four years old, leaving behind a wife and four children. One of his children, Joe, is now in the wrestling business himself.

After coming into TNA for those couple of tune-up matches and helping draw interest and ratings for the promotion, Hawk and I started to wonder if we might try one last go with the WWF, now known as WWE (World Wrestling Entertainment) due to a name conflict with the World Wildlife Fund. After putting feelers out to WWE, we got a call in May from my brother John, who worked for Vince since WCW was bought out.

"Joe, I've got some great news," he said. "Vince needs some prospective teams to feud with Kane and Rob Van Dam (RVD) for the tag titles. He wants you to have a couple of tryout matches on *Raw* and *SmackDown*."

Hawk was beside himself with excitement. It was an opportunity he had waited for to redeem himself. "You watch, Animal. I'm going to do the right thing and go right in there and shake hands with Vince. I'll tell him we want to come in and do some good business for the company. Hell, I'll do the job personally to those guys."

Ever since we'd bombed out of the WWF the second time in '98 and had to sit out a year, Hawk found every reason in the book to push the blame entirely onto Vince. He kept a black hole of negativity and bitterness centered right in his gut. When he and Shawn became born again at the AIMC, Mike was finally able to see that everything in life is a two-way street and there needs to be compromise to make things work.

The Road Warriors showed up for work on May 12 at the First Union Center in my old hometown of Philadelphia. That night, when our classic WWF entrance theme sounded over the PA, the Road Warrior pop was alive and well. The crowd gave us a standing ovation and were chanting, "LOD, LOD." It felt as if we'd never left.

When we hit the ring and started the match, Jerry Lawler turned to Jim Ross and said, "You can call them the Legion of Doom, but they're more like the *Legends* of Doom."

Coming from "The King," that compliment was as good as gold.

The rest of the match was pretty much a test from Vince to see how much we could sell for Kane and RVD, although I did get a nice powerbomb on Rob near the end. When it was time to take it home, RVD ducked Hawk's Doomsday Device clothesline, setting up his Five-Star Frog Splash finisher. After getting pinned for the three-count, Hawk didn't really stay down too long, and it came off as if he half no-sold RVD's splash. Take it from me, after coming in and offering to do the job for Vince personally, Mike didn't intentionally pull the roof down over his own head.

A couple days later at the *SmackDown* taping in Baltimore, I noticed our scheduled TV match was switched to a dark match[18] with no explanation. In about four minutes, we destroyed a much younger CM Punk and some other jobber with the Doomsday Device to the deafening pleasure of the fans. I remember right after the show, one of the guys from the road crew came up and told me our pops were so big that Vince's backstage promos kept getting interrupted.

"What in the world is all that commotion out there? It's ruining my interviews," he'd said.

He was told it was the LOD.

After the show, we were told we'd get a call. The phone never rang.

At first I thought, *Maybe Vince thought we disrespected him because of Hawk's unintentional no-sell. Or maybe Vince thought we were too old and didn't fit in with his new WWE. Didn't he see the way the people reacted to us?*

The truth is, we wrestled a solid match, and if Vince truly had any intention of shaking up his tag team division, he should have had us win the belts right then and there on *Raw*. None of it really mattered anyway. It was over. Hawk and I had wrestled together in a WWE ring for the last time together. Mike was crushed.

After this disappointment, we did a couple of independent shows, including one with Paul Ellering for our twentieth anniversary together on June 7, 1983. "Precious" Paul even bleached his hair and goatee and pulled out one of his vintage blue suits for the occasion. I'm happy the three of us got to share that last moment together.

On October 19, 2003, the phone rang late in the day. I had a sinking feeling.

"Hey, Joe, did you hear?"

Hear? Hear what? "No. Why? What's up?"

"You mean nobody told you?" the voice replied.

Now I was getting annoyed. "Man, what are you *talking* about?"

"Mike died last night, Joe."

I heard the caller say it, but I really didn't believe it. I didn't *want* to believe it. Nobody had thought to call me all day. My thoughts were racing, and it was all a blur. I finally snapped out of it and called Dale. She said Mike had been moving boxes the previous day into their new condo in Indian Rocks Beach, Florida. After he'd made his last trip, everything was fine and they went to bed. Mike never woke up. He died of heart failure in his sleep.

My eyes started welling up when I got off the phone. I told Julie and James and Jessica the news, and we hugged and prayed. After forty-six years of hundred-mile-per-hour living, including twenty years of being the most imposing and comedic character in professional wrestling, Michael Hegstrand, my partner and dear brother, moved on to the next life. The mighty Hawk had made his last flight.

Mike's body wound up being cremated and there were actually two funerals, one in Florida and one in Minnesota. Kenski even flew all the way from Tokyo and spoke at the service in Minnesota. In a very emotional speech through a translator, Kenski thanked Mike for being an honorable friend who'd unselfishly helped him become an established name in the business eleven years earlier. It was nothing but the highest respect.

The very next night on *Raw*, the show started off with a graphic of Mike along with the announcement by Jim Ross and Jerry Lawler of his passing. I'll never forget the first match of the show when WWE Tag Team champions Bubba Ray and Devon, the Dudley Boyz, came out to face La Résistance (Rene Dupree and Rob Conway) with black armbands imprinted with *Hawk*.

In one of the greatest tributes Bubba Ray and D-Von could have paid Mike, they won the match with the Doomsday Device and celebrated their win by pointing to their armbands and then to the sky. Somewhere, Hawk was looking down and smiling. I know it.

You know, I think of Mike all the time and remember how he kept pushing everything to the edge. All of his death-defying antics and close calls were just part of his method of operation. Whether Hawk was at a bar, in a ring, or on the road, he pushed his life to the extremes in front of anyone who became an audience until he'd finally pushed everything completely over the cliff into oblivion.

It's like I remember him saying to Paul and me one day while the three of us were driving to a show in the early Georgia Championship Wrestling days: "Hey, this is what I want you guys to put on my tombstone. 'Here lies Hawk. He did everything, and everything did him in.'"

20

THE LAURINAITIS LEGACY

After Mike died, I continued by myself for the next couple of years. My itinerary became filled with autograph appearances and mixed tag matches with an assortment of local guys from each hometown I entered. It was extremely odd for a while not to have Hawk by my side and to have people everywhere kind of pat me on the back and offer their condolences.

That whole period of time was a mourning process not only for me but for the many fans of the Road Warriors who'd lost a little piece of their childhood, or any special time during their lives, because one of their heroes was gone.

It still didn't seem quite real to me. I kept half expecting to turn around and see Hawk in full paint and spikes come storming up to me as "Iron Man" blasted. *Well, are we gonna go out there and bust a few heads or stand around here like a couple of confused clam heads?* Man, I could hear him clear as day. Still can.

In the spring of 2005, the WWE wanted to do a DVD

anthology of Hawk's and my career called *Road Warriors: The Life and Death of the World's Greatest Tag-Team in Wrestling History.* For a couple of the matches, I was flown up to Stamford to record modern-day commentary along with Jim Ross. It was a great time getting a chance to call some of the Road Warriors' greatest moments.

Being honored with our own anthology was like coming full circle. It took me back through my entire career and brought up feelings and memories I thought were buried with my partner. I decided to use my new good graces with the WWE to secure an agent position, but Stephanie McMahon, who was all grown up now and a powerful part of the company, suggested something different.

"Joe," she said, "we want you to consider resurrecting the Legion of Doom with another partner we have for you."

It was a terrible idea. I hated it. I should have said no.

I said yes.

By dangling the proverbial carrot of an agent's position with World Wrestling Entertainment in front of my face, Vince and Stephanie led me right into a regrettable situation. They quickly paired me up with John Heidenreich, a six feet five, 300-pound German who was struggling as a singles performer.

Like so many times before, from the Hell Raisers with Kenski to the LOD 2000 with Droz, it was another try at establishing someone who needed a boost by strapping on a pair of shoulder pads and putting on the paint. In a word, the whole thing completely sucked. Everything was way off and worse than I expected, except for one thing: the people.

Right before my very first reappearance on *SmackDown* on July 14, Vince came up to me with a funny smirk and a classic old question he'd asked me many times over the years. "Are we going to hear a Road Warrior pop tonight out there, Joe?"

I laughed. "Well, you know. We'll see what happens, Vince."

When I walked out, it was like every other time I'd had in the WWF/E. The people jumped right out of their seats and saluted me with an ovation that made me think of Hawk and how he should've been there with me.

No matter how things ever went in my career, from the highest moments in the AWA, NWA, Japan, and the old WWF, the fans stayed with me like old friends. I will always love and respect them for that.

You know, everyone from the office guys to other wrestlers to bloggers can say whatever they want, good or bad, but in the end they *all* know exactly where Road Warrior Hawk and Road Warrior Animal sit in the grand scheme of professional wrestling tag teams: at the very top of the mountain. I'll take that with me wherever I go for the rest of my life.

As I mentioned, the WWE's attempt at bringing me back for an LOD reboot should've died during the idea stage. Here's why: the only thing slightly reminiscent of the old team was my new partner's unpredictable personality. John meant well, but due to a certain lifestyle we were all way too familiar with, it was always uncertain which Heidenreich would show up to work, if at all. Within a few months, he was released from the company.

From there I was paired up with Matt Hardy and, God bless him, he was a good businessman and a great team player who had the kind of work ethic that reminded me of me. I remembered working with him way back in '98 when he and his brother, Jeff, were starting out in the WWF. When it came to working with Matt, we got along great, did the best we could, and probably both felt like we were in the wrong situation. It too quickly came to an end, and we parted ways, but Matt Hardy has nothing but my well-earned respect.

By the very dismal end of it all, they made me take the paint off and actually had me reprise my original Road Warrior gimmick from the Georgia days. I even had the jean shorts, chaps, and leather vest.

When I looked in the mirror I almost passed out. *What have I gone and done?*

Somewhere Hawk was laughing.

It didn't last long, and I thanked the Lord when they finally released me. And guess what? No agent position. No nothing. And you know what? It's their loss.

If Vince ever wakes up one day and realizes he could have a gold mine of a tag team division like wrestling used to have, I know he'll think of me and pick up the phone or have my brother do it.

You see, when I was released, Vince made sure to have my brother John, who was now head of talent relations, call and do the honors of firing me. Nice touch. How ironic is it that once upon a time I did everything in my power to get my baby bro into the wrestling business only to have him announce the end of my career years later? (It's like something out of a *book* or something.)

With my wrestling career officially and finally retired into memories that fade more and more by the day, I could finally concentrate on the most important years for my family: the current ones.

After finishing up boot camp and being stationed in Bamberg, Germany, with the National Guard, Joey had been in the middle of seeing the world when the events of 9-11 compelled him to go over to Iraq. He had been on one of the very first missions to search for weapons of mass destruction.

A family goes through so much when they have a child involved in a war. Julie, James, Jessica, and I were always glued to the TV and waiting for any word from our hero. After serving several years in the Middle East conflict, my son finally came home safely.

Back home, Joey decided to go into the police academy in Dayton, Ohio. He's now an officer in the area and, along with his beautiful wife, Andrea, gave his old man a precious little grand-daughter named Claire. It's official. I'm now Grandfather Animal.

James, of course, became an amazing high school football player as a linebacker and got a full ride to Ohio State University (OSU) in 2001. He was the first player from Minnesota since legend-ary NFL coach Sid Gillman in 1930 to receive a full scholarship to become a Buckeye. While at OSU, James did the Laurinaitis name proud, as always, by becoming a three-time Associated Press First-Team All-American and winning several prestigious awards, such as the 2006 Bronko Nagurski Trophy, the 2007 Dick Butkus Award, and the 2008 Lott Trophy.

In 2009 James was drafted to the St. Louis Rams as a line-backer and was honored with the Carroll Rosenbloom Memorial Award, given out each year to the team rookie of the year. And through it all, James is still the down-to-earth, bighearted Christian he was when he held my hand as a thirteen-year-old boy at the Living Word.

Jessica exploded with athletic talent in high school. In softball, she was a two-year all-state first team player. During her senior year, she didn't commit a single error at shortstop and led the softball team in batting average two years straight.

Not only that, but Jessica, not to be outdone by James, stepped onto the football field for her high school's annual all-girls powder-puff games. In her junior year, she came running at an angle at this one girl and hit her like Ray Lewis, separating her shoulder. The next year, she did the exact same thing to another girl, only this time she actually stepped on her opponent's chest as she walked away. When it comes to Jessica, Joey and James will be the first to tell you, she's an absolute *stud*.

It was in ice hockey, though, that Jessica really found her calling. Overall, her high school career at Wayzata looked like this: four years varsity, all-conference honorable mention her freshman and sophomore years, captain her senior year, and all-state first team her junior and senior years. Get the picture? As of this writing, Jessica is now in her freshman year at St. Olaf College, where she's going to continue challenging herself on the rink and in her academics. Don't be surprised if you see Jessica make a big name for herself as an interior designer in the near future as well.

With all of our babies out of the house now, Julie and I are excited to see what the future holds for our amazing Laurinaitis family. At the end of the day, when Julie and I lie down together at night, we always talk about how blessed our time together so far has been. We have our health. We have each other. We have three beautiful children and a sweet little granddaughter to make the holidays at our house a PPV-quality event. And it's for all of those reasons and much, much more that I thank the Lord Jesus Christ.

As far as the Road Warriors legacy goes? Well, simply put, when I think back over the twenty years that Hawk and I were together, I'm proud of what we accomplished. When we came in, we were big, tough kids with attitudes, but people recognized the raw talent we had. People like Eddie Sharkey, Ole Anderson, and

Giant Baba gave us golden opportunities that, with the guidance of Paul Ellering, we ran with all the way to the bank.

I've said it before, but it has to be said one more time. When Mike and I were coming up, *no one* with so little time in the ring was given that kind of push. We were absolutely blessed to have been given the seeds of an amazing gimmick that would take us around the world ten times over.

Today I'm convinced that if Hawk and I were just now breaking into the business as the Road Warriors, the result would be exactly the same. We would become the greatest tag team in professional wrestling history.

THE ROAD WARRIORS IN THE GOLDEN ERA OF OUR PRIME. 1985.

AFTERWORD
THE IT FACTOR

If ever in history a tag team had the "it factor," that unique something attracting fans and friends at every turn, it was the Road Warriors. Some of Joe's professional wrestling peers whom he is honored to call lifelong friends offered their perspectives on working with Joe and Mike at various stages in their careers. Read on as these eleven all-time greats in the business reflect on their experiences with the indomitable Road Warriors:

"Nature Boy™" Ric Flair®

"The American Dream" Dusty Rhodes

Bret "The Hitman" Hart

"Rowdy" Roddy Piper

Booker T

Rob Van Dam

Jim "J.R." Ross

"The Russian Nightmare" Nikita Koloff

"The Living Legend" Larry Zbyszko

Sean "X-Pac" Waltman

Terry "Warlord" Szopinski

"Respect" is the only word that comes to mind when I think of them. I would like to thank each of these professional wrestling greats once more, here in print, for definitively placing a loud, collective exclamation point on this testament of Animal and Hawk.

—Andrew William Wright

"NATURE BOY™" RIC FLAIR®

One of the most successful professional elements Animal and Hawk had was that their characters matched their personalities. They *were* the Road Warriors. Honestly, I never called them anything else. Some guys tried to be something they're not, but not those guys. Hawk especially was just as charged up and loud out of the ring as he was in it and was definitely the wilder of the two. Joe was the Milder Warrior, so to speak, and that's exactly why they did so well together, both professionally and personally.

I remember meeting them when they first came into Georgia. They were men. Sometimes you talk to twenty-one-year-olds, and they're still kids. Not Animal and Hawk. They were respectful, possessed positive attitudes, and had a huge presence backstage in every way. And back then, believe me, wrestling was a tough, man's man business. They never complained, always worked hard, and were in great shape.

For a couple years there, it seemed like I was wrestling them every night in six- and eight-man tag matches. I loved every second of it.

I think the Road Warriors are the most recognized name in the history of tag team wrestling, and more importantly, Animal and Hawk were great guys—just fantastic people. Animal used to buy my kids toys in Japan and take them to my house, and I'll never forget it. I've got nothing but great thoughts of Joe Laurinaitis and Mike Hegstrand.

Oh, and Joe? I know you're reading this. I didn't forget about Terry Funk and the hotel door in Japan back in '85. You still owe me $1,500!

"THE AMERICAN DREAM" DUSTY RHODES

The Road Warriors revolutionized the way we all looked at characters in our industry. It was amazing for me to have had the opportunity to mentor Joseph and "Hank" (my nickname for Hawk) when they first came in, knowing they were so fresh and new, especially with that entrance music, that there'd be imitations. You know, there would be other guys throwing big clotheslines or maybe wearing spikes, but none were as powerful and devastating, not only in the ring but to the television audience at home and in terms of generating revenue.

Joe and Hank were my "babies," as I used to call them, and were just as much a part of me as I was part of them. In the early days at the TBS studio, they'd always come running back after their match to get my thoughts; it was endearing. They were just so excited and wide open about everything. It was also clear to me that Hank was running wild like James Dean while Animal was the captain of the team, *if you will*.

I can't take too much credit for the Road Warriors, though. At TBS at the time, I thank God I was lucky enough to be the golden boy and put on the map on a national level because I also had a knack for recognizing talent. With the Road Warriors, I was kind of like a quarterback who saw these two charging at me from the corner of my eye with a big hit that laid me out, making me wonder, *Who were those guys?* I'll always be proud to say that I am very happy to not only have developed a close friendship with Joseph and Hank but to have worked alongside them during the greatest period the industry's ever seen.

BRET "THE HITMAN" HART

I can remember seeing photos of the Road Warriors when they first started. They were truly awesome-looking, radical, ripped— and they put fear in me. It wasn't long before I caught them on an AWA TV show and watched them destroy some team, concluding with Animal propping a dazed jobber on his shoulders and Hawk deftly climbing to the top corner and clotheslining him to the mat with a thud. I can remember being instantly blown away by them.

I think the Road Warriors, or LOD, was one of the greatest wrestling tag teams of all time. They had a great look and, although Mike and Joe had different styles, they only complemented each other. They had two of the most impressive powerhouse physiques the wrestling world ever knew. They were bone-chillingly real during interviews and promos. Quite simply, they had the look, the walk, and the talk.

Regardless of what anyone ever says, the Road Warriors drew big money, worked hard, and helped raise the bar every bit as high as either the Hart Foundation or the Bulldogs, or any other team for that matter. I only worked with them one time in my old Hart Foundation days. They were great, and it makes me mad and sad that it was all we ever got. Hawk was a close friend, and all I can do is shake my head and smile at the memory of a spiked up Joe saying, "Tell 'em, Hawk!" and Mike with that crazy mad look on his face, his tongue hanging out, barking out, "Oh . . . what a rush!" Both Joe and Mike were first-rate pros who were loved and respected by all who knew them.

"ROWDY" RODDY PIPER

At the time Joe and Mike came into the business, it was really difficult. There were a lot of A players. The bar had been set pretty high by big, powerful guys like Don Muraco, Paul Orndorff, and Edward "Wahoo" McDaniel. Holy cow, those guys would beat you up pretty quick, but Joe and Mike jumped right in there without any real road map or game plan, and they just . . . belonged there.

And they had respect—you know, "yes sir, no sir"—which got them over in the beginning with all of us and endeared them in the inner circle backstage. As soon as you sat down with them, you knew there was something special.

And you know what else? They were believable. Whatever people say about pro wrestling, when they come to the arena, they want to see something that makes them say, "Whoa! That wasn't supposed to happen!" Joe and Mike brought that element. The Road Warriors kept it simple, were as powerful as they said, and what they did in the ring left people with no doubt in their heads that what they saw was real.

In a time when the pro wrestling was drawing a huge amount of attention and all the top spots had been taken over and seasoned, the Road Warriors came in like a breath of fresh air. Joe and Mike weren't polluted by politics, maintained the ethics of the business when it needed it most, and their convincing style made people proud to be wrestling fans. No one could've done a better job.

BOOKER T

Innovators. That's what the Road Warriors were. At the time they were getting started, Mel Gibson's Mad Max movie was really popular, and they were the first to take a theme from a movie and bring it to the wrestling world. The Road Warriors were able to create something totally different visually with the spikes, the paint, and their size for the audience to really get behind.

The first time we saw them on TV, my brother (Stevie Ray) and I were like, "Whoa!" Hawk and Animal were way bigger than anyone else we'd seen, and they were just killing everybody. And that's what people wanted to see back then.

When I was in Harlem Heat back in WCW, you know the Road Warriors were top dogs, and Stevie and I were on our way up. We had the chance to wrestle them once and it was a huge opportunity to make a statement to the world what Harlem Heat could do. I'll never forget that.

And of course you know there's a saying in wrestling that you don't really get a pop from the crowd until you get a Road Warrior pop, and that's definitely true.

ROB VAN DAM

Growing up in Michigan, with no cable in our house, I was exclusively exposed to the World Wrestling Federation. They hooked me in with their bigger-than-life characters that impressed me through the television. Eventually, as my fan drive grew, I learned that there were other wrestling groups, but I didn't know much about them. Very few of these other superstars broke the barrier of my focus. Then, there were the Road Warriors.

The first time I witnessed Animal and Hawk entering the arena to take care of business, I was in awe. From their hardcore music to the welcoming roar of the crowd, I felt the immense energy build as they approached the ring, and I had no doubt that these guys earned massive expectations from their fans. And the Warriors didn't disappoint.

They were built like bodybuilders, wore shoulder spikes and painted their faces to do battle. If you weren't intimidated before the action, you'd see them devour their opponents in a fashion that made them stand out like the last guys you'd ever want to fight.

Animal and Hawk earned legendary status with their long and extensive careers and have influenced wrestlers for many generations to come.

JIM ROSS "J.R."

The first thing that comes to mind when I think of Hawk and Animal is that they were arguably the greatest pro wrestling tag team *attraction* I ever saw. And I definitely don't mean *attraction* in a negative sense, because the greatest singles attraction I ever saw was Andre the Giant. Was he the greatest wrestler? No. But when used properly by a promoter as a special attraction and bringing him out for main event matches, he drew people and generated great ticket sales. Like Andre, the Road Warriors were a qualified and proven attraction that promoters could get a lot of mileage out of and do good business with. There is no other team in wrestling that I could put in front of them in that context.

Hawk and Animal generated phenomenal success and became "water cooler talk" stars with a great presentation. From bell to bell, their package was perfectly projected with a huge arsenal of awesome power moves I'm sure their opponents weren't too happy about. They also had the positioning, thanks to guys like Ole Anderson and Paul Ellering on their side, to start at the top, and that's a rare testament to the talent and charisma they brought to the table.

From the very beginning, the Road Warriors were always main-eventing, and if they weren't the champions of whatever promotion they were in, they were certainly in the hunt. The music was perfect, the image was perfect, and they'll be remembered by historians of professional wrestling as one of the all-time great tag teams.

"THE RUSSIAN NIGHTMARE" NIKITA KOLOFF

Their reputation certainly precedes them. Animal and Hawk are unmatched by any other team in wrestling, and that's not to slight any other great tag teams, but the Road Warriors dominated the business and made quite a name for themselves on a worldwide scale.

I remember that match at the Great American Bash '85 when Animal and Hawk had that big babyface turn against my "Russian" allies Ivan Koloff and Krusher Kruschev. The three of us spent a lot of time in the Carolinas building up huge heat, and when the Road Warriors came in as American heels, it was fun to watch as 35,000 instantly cheered them as heroes. They were completely catapulted into another level of fan popularity that never left them.

The Road Warriors were two guys perfectly in sync, and that was the key to their success. You know, I'm certainly not familiar with the entire scope of the history of professional wrestling, but to put it in terms of the teams I do know, they're the most dominating force to ever come out. I have marveled over the fact that Joe and Mike sustained the longevity they did, spanning a twenty-year career with all of their fantastic achievements. I think that says it all.

"THE LIVING LEGEND"
LARRY ZBYSZKO

You know what? The Road Warriors were the first of an era with their hairstyles and face paint. I remember working for Ole Anderson in Atlanta when Mike and Joe first arrived. They were just these giant guys with flattop haircuts and really nothing besides that in terms of a gimmick. And then, all of a sudden, the next time I saw them, they had the paint and the wild hair. I heard Ole had something to do with it all. There they were, and there was nothing else like it. The crowds went ape shit for them. It was something they'd never seen.

Mike and Joe were coming into wrestling at a time when the bad guys were becoming cheered like good guys, and the good guys were coming off like saps. It was all getting pretty stale to be honest. But the Road Warriors were two tough, take-no-shit guys with the right look and just exploded onto the scene when not only wrestling fans, but the whole world seemed to be coming out of this whole naïve mind-set about things.

Hawk and Animal became the forefathers of a new generation of wrestlers in the 1980s with similar looks and style while the old-school guys like Harley Race, Bruno Sammartino, and even myself were in the twilight of our careers. It was just a natural transition of old into new, and the Road Warriors were the perfect guys for the job.

SEAN "X-PAC" WALTMAN

All I can think about when I hear the name Road Warriors is when "Iron Man" would hit and Hawk and Animal came running out. Shit, I've got goose bumps just thinking about it. Those were way before the days when Vince McMahon came out and said wrestling was just entertainment. And even though there were a lot of people who knew what the deal was, when the Warriors came out, they were so big and so bad that everyone said, "Whoa, these guys are real!" Even the guys who'd say it was all fake had second thoughts when they saw Hawk and Animal.

When I was ten years old, I had the chance to help set up the ring for Georgia Championship Wrestling. I'd become obsessed with wrestling and gotten my way into helping the crew. I'll never forget when the Road Warriors wrestled the Sawyers; the place went nuts. I mean, Hawk and Animal were the heels and, yeah, they got the bad guy reaction, but the thing I remember most is that they were being cheered like big-time stars. To me, they were the first guys who stepped over that boundary to be turned babyface by the audience and not by a promoter.

The Warriors will go down forever as the greatest, most imitated, most influential tag team of all time, and you can't just say that about anybody. I don't care if they weren't the most technical workers, because none of that matters. At the end of the day, it's the people who decide who the best is, and they chose Hawk and Animal.

TERRY "WARLORD" SZOPINSKI

As far as the Road Warriors' legacy is concerned? They're the greatest tag team of all time, and no one can touch 'em. They came out with those spikes, that look, and that size and completely changed professional wrestling. You can take the Steiners or the Rock 'n' Roll Express or even the Powers of Pain, and it doesn't matter. Joe and Mike were so ahead of their time that they hold a special place in history. No one can question that. You look at tag team wrestling today, and it sucks. Where did it all go? Everything that's still out there on TV is just thrown together, and it shows, but they try to hide it with a bunch of flips and crap. Again, it sucks.

I think tag team wrestling died when Mike passed. It was the end of not just a great life but a big chapter in the wrestling history book itself as well. Joe and Mike came from the old school when they busted their asses on the road, whether it was in the gym, in Tokyo, or some small town in Alabama. They took on a bigger-than-life status and carried it like pros, always making sure the crowd was just as much of the match as they were, and that was the difference.

Joe and Mike were the best. Just the best. If it weren't for Joe in particular, there never would've been a Warlord or Powers of Pain. I've always looked up to Joe for that, and I always will. If Joe ever wants to come back for one more run, he's got a partner right here in a second. It would be an honor.

MEDALLION
P R E S S

Want to know what's going on with your favorite author or what new releases are coming from Medallion Press?

Now you can receive breaking news, updates, and more from Medallion Press straight to your cell phone, e-mail, instant messenger, or Facebook!

Sign up now at www.twitter.com/MedallionPress to stay on top of all the happenings in and around Medallion Press.

Be in the know on the latest Medallion Press news by becoming a Medallion Press Insider!

As an Insider you'll receive:

· Our FREE expanded monthly newsletter, giving you more insight into Medallion Press

· Advanced press releases and breaking news

· Greater access to all of your favorite Medallion authors

Joining is easy, just visit our Web site at
www.medallionpress.com and click on the Medallion Press Insider tab.

For more information
about other great titles from
Medallion Press, visit
m e d a l l i o n p r e s s . c o m